THE
REALIST

Book Launch Party
Saturday, December 16th, 2017

ClampArt
247 W 29th St
New York, NY 10001

Sarah Coleman

THE REALIST

SARAH COLEMAN

THE
REALIST

A NOVEL OF BERENICE ABBOTT

SilverWood

Published in 2017 by SilverWood Books

SilverWood Books Ltd
14 Small Street, Bristol, BS1 1DE, United Kingdom
www.silverwoodbooks.co.uk

ISBN 978-1-78132-730-2 (hardback)
ISBN 978-1-78132-729-6 (paperback)
ISBN 978-1-78132-744-9 (ebook)

British Library Cataloguing in Publication Data
A CIP catalogue record for this book is available from the British Library

Page design and typesetting by SilverWood Books
Printed on responsibly sourced paper

For my mother

AUTHOR'S NOTE

This novel is inspired by the life and work of Berenice Abbott, but it is a work of fiction. While I have adhered to the broad outlines of Abbott's life, scenes and conversations have been imagined, and several characters are composites. Detailed biographical facts regarding the characters in this book should not be sought in these pages. Readers whose interest is piqued by this story may want to explore the nonfiction accounts I have listed in the Further Reading section at the back of the book.

1951

The lecture hall is fan-shaped, large and bright, with a fresh-cut pine smell that suggests recent construction. Outside the windows, silver birch trees shed white curls of bark, and through them Berenice can see slivers of the cobalt lake, the violet mountains with their licks of snow. Light streams in, painting heads and shoulders as people take their seats, laughing and shaking hands. She cranes her neck, surveying the collage of dark suits, ties and beards, with just a few dresses adding a splash of color here and there. Her stomach tenses. These men probably won't be smiling when they've heard her out. *But so be it,* she thinks.

"Ready to throw some rocks?" Beaumont leans in, flashing a smile. She cocks an eyebrow at him.

"Am I that awful?"

"Not at all. But I trust you not to be boring."

She's glad he's there, her old friend, tall and solid as one of the trees outside. When he stands and strides to the podium, she feels bereft. Beaumont holds up a hand for silence, and the murmuring dies down. In his introduction, he calls her "a clear-eyed observer of city life," and "one of our foremost documentarians." There's applause, and then it's time for her keynote speech.

She stands up, legs unsteady, and braces herself against the chair. The room is full, there must be two hundred people here. Why does public speaking make her feel so jejune? She's fifty-one and has shown her work in museums; she's photographed the *crème-de-la-crème* of the Paris art world. But right now she might as well be her ten-year-old self: awkward, plain Bernice.

Onstage, she manages to smile and shake Beaumont's hand before looking out at the crowd. Seeing the sea of faces makes her feel warm and oddly dislocated from her body. So they've come out, the great and the good, for this first national conference on photography. She spots a Kodak executive, and the photographer Ansel Adams with his bristling beard. Plumb in the middle of the third row sits Edward Steichen, the Museum of Modern Art's photography director, looking sleek and entitled in a dark suit. Just seeing him makes her fingers itch to curl into fists. When they passed each other in the hall last night, his nod was so brief that he might merely have been swallowing.

She retrieves her notes, lays them on the lectern. Her reading glasses are in her pocket; she fumbles them out and puts them on.

"The title of my talk is, *It Has to Walk Alone*," she says, grimacing as her amplified voice reverberates around the room. "I think the reason for that will become clear." She looks up, heart hammering in her chest cavity. For a moment, she almost can't breathe with it. There's still time to back down—but no, she's flown to Aspen for this. She *will* be reckless, god help her.

"In my opinion, the biggest blight on the entire field of photography has been the aesthetic of pictorialism," she says, voice wobbling. "Let me define that term as I understand it. Pictorialism means the making of pleasant, artificial photographs, in the superficial spirit of some minor painters. Using blurriness and ethereality to be 'arty,' as if aping painting is the only legitimate path."

Even from the stage, she can feel Edward Steichen stiffen. Of course he was one of the original pictorialists, Stieglitz's darling. A trite stylist who finagled his way into a top job at MoMA. *Well, let him squirm*, she thinks.

"Don't just take my word for it. Other people have disdained prettiness for its own sake. Ralph Waldo Emerson once wrote, 'Avoid prettiness. The word looks much like pettiness, and there is but little difference between them.'" There's a ripple of laughter at this, and she allows herself to relax and smile. "I believe that's true. Pictorialism gave us out-of-focus images of flowers and women cavorting in forests. Then came modernism, which was about textures and symbols…" She thinks of Alfred Stieglitz, who, though dead, manages to hang around like an odorous phantasm. Alive, Stieglitz confounded the public with photographs like *Spiritual America*, a close-cropped picture of the hindquarters of a castrated horse. What poppycock! Slap a pretentious title on an image and suddenly, a horse's ass becomes art.

"And yet," she continues, "photography is a representative medium. Why stand on our heads to pretend otherwise? Nothing is worse than using mystical terms like 'Equivalents' and 'Spiritual America,' as some photographers have done. They've bewildered the layman and established art as by the few, for the few. Cultural America has been represented by the back end of a horse to people who didn't even know they were being insulted."

Now there are surprised coughs and some laughs, as if she's twirled a dirty garment in their faces. Symbolically, perhaps she has. She has dared declare that the emperor had no clothes—that Stieglitz was a phony. Edward Steichen's stare could freeze lava. But she's not done yet. With each startled frown, she feels herself gaining traction—as if the disapproval is actually fueling her.

"I'd like to tell you about a photographer who showed great acumen at the beginning of the century. His name was Eugene Atget"—an image flashes across her mind, of Atget dying alone in his Paris apartment, his wrinkled face mashed into dusty carpet—"and I was lucky enough to meet him. He roamed Paris every day, capturing delightful scenes with finesse and patience, but was disdained by the art world and died poor. His images were too straightforward, they said. Too simple. Well, I don't know about you, but to me it often seems as if mediocre self-promoters thrive, while quieter talents are overlooked. Particularly," she pauses, "if those quieter talents are women, or otherwise disadvantaged."

This is greeted by *tsk*-ing and angry muttering. She has now gone from being an amusing crank to a troublesome critic. Are they going to rush the stage and remove her? For a moment it seems possible; even Beaumont looks worried. But she sees her friend Margaret Bourke-White, glamorous in red, in the fifth row. Maggie's right fist is clenched with the thumb pointing up.

Gripping the lectern, she leans over it. "Yes, I'm being blunt. Why, you may ask?" *Why indeed.* "Because these issues affect me deeply. I want photography to be for everyone—and I don't just mean the photos that hobbyists take on Box Brownies. I mean the ones in galleries. We've fought for decades to have photography accepted as art, and we've won. But now self-appointed gatekeepers in our own community are declaring that only some images qualify. And which ones? Metaphors and abstractions! Mundane pictures of paint peeling off a barn wall, presented as if they were Monet's waterlilies!"

"Abbott, you're a philistine!" It comes from the second row. There are a few cries of, "Hear, hear!" Everyone watches as Aaron Siskind rises and stamps out, leaving others to applaud his outrage. His images of peeling paint are well known.

Berenice glances at Beaumont. If she's gone too far, he'll let her know. But he gives her a wink, then turns to address the audience. "Ladies and gentlemen! You may not agree with our keynote speaker, but let her speak!"

The murmuring dies down, and Berenice leans forward. "Well, my time's almost up. But before I close, let me say this. It's not just up to photographers to change things. Camera companies: you've been getting away with giving us sub-standard equipment, but you mustn't run away from progress. We need faster film, sharper lenses.

"Next, let the curators not pull the wool over the public's eyes. Lose the pomposity, the mystery! Finally, I say to editors and publishers: *you* must champion the democratic image, for in you rests the responsibility of raising our country's level of culture. Photography can never grow up if it imitates some other medium. It has to be itself; it has to walk alone."

The murmuring has stopped. The room is almost unnaturally still.

"With that, I thank you all very much for your attention."

At first, there's a stunned silence. Mustaches quiver, legs twitch under flannel pants. Silver dust particles hang in the air, illuminated by soft shafts of light.

Then, as the Kodak people shuffle out of their row, as Steichen turns and strides away, she stands there, dazed, as if she's just run through a downpour. So she's done it; she's said her piece. The wagons will circle and she'll be outside, written off as a scold—just as she's already been dismissed as a woman and a "mere" documentarian.

But right at this moment, she couldn't give a fig. As she watches people leave, her heart begins to pump faster, and tiny hairs on her arms rise, like the ailerons of a plane's wing. She's done it, she stayed true to herself. The feeling is bracing, as if she's shed an old carapace and is feeling the air on *her* unfolding wings.

And now, though most people are streaming out of the room, two or three rise and stand in place, clapping. A few more follow, until a dozen or more are applauding. And here is Margaret Bourke-White bounding up the steps to the stage.

"Berenice Abbott!" Margaret shouts, beckoning her over. Berenice walks across the stage, feeling painfully exposed without the lectern in front of her, and takes Maggie's hand. Looking out, she sees seven or eight people staring up, apparently in admiration. Abashed, she gives her new fans a bow.

There's a blinding flash, followed by another and another. Some press photographers have come forward and are snapping away, light zinging from their flashbulbs. A reporter scribbles on a steno pad.

Maggie bends, putting her mouth next to Berenice's head. "Well *that* put the cat among the pigeons," she whispers. Her breath mists Berenice's ear, and her scent—something sweet and musky—stirs an inchoate longing in Berenice's chest. Embarrassed, she tamps the feeling down. It's lucky her friend is there to lean on, because she can barely feel her feet on the ground.

Maggie squeezes her hand, nods at the cameras. Then she leans in again. "My dear, that was staggering," she says. "But what on earth made you do it?"

PART ONE

CLEVELAND, 1910

Engine House, Springfield, Ohio, 1935, by Berenice Abbott

ONE

Of all mornings, the Chillicothe train has chosen this one to be late. It's not yet nine, but already a shimmering heat is making the silver tracks grow fuzzy as they snake off into the distance. Bernice's hair is braided so tightly that her head hurts, but for once she doesn't mind—the pain means that this trip is important. At ten years old, she's about to ride the interurban train by herself. She's going to stay with Aunt Ruby and Uncle Earl while Ma remains in Cleveland. "A week, just to get a few things done," Ma has told her, adding, "Martha's looking forward to your visit." That last bit was an outright lie, Bernice knows: her cousin would rather drink vinegar than see her. Martha always treats Bernice as if she's an exotic, slightly shabby foreigner, and makes no secret of the fact that she'd prefer the two of them not to share a room.

"Here, take this." Quickly, her mother tucks a bill into Bernice's hand. When Bernice unfolds it to look, Ma slaps her arm, hissing, "Put that away! Do you want to get it thieved right out of your hand?"

People push past, bags and umbrellas brushing her skirt. At last the lozenge-shaped interurban pulls in, long poles connecting it to overhead wires. Bernice looks at the train with its sleek green sides and gold letters, the high windows reflecting nearby roof shingles. It's silly, but she imagines she's going to be whisked somewhere faraway—Baton Rouge or Albuquerque—rather than plain old Chillicothe.

At the last moment, Ma closes in for a quick hug. Bernice breathes her mother's scent: lavender soap, salt sweat and starch. Suddenly, she feels uncertain—what if Ma is leaving, like Pa did? A wave of panic laps at her.

"Ma…" she starts, but Ma pushes her toward the train steps.

"Go on, go in now."

On board, she squeezes past a lady's valise and finds a window seat in the middle of the car. Looking out, she sees Ma bouncing on the balls of her feet, peering through the glass. She waves from her seat, and watches Ma's expression soften into a half-smile. For a moment, Bernice sees her mother as a stranger might, the dark hair pulled back in a bun, the profile with its slightly beakish nose. She's used to seeing Ma as a collection of worn parts—blistered lips, wisps of hair—but now, from this distance, they coalesce into the form of a tall, robust woman with tired eyes and a well-patched jacket.

The whistle blows, and Bernice leans into the glass, misting it with her breath. She raps and waves again, but her mother has already turned. As she walks away, Ma's shoulders seem to loosen and relax.

The train rocks down the line, cutting through cornfields and pastures. Cows glance up, their mouths dripping with chewed-up grass. In a few moments, the fruity smell of manure permeates the car. Bernice tries to settle into the seat's stiff leather. A man sitting nearby reads the paper, arms stuck out wide, one hand hovering close to her face even though there's a spare seat between them. He can do that because she's a child. She examines the coarse black hairs poking from his arm like blades of grass. *Why*, she thinks, *does hair end at the wrist like that?*

Pa had arms like that. They were thick and muscular, with pale skin that barely showed under a thicket of dark hair. She would hold onto them, grabbing at the pelt-like hair when he swung her in the air and kissed her. Those sudden appearances had been thrilling. After days away, he would show up with gifts for her and Hazel. A hair ribbon shot through with silver threads, a toffee wrapped in wax paper. A peacock feather, elegantly curved and softly iridescent.

Ma didn't like Pa's kisses. She struggled and pulled away as he grabbed her, his fingers digging into her arms. He said she was a witch and she called him a good-for-nothing who didn't care if his children starved. Their shouting roiled the small apartment; you couldn't get away.

Still, the divorce shocked everyone. Hazel, who was three years older, said that being divorced was like being the only bruised apple in a fruit bowl. Most people didn't want that, so they stayed married and miserable.

On the day he'd left, six years ago, Pa had crouched down and stared into her eyes. "I'll come back for you, Bernice, I promise," he'd whispered, his eyes red-rimmed. She'd nodded, sniffing back her own tears.

"Men are dogs," Ma told Bernice and Hazel after that. She was full of complaints about bad coal, moldy potatoes, feral cats. It made Bernice feel guilty, acutely conscious of the burden she was imposing just by existing. Sometimes, braiding the girls' hair, Ma would spare a kind word for Hazel. But she shook her head over Bernice, tugging her hair and spit-wiping her face with a sigh.

They moved to a coldwater flat in Kamm's Corners, on the ground floor of a building that smelled of boiled cabbage. Music spilled from the Irish saloon on the corner, along with swaying men and the occasional lively young woman. Ma told Hazel and Bernice to keep their heads down and mind their business, because the world was full of men who would take advantage. Exactly how they would do this, and when, was left vague—but that it would happen, sooner or later, was not in question.

Leaning back in her seat now, Bernice peers round the corner of the paper at the man sitting near her. He's chuckling over a Buster Brown comic strip, his fingers grimy from turning pages. His hair is slicked with Brilliantine, and he has small, shapely nostrils—not in the least like a dog's snout. On the other hand, people can look respectable and still be murderers. Just recently, a wealthy gentleman in Cleveland shot his wife and daughters, then hung himself from the ceiling. Ma said he'd lost his fortune in the Panic of '07 and gone wild, and that Bernice shouldn't worry because their family had no money to lose.

Chillicothe is the end of the line. When they arrive in the station, there's no sign of her uncle or aunt. Bernice studies the other passengers, reading stories into their gestures and expressions. A reedy young woman in a straw hat is barely tolerating an older man's avid embrace, loves another fellow, Bernice decides.

Gradually, the throng dwindles and disappears until it's just her. She waits for a while, then goes to sit on the platform bench, tucking her valise squarely under her legs. She can feel her heart pulsing against her ribs, the clamminess of her underarms. In front of her a few pigeons strut, half-heartedly pecking for crumbs in the heat.

For two years after Ma and Pa divorced, life was almost normal. Bernice and Hazel went to school, and Ma, who was talented with a needle, took in sewing. She made the girls' dresses, keeping scraps back to patch them when they wore out. Meals were plain, but they managed.

Then one day, Bernice came home to find Ma sobbing at the kitchen table, a stiff-backed policeman next to her. For a moment, standing at the threshold of the room she shared with her sister, Bernice froze. Then she ran in and opened closets, pulled back blankets, to be greeted by…nothing. The only hint that Hazel had ever been there was a blue hair ribbon, crimped in the places where it had been tied around her older sister's braid. Hazel gone! It was Pa, she learned. He had come and taken her. *You won't find us, so don't try*, his note to Ma read. *This is my due. I deserve one of them.*

"Hazel, Hazel!" Ma keened, as if repetition would bring her back. In a daze, Bernice answered the policeman's questions. No, she hadn't seen her father lately. She didn't expect this. No, she didn't know where they'd gone.

For weeks after that, she walked around bewildered. At the thought of Pa and Hazel together, black jealousy boiled in her stomach. Pa had promised her; *she* should be the one! She imagined Pa and Hazel driving across the country, hair blowing across Hazel's face while a setting sun painted the sky pink. And she was stuck in dull-as-dishwater Cleveland. It was unforgivable.

Ma, too, was numb. She took to bed for a week—and when she finally got up, it seemed as if she'd left the best part of herself behind. She barely cleaned or shopped, so that it fell to Bernice to take money from the mantel box and buy potatoes and loaves. When there was no money, they lived on broth and stale heels of bread.

It was all wrong, their balance tipped—as if one leg of a three-legged stool had been removed. Bernice knew she'd never been her mother's favorite. But Hazel's absence, which could have brought them closer, compounded the faults Ma found in her. She was clumsy, her handwriting a disgrace, she ate too much, or too loudly. She felt like a cuckoo, too big and awkward for the nest.

It wasn't all bad. One summer when she was eight, Ma took her by train to Olentangy Park in Columbus. They stood in line for over an hour to ride the new toboggan rollercoaster. Slowly, creaking, the ride bumped up to a peak from where they could see the park splayed out: the community dance hall, the lake with its jaunty rowboats. A brief pause, then an electric thrill, the pure, gasping joy of rushing through air, screaming and clinging as they rose and plunged again! It was unlike anything she'd felt before, and she'd wanted to ride again. But there wasn't enough money, so instead they ate sugared peanuts out of twisted paper cones. Ma insisted she'd never endanger her life on such a contraption again—but she was laughing, the color high in her cheeks. It's one of the only times Bernice can remember holding her mother's hand.

The air in the station is thick and close. A few people have trickled in.

They tilt over the platform edge, looking down the track. In a few minutes the next train comes in, and Bernice watches passengers disembark, the hugs and happy greetings. Still no Aunt Ruby. For a moment, the panic she'd felt in Cleveland returns, knifing through her guts—but she takes some deep breaths, telling herself to calm down. Her relatives haven't abandoned her, they've forgotten her, that's all.

What should she do? She cranes her neck, looking down the platform to a green door. But she doesn't want to sit in a stuffy office with people talking over her head. She thinks of Dorothy in *The Wonderful Wizard of Oz*. When the Witch of the North tells Dorothy to walk through a land that's both pleasant and awful, Dorothy doesn't wilt or look for help. She puts on the magic shoes and sets off on the path.

Suppressing a slight tremble, Bernice picks up her valise and walks out of the station.

The sun is high. It blazes down, making sweat pool at her neck and snake down her back. A horse-drawn ice truck bumps by and she's tempted to leap on the running board, steal some chips and jump off, as the boys do. But all she gets, as the truck passes, is one glorious blast of cool air.

At least Chillicothe is small. She climbs the incline behind the station, passing a milliner's and a butcher's with a row of plucked chickens in the window. She rears back when a pink blob coalesces into a pig's head, staring at her with its dull blueberry eyes.

A little way on, she comes to a stoop where a woman sits with her skirts pushed up, fanning herself with a copy of the *Chillicothe Gazette*. She nods lazily at Bernice. Jutting out her lip, Bernice blows her bangs out of her eyes and nods back.

It's not until further on that her confidence falters. She's entered a street of houses that look badly cared-for. The front yards are cluttered with broken furniture. A tall tree casts a shadow across her path, and she basks for a moment in its coolness, then takes a step forward, only to find herself almost tripping over something. "Watch yourself!" a voice growls, and instinctively she cries out, "Sorry!"

A pale ankle, a ripped pair of pants. Nearby, an empty brown bottle.

The man peers up, his face breaking into a crooked smile. "Hey, missy! Help me up, eh? Give me a pull."

He reaches a lumpy hand toward her, and Bernice freezes. *Men are dogs.*

This one looks the part, too, with his shaggy forearms and wet, shining eyes. Her heart skitters. She's suddenly acutely aware of the dollar bill in her pocket, her freshly polished shoes. The Bible says to help others, but what if the person you help is wicked? Those daughters shot by their mad papa in Cleveland had done nothing wrong.

She hesitates for a fraction of a second—then, with a jerk, vaults over the man's legs and runs, heart pounding against her ribs, suitcase bumping her legs. *Run.* Feet landing unevenly on cobbles, skirt lifting around her. Through the square, down an alleyway.

At the other end of the alley is a street that—mercifully—is bustling with people. She leans against a wall, heaving. Her ribs are aching and she can feel her pulse in her throat.

A jingle—someone opening a shop door—makes her jump. Across the street is a gas station and a restaurant sign advertising burgers (*hot and juicy!*) at five cents apiece.

What now? Her temples are throbbing, and she scraped her leg against the wall coming around the corner. It pounds with pain, but she won't cry. Ma says tears are for ninnies.

Sniffing back snot and dread, she limps down the street, taking care not to look into any faces. Instead, she gazes into shop windows, feigning interest in fabrics and pies. And so on, until something makes her stop and stare.

The framed picture stands on a display of books. Posed informally, with one hand on her hip, the little girl in it leans against a mossy wall, wearing a dress that is slipping off one shoulder. The oddness of this is compounded by her gaze, which is both direct and faraway. She looks like a wood sprite come in from the forest.

Berenice leans into the window, entranced by the girl's frank gaze and the defiant tilt of her head. She's used to seeing photographs where people hold themselves stiff and prim, but this one is loose, and audacious in the way it presents the girl's raw, thorny reality. It makes Bernice's breath catch, and her pulse quicken—with excitement this time, not fear.

She peers into the shop's interior. Near the front is a table with novels stacked high; in back, a thin-faced woman sits behind a counter. There's only one customer in the store, an elderly gentleman who is bending to examine a title on a low shelf.

Shyly, she pushes open the door. As she approaches the counter, the woman looks up, and seems to grow taller and more pinched. "Yes?"

Bernice licks her lips, finding her voice. "There's a photograph in the window. If you don't mind—" she pauses, "—who is it of?"

The woman gazes down coolly, and Bernice is suddenly conscious of how she must look, with her sweaty face and braids coming undone. But she can't help it, she needs to know.

"Her name is Alice Liddell," the woman says haughtily. "She's the little girl who inspired the book *Alice in Wonderland.*"

"Oh," Bernice says, and then on impulse adds, "curiouser and curiouser."

"You've read it." The woman takes her in more kindly now; she leans forward in a familiar way. "The photographer was Mrs. Julia Cameron, Alice's neighbor in England. She knew all kinds of famous people."

A half hour later, hot and disheveled but triumphant, Bernice arrives at number fourteen Oak Street. The bookstore woman had a map, and she worked out a route and wrote it down on a faded postcard.

On the other side of the door, her aunt's eyes and mouth open wide. "Bernice, my stars! How did you get here? We thought you were coming tomorrow!"

Behind Aunt Ruby, the hallway lamp is a soft-edged orange. Bernice tries to speak, but her throat is dry and words don't come. Relief oozes out of her. That's all she remembers, that and her legs crumpling under her.

When she wakes the next morning there's a lump on her temple, throbbing, purple and tender as a plum.

◆

"What do you have there?" Martha stands above, casting a shadow over the apple box that Bernice is using as a dissecting table. Bees dart nearby, diving in and out of the violet cones of flowers.

Bernice puts the cold body in her palm and holds it up for her cousin to see. "It's a starling, I opened the gizzard. See the worm? That was breakfast."

Martha recoils, all quivering shoulders and swinging braids, then recovers herself and frowns. "That," she says firmly, "is the most disgusting thing I've ever seen."

Shading her eyes with a soil-grimed hand, Bernice looks up at her cousin. She's acutely conscious of the contrast between Martha and herself. Martha is dressed in a buttercup-yellow pinafore dress with white piping around the sleeves. She has a narrow waist and the beginnings of breasts. They are only three years apart in age, but there seems to be a yawning gulf separating them.

"Are you going to be a surgeon?" Martha taunts now.

"No," Bernice says, dipping her head, "an artist." The moment the words are out, she regrets them. She might as well have handed Martha Pa's old penknife and asked to be gutted.

Sure enough, Martha begins to shake with laughter, even doubling up. "Yes," she says. "And *I'm* going to marry the sultan of Morocco!" Abruptly, she straightens up. "Anyway, you're to come in and get clean. Your mother's due any minute." When Bernice squints at her, confused, she continues "I know, she's supposed to come tomorrow. Perhaps she wants you early." Her tone implies that this would be surprising if true. She turns and runs back to the house, yellow skirt swishing around her.

Bernice inspects the dirt under her fingernails. She doesn't want to go in yet. Aunt Ruby's yard has been her sanctuary for the last week. She can happily lose herself rooting around in the damp, cool soil. It's better than being inside her relatives' house, where she always feels as if she'll scuff the varnish or knock over a vase.

"My girl should've been a boy," she once heard her mother tell a friend. "She'd rather play with a knife than a doll." It's true—Bernice has no use for dolls, with their limp limbs and impassive faces. Once, a distant relative sent two dolls for the girls, and Bernice cut the fabric neck and put the china head in a flowerpot, spreading worms over it so that it resembled a small, writhing Medusa.

She is strange. Her mother's face tells her this often. But she can't help herself. This morning, when she'd found the starling on the path, it didn't even occur to her to step over it. Instead, she'd picked up the remains and carried them to the yard, where, penknife in hand, she'd begun cutting. While there was no longer any heart or liver, there was an intact gizzard with, inside, a near-complete worm. Best of all were the wings. She'd bent their hinges, opening and closing the oily fans of feathers, marveling at their clever design. Carefully, then, she'd severed each wing from the body, held them up and tipped them in unison, imagining herself gliding on wind currents. What must it be like, to soar over clouds and leave the Earth behind!

She stands, the bones in her legs cracking from the sudden movement. Ma is coming a day early. Maybe, for all Martha's skepticism, Ma misses having her around. The thought gives her a surge of joy.

In the kitchen, she finds Aunt Ruby standing at the stove, anxiously thumbing through a recipe book. Her aunt looks up, puts the book down and hurries over. Then, looking flushed, she throws her arms around Bernice and squeezes hard.

"Oh Bernice, what do you think? Your sly old mama snuck off and got herself married!"

And just like that, joy evaporates. Deep in the earth there's a shift in the lithosphere, plates jolting and scraping, painfully realigning. Bernice's face is crushed into her aunt's shirt—but even without that, she doubts she could speak. She lets Aunt Ruby hold her. In a minute, her aunt will laugh and say, *Oh Bernice, you didn't honestly believe me?*

"Married," Aunt Ruby holds Bernice at arm's length and speaks with emphasis, inspecting Bernice's face. "Can you believe it? They're coming for dinner and staying over. Wear your green dress, so you look nice. And scrub your face, honey, so you don't look like a savage."

"But…" Bernice can't look Aunt Ruby in the eye, and instead stares at the cracked pitcher on the dresser. Her mother's duplicity stuns her. *A week, just to get a few things done.* False, all false. And what about *men are dogs*? Did it take just a week—six days—for Ma to change her mind?

"How could she…so quickly?" she finally says.

Aunt Ruby pats her forearm. Once prettier than Ma, she has grown round-faced, with pillowy breasts and dimpled elbows. "Apparently she's known the gentleman for some months," she says. "I know it's a shock, but just think—you can move out of that awful flat. And Bernice, you have two parents again! A new papa!"

A new papa. As if fathers can be bought off the shelf! Bernice feels her insides curl. At the same time, she can't help it—a tiny part of her stretches toward hope, like a plant feeling for the sun.

His name is Giuseppe Contadino, called Gus. From Sicily. By trade, he's a tailor—ma met him buying supplies in Shaw's. He's certainly a fine dresser, cutting a dashing figure in his silk waistcoat and homburg hat. She doesn't like how Ma clings to him as if he's a fish that might wiggle away. He's handsome, though, she'll give him that. He has curly black hair and olive skin, and a square chin with a cleft in the middle. Intense, dark eyes; lips the color of cherry soda and plump, like a woman's.

Releasing Ma, Gus strides over to Martha, picks up her hand and kisses it. "Bernice," he says, rolling the 'r'. "I am charmed to meet you."

Martha giggles, turning red. "I'm Martha," she says. "That's Bernice over there."

Gus turns to look, and Bernice squares her shoulders and stands straighter. Earlier, when she'd washed her face, she'd searched her reflection to see if she was a savage, as Aunt Ruby had said. But the girl who stared back at her was unremarkable—just clumsy and plain. Nose too big for her face, receding chin. Dark eyes that look swollen, as if she's perpetually on the verge of tears.

As Gus looks her up and down his eyes narrow, but then he breaks into a smile as he walks over to her.

"We will be friends, huh?"

She can't think of anything to say. Up close he smells lemony, with a musky scent underneath. She wonders why he picked Ma, who's tall and curvy, but not rated a beauty.

Following her eyes, Gus laughs. "Your mama look good, eh?"

It sounds like a boast—but much as Bernice hates this, she can see it's true. Ma looks flushed and happy, injected with new energy. Bernice feels a prick of surprise, followed by a stab of resentment. She thinks about her own futile attempts to cheer Ma.

"...and we'll be opening a store in Murray Hill," Ma is telling Aunt Ruby. "We've already paid a month's rent."

"Oh!" Aunt Ruby mock-fans herself with her hand, "it's so romantic. Don't you think, Earl?"

"Like a picture," Uncle Earl says flatly. Bernice smiles at him. Aside from her, he's the only one who doesn't seem thrilled by this whole affair.

"Bernice, come here," Ma says. "Let me hug you."

Slowly, Bernice walks over. She'd intended to punish her mother by being unyielding. But when Ma's arms are around her, she can't help softening. She clings on and burrows her head into Ma's bust. *Maybe it will work out,* she thinks. They'll settle into their new neighborhood, make friends. Gus will have a big Italian family, and she'll learn to make *zeppole.* She clings on.

Behind her, a car trundles by outside the window. Aunt Ruby bustles forward. "Well, you must be famished!" she says. "Why don't we sit down? There's a lamb pie that won't eat itself!" She darts out, followed by Martha, Uncle Earl and Gus.

As Bernice reluctantly detaches herself from Ma and turns towards the door, her mother puts a hand on her arm and pulls her back. "Bernie," she says, almost gentle, and Bernice's pulse skips. Ma wants to talk to her privately. Perhaps she'll say that the two of them are a team, that Bernice shouldn't worry.

She looks around. "Yes?"

But Ma's grip tightens, her jaw hardens. "Don't be such a baby," she says.

TWO

Miss Morgan is outlining Latin declensions, and Bernice is half paying attention while also sketching the vase of lupines on the windowsill. *Lupinus, lupine, lupino.* She squints at her paper, then sighs. The flowers look stiff; the shading on the vase is clumsy. She's not skilled, yet. It will take time.

Sucking on the end of her pencil, she surveys the teacher's scribbles on the board. She likes the fact that some English words have Latin roots, but in class they only do the deadliest of dead grammar. Art, on the other hand, is alive, forceful, full of color and urgency.

Trudging home after school, she hears footsteps behind her. She quickens her pace, but the other person speeds up too.

"Can I walk with you?" a voice asks, and Bernice sighs: it's the Borlotti girl. They're in the same class, and Vera Borlotti—whether because she's studious or homely—is shunned. Now Vera has figured out that she and Bernice live close, and wants to be friends—so much that she can't hide the wobble of desperation in her voice. For her part, Bernice is wary. She doesn't want to be lumped in with an unpopular girl for lack of better options.

"Can we walk together?" Vera asks again. Without slowing down, Bernice shrugs, as if to say, *I can't stop you.* She glances at Vera, whose braid of frizzy black hair is unfurling. Her father owns Borlotti's, the big bakery near the new library.

They walk along Mayfield Road, then turn left onto Murray Hill. Bernice feels her spirits lift at the sight of glass dishes in a window, sunlight teasing rainbow hues from their sides. She loves this neighborhood. Plump women lean out of windows to gossip; sweet smokiness wafts from the doors of restaurants serving *ragu* and *pasta e ceci*. They walk past a shop where a fat ginger cat basks in the window, all curves. Like the Irish of Kamm's

Corners, these southern Europeans are loud and dramatic. But Bernice thrills to their cries. Even the insults have a lush, musical sound.

"…because you like music," Vera is saying, and Bernice turns to her, confused, as if the girl had read her thoughts.

"How do you know?"

"There was a man playing violin across the street at recess. I saw you listening. Your eyes were closed." Bernice casts the girl another glance, both flattered and perturbed at being watched so closely. "I'm learning the clarinet," Vera offers.

Now, Bernice turns to look at her companion properly. Vera has squinty eyes above plump cheeks, but her dress is well made, with silk trim on the sleeves. Jealousy tugs at her—business must be good at Borlotti's. "I'd love to learn an instrument," she says.

"Why don't you?"

Irritated, Bernice hefts her bag onto her shoulder. "This is my house." The sign—*Contadino's Tailoring*—floats above a window just big enough for a single mannequin, who holds his arm out gamely, as if about to escort a lady to the dining room. Beyond, she can see her mother in the back, frowning as she works the wheel of a sewing machine. Funny how Ma is always working, while Gus flits around "buying supplies." Months ago, it became apparent to Bernice why Gus married her mother: to gain a free cook and seamstress.

"May I come in?" Vera asks.

"Better not. My stepfather's crazy."

Vera peers into the store window, looking disappointed when the interior fails to reveal a madman frothing at the mouth. "All right. I live above the bakery. Come over some time. You can try my clarinet."

She plods up the street, and Bernice unlocks the street door. A door to the right leads to the tailor's shop, beyond are stairs to the second- and third-floor apartments. She never likes going along the hallway, it always feels as if someone could be lurking under the stairs. The blood-red wallpaper doesn't help.

She turns the key to their first-floor apartment. It's cramped, not much better than Kamm's Corners except for the indoor bathroom. This, she has to admit, *is* a gain. There's no more standing in the courtyard, shivering as Deirdre Flanagan's father empties his bowels. No more baths ina cold, cramped tub in the kitchen.

Inside, there is the rich, earthy smell of Gus's coffee. Bernice puts her bag on the dresser, trying to avoid looking at the wedding photograph, though she knows it by heart: Gus in a wicker chair in the foreground, her mother behind, half-obliterated. It's a standard wedding pose, she knows, but she can't bear how Gus sits there, legs splayed as he lords it over her mother. If *she*'d taken the photograph, she would have put herself and Ma in the foreground and made Gus a dark shadow falling across them.

Next to the photograph is a more pleasing image. Perhaps conscious of his heritage, Gus has tacked up a sketch of an old man in profile by an Italian named Da Vinci. The left edge is ragged and the bottom corner is missing but, torn or not, the drawing is fully, searingly alive. With just a few clean pencil strokes and some crosshatching, the artist has managed to convey the man's sagging flesh and his weariness. When she looks at it, Bernice feels a thrill in her fingertips, a giddy happiness that it exists.

She hangs her schoolbag on a chair, then goes to see Fredo in the courtyard. The pitbull lies asleep by his kennel, a rusted chain draped over his leg. She reaches down and runs her finger along the nicks in his ear, then feels in her pocket for the morsel she saved for him. It's not much, just a lump of cheese, but she puts it under Fredo's head and watches his nose twitch and his eyes fly open. He glances up quickly, then bolts down the scrap. Done, he butts her hand with his head until she strokes him.

Six months ago, when she'd first approached him, Fredo had bared his teeth and snarled. She should have kept her distance, but curiosity—Ma would say cussedness—called her back. At first she started to sketch him from the other side of the courtyard, trying to dissect him with her eyes. How wonderful if she could make him live on the page, like Da Vinci's old man! But hard as she tried, her lines bore little resemblance to the sleek, live animal.

Awake, Fredo at first regarded her with narrowed eyes and a wary, twitching nose. But gradually he softened, allowing her to scratch him under the chin, even wagging his tail when she came out to the yard.

So it was alarming, one morning, to be woken by the sound of crazed yipping. Looking out of the window, Bernice saw Fredo roped in the corner and Gus in the middle of the yard, moving a slab of beef from hand to hand. Fredo lunged at the meat, but before reaching it was whipped back by the rope, making him yelp in surprise. It happened again, then again. Thinking to get the meat each time, Fredo kept backing up and running at it, each failure making him cry with more frustration and pain.

Feeling sick to her stomach, Bernice ran to her mother's bedroom. "Have you seen what he's doing? He's got the dog and…"

"Bernie…" In the dressing-table mirror, a pained expression flashed across Ma's face. "I can explain…"

"I'm going to stop it."

"No!" Her mother's arm flew up, catching her wrist. "It looks bad, I know, but Gus has a reason. This is part of Fredo's training. Pitbulls are bred to be aggressive—he's learning what's in his nature."

Bernice blinked. "So we're to ignore this?"

"Yes. Fredo is a fighting dog. He makes money for Gus, which means he makes money for us."

Regarding her mother then, Bernice felt both sick and scared. The old Ma would have stepped in and shut this down, but now she was under Gus's thumb. And Bernice had her own guilt, too, because she was failing Fredo. Without Ma's support, she was afraid to challenge her stepfather.

Something changed that day. Gus, formerly an inconvenience, became her adversary. She started thwarting him—hiding his suspenders, putting pill-bugs in his coffee. Best was when she took a book to the bathroom and sat on the toilet, waiting until he rattled the door. "Just a minute!" she'd call innocently.

But then the bathroom lock broke and wasn't replaced, and one day, Bernice was sitting in the tub when her stepfather strode in and casually began unbuttoning. "What—" she crushed her knees to her chest and squeezed her eyes shut—even so, it was awful. The splashing arc was less than two feet from her head; she could hear the liquid ping against the bowl and smell its sour, fishy odor. He must have planned this, waiting for a time when Ma was out.

It went on for what seemed like hours. And then, with a cheerful whistle, her stepfather buttoned up and left the room.

◆

At four-ten on the afternoon of 24 October, 1911, the aviator Orville Wright manages a difficult feat. Making a new world record, he stays airborne in a glider for nine minutes and forty-five seconds. *Soaring beside a hawk, or looking down on clouds whose edges are burnished by the sun,* Bernice writes in response to Miss Morgan's prompt. *Such are the giddy pleasures afforded to one who is airborne.* For a moment, while writing, she's gliding on air herself. When

Vera nudges her elbow, she is brought down to earth with a bump.

That night, Ma makes *polpettonne*—Italian meatloaf. Gus gets in late, banging the door behind him. He doesn't want to say grace, just waves a hand and tells Ma to serve.

Ma lays a slice of steaming meatloaf on his plate. "What's the matter?"

Gus grunts. "Ehrenzweig is cheating me. Last month he charge fifty cents for a roll of thread, now seventy-five. Say the price of dye has gone up. For what the price of dye should go up? He get greedy, is all."

"Can you use another supplier?"

"Yes, but his colors are, how you say, *unico*. So *ecco*, I must buy from a lying Jew."

"Well, you can relax now, *amore*. Enjoy your food." Ma puts a hand on his arm. "I'll make you a *tisana* afterward—with whisky." Her servile tone makes Bernice cringe, and she juts out her lip sullenly to balance things out.

Gus shakes Ma's hand away. "No *tisana*. I have business." He glances toward the courtyard and Bernice sits up straighter. Is Fredo "making money" for Gus tonight? Casually, she lifts a forkful of meat to her mouth, watching her stepfather chew as he drums the underside of the table with one hand.

After dinner, she asks permission to go to a friend's, then walks uphill. Outside Borlotti's, the sugary smell is intoxicating. Resting in the window are pastries shaped like shells and little pillows. *Sfogliatelle, bombolone.* Even the names are delicious.

Inside, the air is perfumed with cinnamon and roasted nuts. At the counter, a plump man with close-set eyes like Vera's is arranging loaves on a back shelf. When she asks, he nods at a back room.

"Eh, go look."

She opens the door, and is met by a wall of scorching air. An enormous oven takes up most of the room's back half, and in front of it, two women are kneading and braiding dough. Next to them, a flour-dusted Vera is brushing beaten egg onto the finished twists. When Bernice walks in she looks up, astonished.

"What are you doing here?"

Bernice walks over. Their friendship barely exists, but there's no one else to ask. And she can't do this alone.

She bends down and whispers, half-expecting a demurral—but when she meets Vera's eye, the other girl looks cross-eyed with excitement. After firing off some sentences in Italian to the two women, she unties her apron and throws it over her chair. On the way out, she grabs two pastries from a tray.

They wait in the recessed doorway of the funeral home opposite *Contadino's*. Vera hands her the still-warm cake and Bernice bites through layers of flaky, buttery pastry into a sweet almond paste. *Holy saints*. No wonder Vera is plump.

"Oh," she says through a mouthful of sugar, "here he comes."

Gus is coming out with Fredo on a leash. A newsboy hat is tipped over Gus's brow, and Fredo trots by him, happy to be outside.

Bernice pulls Vera out of the doorway and the two of them follow, keeping at a distance as Gus walks Fredo down the hill, then veers left on Mayfield Road. When he gets to the *Società Fratelli di Napoli*, he crosses over and turns right. A little way down the road is an abandoned warehouse, its windows boarded with rain-buckled wood. Man and dog disappear around the side.

The girls follow, Bernice's heart pounding. At the back of the building, there's a row of overgrown bushes and a path lined with rusting machine parts. They watch as Gus and Fredo enter through a scarred metal door.

Bernice looks at Vera. "If you're scared, go home now," she says. Truth be told, *she's* frightened—who knows what they'll find in this place? She imagines bats and snakes, maybe skeletons. And men, a lot of men like Gus.

Vera's lip quivers. "I'm not scared."

"Sure?"

"Sure."

Just then, Bernice hears voices behind them. In a flash, she grabs Vera's arm and pulls her behind the bushes. Thorns prick her arms, and it takes all her energy to hold her breath and stay still.

Two men emerge around the corner, cigarettes in hand, arguing in Italian. Loping behind them is a dog, probably a whippet, with a zigzag scar running down its back. The taller man has thick eyebrows and a crooked nose; the other is young and twitchy with nerves. They throw down their cigarettes before climbing the stairs and entering the building.

Bernice releases her breath in a *whoosh*. The sight of the men has injected a note of danger; the tall one looked mean. It's obvious they won't listen to eleven-year-old girls. "We need to find a policeman," she says.

"We should go to the Naples Club. My dad gambles with policemen there," Vera says. So they run to the *Società*, past the American and Italian flags, Bernice almost tripping in her haste to get up the steps.

Inside, in breathless Italian, Vera explains the situation to a receptionist. Bernice watches the woman's face turn pinched and red. "*Signor Fiorello!*" she calls, and a man in the room beyond looks up. Though he's out of uniform, Bernice recognizes him: tall, broad-shouldered, with black hair and stubble so thick that it looks painted on. She has seen him patrolling the neighborhood, inspecting licenses and munching free *calzone*.

The officer lumbers forward, looking stern until the woman explains their presence. Then he raises his eyebrows—so high that Bernice can't tell if it signals alarm or amusement. "Ok, *ragazzi*. We go see."

Back at the warehouse, he tells them to wait by the door. A moment later, he is swallowed by the dark interior.

Bernice looks at Vera, and can't help thinking that the girl looks porcine, with her close-set eyes and round, pink face. Perhaps she'll talk about this at school, inflating her own role and painting Bernice as a coward. The thought is painful.

"Stay here," she says, "I'm going in."

"But he said…"

"I know. I'll be careful. If you hear anyone coming, open the door and shout 'Geronimo.'"

Vera looks unhappy, but nods. "Come back quickly."

Bernice has to push hard to get the door open. There is a mushroom-y smell as she steps across the threshold, and from faraway comes a thin, warbling sound. Then the door closes behind her, and as the inky darkness floods her vision, her pulse seems to be everywhere, and her breath becomes a whimper.

Slowly, her eyes adjust enough to see a corridor. Trembling, she moves forward, sidestepping greasy puddles. At the end of the passageway, steps lead to a door with dirty glass panes at the top. She creeps up and, standing on tiptoe, peers through the glass.

Skylights; a pitched roof. The backs of five or six men blocking her view. She can hear murmurs, and above them the shrill noise she heard before, which now resolves into individual barks and squeals.

Then one of the men moves, and she gasps because she catches a glimpse of something just beyond him. A crudely made pen, inside which two dogs are rolling and squirming, bodies covered in sawdust, jaws clamped around each others' necks. Bernice bites her lip, then exhales in relief when she sees that neither dog is Fredo. Frantically, she scans the room and sees Gus in a corner and Fredo by him, tongue hanging from the side of his mouth like a carelessly knotted tie. Officer Fiorello stands next to the two, relaxed, as if he's catching up with an old friend.

She watches, growing more enraged, until the two men shake hands and Fiorello walks toward the door. When he emerges, she practically jumps on him.

"Did you stop it?"

The policeman rears back. "*Merda!* Didn't I tell you to wait outside?"

"I couldn't. So, did you stop it?"

He peers at her. "There was nothing I can do. Inside there is clean."

"But it's against the law!"

"*Si*, if money is changing hands. But your stepfather and his friends are doing it for sport, for fun."

"That's not true! They make money!"

"You have proof of this?"

"No, but stay! You'll see it happening!"

"I have other business to attend. Go home now, *signorina*."

He turns to go, but she grips his arm. "Playing cards? Is that your business?"

Officer Fiorello draws himself up to his full height. "You want I take you home? Your mamma would like this?"

"No." Bernice looks up at this thick column of a man, with his sweat-stained shirt and thick stubble. He's a policeman, but is no better than the men in the room beyond. Crestfallen, she lets go and watches him walk away.

When he's gone, she sits on the steel steps and puts her head on her knees. A moment later, a bark makes her jump up and look through the glass, but the men's legs are shielding her view. When one turns and looks toward the door she ducks down, her stomach flip-flopping in fear. And then, crouched down, she hears a yelp that rends her heart. It's Fredo; she recognizes his cry.

She leans into the closed door, her heart pumping as the yelping turns to shrieking, its pitch so high and pure that it's almost musical. The sound drills through her gut. Unable to bear it, she stands up, turns the handle and runs into the room.

"Stop it! Stop!"

The men look around, their faces a tangle of surprise and guilt. She runs, pushing bodies aside, thinking only of getting to the ring. But her arm is caught and she is jerked back. "Eh, *ragazza, calma.*"

The ring is in front of her. She can see Fredo. He's caught under the reddish-brown ridgeback she saw earlier, who's pinning him to the ground. She can hear his whine, like chalk on a board. The room smells of metal and sweat and something else, sweet and putrescent.

She sinks to her knees and looks at the men, some of whom are decent enough to hang their heads. Gus stands nearby, his hands balled into angry fists. A man calls out and the ridgeback stops nipping at Fredo and retreats to a corner.

"Fredo!" Tears blur her vision, stinging her cheeks as they flow down. She's aware of Gus striding to her, putting his hands in her armpits and hauling her up, then clamping an arm around her shoulders. She can feel his stomach against her spine, his fingers digging into her arm. He's rattled, she can tell, both by her sudden appearance and by Fredo's inability to stop the ridgeback's attack. This was not expected. Gus is watching part of his livelihood drain away, and is either too proud or too stupid to stop the fight.

"Watch," he whispers in her ear. To the men, he says, "*Risucita.*"

A man goes to Fredo and splashes water onto him, exposing puncture marks on his neck. Fredo's eyes are open and he's looking at the ceiling, just barely whimpering. With a sinking heart, Bernice realizes he won't recover.

"Fredo," she calls softly.

The ridgeback walks around, growling as he surveys Fredo's prone body from different angles. Then, with surprising lightness, he springs forward and buries his teeth in Fredo's neck. Fredo flops under him, his body rolling in the sawdust, submitting to his fate. Bernice closes her eyes, waiting for the end. There are some low growls, a thin whine. Then silence.

"Salvatore wins!" a man cries.

Slowly, Bernice opens her eyes. Fredo lies on the ground, his throat in ribbons. The ridgeback has leapt the barricade to his owner, who is wiping the blood from his muzzle. It's sickening. With a strength she didn't know she had, she stiffens her neck and rams her head backward into Gus's nose. He shrieks and releases her, and in a flash she has leapt the wooden boards into the dusty ring.

Once there, she drops to her knees and puts Fredo's head on her lap. Blood soaks her dress and is joined by splashes of tears. She strokes Fredo's face and still-warm ears, whispering, "There, now. You're safe."

Outside the ring, the men shuffle and murmur. She sees a man thump

Gus on the back, and beyond that Vera in the doorway, looking helpless. Bernice turns away. She feels she might vomit, but doesn't want to give Gus the satisfaction. So she swallows the acid bile back in her throat, feeling the burn as it slips down.

And then, with piercing clarity, she realizes something. She, too, is responsible for this carnage. Her nurture made Fredo soft. If she hadn't secretly fed him, he might have been meaner, more aggressive. He could have won.

She cradles his muzzle in her hand, feeling hope fade along with his warmth. *Men aren't dogs*, she thinks. *Dogs are better.*

THREE

"Come here, Bernie. On the platform."

Bernice looks up from the table where she's sewing the seam of a skirt for Ma. A few moments earlier, Gus had entered through the street door with a package in hand. Ma had joined him as he cut the string and unwrapped the paper, and from the corner of her eye, Bernice had caught a flash of crimson.

Warily, she puts down her sewing and goes to the alteration platform. Once up there she's less than a foot above the floor, but the room looks different, with threads and trimmings spilling over shelves. She can see the dusty top of the gaslight, and the places where her mother's iron has left scorch marks on the board. Ma and Gus look different too—especially Gus. With his eyes at the same level as hers, he seems smaller and less intimidating.

"Here," he reaches around, draping fabric over her, and she can't help but feel a thrill at its silky weave. "Like this, see? Or more?" His hands cinch her waist, drawing the cloth close.

"Hm," Ma tilts her head to survey the drape, either oblivious or indifferent to her daughter's discomfort. "Not too tight?"

"*Niente*! Is the new fashion. I see in Brodman's."

"I'll make a mock-up in cotton. We'll see what the ladies say."

Bernice holds her breath. One of her eyes is itching, but she won't draw their attention by scratching it. As he lifts the fabric off her, Gus's hand brushes her hip and—unless she imagines it—lingers there for a moment. Again. In the last six months, as her body has swelled and sprouted, he has grown more affectionate and attentive. As if that weren't bad enough, four months ago she'd undressed and found her undergarment bloody. Horrified, she'd run to

Ma and asked if she was dying. Ma just laughed, then took her to the closet and showed her a pile of small, stained towels. The sight of those pink-tinged cloths made Bernice want to retch, and the idea of sharing them with Ma was gruesome. The whole business made her ashamed, and sorry she hadn't been born a cat or a cockroach.

"I can't wait to leave this place," Henrietta Patrick says the next day as they eat lunch in the schoolyard. Henrietta Patrick, Vera Borlotti, Beata Basek: these are her friends, the plain, sensible girls. The ones who might, if determined, do something. But their ambitions are woefully modest.

"Yes," Beata agrees, "I only have to wait two years. Then I can work in my parents' shop."

"Don't you want to go places?" Bernice says.

Beata gives her a sideways look. She has shapely red lips, but the effect is spoiled when she speaks and reveals buckteeth. "Like where?"

"Oh, well," Bernice feels herself blush. "New York, or Paris. Chicago, even. Places where people make art." Make art! How ludicrous it sounds, even to her, right now. But she has to believe it can happen. Defiant, she picks the apple out of her lunch pail and takes a bite.

Henrietta looks over, her eyes squinty. "Well, *I'd* rather learn to butcher a pig. Or know what to do when a boy's trying to get me underneath him."

"Henrietta!" Vera and Beata laugh, but Henrietta just juts out her chin.

"What? It's the truth. They should teach us how to stretch a dollar, and what to do to stop a baby from coming. Things we'll need in life."

Bernice looks up. "You can stop a baby from coming?"

"Oh, Bernice!" says Beata. The three of them look at her and laugh, until, embarrassed, she dips her eyes to her half-eaten apple.

That night, she's closing up the shop for Ma when Gus enters from the back. His womanly lips are set firm, his eyebrows tensed. Wariness flares up in her. She must get past him, to the door beyond.

"Excuse me, I need to finish cleaning up." She steps forward lightly—but just as she thinks she's safe he reaches out, grabs her forearm and twists her around. He presses her to the wall, his fingers digging into her arm, and there's the feeling of something warm and slick on her throat—saliva. "Ugh!" She butts his chest with her head, but he has her by both arms now and is pushing her into the storage closet, bumping them both against the shelves.

Just then, a jingle at the door makes him freeze in his tracks. Bernice half-closes her eyes. Her heart is pounding so violently that everything sounds faint. Still, she hears someone rustle into the shop, not twenty feet away. It must be Ma. She's the only one with the key.

Flashing Bernice a warning glance, Gus pulls away, spits into his hands and uses them to flatten his hair. He walks out of the closet with a smile, and Bernice hears him greeting Ma, playing the part of the devoted husband.

For a moment she's frozen, caught in the animal reek of his need. She's tempted to walk out of the closet like this, mussed-up and shaky, and let Ma see. But it would be her word against his—and the awful thought occurs that Ma might side with Gus. She still loves him, or wants to.

So Bernice retreats to the closet's shadows, holding her breath until Ma and Gus have left. She'll have to be patient, and wait until she can prove what he's doing. But she'll do it. She's not Ma; she won't buckle under him.

◆

The new dog, Cesare, is all black, with wary eyes above a quivering muzzle. Unlike Fredo, he seems aggressive and witless, happy to collude in his own corruption. Bernice tries not to listen to the yipping and howling from the courtyard in the morning, or the furious gnashing when Gus finally slings a bone across the cobbles. On the rare occasions she goes to the courtyard, Cesare's growl makes her dart back into the kitchen.

In the public library on Mott Street, she's browsing one day when a title catches her eye: *Around the World in Seventy-Two Days*. The book recounts the attempt by Miss Nelly Bly, a lady journalist, to beat the global circumnavigation achieved by Jules Verne's fictional hero, Phileas Fogg. *I have always had a comfortable feeling that nothing is impossible if one applies a certain amount of energy in the right direction*, Miss Bly writes. *When I want things done, which is always at the last moment, and I am met with such an answer: "It's too late. I hardly think it can be done," I simply say: "Nonsense! If you want to do it, you can do it. The question is,* do *you want to do it?"*

Before Bernice knows it, two hours have gone by and the sky outside the windows is dark. It turns out that Miss Bly not only succeeded in her round-the-world quest, but did so in the face of violent storms, lost luggage and a doubtful press. She visited Egyptian gambling dens, learned to love curry, and rebuffed the men who tried to make love to her.

Transfixed, Bernice clasps the book as if it will disappear with the sun.

The words thrill, holding out the promise of new worlds. You can be a woman and live a rich, full life—travel, get educated! The miserable marriage, the squalling babies are not inevitable.

At school, in an essay about heroes, Bernice writes, *Miss Nellie Bly has shown us a fine example of the New Woman. She is someone who cares more for conversation than fashion, is nourished by ideas as well as food. Like Miss Bly, I will seek experience and challenge the limitations of my sex.*

When she gets the paper back—an A, with *Good ambition!* written in Miss Morgan's tight cursive—she feels a flush of happiness, followed by something like despair. For how, exactly, will she challenge the limitations of her sex? Until she leaves home she might as well be a fly trapped under a glass—and it's not clear how she might escape.

All too soon, it is the end of the school year. Her friends are impatient; they want their freedom. But Bernice dreads summer, when she'll work in the store every day.

June seventeenth is Ma's birthday. Gus arrives home with a limp, dead rabbit and Ma uses her strength to strip it, ripping skin from muscle, revealing translucent pink. The rasping noise is horrible: Bernice is glad when she's dispatched to the store to buy beer and ginger ale.

When she gets back, Gus has oiled his hair and put on a good blue shirt. He comes out of the bedroom whistling, hands behind his back, and approaches Bernice at the sink.

"A gift," he announces. Then, holding two fists in front of his chest, "but you must guess which hand!"

Bernice looks down at the black hairs curling over his knuckles. She doesn't want to touch him. What could he have in there? A candy, a coin? She backs up, her hip making contact with the sink.

"Go on," her mother says from across the room.

Hesitant, Bernice nods at his left hand. Gus turns it over and uncurls the fingers, but his palm is empty, just some sweat in the ridges. Bernice breathes out. Maybe there's nothing in the other hand either.

"Eh," Gus says, "you guess wrong. But it is Mama's birthday, so I am generous." He opens the other fist, revealing a glint of gold that makes Bernice cringe. It's a delicate chain with a filigree butterfly suspended from two rings in the center. The piece is pretty, finely crafted. It occurs to her that he might have stolen it. She'd like to believe he did, because the alternative—that he went into a store and spent money on her—doesn't bear thinking about.

"It's beautiful," she says. Then, quickly, "But it isn't my birthday, it's too much. You should take it back."

"No," Ma has come up, and is looking into Gus's hand. "Gus chose this for you. Take it, Bernice." Her eyes flash a warning. "Put it on."

"Turn around," Gus says. "I fix for you."

There's nowhere to go. Bernice turns and faces the sink, her skin crawling in anticipation of her stepfather's touch. His hands reach around, and she tries not to recoil as his fingers trace a path back around her neck. As he fastens the clasp, the butterfly comes to rest in the bony hollow between her clavicles, the wing-tips poking into her, the metal clammy and warm. She imagines the chain's malign imprint seeping into her skin, leaving a ring of indelible black.

"Turn around," Ma says. When she does, Ma and Gus both look her up and down, as if the necklace could effect a magical transformation. Bernice is acutely conscious of her breasts straining against her dress, her heart beating under them.

"*Bella*," Gus finally says.

"Already growing out of that dress," her mother observes. Mortified, Bernice turns back to the pitcher.

At dinner, the three of them grow unusually polite. Ma has spread the good cloth on the table; candles flicker on the dresser. The rabbit is moist and rich and Gus is jolly, joking about the lady who comes every week to have her seams let out. The candlelight favors Ma's face. She looks young, rosy. Bernice sucks meat off the rabbit's bones and uses her bread to mop up the rich gravy. She looks at her mother and stepfather, and experiences an odd feeling. For a moment, they seem almost lovable.

After dinner, Ma looks stricken. "Oh, I borrowed Grazia's boning knife. I have to take it back."

"Let me!" Bernice stands so quickly that she almost tips her chair over.

"All right," Ma laughs, "since you're keen. Oh," she shakes her head, "I forgot. She wants me to show her how to mend a collar. I promised I'd take my threads and get her started. I'll go myself."

Bernice sits down heavily. She casts a quick glance at Gus, who is at the icebox, getting himself a beer. "Can I come?" she whispers.

Ma blinks. She's a little tipsy. "No, Bernice. Skinning that rabbit took my last ounce of strength. Now do your part, stay and clean up this mess."

When Ma has gone, Bernice turns to survey the kitchen. The remnants of their feast are on the table: empty glasses and bottles, greasy plates, piles of small grey bones. Gus has gone to the courtyard, leaving the door ajar. She can hear him murmuring to Cesare, and Cesare answering in a guttural growl.

Sighing, she sets water to boil, then turns to clear the table. When it comes to picking up the pile of bones by Gus's plate she draws back, reluctant to touch things that have been in his mouth. Finally she retrieves the pail from under the sink, takes it to the table and, in one quick gesture, sweeps up the bones, which clatter dully against the metal.

When she's washed the empty beer bottles, she sets them to dry on the windowsill. They're quart bottles, thick and nacreous, and as she looks through them the courtyard bricks seem to swell and undulate. A fading light comes through the window, casting a pink glow over the wet bottles, turning the potted lily next to them into a rose-tinted, translucent trumpet. Observing this—the waxy petals against the gleaming bottles, the wavy lines of mortar between the bricks—Bernice feels a surge of joy. The impromptu still life strikes her as something transcendently beautiful, a composition in which each element harmonizes with the next and lifts the whole, like voices in a choir. It surprises her—she hadn't realized that anything as prosaic as a beer bottle could be beautiful. She looks at the bottles and tries to imprint the scene in her mind, with the light falling on the lily petals and curves of glass.

She's standing at the sink, up to her elbows in suds, when Gus comes in. Though she doesn't turn, she's painfully aware of his movements as he strides to the dresser, opens a drawer and fumbles for his smokes. When he lights up, the smoke wafts across the room, a gray, foul-smelling miasma.

"Come, Bernie, have a cigarette with me," he says. It's the first time he's used her nickname. Under the water, her hands freeze and hold the plate so tightly she thinks it might crack. "What? You think Mama does not like you smoke? *Va bene*—we not tell her, eh? It is our secret."

Ignoring him, she resumes scrubbing the plate with force. After waiting a moment, Gus blows out more smoke, then she hears him walking slowly to her, each step seeming to spike her heart rate further. He's finally close enough to hold the cigarette up to her face. It hangs from his fingers, smoldering. A couple of ash flakes fall and sizzle against the water. At the other end, his lips have made a damp imprint. Bernice has to stifle her digust at the grey, wet paper.

"*Vai*, you are thirteen soon. Go ahead. I share."

"No thank you."

"Go. You will like." He comes closer, his body almost touching hers. She can smell his beer-laced breath, and feel his brawny energy. Smoke curls from the end of the cigarette, rising in lazy spirals to the ceiling. He moves the end closer to her lips, so she can feel its heat.

"Don't!" She brings her arm up, swiping his hand away. The movement throws him off balance, and he stumbles backward. Hurrying to recover, he straightens up and pulls on his waistcoat, then puts the cigarette in his mouth, draws on it and blows smoke at her ear. "You are not nice," he says, his voice high, an aggrieved child. "You live in my house, eat my food. But you have no respect."

Stay calm, Bernice tells herself. She'd like to take the greasy water in the washbasin and throw it on him. She'd like to shove the burning cigarette down his throat.

"I'm sorry," she says quietly. "You're very good to us."

"Ah! Better. But…" he throws the cigarette stub to the floor, crushes it under his heel, "one more thing. You must thank me for your gift."

She'd almost forgotten the butterfly chain around her neck. At his words, it becomes burningly present. "Thank you for my gift."

"Not so cold. Like a real daughter."

Stay calm. She takes her hands out of the sink and wipes them on the dish-cloth at her waist. Then she turns to him, forcing a smile. "The necklace is beautiful. You had such good taste to choose it. Thank you." She watches the flattery sink in, eliciting a smug smile. And now, while his guard is down, she begins to edge past him. She's about to make for her bedroom when he reaches out and grips her above the elbow.

"Kiss me. For the necklace." He points to a fleshy spot below his cheek-bone. "One kiss here, then I let you go."

"I'm tired," she pleads.

"Come, just one. I am not a monster."

Bernice looks at his cheek, at the ridge of bone and the shadow of stubble creeping up from his jaw. His skin has an insistent olive tint. Ten Midwestern winters have not managed to blanch it.

"Promise you'll let me go?"

"*Si, certo.*"

Leaning forward, she reaches her mouth to his cheek. The reek of beer seems to emanate from his skin. Holding her breath, she presses her lips quickly to his cheekbone, then draws away.

"There. Let me go."

In response he snorts, then wheels her around. The next thing she knows, her back is against the wall and his knee is between her legs. The wings of the butterfly dig into her, the chain almost choking her. He bites her ear and whispers he can't take it, he must be with her, she is driving him crazy.

And now Bernice feels fear, pure and bright. His forearm is across her neck, she can barely breathe. What is he capable of? They know so little about him. Next to them, clean plates rattle in the drying rack. She forgot to give the faucet an extra quarter-turn. It's dripping steadily, water drops plinking into the sink below.

Moving her head from side to side, she manages to lessen the pressure on her throat. "No!" she cries—then, as loud as she can, "Mama! Help me, *Mama!*"

At this, Gus brings his fist up and punches her top lip, so hard that for a moment, stunned, she forgets to cry. Then his hand is over her mouth and he's pushing her head against the wall, and the fear is swirling. He's reaching behind her, to her buttons.

Let him, a voice whispers. For a moment she listens, and slumps back. This is what women do. But then Cesare whines outside the window, and the thin, doleful sound floods her with rage. Her eyes snap open. She looks left and right. And there, as if she'd placed it on purpose, is her answer.

Fearful, she stares at it. Can she? Gus's hand is over her mouth, her head is against the wall. He's grinding against her, she can feel the grotesque hardness in his pants. *No.* She thinks of Nellie Bly. *Nothing is impossible.*

Raising a hand, she puts it on the side of Gus's face, running her fingers across his stubble. That gets his attention: he pulls back and looks at her, quizzical.

"All right," she says, "but cool your fire. Let me unbutton."

Gus nods. Taking ragged breaths, he steps back, his pants ridiculously stretched by the obscene projection at his crotch. He looks on, panting with approval as she unbuttons her dress and lets it fall and pool, leaving just her petticoat and undershirt.

And then, as he moves in toward her, she sidesteps and reaches out.

Grabbing the bottle by the neck, curling her fingers around it, smashing it down. With only one chance, she uses full force. There's the impact, the awful sound of the thick glass shattering as it meets his skull. Confusion on his face as his body crumples and falls against hers, her pushing back and watching him drop to the flagstones, striking his head. A twitch, some groaning. Then stillness. She drops the bottle's jagged neck, which falls on her discarded dress with a thump.

For a moment, she can't move. Her heart is knocking, and her breath sounds unnaturally loud in the room's sudden hush, which is broken only by the faucet drip-dripping into the sink. Still shaking, she turns to the sink and lets water trickle into her hands, then brings them to her face. She stays there, trembling violently, aware of the stillness behind her but afraid to turn around. A minute ago she was wondering what he might be capable of. Now she has discovered her own gift for violence.

After what seems an age, there's a sound at the door. For an instant, she feels certain that the neighbors have heard the commotion and run for a policeman. In a minute she'll be in a wagon, in shackles…

But when she turns, the shoulder that comes around the door is a familiar one, with a sewing bag swinging from it. Ma steps lightly into the room, looking at the cleared table with an air of satisfaction. It isn't until she glances at the sink that she stops cold. As she takes in the broken shards of glass, the prone body and Bernice in her petticoat, her face does a dance through different emotions: horror, suspicion, disgust. They look at each other for what seems a very long moment. Then Ma crosses the floor to Gus, crouches down and holds two fingers under his nose.

"Have I killed him?" It comes out as a whisper.

Her mother looks up. "No, he's breathing. He'll wake. But who knows what he'll do when he does."

"Ma," Bernice is crying, "I didn't…he made me…"

"Pull yourself together and get dressed. Go pack a case. Quick as possible. Just essentials, you hear?"

"Yes."

In her room, Bernice looks around wildly. She has no idea if she and Ma are leaving together, or if Ma is sending her away. She pulls the valise from her closet, opens it and throws in some undergarments, a shirt or two, her green dress. Casting around, her eye lights on a drawing of Fredo. She rips it off the wall, rolls it and stuffs it into the case.

"Come," her mother beckons from the door. "Quick."

Bernice sees that Ma has a carpetbag with her. Hurrying through the apartment, she tries to avert her gaze from the body on the floor, but can't help noticing that there is blood, a lot of it.

"Move!" Ma pulls her down the hall, then unlocks the door to the shop. As Bernice stands guard, her mother runs to a drawer, where she rummages around and pulls out an envelope. Then she goes to her sewing machine and starts tugging, trying to loosen the machine from its base.

"Bernice, come help."

"Ma, there's no time."

"Yes there is."

Bernice glances fearfully at the apartment door, then back at Ma, who is obviously not going to leave without the machine. After a moment, she runs over and helps to pull. At first, it seems hopeless—they strain and tug, but although the machine is only the size of a small cat, it's stuck fast. Bernice can hardly concentrate. She's convinced that, at any moment, Gus will stagger down the hall and kill them both.

At last, after a few heaves, the machine comes loose and they pull it out of its grooves on the base. Ma hauls it under her arm and they run, hurrying down the street.

"Ma—" Bernice huffs, "where are we going?" She looks over her shoulder, but the sidewalk is empty. Ma doesn't answer, just presses forward, her face grim as she struggles with the machine.

They've walked for half an hour or more when Ma stops in front of a rowhouse with a 'Vacancy' sign out front.

"We'll stay here tonight," she says, "then leave for Columbus tomorrow."

Columbus! Bernice almost trips over her feet. She has only been there once, the time they went to Olentangy Park for her birthday. As far as she knows they have no relatives there, no friends. Mute, she follows her mother into the hotel lobby, which is dark and gloomy, with frayed red velvet curtains. Behind a high wood counter sits a clerk, a sickly-looking man whose thinning white-blond hair glimmers palely against the wall behind him.

Ma marches to the counter. "I'd like a room for myself and my daughter."

The clerk looks up and stares rudely, his watery eyes lingering with interest on Bernice's swollen lip and the sewing machine under Ma's arm.

"No visitors," he says at last.

"Of course not," Ma replies tartly. She signs a ledger, then pulls from her pocket the envelope she retrieved from the shop. Though she's careful to keep its contents hidden from the clerk, Bernice can see a thick stack of bills in there. Carefully, Ma counts out three and exchanges them for a key attached to a metal ball.

Their room is on the third floor, up a series of slanting stairs. It's tiny, with space for not much more than a double bed, a desk and a sink. The carpet is worn and the flowered wallpaper ripped, but the sink and bedding look clean.

"Get undressed," Ma says.

Bernice puts her valise down by the desk and stands there, arms wrapped around herself. She doesn't want to take off her dress and expose herself, even to Ma. It's less than an hour since she undressed in front of Gus, stripping down to her petticoat, feeling the intensity of his gaze on her neck and breasts. She thinks of how, in that moment, he both desired and despised her. She wonders if Pa despised Ma, or just grew bored of her.

"Get undressed," Ma repeats, "we've a long day ahead of us." She has taken off her dress and is shaking it out, getting ready to fold it over the desk chair.

After a moment, Bernice unbuttons her dress and slips it off her shoulders. She lays it on the bed and folds it, then takes off her petticoat, folds that too, and lays both on the chair. Ma's dress hangs over the back, its bodice stiff with starch. Bernice goes to the sink and splashes cold water on her face: it feels good where her lip is swollen, and on the places where tears have made tracks down her cheeks.

Before she gets into bed, she approaches Ma, holding out her arms. "Ma. I'm sorry."

Her mother looks around. For a moment she squints at Bernice's outstretched arms, as if the gesture is some quaint foreign custom. Then she reaches out and slaps Bernice, hard, across the face. The move is so shocking that at first Bernice barely registers it—all she can see is the anger on Ma's face. She looks at her mother in confusion, cradling her slapped cheek in her hand.

"I should throw you out," Ma says.

"But…he attacked me."

"And you did nothing, I suppose? With your thighs rubbing together and your bosom half out of your shirt?"

Tears spring to Bernice's eyes, and it takes all her strength to keep them from falling. "Don't you want to know what he did? If he hurt me?"

For a moment, Ma hesitates. Then she looks pained. "There's only one thing I need to know. Could you be…with his…?"

It takes a moment for Bernice to understand. When she does, she drops her head and shakes it.

Her mother huffs out a sigh. "Then there's nothing else to say. We won't speak of it again. As of this moment, we start a new life." She turns her back, gets into bed and pulls the covers over her.

Bernice stands by her side of the bed. This is worse than when Pa left, worse than when he came back for Hazel and not her. Worse than when Ma married Gus—because then, her mother didn't outright hate her.

She looks at the flowered wallpaper, struggling to comprehend how, in the last two hours, her life has changed so much. She thinks of Pa bringing home treats, his eyes dancing as he made a penny appear from behind his ear. The memory brings with it a wave of longing so strong that she almost cries out. Where are Pa and Hazel now, what are they doing? Do *they* ever think of her?

In bed, she pulls the thin sheet across her shoulders. Behind her, Ma lies with her back turned, stiff and unyielding. She's obviously not asleep, but there's no reaching her. They're six inches apart, but there might as well be a brick wall between them.

PART TWO

COLUMBUS, 1918

Dorothy Whitney, 1926, by Berenice Abbott

FOUR

Sullivant Hall seems designed to intimidate. Below its portico, sweeping marble steps ascend to an entrance flanked by tall columns. It's hard to imagine walking up the steps, showing her library pass and sitting at a desk. Hard to believe she belongs here. But her enrollment letter is in her hand, its type black and solid. The paper bears damp indents of her fingers where she's been clutching it.

Beyond the library, the campus of Ohio State University stretches all the way to the Olentangy River. Bernice tucks her letter in her pocket and follows a path by the side of the building, jumping to one side as a student on a gleaming bicycle weaves around her. It's all so foreign: she might as well have crossed an ocean and not come from the other side of town. There are no rats here, no rotting food in the gutters. Instead, flowers bloom in beds bordered with overlapping hoops of black-painted iron.

At the end of the pathway stands a cylindrical bulletin board strewn with posters. Coming closer, she sees that most of them are war-related. Buxom girls draped in the flag reach out, urging young men to *Volunteer! Your country needs you!* It looks as though OSU is fully behind President Wilson, now that troops are dispatched—though she does see, scrawled on the bottom of one poster, *Sure, I want to die! Sign me up!*

She's reached the Oval, an emerald lawn bisected by paths into a series of triangles and diamonds. Around its border lie bicycles with their wheels tipped to the sky, and in the middle, a bronze scholar frowns from a plinth at young people sprawled on the grass. The women wear drop-waist dresses whose fashionable cut and style makes Bernice ashamed of her own worn smock. On the jade turf, with the sun behind, the students' bodies have a luminous, otherworldly glow.

"Cheat!"

A ball sails through the air, lands ten feet in front of her, then bounces once, twice, and rolls closer. Bernice looks up to see a girl sprinting toward her, braids swinging. As the girl comes closer, she feels blood rushing through her veins, surging and pulsing. Exhilaration, then panic—she should scoop up the ball and throw it. But she can't, she is frozen to the spot.

When the girl gets close, she stops and for a moment takes Bernice in. Then, with a smirk she bends her willowy body and, in one gliding movement, retrieves the ball, straightens and turns.

Watching, Bernice feels herself blush to the roots of her hair. It's unnatural, this reaction she has to girls—yet she can't suppress it. She has tried. She even let a boy kiss her once, holding out hope that when their mouths met, something would ignite. Instead, it was wet and repellent. His tongue flopped in her mouth like a hooked fish, and all she felt was an urge to flee.

She has revisited that kiss numerous times, turning it over in her mind as if it were a broken toy she could fix. Maybe it was his breath, her mood, their age…in the meantime she resolved to keep the other feeling hidden, in that same deep place where she kept the thought of what she'd done to Gus.

Then six months ago, she'd come home to find a letter addressed to her from Ohio State University. Snatching it, she'd run to her room and emerged a few minutes later, waving the paper. *Ma*, she'd cried, *I got a scholarship! May I go?*

Foolishly, she'd expected a moment of shared excitement. Instead, she got a look as dark as molasses. "Of course," Ma said. "Why should you help put bread on the table?" Her mother's tone was so bitter that the air went out of Bernice like a balloon.

Now, standing by the lawn, she feels a tear sting the corner of her eye. *Ma's right*, she thinks, *I should get a job.* She will go back across town and do what class and patriotism demand: work in a munitions factory, mixing gun cotton with chemicals and kneading it into cordite. Making money to make Ma's life easier. Tamping down her ambitions until they're no more than bitter dregs that she tastes now and then.

But the next morning she wakes feeling different. She goes back to campus, donning her lilac dress and making a hairband of a purple ribbon. Her face, with its big nose and weak chin, will never win prizes. But she has thinned her eyebrows and rouged her cheeks.

In the enrollment office, she hands over her selection of classes. The clerk studies it, then shakes his head. "All of these are fine except Anatomical Drawing. It's a senior-level course. What's your back-up?"

"Oh—" she thinks of the offerings. European Philosophy, Journalism, Mythological Influence. How can she choose? "I'll come back later," she says.

She drifts over to the wall, where posters advertise ice cream socials and college clubs. One flyer, for a cycling club, features a pen-and-ink drawing of a girl sitting astride a roadster beneath the words *Relish the road*! The girl, who is waving to an unseen companion, looks wonderfully loose and free. This is emphasized by her shockingly short hair—a bob, it's called. Bernice leans in, inspecting the blunt-cut locks. She has seen the style in ladies' magazines, though never yet in life.

As she's standing there, a group appears in the doorway, three young women and one young man, all in boisterous high spirits. The girls are dressed in patterned skirts and colorful shirts, the boy has long hair and a velvet jacket.

"No, Sy," says the tallest, "we have to eat, or we'll die. You can meet us at Kamp's when you're done."

"Lucy will keep your seat warm," says another, at which the tallest girl swipes her arm and the other one giggles.

Bernice inches closer, wishing she could be swept along with them. What would it take for them to invite her? She catches the eye of the tall girl and smiles, then, in a burst of courage, says, "Hello, I'm new here."

There's no mistaking it, the girl snickers. "Yes, you look green. Or should I say purple?" Her companions giggle, and they turn to leave. As they hurry down the hall, their laughter seems to echo hollowly in Bernice's stomach.

What is she doing wrong? In the bathroom mirror, she surveys herself and, to her horror, sees a different girl than the one who left the house this morning. She'd thought she looked sophisticated, but now her lilac dress looks cheap and gaudy, the hairband childish. Deflated, she scrubs at the slashes of rouge she put on her cheeks. How could she have thought this get-up suitable? She looks like a factory girl trying to claw her way up the social register.

At lunchtime, she walks down North High Street, surveying the shops catering to the college crowd. There are stationery stores, candy concessions, bicycle shops. Lots of cafés crowded with laughing, gesticulating students. Passing, she glances into the steamed-up windows at cheerful, absorbed faces. She feels as if she could drop to the ground without anyone noticing or caring.

And then she glimpses something down the street. Her pulse quickens as a crazy idea bubbles up. Might she? If she did, they'd notice her for sure—but Ma would never live it down. Is it worth paying that price?

She inches forward until she's under the red-striped pole and peers into the barbershop. It's a narrow space, just three cherry-red chairs in front of a water-stained mirror. One chair is occupied by the barber, a white-haired fellow who sits with a newspaper spread over his lap.

At the ring of the bell above the door, he looks up. He's small and withered as a prune, with deep-set eyes and a neatly waxed white mustache.

"I was wondering…" she stops, her throat thick with doubt. It's not too late to turn around and walk out. A whim blew her in, another could carry her back out again. But something roots her to the spot. The picture of the girl cyclist flashes through her mind. "How much to bob my hair?"

On impulse, she reaches up and unfastens the pins holding it up. The dark mass of hair falls, tickling her neck, cascading over her shoulders. It's thick and weighty, like the pelt of an animal. Inky-dark, almost black. She raises her hand to her chin to indicate where she wants it cut.

The barber stands, creaky on thin legs. He looks as if he's wondering what idiocy is leading her to jettison her only good feature. But all he says is, "Are you sure, Miss?"

"How much?" she repeats.

He moves closer, his bird eyes twitching up and down. "A dollar if you keep the hair. Free if you give it to me."

Bernice imagines her hair on a mannequin's head, teased and curled into glossy fountains. An elegant wig. The hair falls to her waist, it's a good harvest. How much will it fetch? Judging by the glint in the barber's eye, it must be more than a dollar. It doesn't matter. Free is the right price.

"All right," she says, "you can keep it."

In response, the barber motions to a chair and she sits, her heart racing as he spreads a sheet across her and lifts a tress of hair. "Last chance, Miss." He has dropped his hand. "Tell me you won't be here tomorrow, crying and complaining?"

"I won't."

The barber lets out a soft sigh. There's a metallic *snick!* as the blades cut through hair, and she opens her eyes and looks at the severed tress on the counter. Her breath catches. The Rubicon has been crossed, there's no going back. She thinks of Ma, and guilt pricks at her. Really, though, can she be blamed? If nothing else, Ma's experience has persuaded her—more thoroughly than any manifesto could—that marriage is made for fools.

Men are dogs. They were, in Ma's case. Even so, it took three years before Ma could leave her second marriage. In the end, she chose Bernice, but at a cost. *I'm done,* she'd said after Gus—*used up, finished.* After moving to Columbus she grew stout, her hair grayed. At first she tried to hide the bottles, now she doesn't bother. She takes her first slug after breakfast and keeps on going.

Sometimes, Bernice thinks of the harsh words she and Ma have exchanged. What would Ma be like if Bernice had been more dutiful, or if Hazel had been left? Better, perhaps. Though it feels as if Ma's course was determined long ago, from the day Charlie Abbott turned the beam of his charm on her.

"Wait a minute," the barber says. He goes to the counter and comes back a moment later with a straight-edge razor. There is hair scattered around her shoulders, in her lap, pooling on the counter. Back in Cleveland, Gus would sometimes pick up one of her braids and brush its end across her neck, like a painter making a brushstroke. Taunting, teasing. Making her want to spring up and rip into his face.

"Hold still," the barber is saying. He brings the razor's edge to her skin, moving the sharp blade slowly. Falling hair tickles the nape of her neck, and she shivers. Her hands are almost as white as the sheet they're resting on.

"Done," the barber announces. He picks up the edge of the sheet and wipes it roughly across the back of her neck.

Bernice looks up, meeting her eyes in the mirror, and sees them crinkle in surprise. New Bernice has blunt triangles of hair on either side of her face: her eyebrows have become more prominent, and her cheekbones too. With hair on either side, her receding chin is less feeble, more jaunty. She looks strong, sensual. Like the painting of Joan of Arc she once saw in a book.

And she *feels* stronger. Suddenly, she realizes that she doesn't have to be hemmed in by the past—she's at liberty to invent herself. The feeling is heady, almost intoxicating.

The barber lifts the sheet off her. "I hope you're happy, miss. Got what you wanted?"

Bernice turns left and right, surveying her profile in the mirror. It's a shock to be like this, so mannish and sophisticated. She's at once herself and someone she hasn't yet met. But she wants to make this girl's acquaintance.

"Yes," she says hoarsely. "I love it."

◆

Rollo's café is roaring with students. They spill out of the booths, four bodies crammed where two should go, laughing over bowls of soup and buttered rolls. Despite wartime shortages, Rollo's is still churning out its famous fish chowder by the kettleful. If the soup is more watery, with a lone chunk of clam floating on top, no one seems to mind.

Bernice sits on a stool at the lunch counter, trying to read *A Doll's House* while alternately smoking and forking pancakes from a nearby dish. Coordinating this trio of activities is challenging—she could drop ash or syrup on the book at any moment. New Bernice manages it, though, as she's managing so much else these days. New Bernice wears a skirt that stops a good three inches above her ankle, and a red shirt with a low neckline and ruffled sleeves. She holds an ivory cigarette holder, in which her smelly Camel smolders defiantly.

The café door opens and closes, letting in gusts of air that make the shaved hairs on her neck stand up. She shivers. It's been a week since the bob, and she's still getting used to that naked feeling at the back of her head.

Her transformation to New Bernice had started the moment she exited the barbershop, when she walked along North High Street to the accompaniment of raised eyebrows and swiveling heads. To her surprise, the murmuring and pointing didn't make her want to shrink. Instead, she squared her shoulders and smiled all the way back to Sullivant Hall.

On campus, the positive attention continued. Girls eyed her, a boy whistled appreciatively. The instant acceptance was worth everything—including her mother's fury when Bernice finally got home.

"How could you?" Ma screamed. "Men won't look at you now."

"Good!" Bernice shouted, slamming the bedroom door behind her. The next morning, she left before Ma was up. And for once, she didn't feel guilty as she strode away from the tenement.

Later that week, she surprised herself in Drama. During a discussion of *Hamlet*, she raised her hand and suggested that Ophelia should have pulled herself together. In the brief silence that followed, she feared she'd been brash—but then there were chuckles, and after class, she was invited to join a group for lunch. The girls ate greasy pasta and chain-smoked as they gossiped about professors and grades. Bernice didn't say much, but she didn't have to. Her hair spoke for her, it was her magic ticket to the table.

Chewing on a piece of pancake (cold now, and mealy-textured), she turns her attention to her book. She's near the beginning and can't understand why the professor said *A Doll's House* would be especially interesting for the female students. Nora, the heroine, seems like a fool. She lets her awful husband treat her like a child, and tactlessly gloats about her wealth to a penniless friend. Bernice is beginning to wonder if she wants to spend three acts in the company of such a simp.

The café door opens, letting in a rush of air that blows Bernice's bookmark clean across the counter.

"May I sit here? It's the only place left."

She looks up, ready to be annoyed. But the girl she sees is slim and lovely, a delicate redhead with freckled cheekbones and a wide smile. Her heart punches out a beat, and she moves her bag from the next stool. "Please."

Sitting down, the girl reaches a slim arm over the counter to retrieve Bernice's bookmark. Her sleeve is green, embroidered at the wrist. As she leans over to replace it in the book, she says, "Oh, *A Dolls House*. Freshman year? I saw it in New York, and it changed my life." She opens a small bag, extracts a pack of Fatima cigarettes and shakes one out. "Got a light?"

"Sure." Bernice strikes a match and leans over. Sitting back, she stares as the girl exhales a plume of spice-scented smoke. Questions rattle through her mind: *Are you in New York often? How did a play change your life?* "What was it like?" she finally says.

"The play, or New York? Glorious, both. I'm moving there first chance I get. This place is so dead."

Bernice picks up her cigarette holder and fiddles with it, lest she speak too soon and reveal her ignorance. As she sucks on the Camel, she casts a sideways glance at the girl. She has a small nose that's ever so slightly turned up at the end, and a sprinkling of freckles over creamy white skin. The effect is bewitching.

"I don't know why I'm looking at this," the girl throws down the menu. "I came in with a craving for buttered toast. Though your pancakes look all right."

"Don't be fooled," Bernice says. "They're like soggy cardboard, but you can keep them going for a while with syrup." At this, the girl lets out a deep, warm laugh. She sticks out her right hand.

"Lilian Watkins."

"Bernice Abbott."

They shake with mock formality. Lilian's slender hand is surprisingly calloused, and her grip is firm. As she signals to the counterman and orders her toast, Bernice gets a chance to sneak more glances at her. She has a long neck, and under the green shirt she's almost completely flat-chested. She'd be boyish if she weren't so delicate. Beside her, Bernice feels as bulky as a farm animal.

Swallowing, she tries to look relaxed as Lilian gives her a quick glance. "I love your hair," Lilian says. "I've been thinking of getting bobbed, but I want to act professionally and I'm worried I might bob myself out of the good parts—like our Nora in *A Doll's House*."

At this, Bernice forgets to inhale and is forced to cough out a cloud of smoke. College girls aren't supposed to aspire to act—much less admit it happily.

"Is it really a good part?" she asks. "Nora seems like a bore."

"Oh, but you're only on Act One. The play is about her development. Be patient. If she had nowhere to go, there'd be no point, would there?" "I suppose not." Lilian's wrists are so thin that the knobby bone under the skin glows white. Bernice pictures touching that skin, pushing down and feeling the butterfly beat of the girl's pulse. Shame pulses through her as Lilian leans forward. "So what kind of animal are you, Bernice?"

Bernice's heart does a flip: has she been found out? "Huh?"

"Artist? Writer? Historian?"

"Oh!" Exhaling in relief, Bernice feels herself blush to the roots of her hair. "I'm—nothing. That is, I haven't declared yet. I'm taking freshman courses in Biology, Drama and Sculpture."

"Ooh, ambitious! Are you in Professor Clark's Sculpture class?"

"No, Gertler."

Lilian nods. "The German? I've heard he's good. You're lucky—or will be, if they let him stay." Leaning over, she whispers, "Enemy alien—that's what they're calling them. Disgraceful, isn't it, after they've lived here for decades?"

The warmth of her breath brings a rash of goose bumps to Bernice's skin. Thrilled and mortified, she pulls away. "Could they really send him away?"

"Sure, it's happening all over. A German professor just got sent back from New York University. My friends told me. The students protested, but it had no effect. First whiff of war nationalism, good sense goes out the window."

The counterman sets Lilian's toast in front of her, and she lights into it as if it's the first meal she's had in days. She doesn't seem to mind about eating daintily. Melted butter glosses her lips, and blackened crumbs stick there like flies on flypaper. A thin line of butter dribbles down her chin, and Bernice has the urge to reach out and wipe it away. The thought makes her light-headed, and she pushes it away, instead picturing small, dynamic Professor Gertler getting an order to leave the country.

"Maybe we could organize a petition. For Gertler."

"That would be swell!" Lilian wipes her mouth with a napkin, leaving a smear of red lipstick and crumbs on the paper. "You should definitely get that going."

"Oh, but..." Bernice feels herself color. She hadn't meant to imply she would spearhead the effort. But Lilian is already pushing her plate away and sliding off the stool.

"It was a pleasure, Bernice," she says. "I have to go to class now."

In a moment she'll be gone, absorbed into the swirl of students outside. "Wait!" Bernice blurts out. "Would you—can you recommend any other plays?"

"Sure," Lilian smiles. "Look, if you're serious about drama, some friends and I are mounting a production of *The Persians*. We could use extra hands. Want to come to my apartment later? The others are coming at six. If you come at five-thirty, I could catch you up." She opens *A Doll's House* and scrawls an address on the bookmark. "But if you've got other plans, don't worry."

Then she's out of the door, a flash of yellow skirt disappearing around the corner. A slight depression in the black vinyl stool cushion, a crumpled napkin on a plate. Those, and her address, are all that's left.

Bernice blinks once, twice. She looks down at the bookmark, then lifts the thin strip of paper and blows on it. Something has just happened. She's doesn't know what, except that it feels momentous. Her nerves are buzzing, the roots of her hair are tingling.

She must definitely read more Ibsen.

◆

To get to Lilian's apartment, Bernice has to cycle down North High Street, then take a left on Kossuth Street. She rides into the wind, standing up on the pedals to scale a hill, her bobbed hair whipping at her cheeks.

This neighborhood, Germantown, is poor but clean. She passes a brewery reeking of malt, a butcher's shop with necklaces of sausages strung in the window. Posters supporting the war effort are everywhere, but there are few people on the streets.

At last she comes to the address on her strip of paper, a two-storey brick house with faded blue shutters. In the tiny front yard, a spidery crabapple tree pokes through the earth, wormy brown apples lying around it.

She leans her bicycle against a wall and, following the directions scrawled on the paper, walks to a door at the back of the house. It's open, and she peers into a small, cluttered kitchen.

"Hello?" she calls, "it's Bernice."

"I'm coming!" There's a patter of feet, then Lilian stands in the doorway, loose hair tumbling over her shoulders, her smile radiant. "You came! I'm so glad. Come in, come in!"

She's wearing a different outfit since the morning. Her dress is purple and she has outlined her eyes in kohl, making her green irises stand out against the gorgeous flame of her hair. Through the dress's thin fabric, Bernice can see a silk camisole and the outlines of her tiny, perfect breasts. The sight makes her warm and she turns to look at the wall, where a playbill for *Peer Gynt* has been pasted over a crack in the plaster.

"Would you like coffee?" Lilian asks.

"Sure."

"Good!" Rummaging in the sink, Lilian pulls out a copper pitcher with a long handle. She fills it with water and puts it on the stove. Then she opens a tin of coffee so fine-ground that it looks like cocoa. "It's Turkish," she says. "All I have, I'm afraid."

"It looks wonderful." Bernice likes the scent, redolent of spices she can't identify. "Is this your parents' house?"

"Gawd, no! My mother would faint if she saw this place! They're in Boston."

"Is that where you grew up?" As Lilian lifts cups from the shelf, Bernice looks at her dainty wrist, at the blue veins snaking under almost translucent white skin. She feels an enormous hunger to know everything about her new friend.

"Yes," Lilian says, putting the cups down. "My parents are good ol' Yankees. Needless to say, they don't approve of my acting. They've disowned me, more or less. But we all have our crosses to bear, don't we?" At this, she looks up so intently that Bernice can't hold the gaze, and looks away. She'd like to pour her heart out to this agreeable girl—about Ma and Hazel, Gus and Fredo, and her ever-present ache of loneliness. But she is afraid she'll seem like a circus freak.

Fortunately, the coffee starts bubbling and Lilian is occupied for a minute with stirring, adding sugar and pouring. She hands a cup to Bernice.

"Sorry it's chipped. Let's go into the parlor, shall we?"

They walk through a hallway to an exuberantly messy room. Scarves and shirts are flung over chair backs. On low tables, lipstick-kissed wine glasses sit next to ashtrays overflowing with crumpled cigarette butts.

"We had a late session last night." Lilian reaches a foot out, hooks a stocking on her toe and flings it under a dresser, then sits down. "Just push some stuff aside and find a seat. So, how much do you know about the Greeks?"

"We read *Medea* in class."

"Ha!" Lilian rolls her eyes. "Hysterical matricide, that's Professor Hayden's idea of fun. Well, *The Persians* came before that. Aeschylus served in the Greek-Persian war, so he wrote it from experience. It's considered the first anti-war play." She leans forward. "Performing it now will be controversial, we think—or rather, hope. We want to challenge the portrayal of the Hun as a savage beast. Shake up all that Uncle Sam propaganda. Theater *should* be political, don't you think?"

It's all almost dizzying. To give herself time to think, Bernice takes a sip of the strong, sweet coffee. Mounting an anti-war play when the country is at war seems provocative, even dangerous. You could probably be arrested even for speaking against the government, as Lilian just did.

"You're against the war, then?"

"Of course. I'm against all wars." Lilian sits up, looking proud. "I'm a member of the WPP."

"Oh." Bernice's cup wobbles in her hand. She's embarrassed to admit that she doesn't know what the WPP is. "But don't you risk getting suspended? Or worse?"

At this, Lilian throws back her head and laughs. "Possibly. But it's worth it, don't you think? Anyway, I told you I'm going to leave for New York soon. A college degree is only one means to an end, you know, and not necessarily the best one." She sits back. "But if it's too much of a risk for you, I'll understand."

Bernice takes another sip of coffee, stealing a glance over the cup's rim at her companion. Her admiration for the other girl has reached a pitch that's almost painful. She looks at Lilian's wrists, at the perfect curve of her chin. A blue vein pulses in Lilian's pale neck, and looking at it, Bernice feels a strange, voluptuous hunger. *Focus*, she tells herself sternly.

"I'll do it," she says. With the words comes a sense of relief, as if she's stepped from a nodding boat onto *terra firma*. Like her bobbed hair, this decision has refined the work-in-progress that is New Bernice. What kind of animal is she? Well, as of this moment, she's an animal who'll be in a political theater group—with Lilian.

"Swell!" Lilian springs forward, and Bernice finds her hands being clasped and pumped. The force of the enthusiasm makes her bounce on the chair, and she laughs until something sticks in her rear. Reaching down, she pulls out a silver cufflink shaped like a four-leafed clover.

"Yours?" She wouldn't be surprised if Lilian wore cufflinks, to "shake things up." But Lilian shakes her head.

"Oh, that's Johnny's. He's a slob. Most of the junk in here is his."

Bernice looks around, and sees a long leather shoe, a silk tie, pants with suspenders. She hadn't noticed it before; she was too busy trying to look as if she saw this kind of slovenliness every day.

She feels a flush, and a stab of jealousy. Who is this Johnny who can scatter his wardrobe all over Lilian's floor? Staring at the debris, she tries to read a pattern into the strewn garments, like a gypsy with tea leaves.

Lilian leans forward and pats her knee. "I can see you've figured it out. Yes, we're living together. Don't be shocked. It's cheaper for me to bunk here than to keep my own place. And Johnny knows how to keep any unwanted packages from arriving, if you know what I mean."

As Bernice is struggling to bend her mind around this, the front door slams and a voice yells, "Lil?"

"In here, Johnny," Lilian calls.

There are footsteps down the hall, and a figure appears in the door. Bernice looks up and blinks, confused. Johnny is dressed in a khaki uniform, with stripes on his shoulder and a bayonet in his hand. A domed tin helmet is tipped over his eyes.

She freezes. Has she been played for a fool? Is Lilian a spy, tasked with ferreting out students who are antiwar sympathizers?

"Oh, John, you did it!" Lilian leaps up and runs to the door. "How many?"

"Eight like this," comes a muffled voice from under the helmet. "My man at the supply store came through."

"You genius!" Lilian removes the helmet, revealing a tousled-hair young man with electric blue eyes. She stands on tiptoe and kisses him on the nose, and he pulls her to him. Bernice watches with drawn breath, shocked at their openness, but unable to look away. She's thrilled by the force they radiate, the glamor and heat of it.

After what seems like minutes, the kiss ends and Johnny straightens up. "Hey! Didn't realize we had company."

Lilian looks around as if she, too, had forgotten. "Ah! Bernice Abbott, freshman, meet John White, director and actor. John, Bernice is joining us."

Johnny strides toward her, hand outstretched. "Welcome! We're a small group, full of energy if lacking in resources." He crouches in front of her, his soldier's breeches bunching over his thighs. "So what brings you here, Bernice? If you want to act, we could use another chorus member."

"Oh, I'd rather be behind the scenes."

"Sure, sure. Props, set and costumes need work. If you can paint, we'll love you for the rest of time."

"Sounds like a deal," Bernice looks down at him. She wants to dislike him, for his effortless charisma and its effect on Lilian. But his smile is so wide and genuine that she can't help smiling back. "But why the…" she gestures at his outfit.

"Oh, the duds? Didn't Lil tell you? We're updating the play, setting it in modern-day France. To get the point across."

"You are?" Bernice is taken aback. Performing an anti-war play just now is controversial enough, but in U.S. army uniforms? It seems foolish, reckless. She doesn't know whether she's more frightened or excited, but the flutter in her stomach as she grins at Lilian is oddly pleasant.

Before long, other students trickle in until there are twelve in all. After a brief discussion, it's decided she'll paint backdrops. Johnny holds the uniforms up like trophies, and there are whistles and cheers. Then the rehearsal starts, with actors crying out lines about mortal wounds and battlefields. She watches, captivated by the rich language and dramatic gestures.

Afterward, someone suggests they go dancing. Bernice is surprised they can change moods so quickly, but everyone leaps up as if they've been waiting all week for the chance. They mount their bicycles and cycle out to Olentangy Park.

Riding through the cool evening air, with bicycles on either side, feels dreamlike. Lilian is in front, tendrils of red hair escaping her hastily pinned bun as she pedals furiously, her skirt twisted between her legs. Watching her,

Bernice feels like a plant soaking up rain. To think that she is part of this group—accepted, wanted!

In the park, music filters across the warm night air as they bump over grass to the dance hall. The pavilion is hung with Chinese lanterns, balls of glowing crimson. Underneath, couples twirl around on the springy dance floor, dipping and laughing. It seems hard to believe that across the Atlantic, boys their age are crouched in trenches, facing mustard gas and bayonets—wondering, perhaps, if they'll wake the next day.

"Want to dance?" asks a long-limbed boy named Arthur a little later. Bernice is standing on the side, bobbing her head to the music, watching Johnny and Lilian. The two of them look welded together, their movements fluid as molten glass.

"I don't know how."

"I'll teach you. Over here, where it's not so crowded."

He shows her the steps for the Turkey Trot, and Bernice picks it up almost instantly. To her surprise, her feet take on a life of their own. They skip and shuffle, agile and eager, and for once she doesn't feel clumsy. Stranger still, she senses herself as graceful—as if she belongs to the music. Before the end of the evening, she's able to progress to the Bunny Hug and the One-Step.

"You're good at this," Arthur observes.

"Am I?" She has no basis for comparison. All she knows is that dancing feels absurdly wonderful. Not to be held by Arthur—who has an overbite and pimples—but to move lightly across the floor, skirt fluttering, feet barely kissing the ground. Looking at Arthur, she laughs. How has she lived this long without doing this?

They spin around, almost bumping shoulders with Johnny and Lilian. Bernice's face and neck are covered in sweat, damp hair sticks to her forehead. She's disheveled and exhausted and almost deliriously happy.

"Don't wear her out, Art," Lilian calls, "we need her to paint!"

"Worry about her wearing *me* out!" he yells.

Bernice smiles at Lilian's receding figure. Even in this crowd Lilian stands out, in her purple dress with her flaming hair and black-rimmed eyes. She and Johnny have a natural ease, the biological aristocracy conferred by good looks. They're like two brilliant, glossy-winged butterflies.

And then, as the Bunny Hug music winds down and she and Arthur come to a panting stop, as Arthur smiles at her and Bernice looks at Lilian still breathlessly entwined with Johnny, she gets a peculiar feeling in her chest. It hits her just under her heart, at the side. Not pain, exactly, but hollowness, as if a rib has been removed.

The feeling of finding what you want, and knowing it's out of reach.

FIVE

"He's interested, Neecey," Lilian is saying. They're walking across the Oval to Piper Hall, where the dress rehearsal of *The Persians* is imminent. Fall is slipping into winter, and groundskeepers are raking crinkled leaves into piles. Storm clouds hang above, sullen and purple, ready to unbuckle themselves.

"I know," Bernice says. It's been clear to her for the last month that Arthur likes her. Nothing direct has been said, but he hangs around her after rehearsal, complimenting her painting, mentioning books she might enjoy. It's as if he's realized that they belong together: the gangly, awkward boy and the homely girl. Nature's cruel system of matchmaking.

"You should put him out of his misery. He's smart and open-minded, and his parents have money." When Bernice raises an eyebrow, Lilian adds, "I know, you don't care. But still—why starve, if you don't have to?"

"I can't get into anything right now," Bernice says, thinking, *I'm already in something*. It's her secret; no one must guess. Like a child with a forbidden pet, she hides her infatuation during the day, then takes it out at night and indulges it. A scrap of casual conversation, a remembered smile can keep it fed for hours.

Lilian won't give up. "Looks aren't everything," she says. "He's a gentleman and a good dancer. And I'll bet he's attentive when the lights are out." When Bernice stops in shock, she laughs. "What? Don't pretend it's not important."

"Did he ask you to do this?"

Lil pouts. "I'm trying to help. He's mooning, and you've got no one, and it seems a shame."

"Wouldn't it be a bigger shame to lead him on?"

"Come on. Where's the harm? So it won't be serious. You'll have some fun and move on, and he'll remember your dark eyes and the way you danced the Turkey Trot."

She makes it sound so easy, even though what she's suggesting—sexual relations, pleasurable and free of consequence—is scandalous to Bernice. Of course she won't admit this to Lil, who clearly thinks she has experience. She couldn't bear it if Lil thought her a prude or a bore.

Nor can she admit how much she has studied Lil. She knows Lil's favorite indulgence (coconut chiffon cake), her heroines (Mary Alden and Irene Castle), and the names of her childhood pets (Zeus and Belle). They've traded secrets—Lil has talked about her fear of water and her ambition to get into moving pictures. In return, Bernice told Lil the story of her parents' divorce, and of Pa coming back for Hazel.

"I always wanted to find him," she said, "but I left it too late. By the time I looked, he'd died. Hit by a steel beam at the construction site where he worked."

In response, Lil had pulled Bernice close and held her, and Bernice had let her, feeling as if her insides were inflating. The loss of her father hit her with new force, but at the same time she felt *seen*, in a way that was almost overwhelming. And, inescapably, there was something else, a giddy, dizzy hope that started in her belly and expanded with alarming speed. It was all she could do to stop herself from blurting out something that she would surely regret.

Since then, the two of them have been close. Bernice lives for the times when they're running lines or grabbing a sandwich at Kamp's. Lil makes her feel interesting, and—perhaps more important—safe. As a result she takes risks, making jokes or being clever about an advertisement for stockings.

But there's more. At night, she has fevered dreams, of such intensity that she fears waking her mother. In the dreams, she and Lil are lying together on a bed, whispering secrets. This leads to kissing, which in turn leads to a fervent exploration of each other's bodies. She wakes, gasping in fits of pleasure—and, on realizing she's alone, feels relieved, then deeply disappointed.

In the beginning it made her feel ashamed. Now it has acquired its own tortured beauty, like Pygmalion's statue.

They reach Piper Hall, where they walk through a side door and down a corridor to the stage door at the back. Through the wings, Bernice spies Johnny in front of the backdrop of barbed wire and trenches. Arthur is there, his eyes piggishly small without his glasses. Imagining his hands on her skin makes her shiver, but not in a good way.

"There he is." Lilian gives her a look full of meaning. "Just remember, tonight might be your last chance, we'll be dispersing after this. I'd better get changed." She blows Bernice a kiss and Bernice watches her lithe figure recede. *We'll be dispersing after this.* Surely she means the others, not the two of them? The idea of not seeing her on a daily basis is painful.

"We're going to slay it!" Johnny announces backstage before show time. The curtain is down; the audience is beginning to trickle in. Holding hands, the actors and crew recite Rupert Brooke's sonnet *Peace*. They check each other's costumes and make-up, and whisper encouragement. *You look stunning. You're going to be great.*

In costume, Lil is a vision. As Atossa, queen of the Persians, her lips are painted blood red and her copper hair is piled high on her head. She wears gold bracelets and a heavy necklace, and her dress hugs her narrow hips and fishtails to the ground.

And then it's time. The curtain goes up, the lights are on, and the chorus comes on stage in its army garb. The silence that greets this is thick, stunned. The audience is taking it in: the men, the uniforms, the flag above the barracks. Someone hisses, and there's muffled laughter at the back of the house.

Then it dies down, and Bernice watches from the wings as the play gets underway. Arthur rushes on stage, a messenger delivering news of the Persian defeat, met by Lilian/Atossa.

Alas, thy tale is as a mountain steep
Of grief; yea, shame and lamentation deep
in Persia.

On cue, the chorus begins to moan, which elicits giggles from the audience. The tension is broken. Now there is rustling and coughing.

"Cowards!" The cry comes, loud and clear, from the front row. "Chicken hearts!"

"Support the troops!" comes another. "Support Wilson!"

A missile comes sailing through the air and explodes, with a crack, over Lilian's dress. It's an egg, brown and rotten inside. "Traitor!" comes a cry. Something else is thrown, aimed at Arthur this time. Tomato juice erupts over his khaki pants, then sprays onto the stage.

After that, it's a free-for-all. Plums, eggs, carrots come raining down.

Ribbons of brown apple peel scribble through the air, like tarnished scrolls unfurling. The players shield their faces with their hands and Johnny rushes onto the stage, but slips and falls. Lilian runs to him, sliding but managing not to go down. Some of the actors kneel and start picking things up from the floor, hurling them back at the audience.

Watching from backstage, Bernice is at first paralyzed. Then, realizing what she can do, she runs over to a heavy lever and pulls it down, making lights flare over the front of the house.

Once visible, the vandals grow less bold. Under cover of darkness they were daring protestors, now they're just students armed with crumpled paper bags. Still, they continue hurling things, if less aggressively. And then there's a flash from the front, a photographer is taking pictures.

"Who are the cowards now?" Johnny shouts. "Bowles, I see you! I know who put you up to this!"

"Have some respect!" a man in the second row calls. "You're scared to put on a real uniform, but others aren't!"

"Where's yours, then?"

"Shut your face!"

"Admit it. President Wilson sold us out!"

At this, the fighting erupts again. The rotten food matter has been exhausted, but the crowd has come with back-up: wet wads of newspaper begin to fly. They slap against the wooden boards and squelch underfoot.

Bernice looks for Lilian, and sees her at the other side of the stage, wiping juice from her eyes. Just then, a wad of newsprint hits Lilian on the forehead, and the force of the blow makes her teeter backward. Before she can think, Bernice is rushing across the stage and grabbing Lil's hand, pulling her into the wings.

Lil's dress is splotched all over with juice, and she smells of rotten egg. Coils of her hair have come unpinned, and there's a cut above her eye.

Bernice reaches out. "My god, they hurt you."

"It's nothing." Lil grins. "I'll call it my war wound."

"What about Jimmy?"

"He can handle himself. Don't be fooled, he's loving it out there. He's General Meade and this is his Gettysburg." Her eyes are shining. She seems invigorated, even exuberant.

"I don't understand. Do you mean this is good?"

"Of course. Don't you see, Neecey?" A tomato seed is stuck to Lilian's cheek, and its jelly-like casing glistens in the light. "We talked the play up beforehand and made sure to mention the costumes. We *wanted* this. There'll be all kinds of chatter now, articles in the paper. Johnny made sure to invite photographers. The papers will interview us, we'll speak our piece. That beats a campus performance."

For a moment, Bernice is at a loss. With Lilian and Johnny she always feels as though she's two steps behind. It makes her feel stupid, but flattered. They must think she has the potential to catch up.

"Anyway," Lilian says, "it's been fun, but it's time to move on. No more campus theater for me."

"Are you going to try out for the Columbus Theater Company?"

"God, no! Victorian melodramas and vaudeville? I've got my sights set higher." She leans forward and whispers, "Don't tell anyone, but Johnny and I are moving to New York next week."

Bernice's face freezes; inside she feels a sickening jolt. "But…what about graduation?"

"Oh, please! A university degree won't help me land a part. Anyway, this place is creepy these days. Now, Neecey, don't be sad. You knew this was the plan."

"Yes." Bernice is glad it's dark backstage, so Lil can't see her gloomy expression. "I just didn't know it would be so soon." She dips her head—for she knows now, with abrupt certainty, that to Lil she is dispensable. They've shared an intense experience, but Lil has plans and dreams, and nothing—certainly not a drab, needy Ohio girl—will hold her back.

Lilian nudges her. "Why don't you come?"

"To New York?" Bernice almost laughs. "I don't have the money. And my mother would kill me."

Lilian *tsks*, as if these are minor points. "She'll get over it. And you could find a job. You could live in the apartment Jimmy and I are moving into—which is enormous, by the way. And it's cheap."

Why don't you? Bernice thinks of her high school teachers, of their insistence that she go to university. *Education will open the world to you, Bernice!* To have made the effort to get here, only to abandon it, would be scandalous. On the other hand, OSU is a poor excuse for a college these days. Many of the younger professors are fighting overseas, and others—the anti-war ones—are keeping a low profile. Professor Gertler was deported, even after she and her classmates collected eighty signatures.

How would it be, living in New York with Johnny and Lil? Leaving Ohio? The thought of getting on a train and beginning another life, just like that, is thrilling. She could get a job, make art in the evenings…

But then, wouldn't living with Lil be like getting constant slaps in the face? Always knowing *she* was the one who needed more, loved more?

"I don't know," she says.

"You don't have to decide right away. Think it over."

Bernice has a vision then of two girls on a fire escape, looking out over rooftops, wineglasses in hand. Behind them, a party and dancing.

She wants to be on that fire escape, so much she can hardly bear it. *And I will*, she tells herself. *Some day I will.*

PART THREE

NEW YORK, 1919

Blossom Restaurant 103, Bowery New York, 1935

SIX

The train pulls into the station with a long squeal of brakes. Steam billows and rolls back over the platform, obscuring bodies, so that Bernice's first impression of New York is of a forest of trousered legs.

She peers at the platform and crowds, wondering if she can truly be here. Things she's read about the city come back in scraps: gangs, murders, strikes. Millionaires like Astor and Rockefeller, with their servants and decadent parties. The artistic ferment and sexual depravity of Greenwich Village.

None of which is visible from the station, of course. All she sees are high steel arches, luggage trolleys, and people, people everywhere.

She'd told herself she wouldn't come here. Better to stay in Columbus, finish her studies and find a job. She could get out later, maybe to Chicago. But then she sat in near-empty halls, listening to lectures that seemed to meander everywhere and get nowhere. She wrote a paper on *Ode on a Grecian Urn* that was as studied and dead as the poem's language was alive and beautiful. It was suffocating. Without Lil and Johnny, the campus was dead and her own potential seemed to have evaporated.

One day, when her restlessness was at a peak, she went to the Air Corps recruiting office on Main Street. The idea of flight still fascinated her; the Wright Brothers had left their mark. She might not be able to go into combat, but perhaps she could train to ferry supplies to the troops.

But when she stepped into the office and asked for a form, the reaction was crushing. "It's called the *cock*pit for a reason!" called one wiseacre. Another would-be recruit swooped and buzzed around her, and even the officer behind the desk joined in, offering, "There's no powder room up there, miss—ya gotta squirt into a bottle!" It was both puerile and menacing—and clearly, a taste of what to expect if she persisted. She ran out, her cheeks burning with rage.

Then, like a sign, the letter had arrived the next day.

There was a 'starving artists' party at Emanuel's the other night, Lil wrote in her looping hand. *A girl there looked like you and had a whiff of your intensity. Seeing her, Johnny and I were struck by the same idea—right away, we took up a collection to pay for your train ticket. Oh, Neece, I can see your face, but don't be angry—we only said a friend needed some assistance! Your letters have sounded so gloomy, we thought you could use a break. I've wired twenty dollars in your name to the Western Union on North High Street. You could send it back or donate it to war widows, but you won't, will you? Come, at least for a while?*

She read the letter twice, then a third time. They had taken up a collection for *her*, they wanted *her* to come. It was too much; it made her ache. She was glad Lilian wasn't there to witness how she fell onto the bed and curled into a ball, weeping with relief.

Now, she steps carefully down the train steps to the platform, dragging her case behind her. People swirl around, a colorful blur of capes and furs, hats and long coats. In front of her a feather from a woman's hat bobs in the air, almost tickling her nose.

"Neecey!" Suddenly they're upon her, the two of them, Johnny with a new, wispy moustache, Lil in a dress made from patches of blue and green. They're laughing, Johnny grabbing her case and hoisting it on his shoulder, Lil embracing her and shouting, "You came! You came!"

"I did!" She hugs Lil back, breathing her friend in—rose water and Turkish tobacco. Lil feels warm and alive, throbbing with purpose as she leads Bernice down the platform. Is she thinner since *The Persians*? Maybe. Her hair is shorter—her braid brushes the tops of her breasts as she walks. But she's as incandescent as ever.

"We'll go straight to the Village," she's saying, "and set you up in your room. And don't worry, you won't pay rent until you find a job. Everyone agrees."

"Everyone?"

"We're five in the apartment, didn't I say? Now we'll be six. We're having a salon on Sunday night, so you'll meet everyone then. Here's the subway, look."

Bernice barely has time to register the architecture of Penn Station— soaring, criss-crossing steel arches, blocky shafts of light filtering from high windows—before she's hustled down to the subway. And she barely has time to take in the wonder of the subway—swaying straps, advertisements for hair oil and cigars—before Lilian and Johnny are filling her in on their latest developments.

They've gotten involved with a theater company, the Provincetown Players. It's a new kind of theater staffed by amateurs, influenced by psychology, and dynamically opposed to the bloated, contrived confections of Broadway. Right now, for example, they're working on a play called *The Angel Intrudes*, in which Johnny plays the lustful guardian angel of a young Village poet…

They're still talking a mile a minute as they get out at Christopher Street. Shops and cafés flash by, along with tantalizing smells from a bakery. Lil and Johnny hustle her along, forcing her to scuttle to keep up.

"Slow down," she says, laughing, "I want to see everything."

"Time for that later," Lil says.

So Bernice absorbs what she can. A red soda-fountain sign, a shop selling phonographs…Jones Street, Cornelia Street…then in front of her, a sight she knows from literature. "The ideal of quiet and of genteel refinement," Henry James called it in his novel. Now, eighty years after he wrote of it, Washington Square would shock James. There are bottles in the gutter and acrobats in the park. But the surrounding townhouses are still elegant, and the Washington Arch is magnificent. Bernice recalls Lil writing to her about how a group of artists broke into the Arch at night, shot cap pistols from the top and proclaimed Greenwich Village a "free and independent republic."

In the apartment, she's shown her quarters—a tiny maid's room behind the kitchen—and introduced to Malcolm Cowley, a gaunt young man who shakes her hand and says, "Hello, hello, make yourself at home," before disappearing. He's a promising writer, Lil whispers. The apartment is huge and ramshackle. Pipes lean windows sit crookedly in their frames, radiators rattle and hiss. The kitchen is shockingly filthy, with dirty plates over the counters and a smell of spoiled milk. But the parlor is cozy, with squishy divans and paintings on the wall.

"How did your mother take it?" Lil asks later. The two of them are sitting in the restaurant below the apartment, Polly's, smoking and eating goulash. To the famished Bernice, the creamy stew seems the most delicious thing she's ever eaten. "Was she horribly upset?"

"She was disappointed," Bernice says. That's not quite the word for her mother's reaction, which veered between smoldering anger and cold contempt. Not only was Bernice moving to degenerate Greenwich Village, her mother reminded her, but she was doing so at the height of the Spanish flu pandemic. "Don't blame me if you kill yourself," she'd said, at which Bernice had retorted, "I'll hardly be able to blame you *then*, will I?"

"I know what that's like," Lil says. "Never mind, poor thing, you're here now." She leans forward and pats Bernice's hand, and the soft look in her green eyes makes Bernice's heart dance. "But listen, I have to go to a rehearsal this afternoon. Make yourself at home, then tonight we'll go to the Hell Hole."

"The Hell Hole?"

"A bar. Its real name is the Golden Swan, but nobody calls it that. Don't look so scared, Neece, I'm not taking you across the Styx. Just to Sixth Avenue."

Back upstairs, the apartment seems echoing and lonely without Lil. In her room, Bernice unpacks her belongings—it doesn't take long. There's no closet, so she hangs her few dresses from the curtain rail and uses her trunk to store her shirts and undergarments. Above her bed is a recessed shelf, where she places a few books.

A cough at the doorway makes her jump. Turning, she sees a stylish woman with dark hair leaning against the doorframe. The woman wears a polka-dot shirt, open to reveal a braided gold chain around her neck. Her lip is curled in a smile.

"The new arrival, I take it. Beatrice, isn't it?"

"Bernice."

"Hm, that's uglier," the woman looks her coolly up and down. "Awfully young, ain't you Bernice?"

"I'm nineteen."

"Really? I'd have taken you for sixteen. It's the eyes." Stepping into the room, the woman bends forward, and—rudely, Bernice thinks—starts inspecting titles on the shelf. "Mark Twain, Charles Dickens. Ooh, and *Herland* by Charlotte Perkins Gilman. How did you like *that*?" She straightens up, looking so piercingly into Bernice's eyes that Bernice takes a step back, daunted. It feels as if she's in a lecture hall and the professor has called her to the front of the class.

"I thought…I thought it good," she says in a half-whisper, angered by her own timidity.

"Good?" The woman rolls her eyes. "You might as well call the war 'rough.' A view like that isn't worth spit." She turns to go, and Bernice feels her anger welling up, directed now at this harsh critic as well as herself.

"The ending was weak," she blurts out.

At this, the woman spins around. "How so?"

"It was cowardly. She created a women's utopia, then allowed men to stay. She should have had the courage of her convictions."

At this the woman grins, revealing teeth that, though straight, are an unappealing shade of yellow. "So you *do* have some fire, Bernice. Nice to meet you. I'm Djuna Barnes, I have one of the rooms here." She sticks out a hand. "You may hear my typewriter, I hope it doesn't disturb. I'm a journalist."

A journalist! As Bernice takes the woman's thin fingers in her own, she feels herself quivering. She's sharing an apartment with a real woman journalist, a bona fide Nellie Bly! Djuna looks the part, too, with her long neck and high forehead, her penetrating gaze.

"Which papers do you write for?" she asks.

"The ones that pay me."

"I'd like…could I read your articles?"

"I'm sure it could be arranged." Languidly Djuna moves forward and, raising a hand, runs a finger speculatively along Bernice's cheekbone. The audacity! Bernice freezes, goose bumps rising on the back of her neck, her heart knocking against her ribs. "Cute," Djuna murmurs, "and so young." Then, just as abruptly, she drops her hand and walks to the door. "Well, nice to meet you, kid. I have a deadline to make. Welcome and all."

Left alone in her room, Bernice feels her heartbeat slow. She flips over the three dresses she hung up, which now look drab and provincial next to Djuna's stylish get-up. All of a sudden, she feels panicked by the enormous change she has wrought in her life. What was she thinking, coming here? She has no job, she lacks a clear purpose, and she has thrown away her best chance for a safe future. How will she spend her days? Back in Ohio, she'd told herself she was coming to be an artist—but that hope now seems naïve. Everyone here is a kind of artist, it seems, and most have more talent than her. Was Ma right, is she ruining her life?

She lies down on the narrow bed. Tears sting the corners of her eyes, and although she feels ashamed for being spineless, she can't shake off her fears. In a few moments she closes her eyes and lets exhaustion take over.

That night, true to her word, Lil takes her to the Hell Hole. They enter through a side door, crossing into a place that, to Bernice, seems enchanted. People of every skin color—from pearly white to deepest black—mingle freely, as if in a fairy tale. Women smoke pipes, men wear necklaces, someone sports a turban. A Negro sits at the piano, playing thumping bass chords with trilling notes laid on top.

"Who's that?" she nudges Lil, tipping her head at a huge man with a sunken, sealed-up eye.

"Him? That's Big Bill Haywood, leader of the Wobblies. People call him the Cyclops."

"Wobblies?"

"It's a nickname for IWW, Industrial Workers of the World. They're for workers' rights. Big Bill looks fierce, but he's a darling really."

Bernice blinks at the one-eyed man, who's holding forth to a table of rapt listeners. Her eye darts to a pair of pretty blonde girls. "And them?"

"Oh, that's Lenny and Nora. Lenny's a peach, she's modeled for the painter John Sloan, and Nora's her cousin from Wisconsin. Lenny used to be a prostitute."

"Oh!" Bernice feels herself blush to the roots of her hair.

"Oh dear, Neecey, it's all a bit shocking, isn't it? You'll get used to it, though. Come, let's get a drink."

"Lilian, my dove!" A man is approaching them—gray hair, doughy face. "Have you been writing?"

"No, I've been learning my lines! Jig Cook," Lil turns, "meet Bernice Abbott. Bernice, Jig is the founder of the Provincetown Players. Our maestro. He's been encouraging me to write."

"Your friend has talent, if she'd believe in herself!" the man says.

"Jig's too kind," Lil tells Bernice, though it seems she's saying it more for Jig's benefit. "Bernice is just off the train from Ohio, I'm showing her around. The Players can find a place for her, can't they?"

"Oh, I don't—" Bernice starts, but at the same time Jig says, "Wonderful! Let me buy you girls a drink!" and Lilian turns and winks as he leads them to the bar.

At the bar, Jig and Lil begin a heated discussion about their play of the moment. Bernice listens for a while, but when they get into details, she takes her whisky glass and moves to a nearby pillar. Leaning back, she observes the bar's denizens, who look like a flock of colorful birds. Empty beer glasses sit on tables, laced with foam. Smoke drifts lazily to the ceiling. Every once in a while, the walls vibrate and there's a terrific din as a train barrels past on the elevated tracks on Sixth Avenue.

"How are you?" A man has appeared in front of her. Short, middle-aged, he sports a head of graying curls and a foreign accent. He's grinning as if he knows her.

"Quite well, thank you."

"You don't recognize me, do you?"

"Should I?"

"I served you earlier, in Polly's."

"Oh yes!" It comes back to her, the homey atmosphere, the rich goulash. As a waiter, the man was sloppy but eager. "The food was delicious," she tells him.

"I'm glad. Are you adjusting now? In the café, you were talking to your friend about just getting here from Ohio."

Bernice feels her ears go hot. Does everyone in the Village eavesdrop and intrude? Privacy and manners don't seem highly valued here.

"It's all a bit of a shock," she falters.

"I imagine. I have been to your famed Midwest. I lived in Chicago some years ago. Cold, very cold. But in other ways, hot." He waggles a finger in front of her eyes, in a way that seems vaguely sexual. "If I can say, I saw how you ate my goulash. Gobble, gobble. Good, no? A recipe from my grandmother. You see," he smiles, "I am waiter, cook, dishwasher and rat-chaser. Oh, and editor of *Revolt*, a journal of anarchist philosophy." He bows deeply. "Hippolyte Havel, at your service."

Berenice feels her heart thump. "Are you really an anarchist?"

"You don't believe me? Perhaps you think I need a gun on my back and a bomb in my pocket?"

"No, but—"

"It's all right, my dear. The government would have you believe we're murderers, it excuses *their* violence. And speaking of names…?"

"Oh! Sorry. Bernice Abbott."

"Bernice? Maybe you will come to listen to my speech on Sunday in Washington Square. I talk from two to four, about wage slavery and the proletariat."

"I'll try."

"Good. But let me introduce you!" He grabs at a passing arm, and a man turns. He has a shock of black hair and looks vaguely oriental, the look accentuated by a monocle that magnifies one of his almond-shaped eyes. "May I present Sadakichi Hartmann—poet, playwright, philosopher, journalist. He can't make up his mind. It comes from having a German father and a Japanese mother."

Hartmann bows deeply from the waist. Unlike Havel he is tall, with a narrow, elegant face. Straightening up, he looks at Bernice the way everyone has since her arrival: frankly, with open curiosity.

"And *this* is Maxwell Bodenheim." Havel reaches out, pulling over a tangle-haired man in a threadbare coat. "Gentlemen, meet Bernice Abbott. Newly arrived from the Midwest."

Bodenheim stares at her with red-rimmed eyes. "Hey, sweetheart. Buy me a drink?"

"Hsst, Max, it's her first night. Take this," Hartmann thrusts some coins into Max's hand, then leans in to Bernice, whispering, "He refuses to work until the capitalists are defeated. In the meantime he subsists on others' kindness. Such principle! Can you imagine?"

"Not really," Bernice says. She surveys Bodenheim's as he shuffles to the bar. The arms of his coat are coming away from the shoulders. What would her mother say if she knew that Bernice was fraternizing with drunks and anarchists on her very first night in New York? It would confirm all her fears about the cesspool her daughter has cast herself into.

Hartmann looks at her. "And you, Bernice? Are you an artist?"

"No—well, I've done some sculpture. And I'd like to paint. Or write." Conscious of how indecisive this sounds, she looks down at her feet. "Right now, though, I have to find a job."

"Find *yourself*," Hartmann announces, with the assurance of one who has plenty of change rattling around in his pockets. "That comes first. Right, Hippo?"

"Yes," Havel beams. "And let me advise you, dear girl. As of this moment, you are free to be whatever you want. Here—" he grabs a glass of wine from a nearby side table, "I will baptize you. May you take your place in this gathering of souls, this beautiful hell-hole we call Greenwich Village."

He reaches up and daubs some wine on her forehead, and Hartmann puts his palms together and bows. Bernice giggles. *They're a little insane*, she thinks, *but it's a good kind of insanity.*

She looks around. The place is humid, smoky, and smells of something burned. Bodies are everywhere, pressed to the wall, entwined, a giant fleshy blob with hands and necks and breasts. She can just make out Lilian, standing on the other side of the room in her purple dress, smiling. An unfamiliar feeling surges through her and she recognizes it as happiness, the sense of fully inhabiting her body. She realizes she is a little drunk.

Taking a step forward, she looks at Havel and Hartmann.

"Hey," she says, "do either of you like to dance?"

SEVEN

"I didn't mean it was bad music," Johnny glances to the side, eyes crinkled. "It isn't. It's the beastly memories the damn thing brings up. Something about the rotten thing makes me think of, well, oh, the devil!"

In the wings, Lilian squeezes Bernice's hand. "He's good, isn't he?"

"Very," Bernice admits. She's come to think of Johnny as an older brother, a charismatic, overgrown boy who bolts his food and leaves his socks on the floor. But in character, he has a gravitas she hasn't seen before. Looking at him now, she can see how he's matured even in the weeks since rehearsals on the new play started.

She looks at Lilian. "Do you know your lines?"

"I think so," Lilian shakes her shoulders as if shimmying into the colorful dress of the West Indian girl she's playing. Reaching up, she strokes Bernice's face, causing a delicious tremor to shiver down Bernice's spine. "Ullo, pretty boy," she says in a lilting voice. "Whatcha doin' out here all alone by yourself?"

Bernice clenches her fists, forcing herself to stay calm. She's been running lines with Lil for the last few weeks and has the scene down cold. If necessary, she could understudy for Johnny.

"Thinking," she growls. "And drinking to stop thinking."

Lilian sidles up, coming so close that Bernice can smell her breath, a tinge of violet candy with a sour note underneath. "You oughtn't drink so much, pretty boy, don you know dat? You have a big headache come mawnin." She presses forward, grinding against Bernice's hip. "Ah likes you. Ah don like dem other fellahs. They act too rough. You ain't rough. You're a genelman."

Bernice closes her eyes. The nerve endings under her skin are popping and fizzing, her nipples are puckered. She hopes Lilian can't feel this through the fabric between them, or somehow intuit it. Smitty, the character Johnny's playing, is supposed to be disgusted by Lilian's character, Pearl. But Bernice wants nothing more than to grab Lilian by the waist and…

Unnatural. Her desires are sinful, immoral.

Or are they? Since coming to the Village, she's witnessed extraordinary things. At the Hell Hole, Romany Marie's or the Brevoort, a man and woman might kiss and stroke in front of the woman's husband, who doesn't so much as blink. That's one thing—but then men kiss men, and women rub against women, and sometimes these pairs leave the place together. They—the liberated, the uninhibited—call it free love. But she's aware of another, powerful 'they' out there that calls the Village an abomination, a contemporary Sodom and Gomorrah. And for the most part, it's the other 'they' that calls the shots.

Lil's body is against hers, so close, smelling intoxicatingly of rose water. She's alert, waiting for Bernice to speak. But Bernice can't. She's overcome with the thought of what would happen if she let herself go. To fall down that rabbit hole, touch a girl and be touched back. The thought is overwhelming, but no longer entirely unimaginable. Just the other night, when they were sipping tea before bed, Lil had looked at her and said, *You have lovely eyes, Neecey, you know? Like velvet.* So maybe it's not crazy to hope…

Lil gives her a dig in the ribs. "Thank you for the compliment," she prompts.

"Thank you for the compliment," Bernice squeaks. As she lowers her voice, it takes on some of the bitterness Mitchell wants. "But you're wrong, you see. I'm merely a ranker. And a rotter."

"A ranker," Lil pulls away, breaking character. "What d'you suppose that is?"

"I don't know. Someone ordinary? From the bottom of the pile?"

"I've never heard it before."

"Nor me. But I like the rhythm of ranker and rotter."

"Yes. Our Gene is coming along."

Gene O'Neill, a young Irish-American, has recently hitched himself to the Provincetown Players. They're rehearsing his new play, *The Moon of the Caribbees*. It's more of a mood piece really, a one-act dramatic poem that's meant to convey the rhythms of life at sea. The plot—insofar as there is one—concerns a group of sailors who get into trouble with some Caribbean women while their boat is anchored offshore. There isn't much action to speak of, but that's the point. It's a new kind of drama, something loose and free, more naturalistic than the stilted fare of Broadway.

When she first came to watch rehearsals, Bernice didn't intend to get drawn in. She wasn't a performer, she said, she preferred to work with her hands. But the company needed more bit-part players, and she was cast as one of the lesser island women. She doesn't mind—all she has to do is laugh and dance a bit, and she gets to be around Lilian. And she enjoys O'Neill's lush language, even if the playwright himself is noxious. At rehearsals he smolders in the third row, jumping up occasionally to shout at the director, a minor Broadway actor brought in to impose order on the group. "The sea!" he roared once, "don't you understand, Mitchell, the sea is the hero here!"

"Where the heck is Ralph?" The boards are shaking under Mitchell as he paces the rickety stage. "This is the third rehearsal he's missed!"

"He's sick," someone says, "with a fever."

"Yeesh, it'd better not be the flu. What about Theo? What's his excuse?"

"He has a night job Tuesdays."

"Why'd he take the part, then? God help me!" Mitchell runs a hand through his hair. "I know you people are amateurs, but I expected *some* standards."

He glares into the wings, and Bernice feels a tug of irritation. She has a job now, too—Lil helped her get it. She works as a dyer in a yarn factory on Lispenard Street and is constantly in motion, dipping skeins of threads into vats of dye, wringing them out and hanging them to dry. Her back aches from all the standing—yet she, like the other cast members, shows up for rehearsal. She thinks Mitchell should ease up on them all.

Johnny puts a hand on his chest and barks out a cough. "I'm feeling lousy too, to tell the truth."

"Oh, for goodness sake," Mitchell raises his eyes, as if looking for hope among the ropes and pulleys above. "Go home, everyone. Get a good night's sleep and we'll reconvene tomorrow, all right?"

So saying, he disappears, and there's some shaking of heads before the cast starts to disperse. Johnny comes stomping into the wings, waving a bottle.

"What's in this fake rum?"

"It's burned toast," Lil says. "You use it to color the water, then strain it out."

"God, it's disgusting!"

"Sorry, John. I'll use tea next time." Turning to Bernice, Lil contorts her face in a private language that Bernice can read fluently. *He's in a mood*, her expression says.

"Let's go home," Johnny says, "I feel godawful."

Lil's mouth makes a moue. "Oh, Neece and I were going to Polly's and the Hell Hole. How about I bring you up some goulash?"

"I couldn't eat."

"Go home and sleep, then. You'll feel better tomorrow." She pats his shoulder and turns to go, but Johnny catches her arm and pulls her back. As she embraces him, Lil rolls her eyes at Bernice, and Bernice feels a flutter in her stomach. Is it possible her friend is cooling toward Johnny? That his charms are wearing thin?

She grins at Lil. The feeling that's always under the surface rises up, suffusing her skin with heat. Shy longing, a clandestine hunger. It's enough to bring tears to her eyes, wondering if it will ever be sated.

◆

"We'll be lucky to get a seat in here," Lil says as they enter Polly's. It's Saturday night, a time when even Communists and Wobblies recognize the need to have fun. Sure enough, the place is packed. Flu masks lie discarded and sodden on tabletops, hands and faces emerge from smoke clouds, like apparitions at a séance.

"Should we go someplace else?" Bernice asks.

"No! We'll squeeze in." Lil points at a table for four occupied by two men, one small and dark, the other blond and tall. "Over there."

Bernice shrugs, vexed. She'd wanted Lilian to herself, but Lil is determined. She pushes her way around tables, pulling Bernice after her.

As they get to the table, the short man jumps up and pulls out a chair for Lilian. The other fellow merely nods, so Bernice is obliged to pull out her own chair. But when she sits down he leans forward, fixing her with an intense stare. He's lanky and long-faced, with melancholy green eyes and a narrow, straight nose. As he surveys her, his lips purse in a contemplative line.

"What's he doing?" she asks his friend.

"Oh, Marcel likes to study people. He's French."

Bernice raises an eyebrow. The man called Marcel is still staring, so she sticks her hand under his face. "Hullo. I'm Bernice."

"Appy to mee chou." Raising her hand to his lips, Marcel kisses her on the knuckles. He then turns to Lil, swoops in and kisses both of her cheeks, rattling off some phrases in rapid-fire French.

"He says your beauty is a pulsing machine that, if let loose, would grind his liver to cat meat," the short man says. "Or something like that. He's rather drunk."

"Thank you," Lilian tells Marcel, who bows.

"And I'm, uh, Man," the other fellow tells Bernice.

"You're a man?"

"No—I mean yes, of course. But my name is Man. Man Ray."

Pretentious, Bernice thinks. He has a crooked nose, intense black eyes and a pronounced widow's peak, a deep V from which wiry black hair bristles back over his head. He seems haughty and a little pleased with himself. Still, she supposes some women might find him attractive.

They order wine, and Man tells a story about an artist he knows who, as a 'happening,' trained a parrot to squawk 'philistine,' then took it to a party full of wealthy art patrons. "Genius," he says. "Much better than his paintings, which are shit."

Soon they're knocking back wine and eating Hippolyte's goulash. Of course both men are artists, and Bernice nervously tallies their wine glasses, wondering if they'll split the check. But Man is a making them laugh. He tells them about an artist, Goldknob, so called because he once painted his genitals gold and couldn't get the paint off for weeks. There's something about him, a fierce intensity in his glittering eyes. His ideas are refreshing. He tells Bernice how he hates art museums and their "bourgeois values." Nothing interests him in art, he says, unless he's never seen it before.

"Want to come to a party?" he asks.

Bernice looks at Lilian, who's squinting down at Marcel's hand, trying to read his palm. Lil is drunk, for sure—she's blinking too much, her eyes inches above the Frenchman's hand. Now she looks up, grinning. "A party? Sure, we'd love to. *Allons-y*! Let's go!"

A minute later, in the powder room, Bernice holds Lil's elbow and pulls her back. "What about Johnny?"

"Ach, he'll be sleeping. Anyway I'm not tied to him like some goddamned pet. I'm entitled to some fun."

"I just think…"

"Think, plink. Come on, Neecey! Forget the war and the damn flu. Have some fun, for Chrissake?" She leans forward and kisses Bernice on the nose, and Bernice is a little stung to think that Lil sees her as such a drip.

"All right," she says, "let's go."

"Weel you mind?" Marcel asks when they come out. "I must to my 'ome first, peek up a drawing."

"Sure, we can go your *ome*," Bernice says, raising an eyebrow at Lilian. But Lil has already taken Marcel's arm. The two of them totter down the street, and Bernice and Man follow in silence, pointedly not touching each other on the narrow sidewalk.

"I've been trying some new photography," he says at last. "You'd make a good subject. You have cat's eyes. Would you sit for me?"

She looks at him askance. Nobody has asked her to model before. Her face, with its broad plains and lumpy features, could never be called beautiful; at best it has an arresting quality, a dark allure. For a moment, she's flattered. Then her natural wariness flares up, like a match struck in the dark.

"You'd want me naked, I suppose?"

He gives her an appraising look. "No, something tells me you'd be better clothed. More focus on that curious face."

"Oh." She's not sure whether to be flattered or insulted. "Well, I'll think it over."

"You would do me an honor."

They're walking down Barrow Street, toward the river. A gibbous moon hangs over New Jersey, shedding a pale light onto the thin clouds around it. They pass a hobo, flattened against the side of a building, dirty shirt ripped open to his waist. Around him lie squashed, empty tin cans, like the droppings of a great silver bird.

Ahead, Marcel ducks into the doorway of a building with mildewed walls and boarded-up windows. It looks like a bums' den, an unmitigated fire hazard.

"This is where he lives?"

Man Ray shrugs. "It's cheap. And he needs space for his art. Come on, I think you'll like what you see."

Hesitant, Bernice follows him into a dark hallway. As they ascend the rickety stairs, Lil's laughter peals down from above, making her uneasy. It occurs to her that the men paid for the wine—a gesture they insisted on, which now seems like the kind of thing men do when they're looking for a warm bed for the night. If a sticky situation arises, will she be able to get the two of them out of it?

But when they reach Marcel's apartment on the fifth floor, her suspicion is replaced by pure astonishment. She looks around, wanting to laugh out loud. It's as if she's a child and has entered a museum of curiosities.

Every inch of the space is occupied, and each piece of art she can see is shocking either in terms of technique, materials, or both. On the walls, painted canvasses depict human forms that fracture, splintering into pieces, and somehow the artist has created an illusion of movement through a series of lines that shift and bend, so that it looks as if the forms are dancing through space and time. The floor is almost impassable, taken up with odd and humorous amalgams of everyday objects. A bicycle wheel fixed to the top of a stool, a cage full of broken eggshells. The stuffed head of a deer poking out of a baby carriage.

The strangest piece of all is in the center of the room. It looks like a huge window with wire outlines of chess pieces soldered onto the glass. Painted brown, these chessmen hover around a contraption made of pulleys and cones, while above sits a spindly, insect-like creature trailing an ominous brown cloud.

Bernice moves closer. Though she can't immediately decipher its meaning, she can tell that the piece represents something bold, a break with all artistic rules. Depending on how you look at it, the man who created this is either a madman or a visionary. She recalls a scandal a few years previously, when an artist showed a glass piece at the art show in the Armory.

"Who did you say your friend was?" she asks.

"Marcel, Marcel Duchamp. You see what he's trying to do?" Man looks at her, eyes glittering. "The paintings represent a moment of dynamic, cosmic flux, the passage of time. And the sculptures—he calls them *readymades*. Anti-beauty, anti-taste. The objects are mass-produced, entirely worthless in themselves. It's Marcel's eye that makes them art."

Bernice shakes her head. Everyone in the Village is a capital-A Artist, and most are trying to shock, but not until now has she seen anyone make such a complete and utter break with the past. Who puts a bicycle wheel on a stool and calls it art? *And yet*, she thinks, *there's something here*. With his readymades, Duchamp seems to want to make noticing an act of creation in itself.

"I see it," she whispers.

"*Voila*!" Marcel shouts from across the room. He waves a piece of paper at them, then brings it to his lips and kisses it. "*Trouvé*!"

The drawing is a trifle, a line study of two men playing chess. But it must have sentimental value, for Man Ray is delighted to see it. With this in hand, they descend the five flights to street level.

"Isn't he something?" Lil whispers to Bernice. The two women are walking together, trailing the men. Lil holds a lightbulb in an egg holder that Marcel gave her.

"He is…something," Bernice admits.

"What about Man, do you like him?"

Bernice glances away, avoiding her friend's eyes. "He wants me to model for a photograph."

"Hoo boy. Are you going to do it?"

"I said I'd consider it. Clothed, of course."

"Neecey," Lilian elbows her. "Let yourself go. He's cute."

"It's just a photograph." Next to her, Lil loses her footing on the sidewalk and tips precariously, and Bernice slides an arm around her waist and pulls her close. "Got you," she says.

The party, when they get there, is a riot of music and color, in a basement with purple-painted walls. Music pulses from a phonograph on the floor, and in front of it people are dancing, skirts swing-swinging, shimmying shoulders, bright flashes of jewelry and teeth. Bernice can't help it, her foot begins to tap in time to the music.

"Do you dance?" she asks Man.

He shakes his head. "I don't know the steps."

"I'll teach you."

"Well—"

"Come on, silly. You'll pick it up lickety-split."

Before he can protest, she pulls him over to the dance area and positions him. She takes him through the movements of the Grizzly Bear, and after a few fumbles he gets it. Delighted, he spins her around the space again and again, and when it comes time to make the bear pose, he springs forward with claw-like fingers and teeth bared, convincingly ursine.

"Grrrrr!" he cries. "Look at me!"

They spin to the edge of the room and take a break, and Bernice pants and grins at Man. No matter if she's tired or blue, dancing always puts her in a good mood.

Just then, the door is flung open and in walks a most extraordinary creature. She—if it's a she, for the figure is tall, rangy and bald—wears baggy white pants daubed with blotches of black paint. On top of this is a fur jacket, and visible under the jacket is a brassiere made from two soup cans strung together.

On her shaven head is a mortarboard, and on top of this is mounted a small birdcage containing a live canary.

"Saxophone's steelblast, tangled limbs, riding the moon—to social insanity!" she cries.

"Elsa is here!" someone shouts. Immediately, the phonograph is turned down; the crowd breaks out in applause. "Elsa, you've outdone yourself!" a woman yells. "Give us a poem!" cries another.

Stepping forward, a man takes the creature's hand and escorts her across the room. Keeping her back regally stiff, Elsa steps up onto a coffee table. Her shoes, Bernice sees, are covered in crushed candy wrappers.

"*Affectionate*," Elsa announces gravely. There's an expectant hush as she glances around, eyes narrowed, before beginning:

"*Wheels are growing on rose-bushes*
grey and affectionate,O Jonathan—Jonathan dear
Did some swallow Prendergast's silverheels—be drunk forever and more—
with lemon appendicitis?"

At this, she spirals a hand in the air before taking a deep, extravagant bow. There's laughter and applause, and the canary—bewildered at being suddenly flipped over—lets out an outraged cheep, which brings on more laughter.

Clapping so hard that her hands hurt, Bernice is filled with a sudden sense of awe. To be here, amid such excitement and absurdity—with people who see her, and think her worthy of having her portrait made! She feels light and bubbly, as if she's quaffed champagne.

She turns to Man. "Who is that?"

"You don't know? It's Baroness Elsa."

"Is she really a Baroness?"

Man nods. "She was married to a German baron. A bit of a ne'er-do-well, the black sheep of the family. When war broke out, he enlisted and abandoned her. Now she scrapes by as an artist's model, though as you see, she's also a poet."

Just then, Elsa—who's still on the table—goes down on one knee. She looks at Marcel, who's standing nearby with an arm draped around Lil.

"Marcel, Marcel. I love you like hell, Marcel!" she screams. Someone snickers, and Elsa glares from under her birdcage.

"Oh, and also," Man says, "she's hopelessly in love with Marcel. He sees her as a kindred spirit, but rejects her physically—so her lust goes unassuaged." He leans in and whispers, "It's the source of some of her best work."

Bernice glances at Lilian, who has a hand on Marcel's shoulder and whose mouth, open in laughter, reveals perfect, pearl-white teeth. The swell this causes in her chest—and elsewhere—is, by now, as familiar as breathing. So she and the Baroness have something in common.

"I should like to meet her," she says.

"Come," Man takes her by the arm and, elbowing through a thicket of people, leads her across the room. When they get to Elsa, he pushes Bernice forward like a sacrificial goat. Up close, Bernice sees that the Baroness is older than she first appeared. There are splashes of white on her head from where the canary, a martyr to art, has been liberally shitting itself.

The Baroness looks down at her, and as she did earlier in the evening with Marcel, Bernice gets the feeling that Elsa is either seriously deranged or else some kind of genius, an emissary from the future.

"Elsa, this is Bernice Abbott. She's a sculptor and, as of tonight, your ardent fan. Just off the train from Ohio. Isn't she adorable?"

The Baroness takes a step forward, looming over Bernice. Her clothes exude a sharp odor of mothball, and on top of that a dark, licorice smell.

"Sculptor of what?" she demands.

Feeling a flutter of nerves, Bernice straightens up and looks Elsa in the eye. "I'm working on a head of Edgar Allan Poe," she says. In truth, Poe, with his lopsided face and enormous forehead, has been giving her a headache, and she was tempted to squash him last week.

"Poe!" Elsa taps a finger to her chin, looking dreamily at the ceiling. After a moment, she comes to, singing out, "Pustulous, pernicious, precious Poe!" Swooping forward suddenly, she kisses Bernice on both cheeks. "Sweet thing! Visit me next week, Man will tell you how. Bring your sculpture. You and I shall take tea with the head of Edgar Allan Poe."

She turns away, and Bernice realizes that her audience with the Baroness has ended. Intrigued, she watches as Elsa holds out her hand to be kissed by a young man who goes down on one knee, one hand over his heart. The Baroness looks at him wolfishly, the canary hopping around on her head.

"Satisfied?" Man asks. If attracted, he would touch her now, Bernice knows this. He's fulfilled her wish, she's in his debt. But he just looks at her, eyes limpid under thick brows, and she suddenly knows that his sexual interest in her is as non-existent as hers in him. Seeing this, she breaks into a grin.

"So when would you like me to pose?"

EIGHT

The parlor of the MacDougal Street apartment is in a profound state of disarray. Sofas have been pushed back, tables shunted aside. Twenty or more people crowd the space, all variously drunk or high. Collars are loose, skirts crumpled. Hippolyte Havel is asleep with his head against a bookcase; a writer friend of Djuna's flops on a sofa with a pancake-sized wine stain on her dress. The skunky smell of reefer hangs in the air.

"John, your turn!" Lilian cries. "You've never been psyched."

Johnny grimaces. "Must I?"

"Must he?" Lilian looks around mischievously, and people begin a slow chant: *John-ny, John-ny!* Djuna, who's sitting next to Johnny, gives him a push.

With a sigh, Johnny heaves himself up and makes his way to the psyching chair. Malcolm Cowley, their roommate and tonight's Herr Doktor, peers at him through borrowed horn-rimmed glasses.

"Your muh-zza, young man?"

Johnny blinks. "Beautiful. Put-upon. Had five children in eight years. A gifted artist in her spare time."

"Fah-zza?"

"Disciplinarian, old-fashioned. Would whip my butt if he caught me in a lie."

"Oedipus complex!" cries someone.

"Well, *that* goes without saying," drawls Djuna's wine-stained friend. "The question is, has he gotten over the phallic stage?"

"*Definitely* not," says Lilian. The room erupts in laughter, which makes Hippolyte Havel lift his head and look around. Bernice smiles at him. He blinks, then leans his head back on the bookcase and starts snoring again.

Bernice shifts in her seat. She doesn't like these psyching parties, as prevalent as they are. Psychoanalysis is the new European import, more popular than camembert or Chaplin. Freud is everywhere—you can't so much as go out to buy a loaf of bread without hearing about someone's complex.

"First sex-u-al experience?" asks Malcolm. Johnny looks embarrassed but tips his head, thinking.

"Go on!" prompts Lilian.

"All right! The Adirondacks, 1904. A lake, I was eight. We were there with another family. Imagine a German matron, very strict—my governess. A bit masculine. Hairy armpits. She lifted me up to go in the water, and…"

"Something else lifted too?" suggests Djuna. There are peals of laughter, and someone hands Malcolm a cigarette, which he sucks on deeply. Embarrassed, Bernice looks at the windowsill, where cigarette butts lean in a plant pot like tiny towers of Pisa. Fuzzy-headed, she wobbles to her feet and leaves the room.

In the kitchen, another scene of carnage greets her. The countertop is littered with open bottles, glasses, deliquescent food. Soft cheeses have oozed over plates, wine has spilled into a bowl of deviled macaroni. A half-eaten apple lies discarded, its wet flesh browning.

She could tidy up, but she's tired—and besides, she already spends too much time in the kitchen. When she first moved in, it had seemed only polite to wash dishes and mop floors. If nothing else, Ma had taught her to be fastidious. But cleanliness, it turns out, is disdained by educated bohemians. After a couple of weeks, Lil took her aside, saying, "You mustn't. Everyone will take advantage. You might be in the maid's room but you're not a maid." And so, six months on, she has become almost as slovenly as the others. Only at times like these is she irked by a vestigial urge to clean.

She moves past the worst of it, stepping over a beer crate to get to her room, only to rear back as a man jumps from the bed, cigarette in hand.

"I beg your pardon! I had a headache and wanted some quiet, and you have a cozy spot here. Sorry! I'm Holger Cahill, Malcolm's friend."

"Bernice Abbott." She steps forward and shakes his hand. He writes about art, she recalls, and unlike the guests in the living room, he doesn't look disheveled. His oval face is clean-shaven, and he wears a turquoise shirt that complements his alert blue eyes. He looks pleasant enough but she wants him out of her room.

"Is it safe out there?" he asks.

"More or less. But they're psyching each other."

"Again! You weren't tempted?"

She leans against the doorframe, feeling an ache from sitting cross-legged on the floor. "I can't think of anything worse."

"I know," Cahill says with a chuckle, "me too. I guess Freud would call us repressed. Most people can't wait to spill the beans."

"Most people think they're more interesting than they are."

"Agreed." He takes a drag of his cigarette and blows smoke from the side of his mouth, like a movie star. "I couldn't help noticing your sculptures."

"Oh, they're nothing." Bernice follows his eyes to her desk, where her latest pieces sit. There's a bird, a sort of abstracted raven whose clayey heaviness suggests the pull of gravity rather than the glory of flight. A squat and rather primitive-looking king and queen, the first two pieces of a chess set she's making for Duchamp, who's obsessed with the game. "I'm taking lessons," she says.

"Well, that's good, I guess. But I think your work is charming. If you don't mind my asking, why sculpture?"

Bernice has wondered the same thing herself. "I wanted to paint or draw, but I can't do those well. I like the way clay feels in my hands. My mother can sew—I guess we Abbott women like to work with our hands."

Cahill nods. "I like that. If you ask me, art should be unpretentious—for the proletariat, as our friend Hippolyte would say. Like the early settlers, carving their weathervanes and sewing quilts. Utilitarian, but beautiful." He moves to the desk. "May I?" She nods, and he picks up one of the chess pieces and raises it to eye level. "I like your sense of primitivism. The humble clay, the abstracted features. You've bypassed the genteel tradition entirely."

"Thanks," Bernice says, though she's not sure if it's truly a compliment. It sounds as if he's calling her an oaf. *Perhaps it's just that I lack skill,* she thinks. Certainly, when she crafted these pieces she wasn't thinking about their relation to the genteel tradition. And, much as she'd like to think she'd chosen clay for its homespun quality, it was the only material she could afford.

But Cahill's views, if odd, are intriguing. The artists and writers she's met in the Village like to think themselves radical, but the way they express this—by doing whatever's considered most shocking at that moment—can seem juvenile. What Cahill is saying hasn't occurred to her before, but it makes sense. Using humble materials is a statement, too. Like Marcel's bicycle wheel, it's a rejection of elitism. Why, it's practically socialist!

Cahill replaces the chess piece on the desk. "Have you heard of the Eight?"

"You mean the Ashcan crew?"

"Yes, but don't call them that. The name was invented by a charlatan who fancies himself clever."

"I'm sorry, I didn't know. Actually, Sloan is a hero of mine." It's true. The world John Sloan paints, of poor people doing ordinary things, is one she understands.

She met Sloan once. He dropped into the Hell Hole with his wife Dolly, who proceeded to drink herself unconscious. Hippolyte Havel had picked an argument with Sloan, calling him out for being apolitical. Sloan fired back that he was interested in something more subtle than politics. "Know what, Hippo?" he'd said. "Don't tell me how to paint, and I won't change your goulash recipe." Everyone had laughed, and Havel had called them all bourgeois pigs.

"Sloan has the right idea," Cahill says now. "Art *should* be democratic." His cigarette has burned down. He stubs it out on a saucer on her desk. "But that doesn't just mean painting poor people. It means widening the whole definition of art to include the folk traditions."

"I love everyday things," she tells him shyly. "Shop signs, salt shakers. I find myself wondering who made them, and how."

"Exactly!" He turns his clear blue eyes on her. "I can stand in front of a pawn shop for hours. And I have an obsession with cigar-store Indians."

"Have you seen the one on Thirteenth Street? With his dagger in the air?"

"Of course! I pass it every Sunday."

They look at each other then, and Bernice feels a wave of pleasure distinct from her fading marijuana high. With other people in Lil and Johnny's circle, she often feels like the runt of the litter—inarticulate, naïve. Cahill is one of the first people in New York to make her feel she has something to contribute. Perhaps her little sculptures aren't so pathetic. Perhaps they belong to an honorable tradition of folk art.

"I've been doing publicity for Sloan's group," he tells her. "So far it's all painters, but if we ever get a sculpture group together, I'd be interested to see where you've landed with your work."

Bernice blinks, thinking he must be joking—Sloan's Society! But his expression is steady. Is he out of his mind? Joining the Society would be an unbelievable honor—a miracle. The very idea makes her resolve to work harder.

And to think, she almost hustled him out of her room!

Just then, a tall brunette appears in the kitchen. She puts an arm on the doorframe and leans on it, almost losing her balance.

"Holger, you must come! Malcolm's been hypnotized, and it turns out he fought in the Battle of Agincourt and got an arrow through his leg!"

"Ah," says Cahill. He turns to Bernice, giving her a wink the other woman can't see. "What do you say, Bernice? Will you join us?"

She shakes her head. "I start dyeing yarn in a factory at six."

"A worker." Cahill hands her his dish with the cigarette butt in it, a tinge of apology in his smile. "Well, it was good to meet you, Bernice Abbott. Keep that integrity, won't you?"

◆

A week later, she does a second sitting for Man Ray.

"Elbows on the table, chin in your hands," he directs. "Don't curl the fingers. Hold them around your cheeks."

Taking direction from him makes her feel like a child, but, trusting him, she cedes to his authority. When she sat for him a couple of months ago, he showed her his photographs, which bore no resemblance to the stiff portraits she thought of when she heard the word 'photography.' Taken from unexpected angles, with dramatic lighting and strange props, these portraits were different—looser, more mysterious. They put her in mind of that odd portrait of Alice Lidell she'd seen in Chillicothe all those years ago, and couldn't forget. She saw that photography could be a kind of sculpture, too, where the artist sculpted with light.

He has her rest her head on the table as if it's too heavy to carry. He gives her a black jacket to wear and asks her to glance back over one shoulder. Positioning her in front of a mirror, he shoots her making different expressions at her reflection. Gloomy, surprised, quizzical. Her mouth puckers, turns down at the corners. She's beginning to enjoy herself.

"They're going well," he says during a break. "I'm going to show Stieglitz."

"Who?"

Man Ray tut-tuts. "Are you serious, kid? Alfred Stieglitz is one of the top men in the art world. He's changed the course of photography, and his was the first gallery to show the new art from Europe. Everyone who wants to break through goes to see him. It's practically a requirement."

"He sounds grand."

"Well, he is. He's a bit of an aristocrat, and arrogant to boot. But he has a good eye, and a fine intellect—and if he likes you, he can make your career."

Bernice falls silent. She doesn't like the sound of depending on one rich, bossy man to decree artistic worthiness. She'd thought the Village, with its spirit of open experimentation, was opposed to that.

"Hold that look," Man sounds excited. He clicks the shutter once, twice, then moves to her other side and click-clicks before putting down the camera. "Now I'll show you something." He goes to a dresser and retrieves a booklet titled *Camera Work*, then flips through it. "This is Stieglitz's magazine. See—he took this one to show that a photograph can be as artistic as a painting."

"So he's a photographer too?"

"Not just a photographer. An artist." Man spreads the magazine in front of her, and she sees an image in tones of brown: immigrants standing on the deck of a ship, crowded in with laundry and possessions. A narrow walkway slices across the image, separating an upper deck from a lower one. It is titled *The Steerage*.

She frowns at the image, which doesn't strike her as radical. "I don't understand. Is it because it's an everyday scene, like those Dutch paintings?"

"Good god, no, Stieglitz would detest that comparison! He's interested in shapes, in lines. See the circle of that straw hat, the X of this man's suspenders? And the diagonals, here and here," he traces a finger over a staircase and the walkway, "it's about modernism, form. Subject matter comes second."

Perplexed, Bernice looks at the image. She can see how it might be clever to use formal qualities of painting in a photograph, but to do so at the expense of one's subjects seems heartless. Stieglitz seems dismissive of the immigrants whose "shapes" were integral to his image, and instead much too interested in his own brilliance.

She flips through the magazine, which features more of Stieglitz's work. The images are blurry, as if shot through muslin, and rendered in muddy brown tones. Only one—of train tracks, telegraph poles and a smoke-belching steam engine—appeals to her. The train looks as if it could steam off the page. But Stieglitz has given it a pretentious title: *The Hand of Man*.

"So what are you going to call your portrait of me?" she asks. "*The Ineffability of Dreams?*"

Man Ray takes the magazine from her. "These ideas are difficult for you to digest, I can see," he says, adding cruelly, "you're just a little girl from the Midwest."

Bernice turns her head away. *Maybe he's right*, she thinks. It's been six months since she moved to New York and still she feels out of place, like a turkey among peacocks. At the same time, she's irked by Man's condescension. She may not be a successful artist, but nor is she the hayseed he thinks her.

She flicks back her hair. "I saw Elsa last week."

"Oh?" Man perks up. "How was she?"

"Fine. We talked about poetry." Bernice smiles as she remembers her visit to the Baroness. The basement room on Perry Street was a squalid hole, piled to the rafters with junk. There were a dozen broken umbrellas, a church altar cloth, an old car radiator. Elsa wore men's breeches, a leather aviator hat and a monocle, and during their interview, fed caviar from a silver spoon to a shivering dog called Pinky. Her speech was rambling and largely nonsensical.

But for some reason she couldn't fathom, Bernice got the same feeling she'd had at the party, that Elsa's pronouncements were full of cryptic wisdom. Beneath Elsa's eccentricity lay a vein of integrity, she was sure. Who else could carry off such a persona but a woman who answered to no one but herself? So on impulse, she opened up and confessed everything: her dark thoughts, her doubt she could express herself through sculpture. Her hopeless love for Lil. Elsa listened, squinting through the monocle and sucking her teeth.

"Soak in your love juice," she'd advised at last. "Mold a heart from clay. Then tear it apart." Was she being literal? She put the dog-licked silver spoon back in the pot, scooped out some caviar and ate it with relish.

"She thinks I should go to Paris," Bernice says now.

"Ah, Paris! I want to move there soon." Man fits a cover onto his camera lens. "Montparnasse is the place. It's full of artists, and you can live on nothing. All the good work is being done there."

"Don't people say that about the Village?"

"They do—and it's true if you're from Kansas. But Paris! *Luxe, calme et volupté*! Marcel says the girls are beautiful, even the ugly ones."

Bernice doesn't say anything. She feels suddenly hot, and a wave of nausea washes through her. She coughs into her hand.

"What is it?" Man asks.

"I don't know, I don't feel good." She's exhausted, she realizes. She's been getting up at five most mornings to reach the factory, and staying up late for rehearsals. She looks longingly at the moth-eaten sofa across the room—but if she lay down, she might not get up. "Just tired, I think."

"I hope so. Isn't your performance tonight?"

"Oh god!" Bernice forces herself up. She'd forgotten it was opening night of *The Moon of the Caribbees*. "That's right."

"Well, that's it—you have stage fright," Man asserts. When she coughs again, he recoils. "You'd better get going."

"Maybe I should rest for a minute..."

"No." Taking her elbow, Man steers her firmly to the door. "You need to get home, sleep in your own bed. I'd only disturb you. Do you have your flu mask?"

"I think it's at home."

"Oh, well. Hurry, then." He holds her at arm's length, brow furrowed. "I'll be there tonight, with Marcel and half the Village. But don't be scared, kid, it's in the bag. You'll be great."

◆

A few hours later, Bernice totters along MacDougal Street. She managed to rest for three hours, and has taken some aspirin chased with rum. She feels better, at least, she thinks she does. As she walks, her forehead grows damp and the sidewalk feels uneven. It's tiredness or stage fright, she tells herself. Anything else is unthinkable.

After a few months of calming down, Spanish Flu is back, in a second wave that authorities say could be even more deadly. The mayor has banned spitting in public, and Village shops are hawking "sure protection" in the form of garlic gargle and camphor lockets. Paul Markham, the cast member playing Paddy, came down with it two days ago, causing a last minute reshuffle. So did Bonnie, who worked alongside Bernice at the yarn factory and who is now in St. Vincent's Hospital.

Watching Bonnie succumb was terrible. Bernice will never forget the awful, grinding sound of the girl's cough, or the blue tinge of her skin. By the time the stretcher arrived, Bonnie was coughing so violently that she'd ruptured blood vessels, and there were crimson bubbles at her nose and mouth.

But that won't happen to me.

Fumbling in her pocket for her mask—of course, she left it on the kitchen table—Bernice hurries down the street. She's aware of how late she is, but also

103

knows her presence is far from essential. She has no lines, merely has to swing her skirt, dance and look flirtatious. Someone else could do it, but she won't cede her place. She likes to be with Lil, hovering over her, making sure she's all right.

At the theater, people buzz about, hanging ropes and arranging props. There's been a minor accident. The island, a six-foot cutout, was mistakenly left in the courtyard and ruined in last night's rain. Now Johnny and the stage manager, Neil, are hastily crafting a replacement, Neil sawing through beaverboard while Johnny dabs at it with paint, flicking in stumpy palm trees.

"*There* you are!" Lilian calls. Looking over, Bernice feels a hot wave of pleasure and surprise. Lil is already in costume in her flouncy yellow dress, her face almost unrecognizable under blackface makeup. Red curls bounce on her shoulders, and she has shiny bangles up her arms. "Come," she says, "let me do your face."

Bernice follows her to the wings, where Lil has her sit on a folding stool. She pulls a headband over Bernice's head, and daubs black shoe polish on Bernice's face.

"Your skin is burning, Neecey. Are you okay?"

"Yes, I was sitting for Man Ray, then I overslept and had to run."

"Silly girl. Relax now." Lilian rubs the shoe polish around her face, and Bernice closes her eyes so that Lilian can put it on her eyelids. Her character, Violet, is minor and rather sketched-in—just a sun-kissed, sensual being. She loosens her shoulders, trying to feel the part.

"Hold still, all right? I'm going to do here now." Lilian rubs her shoulders, working the polish in circles, reaching her hand forward and around to cover the chin and neck. Her touch feels absurdly good, gentle but firm, making Bernice's body sigh with pleasure. When the tide of desire wells up, for once she doesn't push it down. Instead, she closes her eyes and allows it to suffuse her, taking shallow breaths while she tries not to shiver. She wonders who helped Lilian with *her* makeup, who touched *her* this way. Jealous, she resolves to get to the theater on time tomorrow.

"Look at yourself," Lilian says at last. Opening her eyes, Bernice sees a woman who is at once herself and someone completely different, a mysterious, carnal being. Her receding chin is less noticeable under the blackface. When she opens her mouth, pointy teeth flash white against velvet skin.

"What do you think?" Lilian says. She leans forward and whispers, "I think you look beautiful."

As she takes this in, Bernice starts to shiver—from happiness, surely, because Lilian has never called her beautiful before. "I like it," she says. "But I feel odd. My head's spinning."

"It's hot in here. And you're probably nervous. Come outside, I've got something that will help."

They go out to the brick-lined courtyard, where the cutout of the island suffered its soggy fate. It's perennially damp out here. There's a smell of mildew, and moss sprouts in the spaces between crumbling bricks.

Lil reaches down and hikes up her skirt, making Bernice's heart stop. But she's only retrieving something. "Here," she says, drawing out a small pipe. She taps it knowingly. "Mexican, the best."

Reefer: the thought makes Bernice dizzy. "Is it a good idea to smoke now?"

"Sure, it's the best thing for nerves!" Lilian looks so animated—so cat-with-the-cream pleased with herself—that Bernice can't refuse.

They stand there, passing the pipe back and forth, talking about what they'll do when the play ends. A prickly heat steals over Bernice's body, but along with it comes a feeling of lightness. *She called me beautiful.* She looks at Lilian, who's blowing an elaborate smoke ring into the air. *If only it could be this simple,* she thinks: *two women saving their best selves for each other.* She and Lil on their own little island.

"Steady," Lil reaches out a hand, "let's not overdo it." Looking down at the hand on her arm, Bernice is suddenly surprised at the sight of her own dark skin. She'd forgotten she wasn't herself, but a dusky Caribbean beauty.

And that's when the impulse strikes her. The spicy smoke wreathing around them makes her bold and, straightening up, she makes her voice deep. "I can't help it," she growls, "I'm merely a ranker—and a rotter."

Recognizing the line, Lilian juts out her chin. "No you ain't," she says in her lilting accent. "You're a genelman. Ah wouldn't have nothin' to do with dem other men, but you is different." She sashays toward Bernice, and Bernice pushes her away with a grunt.

"Don' you like me, pretty boy?"

"I beg your pardon. I didn't mean to be rude. I'm a bit off color."

"Den you do like me little ways?"

"Yes, yes. Why shouldn't I?" Catching hold of both of Lil's arms, Bernice pulls her forward. Lil is smiling, and in a quick movement, Bernice twists her friend's light body around and pushes it against the brick wall. Leaning forward, she closes her mouth over Lilian's and, for a heady moment, feels the soft give of Lilian's lips. Hungry, she thrusts her tongue into Lil's mouth, feeling its texture, tasting violet candy. She presses forward so that their legs are entwined.

"Neecey!" Lilian is pushing at her, struggling, trying to move her head. "Neece! You don't really have to kiss me!"

"I know," Bernice says. "I know." And then the frustrations of the last months well up and she can't help herself, she's frantically covering Lil's neck and shoulders with kisses. Sweat runs down her forehead, leaking blackness into her eyes, dripping it onto Lil. And it seems to her that the bricks around them are tilting, swimming. "I can't help it," she gasps. "I've tried, oh my god, I've tried."

"Neecey—stop!" Lil's hands are on her shoulders, pushing roughly. Bernice takes a step back, confused and delirious. Shoe polish drips into her eyes, but through it she can see that Lil looks disheveled, with shoe polish streaking her hair and dress. Startled eyes stare out of her black face.

"What were you thinking, Bernice? I mean, really? What the *hell*?"

What *was* she thinking? That with enough loving care, Lil's friendship could be coaxed into more? That in this place where individual appetites rule, she could reach out and grasp her own pleasure?

And now, looking at Lil, she feels shame come to claim her, like a rightful owner finding a lost purse. It's so hot out here, and airless. She's burning up, and can hardly see four inches in front of her. Half-closing her eyes, she leans against the moldy bricks.

"Oh my god, Neecey, what's wrong? Your nose is bleeding! Are you ill?"

"I'm sorry…" she mouths, "so sorry…"

But that's all she gets to say. In the next moment she's falling, and the ground is rising up, and everything is going dark.

NINE

The first thing is sound, a ragged symphony of groans and coughs. Then comes smell—a horrid mixture of burned meat, bleach and vomit. Fluttering open her eyes, she sees milky shafts of light filtering through a high window. Briefly, she registers the surroundings—glazed brick walls, rows of beds—before sinking back into oblivion.

For an indeterminate period after that, she floats in a sea of delirium. At times she's aware of her body twitching and jerking, her limbs pushing against some kind of restraint. At other times she sees eyes floating above her: Hippolyte, Elsa, Johnny. Are they really there? Someone holds her hand, but when she turns to thank them, they're gone. There's a distant relative from Westchester, a cousin Frances, who says something about her mother. But it might be a dream. Her bed is a raft, gulls circling above. One day she sees her father, dressed for a funeral, standing on the deck of a passing ship.

Then suddenly, the worst is over and she can sit up for a few minutes. Johnny comes, bearing the miraculous gift of a bar of soap and some chicken soup, which he spoons out of a cup into her mouth. The hot liquid dribbles onto her gown, but she doesn't care because she can taste, and has an appetite again.

"Who else?" she rasps between spoonfuls.

He looks away. "It's bad, Bernice. Really bad. Half the cast came down with it. I didn't want to break this to you while you're recovering, but...Perkins and Westervelt didn't make it."

Perkins, the lighting director; Westervelt, the ship's first mate in *The Moon of the Caribbees*. Both talented, vibrant young men. Scrabbling on the pillow with her elbows, Bernice manages to prop herself up. "Lil?"

Johnny closes his eyes, and she notices dark circles around them. Fear shudders through her. "I was just with her upstairs. She's been bad, like you. Came down a couple of days after you did, and they put her on the third floor. Crazy, it's been crazy. I don't know, I can't..." He bows his head and she watches his shoulders convulse, knowing his worry isn't for her.

After he leaves, she tries to get out of bed. She's barely taken three steps when her knees fold and she falls, banging her hip on the tile floor. For several minutes she tries to drag herself across the floor with her hands, until a red-faced nurse runs over and hauls her back into bed. "Stop this madness—you can't go upstairs, no," she says. "Now be good or get sedated, which will it be?"

Next thing, there's a needle and she's sinking into a dark, foggy sleep.

Luckily, the night nurse, Eileen, is new on the job. An Irish girl with freckles above her facemask, she is tall and solid, a good fit for the job. After hearing the story, she clucks her tongue. "All right, I'll help but I'm pure stupid. Don't blab, or I'll have your guts for garters!"

And so that night, when ratcheting coughs are the only sound on the ward, Aileen rolls in a wheelchair and lifts Bernice into it, as easily as if she were a bag of feathers. They take the service elevator to the third floor, where Aileen wheels her down a long, dim corridor. Bernice grips the wheelchair's arms as they pass a nurse's station where the nurse is snoring, her gauze mask askew. Then they're at the end of the wing and Aileen is pushing her into a dark ward, past rows of cots with humped, sleeping bodies.

The glimmer of orange is the first thing she sees. Lil's hair has been chopped off at the neck, presumably to make the nurses' lives easier. But they can't dim the lovely warmth of its coppery glow.

As they come closer, though, Bernice sees the gauntness of Lil's features. Skinny before, Lil is positively ethereal now, with scooped-out eye sockets above her ridge-like cheekbones. A sheen of sweat gilds her forehead, and around her nose are red stains from where blood has come up through her airways. Beneath, her lips—those lips Bernice has thought about so much they could practically be her own—are dry and cracked. She feels a wave of anger. Couldn't the nurses rub Vaseline on them?

Aileen rolls the chair to the bedside. "I'll be back in ten minutes," she whispers. "Make sure you're quiet."

Left with Lil, Bernice soaks up the sight of her like never before, letting it flood every cell of her body. But then, as she looks at the febrile form in front of her, guilt takes over. Lil's pale brow is wrinkled; her lips mouth silent words and every few seconds her head jerks, as if she's arguing with someone. Bernice is desperate to touch her forehead, to calm her, but after what happened in the courtyard she feels too awkward. If they could go back…but that's a futile thought, she might as well ask to go to the moon. With effort, she leans forward. "Lil," she whispers, "it's Neecey. Lil! Wake up." There's the hint of a twitch at Lil's eyebrow, and she waits, but Lil's face settles into impassivity. If not for the red stains on her skin, she could be Millais's Ophelia floating in the stream. "Lily, you have to. Wake up, please!"

All around, there are wet coughs. From one or two beds come grunts and snores. Between these aural assaults, Bernice can sometimes make out Lil's rasping breath, so faint that it seems to be coming from beneath layers of wool.

She'll come through.

She leans further down, so that her head is just a few inches from the coppery shine of Lil's hair. "Honey," she whispers, "you're going to get better. We'll go back to the way we were. I promise. You believe me, don't you?"

Lil's head jerks as she murmurs something incomprehensible. The damp sheet clings to her, emphasizing her jutting hipbones and the tiny bumps of her knees.

"What?" Bernice says. "What?" But the sounds Lil's making are slurs and groans. The only thing distinguishable is their fevered tone.

Just then, there's a rustle behind her and Aileen puts her hands on the wheelchair. "Time to go."

"No! A few minutes more."

"Jay-sus, girl, I can't! It's more than my job's worth."

Before Bernice say more, the wheelchair is being swung around. She cranes her head to get a last look at Lil, whose lips are moving soundlessly. *I'll be back,* she promises.

For the rest of the night she lies in bed, staring at cracks in the ceiling. She bites her lips until they bleed, feeling a dark satisfaction at the pain. She imagines Lil upstairs, livid with fever, and over and over, relives those moments of kissing Lil's neck, of forcing her tongue into the unwilling mouth. She infected Lil, she's sure. For the first time in her life she prays, not sure whom she's addressing, but doing it anyway. *Please listen. If you take one of us, let it be me.*

The next thing she knows, a lunch tray is being clattered onto her bedside table. Fried liver, boiled cabbage—*ughhh*. She turns away, burying her head in the pillow.

The afternoon drags by, each second its own form of torture. Several times she tries to get out of bed, but although she can manage to sit up and swivel around, she doesn't have the strength to stand and walk. The day nurses shake their heads: *Imagine*, they say, *if everyone wanted to go rambling around!* "Not everyone," Bernice insists, "just me." But they refuse to bend. "Your friend is in good hands. The best thing you can do for her is get well yourself."

Even Aileen, who arrives at five o'clock, protests that it's too risky to go upstairs again. Having anticipated this, Bernice holds out the two silver bracelets she wore for *The Moon of the Caribbees*, and watches the nurse's face turn scarlet. "All right," she says, pocketing the bracelets. "But if you breathe a word, I'll tell matron to hog-tie you."

Later, on the third floor, the sight of Lil makes Bernice gasp with relief—for here is her darling, no better and no worse, but indisputably alive. The fears she's been nursing recede. Two thick leather straps are tied around the bed, over the sheet covering Lil, and this is perversely cheering. It means she's had convulsions, which often come before a fever breaks.

But as Aileen wheels her up to the bed, it makes Bernice sick to see how tight the straps are, how they press the sheet into Lil's flesh. And Lil looks, if anything, more ethereal. As if she could dissolve and melt away.

Once Aileen leaves, Bernice sits by the bedside whispering stories. She talks about getting her hair bobbed, *The Persians*, the night they met Man Ray and Duchamp. She trawls her memories for moments when she made Lil giggle, and does her best to relive them. *Remember when we didn't have money and you wanted that knockwurst? And I said Johnny had a bigger one waiting for you at home?*

After a while, when Aileen doesn't come, she begins to get sleepy. The ward is warm, its air fuggy with rancid exhalations. She's aware, several times, of her head drooping, of jerking it up again. Who knows how much time passes before she is sitting up, hyper-attuned? Something has changed in Lil's breath, it is labored and grating. Bernice looks around for Aileen, who is nowhere in sight. Another nurse? But the ward is still, all she sees are the humps of sleeping patients. Should she call out? Try to push herself to the nurses' station? But then she'd have to leave Lil.

The grating grows deeper, becoming a kind of guttural panting, and now Lil's body is bucking, straining against the straps. "Help!" Bernice cries out, "Help!" But her lungs are weak, her voice doesn't carry.

Panicked, she looks at the convulsing body in front of her. Lil's shoulders are arched, sweat has soaked her gown. Her face is clenched, and her breathing has changed again, now sounding strangled. It's unbearable.

Before she knows quite what she's doing, Bernice has grabbed hold of the leather strap around Lil's chest and used it to pull herself up. She reaches her other hand to Lil's chest, and although she has only the faintest idea of what should happen next, she pushes for all she's worth, trying to pump blood and air into the weak form under her. She can feel her own heart pounding, the blood rushing to her face—but beneath her hand, nothing. *God!* She presses down, grunting with the effort, until she feels herself being caught, an arm circling and restraining her. Before she can cry out, a hand is clamped over her mouth, the fingers digging into her jaw.

"What are you doing?" Aileen hisses in her ear. "Are you mad?"

In response, Bernice writhes so hard that, after a few moments, Aileen is forced to release her. When the hand comes off her mouth she pants desperately, taking in gulps of air. "Please! I'm afraid."

Aileen moves to the other side of the bed, where she bends and puts a hand to Lil's neck. She presses down, lightly at first, then more emphatically. After a moment, she looks up with widened eyes. "Mercy, she's gone."

Bernice gasps, her heart still pounding from the struggle with Aileen. *No. It can't be.* "Breathe into her," she begs. "Give her air."

The nurse shakes her head. "She's gone, I say. If they find out we were here—"

No. It isn't happening. Frantically, Bernice scans Lil's face and sees it, the unmistakable change, the still perfection of death. Unable to look at Aileen, she hangs her head, then lowers her forehead and presses into the leather strap around Lil's chest, wanting it to leave an imprint, to scar herself. She clings onto the strap, willing time to stop or reverse itself—to go anywhere but where it must go, sliding into the next moment and then the next.

A hand on her back. Aileen is behind her. "Will we say a prayer for her?"

Bernice lifts her head slightly and shakes it. What use would that be now? She believes death is final, immutable. Still, she can't relinquish Lilian yet. With her right hand she reaches out, touching the pale skin of Lil's face, running a finger over the still-warm lips. They give under the pressure, as they did in the courtyard, but with a difference. Now there's no life in them, no blood pulsing under the surface.

In the end, being by her side didn't matter. There's no mercy or Lil would have been spared. No justice, or she, Bernice, would be the one gone.

What a joke, she thinks, *what a fucking farce.*

Aileen pulls on her arm. "Come, let go. We can't be here."

Bernice's fingers curl around the strap—how can she release it? To abandon Lil, leave her here—it seems like a betrayal. The moment she loosens her hold will be the last time she gets to look at Lil's face, the last time the two of them will be in a room together. "What will happen to her?" she asks.

"Oh, I don't know. I expect her family will come for her, poor soul. She'll go back to the earth where she came from." *Yes,* Bernice thinks, *the Boston Brahmins.* She imagines Lil's parents coming to claim the body and sees a funeral filled with polite people, all listening to a pastor drone on as if he knew her. The last thing Lil would want.

"Come, now, we can't do aught," Aileen says. The words are like a slap to the face, but she's right. It's useless, nothing can be done.

And so, with one great, heaving sob, Bernice allows herself to be detached from the bed and wheeled away.

PART FOUR

PARIS, 1922

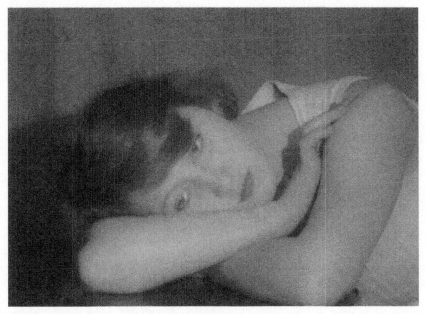

Tylia Perlmutter, Paris, 1926, by Berenice Abbott

TEN

As soon as she enters the sculpture studio, Bernice senses a difference. The air is electric, its molecules disturbed. Looking around, she sees the source—a woman in a faded blue wrapper who stands by the window. She's around Bernice's age, round-faced and pretty, with shingled dark-brown hair and green, slanted eyes. Under her loosely tied robe, Bernice can see the soft edges of her breasts and a slim white column of flesh. She gazes out over the rooftops, her thin fingers languidly moving a cigarette to her mouth. In the center of the room, instead of the usual table with its human skull or stuffed fox there is merely the dais, with a patterned shawl over it.

"Yes," says Professor Mourcier when the students are assembled, "we will be working from a live model today. This is serious business, *mes enfants*. Before making an armature we will observe and sketch, so please fetch your books and charcoal."

By the time Bernice gets back with her sketchbook, the model has thrown off her wrap and is standing naked on the dais and the other students—all men—are looking like cats whose water bowls have been filled with cream. Under angular shoulders, the brown nipples of the model's small breasts point upward. Her belly swells beneath and there's a scar to one side of her navel near her rounded hips, a neat pink line with dots on either side from where stitches were placed.

Following the professor's instructions, Bernice joins the students circling the dais as if the model is the sun and they are distant planets. As she walks, she tries to focus on the things the professor has taught them: where the central axis of the figure is, how weight is distributed. But she can't help noticing the sheen of sweat between the model's breasts, and the bush of dark hair that fizzes at her pelvis. The nearness of these things, the realness of them, is disquieting. It's as if the model is generating voltage that, if Bernice reached out to touch it would instantly singe her fingers and her hair would stand on end.

She has seen naked women before, of course. But not like this, not with an invitation to linger, stare and take everything in. Her past glimpses—of a bared breast at the beach or at a Village party—have been surreptitious, accompanied by shame. Here in Paris, André Gide once took her to a nightclub where a stripper sang as she peeled off her garments—revealing in the finale enormous breasts with tasseled pasties, which she somehow managed to spin around as the audience cheered. Bernice had laughed and clapped along, but felt hot and testy for the rest of the night.

Now, as she holds up her stick of charcoal to measure the model's shoulder width, she notices her fingers wobbling. Sex: it is everywhere in Paris, from the smoky American jazz clubs to the cream-frilled pastries in the *boulangerie* windows, with their sticky red cherries on top. Nothing is considered too perverse—except, perhaps, *not* indulging in the city's erotic pleasures, which marks one out as an oddity.

"Let yourself go," Gide had told her. "Delon likes you." Delon, rangy as a giraffe, had stringy dark hair and sunken eyes, but his paintings, Fauvist explosions of purple and green, were lively. And so Bernice had smiled and let him take her out for *boeuf en daube*—and then the rest, the bed squeaking under them while she contemplated whether she would rather have had the *coq au vin*. It was a grim experience. Delon's breath was sour, his hands flabby and moist as slabs of meat. When he entered her it hurt like hell, and she left quickly afterward, not even bothering to clean up. That was her virginity, then, dispatched with all the grace of an alleyway screw.

She tried another man after that, just to be sure. It proved marginally more satisfying, but only because he had an interesting collection of astrolabes.

A woman, though—that would be different. Sometimes, a smoky-eyed girl smiles at her at a party and she lets her imagination run, the breath catching in her throat. But it's something she hasn't allowed herself. Not since what happened with Lilian.

She moves her charcoal stick over the page, thinking of Lil's slim shoulders, her narrow hips. Four years on there's still an awful, empty ache under her ribs when she remembers her friend. She closes her eyes, thinking of her confession in the back yard of the Provincetown Players, remembering the kiss and

Lilian's aghast expression before everything went dark. Bernice almost died, that was her punishment—but it wasn't enough, she *should* have perished. The disease threw its worst at her, but unlike so many, she lived. If there's a reason for this, it's a mystery she hasn't yet solved.

A soft cough and a firm hand on her shoulder brings her back to the present. "Mademoiselle Abbott," the professor stands behind her, huffing a soft sigh, "there is nothing correct here." *Rien juste*, Mourcier's worst assessment. Are any words more damning? "The pelvis is the center of the body, yes? When we start with the upper torso, our figure is out of balance. Please start again."

"*Oui, monsieur.*" Bernice puts down her charcoal stick and bites her lip, looking at her drawing. The professor is right. Her figure is off-kilter, listing dangerously to one side. One leg is much skinnier than the other, making it look as if the model has polio. It's embarrassing, even worse than usual.

She rips the sheet from her notebook and starts again, feeling herself blush as she looks at the triangle of pubic hair in the model's crotch. *Le pelvis*: Professor Mourcier talks a lot about this. *Le pelvis, c'est le fondation.* Unlike the girls in her boarding house—who discuss their sexual conquests in great detail—his interest is structural. But still it rattles her, this sense of the pelvis as the body's essential core. For if the life force springs from the pelvis, then surely it follows that death and disease dwell there too?

She's only made three strokes with the charcoal in the last ten minutes. Quickly, she begins to sketch, glancing up at the model and trying to visualize the skeleton under the flesh. It's better, there's a sense of solidity now, though the shins are too big and the left shoulder too rigid.

"I like it," someone says over her shoulder during the break. Bernice is surprised to see the model herself, standing with a cigarette in hand. "You've made me look strong. Almost masculine."

"That was an accident," Bernice says, "but I'm glad you approve." The model leans down, her armpit by Bernice's face. Her lilac perfume is mixed with the sour smell of sweat.

"Here, want a drag?"

"Thanks." Bernice takes the cigarette and puts it to her lips, hoping to steady herself. But the smoke almost chokes her, and she blows it out quickly. "The professor thinks I'm a hopeless case."

"Oh, Mourcier is old-fashioned. I've modeled for him before. I wouldn't worry about what he says. You have to remember he's an old stick who had his heyday well before modernism. I'm Tylia, by the way."

"Bernice."

"Burniss?"

"No, Bern*eess*. It's American."

"You don't say."

Just then, the professor looks at Tylia and raps his watch and she smiles at Bernice and slopes off, trailing smoke and lilac perfume.

After class, Bernice goes to her job at the flower market. She stays in the back room, cutting thorns off roses and arranging them in bunches with ferns and sprays of baby's breath. In the front, she can hear Madame Archambault chatting with customers, complimenting their taste and gently prodding them to spend more. Claudine, the other backroom girl, prattles cheerfully as the two of them work.

"…really the funniest song, you should come some time, I know you'd like it. Have you been to *L'Escargot*? No? Expensive, but everything is *so* delicious. Marc took me, and we had the *best* lemon tart…"

"Ouch!" Bernice says. A thorn has pierced her finger, bringing out a bead of blood. She wipes it on her apron, shaking her head. She's not working well this afternoon. Something is off, she can't find her rhythm. Seeing Tylia naked has brought up emotions that have shaken her.

"*Ça va?*" Claudine asks. "You seem distracted."

"No, I'm fine. Just tired." *Seulement fatiguée.* She can't confide in Claudine. The girl is nice enough, but she's not the sharpest creature. She comes from a bourgeois family in Nantes and is simply in Paris to find a nice banker to marry.

"Are we ready, girls?" Jean, the deliveryman, has entered through the side door. His lopsided smile lends a rakish air to his otherwise symmetrical face.

"Almost," Claudine says. "Just two dozen roses and a few birds of paradise."

"*You're* a bird of paradise," says Jean. "Fly with me to the beach, won't you?"

"Oh, leave me be! Go outside and have a smoke."

When Jean leaves, Bernice raises an eyebrow at Claudine, who shrugs back. "What? Not a chance! Sure, he's cute, but a flower deliveryman? No thanks!"

"Maybe that doesn't matter, if you like him."

"Oh, Bernice—be realistic, won't you!" Claudine stabs a rose stem into her arrangement. "Anyway, to get back to the desserts…"

After Lil's death, Bernice's world tipped on its axis. She couldn't go back to the MacDougal Street apartment or any of her past haunts. Instead she found a job at a shoe factory and got a basement room on Barrow Street. It was there Hippolyte Havel found her some months later, with the mold and cockroaches and the dead begonia.

"My dear, why are you hiding in this awful place? Everyone's asking if you died."

"I did. I might as well have."

Hippolyte looked around the room, taking in the curling linoleum, the damp walls. "I see you're not doing any art."

"What's the point?"

At this, the old anarchist came and knelt in front of her, taking her hands and forcing her to look into his eyes. "Listen to me, Bernice. You have to pull yourself together. Nobody wants to see you throw yourself away. What happened was a tragedy—but you're here, you're alive."

Gradually, he coaxed her out of her hovel, taking on the role of a strict but benevolent uncle. He read to her, cooked her goulash. In time she could see a few old friends, and she bought some clay, made some figures. Occasionally she ran into the Baroness, who had grown even more eccentric. She was wearing cooking pots on her head and postage stamps affixed to her cheek, but she was also having some luck. Her poems were being published in *The Little Review*.

"I'm moving to Paris," Elsa told her one day. "Everyone is there, you know." By *everyone* she meant Marcel, who was doing well, getting his work into major salons. Occasionally, he sent Elsa postcards with lewd drawings on them—which Elsa proudly pinned all over her body.

Of course, the idea of going to Paris was old hat by then. When Prohibition was introduced, half the Village flew the coop—or so it seemed. Europeans knew how to live; their governments treated them as adults. The party was moving. In the Village, the old insouciance had given way to cynicism. People had become selfish and petty, just like everywhere else.

On top of that, Bernice had her memories. Every time she passed Polly's or the Provincetown Players, her stomach seized up—and if she saw a slim redhead, her heart would beat so fast that she feared blacking out. Lilian was in the rose scent that wafted from a milliner's, in the canned soup she picked up at a grocer's. The heart of her heart, destroyed by her love. *What were you thinking, Bernice? I mean, really? What the* hell?

And then, one day, she and five others were abruptly dismissed from the shoe factory. That decided it. If she was going to starve, she might as well do it in a beautiful European city.

But before she left, there was a journey to make.

Contact with Ma had been limited since she'd been in the Village. Bernice had sent a dollar or two when she could, and occasionally Ma sent a note back, in shaky handwriting that said more than her few dry words could. When Bernice had been sick, Johnny had asked if she wanted him to call anyone. She shook her head. She couldn't face the prospect of Ma's *I told you so*.

Back in Columbus, Ma greeted her with a litany of complaints. Her landlord was cheating her; neighbors had stolen her towels. The sight of her brought on a crush of guilt, followed by a desperate urge to flee—an all-too-familiar combination. It was miserable, but what was the alternative? Bernice wasn't going to bury herself. Right after Lil died she might have considered it, but not any more. Now she wanted to live, to be on the side of risk and beauty.

When Ma took in Bernice's words about Paris, her face puckered. "New York, Paris—it'll be the moon next, I suppose." Bernice promised to write, at which Ma grimaced. "Well, don't expect me to write any long letters back."

And so it was that on 21 March 1921, she had stepped onto the deck of the *Rochambeau*, holding a portmanteau and a carpetbag. Anxious, excited, not knowing quite what to expect at the other end. Stowed in her carpetbag was a letter from Elsa, who had become disillusioned with Paris—and finally, it seemed, with Marcel—and moved to Berlin. She told Bernice to go see her friend, the writer André Gide. "He's rhythmic and embellished," she wrote. "He dribbles pearls."

The crossing seemed interminable. There were ball games on deck and evening dances, but far too many people in third class. A few third-class passengers tried to sneak onto the upper decks, but were found out and returned to their proper stations. Bernice amused herself by observing her fellow passengers, imagining their lives past and to come.

Paris, of course, was beautiful, but more than that, it was bursting with life. Prices were low, hemlines shockingly high. Montparnasse, the artists' quarter, was a French version of the Village, but more spacious, with wide tree-lined boulevards and elegant wrought-iron balconies. Each night was a party—the cafés and clubs overflowing with people, the sidewalks echoing with cries of, "Hey, it's you! You buying a round?"

On her first day, Bernice went to Gide's house with Elsa's letter in hand.

The writer was just then in the throes of a scandal, having published an article that made a case for pedophilia. In person, he didn't seem like a sexual aberrant. He was courtly, an oval-faced old man in a herringbone suit.

"What will you do here?" he asked.

"Sculpture," Bernice said, self-conscious because her sculpture had been languishing over the last months. "I'm not very good yet. Most of what I make gets squashed." She mimed a crushing action with her hands.

Gide laughed. "You won't get far in Paris, *mademoiselle*, unless you learn to *faites la promotion*. How do you say? To be a noisymouth."

"I'll shout from the Eiffel Tower when I have something to promote. But right now, I need a job."

He took her to his tailor, a ruddy-faced Englishman, and before long Bernice was shelving and managing supplies—Ma's training finally useful. That was her first job in Paris. It lasted a year, until the tailor's nephew arrived from Lyon and took her place.

Gide was married, but it was well known as a *mariage blanc*—one that went unconsummated. One night, he took Bernice to a costume party at a club called *Le Boeuf sur le Toit*. The room was full of gypsies and soldiers, pashas and clowns. No sooner had the two of them stepped in than a tall 'bride' ran up to Gide, pressed up close and kissed him on the mouth. Only then did Bernice notice the 'bride''s facial hair. Embarrassed, she took herself off to the bar, where a white-faced geisha eyed her with interest.

It would have been so easy to let go, just fall. There were so many willing arms to receive her. No one cared, as Gide said, if your tastes ran to men, women or beasts. But every time she got close, something seized up, and she found herself saying, "I can't," and "I'm sorry." She watched others, at parties, carry on as if no one else was there. She went to bars where girls whispered that they knew what she liked. And she shivered and yearned, but still didn't dare.

Now what? She's been working in the flower market for six months, taking Professor Mourcier's class for three. She still has a long way to go, it seems. Unlike Holger Cahill, no one here is raving about work that draws on folk-art traditions. She needs to achieve more finesse.

Once in a while, for a different kind of evening, Bernice and Claudine go dancing at the *Bal Bullier*. Occasionally, young men who work in épiceries or shoe stores take them to a bistro, where they eat *steak frites* or sole in brown butter sauce. Bernice tries to toe the line between helping Claudine land her catch and not leading the second young man on. She can usually extricate herself. Only once has she has to slap a particularly persistent boy across the face.

"Careful," Claudine says now, "you're cutting the stems too short. Madame will have your guts for garters."

Bernice looks down at her work. Claudine is right. "She won't notice. Look, I'll put them in with these ones. Perfect, see?"

"Hm, you're crafty," Claudine laughs.

That night, Bernice attends a salon at Gide's home. The salonistes knock back *vin rouge* and bicker good-naturedly about various *isms*. Bernice rarely gets involved in these debates, though she likes to hear the others talk.

"Look at that." A pale man named Leo Stein points at a Japanese print on the wall. "What you see there is a corpse. Exquisite art is dead."

To her surprise, Bernice finds herself piping up, "Are you sure?"

Stein turns his limpid eyes on her. "Young lady, we live in a time of disillusionment. The war destroyed all idealism. Consequently, beauty in art has given way to disfigurement, ugliness and fragments. It's the only honest response."

The whole room turns to Bernice, as if awaiting the next stroke in a tennis match. She feels herself go crimson, her natural shyness flaring up. Stein is a noted intellectual; how can she match him? "But can't art be both whole and honest? Like…" she racks her brains, "Brancusi? I saw his show the other week."

Stein considers. "Brancusi has talent. But he's a romantic. His rounded forms engender comfort…"

"…like the whores' asses on Pigalle?" someone says. The room erupts in laughter then, and after a moment Bernice laughs too, relieved.

Later that night, she thinks of her own sculptures. She knows Stein would find them conventional—she hasn't progressed beyond a crude kind of realism—but she doesn't see why *everything* must be disfigured. She likes balance; she likes beauty. Also, Professor Mourcier talks endlessly of creating harmony in one's sculpture. *Il faut que ça chant*, he says. *It must sing*. So who is right?

The next day, she works on her armature at sculpture class. When she takes in Tylia's body, she tries to look beyond skin and muscle to the bones beneath, focusing with mechanical detachment. The students have made an armature before, for their animal sculpture, but this one is harder. In a moment of idiotic ambition, she decides to make her sculpture half life-size, then struggles to make the wire form balance on her wood plinth. When she looks around, she sees that the other forms are half the size of hers.

"Ber*neess*, stop!" Tylia calls after class. She trots across the courtyard after Bernice, her heels clicking on the cobblestones. "Ah, do you know where I can get a *soupe* around here?" It's an odd question for someone who's modeled here before—but Bernice directs her to a nearby place where the students go.

"Perhaps you'd come along?" Tylia asks. "I've been inside my own head so much. I'd love to hear someone else talk."

She looks different in her clothes, smaller and less voluptuous. It's windy out, and her hair is blowing across her face. Bernice notices a tiny mole, almost a freckle, on her chin.

"I'm sorry, I have to go to work."

"Oh," Tylia pouts. Reaching out, she fingers Bernice's collar, rubbing the coarse wool between her fingers. "Do you work every day?"

"Yes, except Wednesday."

"All right, let's make a date. Next Wednesday after class. *D'accord?*" And then she turns, running off before Bernice can answer.

It's just two girls going for coffee, Bernice thinks, *nothing special*. But the following Wednesday, she finds herself dressing in her knee-length grey skirt and a new pair of stockings. The morning drags. She tries to sketch, but is too much on edge to sit still. She prowls her room, picking up books and putting them down, opening the window, dusting shelves—as if she is meeting Tylia here and not at the academy.

Then, finally, she's in class and Tylia is on the dais, her weight on one leg, the fingers of one hand curling around the soft curve of a hip. Looking at the area between crotch and neck feels too impertinent today, so Bernice spends two hours molding feet and legs instead. Glancing around the room, she sees twenty-two mini Tylias of varying size taking form. Some are carefully smoothed, others are left lumpy, some are realistic and others less so, but all are the same shade of mushroom-soup gray. Even this dreary color can't dampen Tylia's allure, though. She is carnal, majestic. Intriguing.

After class, Tylia dresses and they head out of the building, blowing smoke as they laugh about Prof. Mourcier's creaky shoes. They end up walking to Saint-Sulpice before even thinking to stop for coffee. Tylia talks about her childhood. She was born Tylia Perlmutter in a Jewish village in Poland, and her parents emigrated to the Netherlands ten years ago. But after a few years there, her father lost his job and Tylia quit school to work in a factory. Then three years ago, when she was eighteen and her sister Bronia sixteen, the two of them decided to move to Paris and model.

Tylia may not be educated, but she's smart and funny. She loves everything American, she says: jazz, the *Herald Tribune*, Buster Keaton. She has read Scott Fitzgerald's *The Beautiful and the Damned*, found it *tres émouvant*. "And what is that thing you have—a dog you eat? With the bread?"

"A hot dog," Bernice says. "Just a sausage, really. With mustard and ketchup."

"*Kett-soup*," Tylia says, and Bernice laughs, because her accent makes it sound so much better than the real thing.

And then it becomes a habit. Every Wednesday they walk together, and Bernice tells Tylia about Ohio and Greenwich Village. She talks about Hippolyte Havel and the party where Elsa appeared with a birdcage on her head. She tells her about college, drama classes, the students arguing over America's part in the war. During the course of these walks, something happens—the pain lessens, and she's able to reminisce without guilt. She loves looking at Tylia's white arms, her delicate nose. She loves the way Tylia holds a cigarette in her thin fingers, blowing smoke and trilling, "*Mon dieu!*" at the end of her sentences.

Tylia too seems to look forward to their outings. She is warm, uninhibited. She thinks nothing of putting her arm around Bernice, or chucking her on the chin. Does it mean something or not? Bernice spends an unreasonable amount of time pondering this question. When Tylia leans close to whisper in her ear, nerves fizz under Bernice's skin and she wants to close her eyes. She's intoxicated by the other woman's presence, her lilac-and-tobacco scent, her accent, the warm breath on her neck.

At the same time, her sculpture is suffering. When Tylia is posing on the dais, Bernice feels so restless that she can barely stay at her station. But then, when she thinks of the confidences she and Tylia have shared, she feels ashamed. Why can't she be satisfied with friendship? Why must she feel things that—whatever Gide says—are peculiar?

Whether it's these nagging thoughts, or something else, the half life-size Tylia is a poor copy of the real one. Her arms are thick, her buttocks sag. The armature is crooked. The piece feels leaden—it doesn't sing, it barely even croaks. At the end of each class she throws a cloth over it as quickly as possible.

"Let's go, I'm starving," Tylia says every Wednesday. "I thought I was going to die up there." And they share a cigarette on their way to whatever cheap café beckons.

Then one cold morning in early December, Bernice arrives at the flower shop to find a *gendarme* guarding the door, rubbing his hands to ward off the cold.

"What's happening?" she asks.

He exhales a puff of white. "Store's closed."

"But I work here."

The policeman raises an eyebrow. "In that case, go in, *mademoiselle*. You may be required to give evidence."

Perplexed, Bernice steps inside, where she is greeted by a fragrant scene of chaos. Roses and baby's breath are scattered on the floor, tulips lie trampled and Madame Archambault is in the corner, hands shackled, screaming that it's *affreux, on se trompe tout le monde*. But it's no mistake. Taking Bernice aside, Claudine whispers that Madame has been found operating a crime ring with Jean and Franc. For several years, when delivering roses to a fancy address, Franc would fuss around placing flowers on a console while Jean would ask to use the bathroom and, while no one was looking, plunder jewelry from the mistress's room. The men were careful to take only a few pieces, so that weeks might pass before anything was missed.

Bernice is at a loss for words. Plump Madame Archambault, so breezy and chatty—and the men, smiling Jean and short Franc—how did they pull this off? The men were always kind to her; they never complained when she was late finishing an arrangement. Yet they were ruthless thieves—probably laughing at Bernice and Claudine behind their backs!

Madame Archambault leans against the counter, her elegant chignon unfurling, her wrists awkwardly shackled. She curses the police, using vulgar words, and for the first time, Bernice sees her not as a formidable *haute-bourgeoise* but as a *arriviste*. It occurs to her that you never really know a person; anyone could be living a double life. Look at Gide, with his English suits and scholar's glasses! If she didn't know better, she would never peg him as a pedophile.

She'd thought she'd found stability, a foothold. But this unmasking of her employer is jarring. It suggests she only has a feeble grasp of what's going on around her, even after four years. Suddenly, everything is lopsided. Her world is unsteady on its base—like her sculpture of Tylia.

On top of that, she's out of a job.

ELEVEN

"*Mon dieu*, how ghastly," says Bronia. "So what will you do?"

"I don't know." Bernice looks up from the croissant on which she's spreading *paté de fruits*. It's hard to hold the knife without trembling. After the trauma in the flower market and her interview at the police station, she didn't want to be alone. This was the first place she thought to come, quickly grabbing some croissants to justify the intrusion.

Bronia and Tylia live in a fourth-floor apartment on the Boulevard Raspail. The place is cluttered but inviting, with books and clothes strewn over the floor. Looking through some paint-chipped French doors, Bernice sees the corner of a wrought-iron double bed with crumpled sheets. Embarrassed, she looks away.

"Do you think I could model?" she looks over at Bronia, then at Tylia, who's buffing her nails on a threadbare *chaise longue*.

"I don't know, have you done it before?" Bronia asks. She's taller than her sister and has a less earthy, more glamorous presence. She models too, for painters and fashion designers, and is apparently much in demand.

"A little bit, in New York. For an artist called Man Ray. He took a photograph of me that won a prize."

"Man Ray—sounds familiar," Tylia muses.

"He's part of that Dada group," her sister says. "With Tzara and Breton."

"Oh, those crazies!" Tylia looks at Bernice. "Were the two of you—?"

"God, no," Bernice says, "just friends. He's not my type at all."

"*Bien sûr.*" Bronia gives a businesslike nod as she tears the horn off a croissant. "Well, modeling. Truthfully, there are far more painters than photographers around. And modeling for a painter is hard, you know. You have to stay like this," she flings out her arms, tilts her chin, "being oh-so-seductive, while all you can think about is that your nose itches and you need to go *pipi*."

"The studios are cold," Tylia adds, "and the bastards never pay as well as they promised, and try to distract you by making a pass. As if their glorious dicks should be payment enough!"

"She could do it," Bronia says, "Don't you think, Ty?"

"Oh, sure. With her smoldering eyes and those tight little ass cheeks." Tylia smiles at her, and Bernice feels her face go red. At the same time, something dances inside her at the thought that Tylia has not only noticed her rear end, but appreciated it. "By the way," Tylia goes on, "did you know there used to be a model market in Montparnasse? You'd stand on a soapbox, and artists would come and poke at you and make an offer if they liked what they saw."

"Fair enough," Bronia says. "After all, we're a bit like prize cows."

"Only with smaller udders," Tylia says. Both of them burst out laughing then, the shape of their mouths and teeth disconcertingly similar. Tylia sticks two fingers up like horns and lets out a plaintive *moo*.

Bernice tries to smile, but it's hard. She's not in the mood for jokes. Disappointment is seeping through her like ink on blotting paper. She'd thought modeling would be easy, but now she sees she wouldn't be able to do it at all. She could never affect the teasing, sensuous air that make Bronia and Tylia so popular. And the idea of being cheated and having to fend off a hairy, paintbrush-wielding man is dismaying—she'd probably punch him in the mouth. At the same time she needs money. Next month's rent is due in a week.

She stands up. "I have to go, anyway. I'm going to check the department stores. Someone told me they like American girls at *Le Bon Marché*." Practically running, she hurries out of the door.

"Thanks for the croissants," Bronia calls after her.

As she makes her way down the dimly lit staircase, Bernice feels leaden, as if gravity is exerting twice its usual pull. The department store errand was made up, an excuse to leave because she didn't want to cry in front of Tylia and Bronia. And she's feeling dangerously close to tears.

It's not just the money. That's part of it, of course—but even more, she needs to know what she's doing with her life. What is her path, where is it all leading? She's been in Paris for four years, and so far she's proven Elsa wrong. She's no closer to finding herself here than she was in the Village. She keeps taking courses, doggedly pursuing sculpture although her improvement in that area has been minimal. If she were going to be a talented sculptor, wouldn't it have happened by now?

Her sculpture of Tylia is no good, she sees this now. What was she thinking, making it half-life size? It seems to her now that she wasn't thinking, she just barreled in, overestimating her talent. A crucial error. Probably she'll never be anything but a middling sculptor, however hard she works at it.

She grips the banister, looking down at the stairs that spiral into darkness beneath her. *Maybe I'm just in love with the idea of being an artist,* she thinks. *Maybe I don't have the imagination, rigor or talent to do it properly.* She can feel her heart pumping as she faces this possibility—which, she realizes, she's been avoiding for years. How much easier it's been to maintain the fantasy that she was making progress, that her art was going to be important! In Montparnasse, everyone is always on the brink of a major breakthrough—a collective delusion, really. She wonders if it would be possible to accept one's failings and live happily as a mediocrity, in constant proximity to brilliance. It strikes her as a depressing existence—yet what else will there be for her if she doesn't become an artist?

"Hey, Bern*eess*!" Tylia is clacking down the stairs, trying to catch up. Bernice hurries down, blotting her eyes, but Tylia is fast. She runs up to Bernice in the lobby, catching her by the arm. "Wait, stop! What's going on?"

"Nothing," Bernice says. And then, all of a sudden the façade crumbles and she leans on the wall, her body sagging. "Oh, my life's a mess."

"Because you lost a job? You'll get another."

"It's not just that." Bernice looks at Tylia's face, with its elegantly arched eyebrows and the little mole on her chin. She wants to explain her self-doubt, but is afraid she'll sound weak and self-indulgent to this girl who's been making her own way since she was fourteen. "Everything is so hard," she whispers.

Tylia leans forward. *"Ma pauvre chérie.* You bear it alone, when there's no need. Listen, Bron and I are having a party tomorrow night. There'll be lots to drink, interesting people, dancing—you like to dance, yes?" Not breaking eye contact, she lifts a finger and runs it along the underside of Bernice's chin, sending a sharp tremor through Bernice's body. "Promise you'll come."

"All right."

"Bon."

Pushing open the heavy door to the street, Bernice blinks in the sudden onslaught of light. The sight of winter's first snowflakes—bright and fluffy, settling on the trees' black branches—should lift her spirits. Instead, it just makes her aware she has no coins for the gas meter in her room.

She's at the intersection of Raspail and Montparnasse, walking past *La Rotonde* when something stops her in her tracks. Inside, sitting alone at a table in the middle, is a familiar figure. Man Ray is affecting a Parisian look, in a tilted black beret with a scarf tossed over one shoulder, but his face—with its pouchy bags under the eyes and the slanted nose—is instantly recognizable. He's hunched over a bowl of *café crème*, staring gloomily down at it.

Bernice leans in to the window, so close that her breath makes a patch of condensation bloom on the glass. Seeing Man Ray right after she'd been talking about him is a strange coincidence. She doesn't believe in fate, but it's odd—maybe he's here for a reason. At the very least he might ask her to pose again and she could get a meal or two out of it.

She pushes through the door, then steers through the tightly packed tables. Even when she's standing in front of him, Man Ray doesn't look up. He's sunk in a fog of self-absorption, and she has to put a hand on his shoulder and shake it to get his attention.

"Man."

He looks up with weary eyes. "Oh, it's you."

"Nice to see you too," Bernice leans down, he half rises, and they meet awkwardly in the middle, kissing on both cheeks. He waves an invitation to sit, and the waiter approaches, a zinc tray under his arm. Bernice orders a *café crème*.

"Are you still sculpting?" he asks.

"Yes. I'm taking a class with Henri Mourcier at L'Académie."

"How is it?"

"Great," she lies. "Traditional, but a solid grounding." Her *café crème* arrives, fragrant and steaming, and she wraps her hands gratefully around the bowl. "What about you, how have you been? I hear you're a Dadaist now."

Man Ray grunts. "That! Well, they've claimed me, I suppose. They like these new camera-less prints I'm doing. I call them Rayographs. Tzara says they're works of genius." He smirks, the closest to happy he's come since she spied him through the window.

"How can you make a print with no camera?"

"Easy. You put objects on photo-sensitive paper and expose them to light. Combs, leaves, a gun, anything. A monkey could do it—which is what Tzara likes. He thinks they're pure Dada." He shrugs. "People find them intriguing.

Cocteau used one on the cover of his new poetry book, and ever since then I can't make them fast enough."

"That's good! And your portraits, are you still doing them?"

"God help me, yes. It's turned into a factory. I have Cocteau to thank for that too. I took his portrait, then he started bringing all his friends around. Now every artist who passes through Montparnasse wants one. Go to the Moulin Rouge, eat *cassoulet*, get your picture done by Man Ray. Three things to do in Paris."

"Geez," Bernice takes a sip of her *café crème*, looking carefully over the rim at him. He's a mess, his shirt is crumpled, and there are coarse black hairs curling out of his nostrils. If this is what success looks like, maybe failure isn't so bad. But something about his misery kindles her protective instincts. "So what are you doing here?" she ventures. "Shouldn't you be in your studio?"

"I should. But *he's* there." Man spits the word out. "I'm hiding from him."

Bernice leans forward. *He*—a client? A lover? As far as she knows, Man only sleeps with women. "What's the matter?"

Man Ray looks around the room, black eyes darting here and there, then leans in and whispers, "It's my assistant, Gas-*pard*. An artist of the first order, at least in his own mind. In my mind, a sonofabitch."

Sighing, he tells her the story. Apparently Gaspard, the son of a wealthy client, has been taking too much initiative in the darkroom. He has his own ideas about printing and departs from Man's directions, adding creative flourishes and expecting his ingenuity to be rewarded. "Whether it's my bad French or his pig-headedness, I can't get through to him," Man grumbles. "And now I can't bear being with him."

Bernice is tempted to laugh. *Is that all?* she wants to say. It seems such small potatoes compared with not being able to pay next month's rent. But clearly it's not small to Man, as no problems ever are to their sufferers. So she nods sympathetically. "Can't you write things down? So there's no ambiguity?"

Man shakes his head. "That wouldn't do. He's got that aristocratic thing going on. *Noblesse oblige*, whatever you call it. He thinks I should be grateful for his presence. No, I've got to screw up my courage to fire him and take the consequences. And then I need to find an assistant I can mold. Someone who knows absolutely nothing about photography."

As he says that, Bernice starts to laugh, because here is her answer, being offered up like a truffle on a silver spoon.

"What about me?"

His body jerks. "You?"

"Why not? I need a job. And I know nothing about photography."

Man looks dubious. "It's not a job for a woman. You have to mix chemicals, and carry heavy containers."

"Oh, pish. I'm not scared."

"But do you understand what the job is? I want a technician."

"I understand," she says impatiently. "And I know I need this, and you need me. We're perfectly matched. You just need to go back to the studio and tell Louis the Sixteenth he's fired."

Man looks at her, half-smiling, cogs clearly whirring in his head. "I could give instructions in English," he muses. "And you say you've never been in a darkroom?"

"Not where photography was being done." At this, Man throws back his head and laughs.

"I can only pay fifteen francs a day."

"That's fine," she says. It's enough to keep the heat on.

"All right. It's a deal." He holds out a hand, and they shake with mock formality. "Come to my studio tomorrow at eight on the dot. And be alert," he looks stern, "you'll be taking in a lot of information. Don't think you can go to bed at four and then stumble in to work at eight."

"I'll be a nun," she says.

Man takes an old bill out of his pocket, scribbles his address on the back and gives it to her. Then, standing, he tugs down his beret. "This is a two-week trial," he says. "If your work is acceptable, the job's yours. Otherwise we part with no hard feelings."

Bernice watches his back, slim and round-shouldered, move toward the door. Her heart is beating fast under her middy blouse. What just happened? It was all so quick, she's hardly even sure it was real. Does she have a job? She looks down at the table, at the coffee dregs in Man's bowl. In the residue of milk foam on the inside rim is an imprint of his thin lips.

Man Ray. She's seen him here and there in Paris, and knew he was doing well, but she didn't know he'd become such a force. He used to call himself a painter, desperately wanting to be Duchamp's equal, but it's his photography that's taken off. Sometimes you have to take what the world gives you.

As for photography, she has never handled a camera or considered doing so. Is it even art? She thinks of the studio portraits of her youth, people sitting stiffly with frozen expressions. But then she remembers other photographs—the wood sprite Alice, staring at her from the window of the Chillicothe bookstore. Man Ray's portrait of *her* where she's looking over her shoulder. Those photographs required vision, and skill. It would take more than a monkey pushing a button to make them.

Besides, she thinks, *I have always liked process.* The dissections she did as a child—pulling back skin, finding organs—had taken patience. Perhaps a medium that combines art with science will be just right for her.

She sits for a while longer, sipping her coffee and idly wondering what kind of boss Man Ray will be. When she modeled for him in New York he was relaxed, a joker, but then she was doing him a favor. To others—lovers especially—she'd heard he could be cruel. Rumors abounded in the Village that he'd whipped a cheating girlfriend with a belt until she begged for forgiveness.

Then again, Man Ray's personal life is not her concern, just as hers has nothing to do with him. This is business, a basic exchange of cash for services. And she's lucky to have gotten the opportunity, no question. This is the only job she's heard of where the major qualification is no prior experience.

She gets up, invigorated for the first time in days, and pulls on her woolen gloves. Now she knows she'll be able to pay for heat, the snow outside looks different. It's clean and lovely, covering the grubby streets with a dazzling mantle of white.

She's putting on her coat, getting ready to dash out when she sees the two empty bowls on the table, and realizes: Man Ray has stuck her with the bill.

◆

The next morning, she wakes up eager to get started. Her hands and feet are icy (no money for the meter yet) as she riffles through her paltry wardrobe, wondering what one wears to a darkroom. Finally she settles on a pleated skirt and crepe shirt—conservative, professional. Breakfast is a sliced apple and day-old croissant served on a chipped china plate. Then she pulls on her threadbare coat and walks down the Boulevard Raspail to rue Campagne-Première, the address on the back of May Ray's bill (which, she notes, is for kid gloves, twelve francs).

Number thirty-one *bis* is a large, modern building of artists' studios with high windows surrounded by sage-colored Art Deco tiles. In the doorway she finds Man's name on a list, along with others that sound vaguely familiar.

She pushes a buzzer and Man Ray lets her in. "You're early," he says, pleased, then darts in closer to peer into her eyes. "And rested."

"I keep my word," she says. For his part, he looks better too, dapper in a clean white shirt, his thick black hair brushed back from its widow's peak.

She follows him to a large room whose walls are covered with paintings and photographs, evidently all by Man. She doesn't care for the paintings, which look like poor imitations of Klee and Duchamp. But the photographs draw her. There are some intimate nudes and one unusual image that shows a white silhouette of fern leaves on a black background. It must be one of the camera-less prints he told her about.

On one side of the room, a curving wooden staircase leads to a gallery room. Man tips his head toward it. "My studio. But my woman is sleeping there at the moment. Come, let me show you the darkroom."

The darkroom turns out to be a bathroom, of good size and cleverly converted, though apparently still in use: there are squares of newsprint in a pile on the commode. The windowpanes have been painted black, and a piece of wood on top of the tub forms a rigid work surface. A counter has been built opposite, and above, shelves bristle with boxes and bottles. On the counter sits a machine that Bernice assumes has something to do with printing photographs. She hopes Man won't find her ignorance too stunning.

Man takes a spiral-bound notebook from a shelf. "This is for you. I don't like repeating myself, so write down what I say."

And for the next hour, she does just that. After five minutes, she's grateful for the book: the volume of information is overwhelming.

Man shows her how to mix chemicals. There are different formulas for developing a negative or a print. After fixing, prints must be washed for ten minutes in running water, then hung from a clothesline to dry. Hanging on the wall are instruments that look like tiny, flattened spoons. These are Man's dodging tools for blocking light to part of a print. They must be constantly jiggled, he says, to avoid creating a harsh line. *Dodge tools: no harsh line: jiggle,* she writes.

After about an hour, Man turns his black eyes on her. "And now, we will make a print." He pulls a box from a shelf and removes an envelope. Carefully, he takes out a rectangle of glass and holds it to the light, handling it by the edges. Bernice sees a man's face, glasses, a beard—but the tones are reversed, so that the face is black and the beard snowy white.

"Who is it?" she asks.

"You don't know?" Shocked, Man blinks at her. "It's Matisse."

"But he looks so conventional!"

"Kid, since when did artists have to look like their work? If they did, Picasso would be in trouble."

To her surprise then, he nods to indicate she should take the negative from him. *Really?* she wants to say, *you trust me?* But it's a test, she realizes. He needs to know she can do this without fumbling.

She reaches up and puts her fingertips around the plate. She doesn't dare breathe, for fear she might break this fragile, irreplaceable document. One clumsy move and Henri Matisse will be lying in shards on the floor.

Man Ray is over by the machine, sliding a kind of frame from its top. He lays it down and shows her how to fit the glass plate into it. Then he slides it into the machine, which she learns is called an enlarger.

"Ready?" he asks. Before she can answer, he flicks a switch and everything—her skin, Man's shirt, the trays on the tub—turns to shades of red.

"My brothel," Man says with a wink. Instinctively she takes a step back, and he laughs. "Don't worry, I'm kidding. I need an assistant too much to try anything."

The next fifteen minutes are astonishing. He explains that photographic paper is sensitive to blue and violet light, but won't react to the red. Then he flicks another switch, the enlarger whirs into life and a fuzzy version of Matisse's face appears on the table below. Man shows her how to focus the image, checking its sharpness by looking through a magnifier for particles of grain. He shows her the difference between the paper's glossy front and matte back—"And don't mix them up, because each piece costs eighty centimes." As the timer ticks off seconds, Bernice watches Matisse's face. Glowing under the enlarger, the *éminence grise* of modern French art stares up at her, his brow furrowed above wire-rimmed glasses, a stern patriarch. She's glad she didn't drop him.

"Done," Man Ray says.

He picks up the paper and slides it under the liquid developer. At first it remains blank, but as Man rocks the tray, a shadowy presence begins to take form. It is a phantasm at first, just a faint outline of a face that slowly fills with melancholy eyes, the dark, clipped beard and finally Matisse's high forehead and big left ear. Bernice can't help but bounce on the balls of her feet. Suddenly she's a child again, dissecting birds—or watching Pa draw a penny from Hazel's ear: *Do you see anything now? What about now?* For surely it is some kind of magic that the light falling over Matisse's face has been captured in every detail, rendering a negative that can be reversed onto paper and fixed there. She watches with delight as the tones darken, adding texture to the artist's beard and his lined, mottled skin.

"Damn!" Man lifts the paper out of the tray with tongs and peers at it. "Too dark, it needs less time. Can't have our Henri looking like a Negro." With a sigh, he drops the paper into another tray, and Bernice bends to look, surprised. She can't see the problem. Evidently she has a lot to learn.

Just then, someone bangs on the outside of the bathroom door with such force that she jumps, knocking her hip on the wood plank over the tub.

"*Ouvre la porte!*" shouts a woman's voice.

"I'm working!" Man cries.

"*Mais je dois pisser!*"

"Get lost!" Man Ray bellows, "Use the jar!"

This is followed by a violent pummeling of fists on the other side of the door and a volley of curses.

Bernice stiffens. "Shouldn't you open it?"

"Oh, she's being dramatic," Man says. "She's got a bladder like an ox."

The door rattles in its hinges and Bernice feels herself growing hot, affronted for the woman on the other side. Men can be such idiots. Her fingers itch to open the door, but she can't risk angering her boss on her first day.

A few minutes later, when the fixed print is washing in the sink—and he's taken his time—Man opens the door. Pushing past, a woman enters, spitting curses. She's statuesque—so tall, in fact, that if not for her beauty she might be taken for a man. Despite her tousled hair and lack of make-up, Bernice recognizes her at once. It's Kiki, Queen of Montparnasse, star of a thousand cabaret posters—and also, it seems, Man's lover. Bernice is impressed. She wouldn't have thought Man could entice such a *nénette*. In person Kiki is imposing, and not just because of her height. She is clearly *bien dans sa peau*, sloe-eyed, with jet-black hair and large nipples visible through her skimpy negligee. Seeing Bernice, she stops abruptly.

"*Qui est-elle?*"

"My new assistant," Man says. "I told you, remember? The kid from New York?"

Kiki scrutinizes Bernice's face with the same close attention Man paid to his print. "*Jolie-laide,*" she announces—*an attractive ugly woman.* Bernice feels as if she's been slapped. Then, taking Bernice's arm, Kiki steers her firmly out of the darkroom, closes the door behind her and locks it. Bernice hears more swearing, along with the unmistakable sound of a long, much-needed piss.

She walks around the drawing room, looking at the art on the walls. Several of the nudes, she now realizes, are of Kiki. She peers at one striking image that shows a woman by a window. The head and legs are cropped out of the frame, and light streaming through striped curtains casts a zebra-like pattern on the woman's torso. She recognizes Kiki's huge nipples, and the way light plays off them sends a hungry throb through her. But if the image is sensual it is also abstract, a study of light and form. It is very modern.

So this is what photography can be. A door has been thrown open; her world has expanded. She already knows she's going to love being here.

After a minute or two, the bathroom lock slides open and Man Ray emerges, clearly discomforted. His eyes dart around, not meeting hers.

"She's a little agitated. I told her about you, but she seems to have forgotten. And she's used to male assistants." Taking some coins out of his pocket, he presses them into Bernice's hand. "Why not go for coffee, eh? Come back in an hour or so?"

Bernice weighs the metal in her hand. It feels like at least two francs. Before she can answer, Man is retrieving her coat. He thrusts it at her and only then does he meet her eyes.

"Women!" he says with a laugh.

Down the street from Man's place is an artists' café, *Chez Rosalie.* With her money in hand (two francs fifty, as it happens), Bernice decides to treat herself to a hot breakfast. God knows, it's been a while. She orders eggs, ham and coffee, and admires the paintings on the walls. Her mind wanders back to the studio, to Man and Kiki. What an improbable couple they are—he, intense and self-absorbed, she, larger-than life and tempestuous. She can't imagine them sharing a conversation, let alone a bed.

When the food comes, she digs into it with unseemly passion. The coffee is strong; the ham is soft, the way she likes it, and the eggs have been cooked in the ham fat. It's the most delicious meal she's had in months.

As she eats, she flips open the notebook Man gave her. Considering the speed at which she was scribbling, her notes are surprisingly neat. *Amidol developer 3:1,* she reads. *Sodium metabisulphate, 10g. Throw out after a week.*

She thinks of Matisse's ghostly image swimming up in the tray. Photography might be a matter of numbers and chemical reactions, but it's also a kind of alchemy, thinks. A process by which light is captured and transformed by metals and chemicals into something durable. An art, too—she can see that now. Man's photo of Kiki by the window is every bit as inventive and original as a painting. In fact, she can't get the vision of the zebra-striped torso out of her mind. It's like Duchamp's kinetic figures. The idea that she might work on such images is thrilling.

Kiki, on the other hand, could be a problem. She's obviously volatile, the jealous type. Perhaps she knows Bernice modeled for Man Ray in New York, and has drawn conclusions. *Well*, Bernice thinks, *that can be handled.* When Kiki's around, she'll simply melt into the background.

All things considered, she thinks she's going to like this job.

◆

Outside Tylia's, Bernice straightens her skirt, then moistens a finger and runs it over her spit curl. Reaching down, she pulls from her purse a half-quart of Rhum Nikola. Finally, with her heart punching a fast beat, she pushes open the door.

The scene inside is as she expected: loud music, louder people. Smoke in the air, raucous laughter. She recognizes Kisling, a painter for whom Bronia has modeled, who is pouring bottles of liquor into a punch bowl with abandon. Kisling's friend Pascin leans against a wall talking to Treize, a model with a perfectly oval face. There's a Japanese painter, Foujita, who, with his curtain of black bangs and round glasses, looks like an overgrown schoolboy. Women cluster around him; one strokes his hair as if he's a poodle.

"Don't *you* look cute!" Tylia appears at her side, gorgeous in a sleeveless black dress gilded with jet beads. She swoops in, kissing Bernice on both cheeks, smelling of gin and a faint tinge of garlic.

"Do I?" Bernice glances down at her polka-dot shirt and gray skirt. They seem drab next to Tylia's finery. "Not next to you. You're like a Fabergé egg." Realizing that this isn't entirely a compliment, she does an awkward little shuffle.

Tylia grins. "*Mon chou*," she says in a tipsy drawl, "I'm so glad you came." Leaning toward Bernice, she seems almost about to kiss her again, but then straightens and raises a bottle of rum. "Kisling needs this. I'll be back, though. Enjoy yourself, *oui?*"

"*Oui*," Bernice watches Tylia move through the crowd, savoring the way her friend's body moves under the black dress. She is intimately acquainted with that body—has absorbed it, obsessed over it, tried to recreate it—but it seems newly enticing under the dress, where so much is left to the imagination.

For the next hour she floats around, sipping punch and observing, occasionally being drawn into conversation. Hart Crane, a poet she knew in New York, tells her he's just had something published in *Harper's*. She's less thrilled to see Reichard, a handsome classmate from the Académie—for a moment she wonders if Ty has been going out for "coffee walks" with all the students. But then she finds out he's a friend of Bronia's and relaxes, returning his broad smile.

When everyone has had plenty to drink and the hashish has made the rounds, Bronia and Tylia roll up the Turkish rug and open up the Victrola. They have some new American imports: *Cutie* and *The Happy Hottentot*. Tylia is a good dancer. She tears it up with Kisling, the two of them shimmying back and forth, shaking their heads and arms at each other. Bernice watches, clapping, her breath quickening at the sight of Tylia's white thighs under her flapper's dress. Pushing away the image, she dances with three or four men herself, having a fine time until she realizes it's almost three in the morning. Good grief! She has to be at Man Ray's studio at eight, and she promised she'd behave. Quietly she slips into the hallway.

She's making her way down the corridor to fetch her coat when Tylia comes out, swaying, and puts an arm across her path.

"Where are you going?"

"Home. It was wonderful, but I'm exhausted and my shoulders ache."

"No you don't, you can't. It's early!"

"Ty, it's three o'clock." Bernice laughs and ducks under her arm, and Tylia laughs too and follows her down the corridor to the maid's room. When they get there, she closes the door behind her. "You say your shoulders ache? Lie down. I'm going to rub your back."

Feeling drunk and more than a little confused, Bernice teeters toward the tiny bed in the corner, where coats are piled. "You don't want to go back to the party?"

"Shh," Tylia pushes down, gently but insistently, until Bernice is lying face down on the coats. "Now, hush. See how good this feels?"

Tylia is drunk too, Bernice realizes, but perhaps that's just as well. It feels as if the two of them are encased in a boozy bubble, floating away from everyone down the hall. Inside this bubble, it seems perfectly natural for Tylia to be rubbing Bernice in long, firm strokes that ripple down her polka-dot shirt, from her shoulders to her waist. It seems natural to sigh and clutch the edge of a wool coat, the pads of her fingertips alive to its rough weave. She can hear Tylia's gentle laugh, as if her friend is saying, *Isn't this a delightful game we're playing?* Then Tylia moves her hands, and her thumbs circle each of Bernice's vertebrae, slowly, with deep, careful force. Bernice lies still, hardly daring breathe lest her breath come out as a moan. Her body is pouring into Tylia's hands and she's floating, succumbing, until Tylia's fingers stop pressing and, reaching down, start to unhook her brassiere. And then she jerks up, a clumsy jack-in-the-box, hugging her brassiere to her chest.

"Wait. Please..."

"May I?" Tylia asks. She bends to kiss Bernice's neck and Bernice sinks back on the coats, instinctively wrapping her arms around herself. Her legs are trembling. How can it be possible that Tylia—her beautiful, self-assured friend—wants *her*?

"What about Kisling?"

"Oh," Tylia laughs, "he's not for me. Bron's been with him, so he thinks I'm fair game. But no," she raises an eyebrow, running a finger along Bernice's cheek, "I'm interested in someone else."

She bends down, and the beads on her dress make a *shushing* sound as she maneuvers herself onto the bed. Bernice holds still, breathing the smoky, perfumed scent of her friend. She thinks of Tylia on the dais, her rounded belly and the whorls of hair beneath, and at this thought, her crotch throbs so powerfully that it's almost painful. She longs to reach out—but how can she? How can she know, when she touches Tylia, that the two of them won't combust?

"I haven't..." she whispers. "I can't." Tears crowd her eyes. "The last time I tried this...something happened."

"Oh," Tylia makes a sympathetic *moue*. "I see. Well, look." She bends down and touches Bernice's lips with her own, so fleetingly that Bernice is left shuddering. "See, nothing bad. And again..." She bends down and this time her lips linger warmly, and Bernice meets them with her own. "Nothing."

"No," Bernice breathes.

"Don't worry," Tylia whispers, "I can teach you."

And before long she has undressed them both. Her fingers move over Bernice's body, expertly stroking and pinching, and Bernice closes her eyes and gives in to the strangeness and wonder of it all. She breathes in the heady scent of Tylia's vetiver shampoo and sighs as Tylia's cornsilk cheek brushes her own. As they kiss, she tastes gin and that faint tinge of garlic, and it is warm and tangy and delicious.

And then—oh! She is arcing, gasping, hardly believing such things are possible. Tylia kisses and teases, her tongue moving from Bernice's navel to her crotch, where it flicks in and out. From down the hall comes laughter and music—and the thought of the others dancing while she and Tylia are doing this makes her feel delirious. The tension builds, and at the moment of release she sees Kiki's torso with its harsh stripes, and moans as her body turns to honey. She imagines Gide looking at her with a knowing smile.

Later, when they're putting on their clothes, Tylia touches Bernice's shoulder. "We must do something about your name."

"My name?" Bernice looks up, shyly clutching her shirt to her chest. "What's wrong with it?"

Tylia wrinkles her nose. "Bern*eess*. It's ugly. It has no music."

"What do you suggest I call myself? Scheherazade?"

"That would be nice," Tylia cocks her head. "But I think just a small change. You see, if we add an 'e' in the middle, you become Bérenice. Elegant, sophisticated. You see? No more American midwest."

"Bérenice," Bernice rolls the name over her tongue. It sounds rich, exotic. "I like it." *A new name for a new person*, she thinks. She feels lighter but also stronger, as if her body has been charged with new energy. What could she do as Bérenice? What *couldn't* she do? The effects of the alcohol and reefer have worn off, but she's intoxicated in another way, drunk on her power to give and receive pleasure. Exhilarated at the thought that—soon, she hopes—they might do it again.

"Bérenice," she repeats.

Smiling, Tylia shimmies into her dress. Her burgundy lipstick is smudged, giving her mouth an out-of-focus look. "What do you think Man Ray will say?"

"I don't know." Reaching over, Bernice pulls Tylia toward her. She is more grateful than she can say, for this dark-haired girl with the cat's eyes and nimble fingers. Putting her arms around Tylia's waist, she nuzzles her mouth against her lover's ear. "And honestly, I don't care."

TWELVE

"I think it needs more texture in the highlights. I can burn it in here, see? I tried twenty seconds, and it worked well."

"Hm." Man looks over her shoulder at the portrait she's holding up. The subject is André Breton, a friend of Man's, a former Dadaist who made a stir the previous year with his surrealist manifesto. He's wearing a black leather coat, looking to the side and up, as if staring at the future. Man shot him from below, as one would a statue, and the light coming from the left gives his round face structure. But there's too much contrast. Berenice's burning-in has given it a softer, more human feel.

"All right, yes," Man says, "that's good." She can feel him looking at her as she washes a print. "You've picked this up fast, you know. You're doing good work."

"Thanks." Berenice basks in the unexpected praise. The work suits her, she knows. She likes the exacting process of mixing chemicals, the adjustments of exposure and filters that can turn a so-so negative into a stunning print. And she prides herself on being a good employee. Each morning, she gets to the studio at eight, and she usually doesn't leave until after eight at night. If there's a rush job—and there are, many—she'll cancel her evening plans. Well before her two-week deadline, she'd done plenty to impress Man, and since then he has told her several times that she's the most reliable assistant he's had.

"I'm going to lunch," he says now. "Listen," he throws this over his shoulder, "if you ever want to fool around with the cameras while I'm out, go ahead. I trust you. Just leave them how you found them, okay?"

"All right," Berenice stares at his back, surprised and flattered. Man's cameras are his babies, she knows. In fact, if a camera and Kiki were both drowning, she has no doubt which Man would rescue first.

As it happens, she'd been trying to nerve herself up to ask if she could use them. Has he sensed it? Seeing him work, watching him get an idea and create it, has made her curious to try it too. Just last week, when Man was shooting a portrait of Antonin Artaud, she'd stood behind him, fingers itching to push him aside and look through the lens herself. It had surprised her, the strength of this urge, and her thwarted desire to set Artaud up in a different—and to her mind, better—pose.

"Bérenice," Man had finally said—emphasizing the extra 'e,' which he kept telling her was a ridiculous affectation, as if he hadn't changed his name from Emanuel Radnitzky—"why don't you go to the darkroom and make some prints?"

"All right." She'd shrugged at Artaud, then slouched down the stairs like Cinderella going to the scullery.

Now she climbs the stairs to the studio, telling herself she'll just *look* at the cameras. Kiki was posing earlier, and scarves and shawls lie discarded on the divan. In the corner, the big Seneca is set up on its tripod, a black cloth draped over the top. Other cameras—the boxy Eastman and the Scovill, with its revolving back—sit on the shelves, eying her with their big black lenses.

Something catches her eye then, a conch shell that Man sometimes uses as an ashtray. If she put it on the sill…she wipes it down and carries it to the window, where the soft north light illuminates its spikes and pearly interior. On a table nearby is a chipped ceramic pitcher with a single tiger lily, Kiki's favorite. Getting an idea then, she takes the flower out of its vase and lays it near the shell. There! Now, all she needs is a dark background to accentuate the objects. Casting around, she sees a purple shawl of Kiki's and fetches it. She spends a few moments manipulating the flower petals. There it is, no masterpiece but an unexpected composition full of textures that—if she gets the exposure right—should come out well in a photograph.

By now, her heart is doing the Texas Tommy in her chest. She looks at the Seneca, majestic on its tripod, all polished mahogany and brass fittings. The idea of handling it is daunting, and her eye goes back to the shelf, to the Eastman. It's not set up, but at half the size it's more managable. She'll just go downstairs, maybe see if she can find a plate for it.

Five minutes later, she's fitting a glass negative into the camera back. She has already set the angle, tilting the lens so that she's looking down on the conch. Her fingers are trembling, but she finally gets the holder into its grooves on the back of the camera and removes the slide. *One, two, three, four, five, six, seven.* The slide goes back, she breathes out. The plate is exposed. Now she'll put the studio back to rights.

An hour or so later, there's a commotion outside the door, a thump followed by boisterous laughter. The door flies open and Man Ray tumbles in, followed by Duchamp. Behind Duchamp is a young man she doesn't recognize—tall, rather good-looking, with a long oval face and cleft chin.

Man Ray stumbles toward her. "Berenice! Marcel and Julien have had an idea for a Dadaist film. We'll be upstairs working on it. Well, come on—don't just stand there. Take Julien's coat!"

Berenice bristles under a forced smile. The more drunk Man gets, the worse he treats her—she's beginning to know how Kiki must feel. Apparently he's forgotten that he promised to work with her this afternoon. Now she'll be up all night, making him look good while he prances around declaiming about Dada—which, if she remembers correctly, he told her he thought was stupid.

To his credit, at least the young man seems embarrassed. Apparently not as drunk as the other two, he hands her his coat with an apologetic look. "Julien Levy," he says, "I've heard you're a good assistant."

"And a good coat rack." Berenice says it quietly enough that Man, who's showing Duchamp some hats, doesn't hear.

Levy grins, revealing perfectly straight teeth. "We'll be going to *Select* later. Will you join us?"

"Thanks, but I'll be working."

"I'm sure the boss would let you take a break."

Is he flirting with her? Or being polite? He's smiling, with the confidence that comes with the blessing of good looks, but there's something else about him, a coolness that reminds her of a shark. She's almost tempted to turn up at *Select,* just to infuriate Man—but that would cause trouble. "No, he won't," she says.

Levy looks put out as if she has no right to resist his charms. But all he says is, "You *are* good."

"Julien!" Man Ray calls. "Look! Isn't she lovely?" He has dressed Duchamp in Kiki's silk hat and a string of pearls, and put plum-colored lipstick on him. Duchamp winks and purrs, *"Allons, mes petits,"* which makes Man and Levy roar with laughter. Berenice stiffens: she doesn't see what's so clever about making fun of prostitutes. Shaking her head, she pushes past them to get to the coat hooks.

Later, Man Ray comes into the darkroom. "What did you do while I was out?"

"Some more prints of Breton. And the spotting you wanted on the Malkine." She won't tell him about her fledgling attempt at photography. Seeing the image of the conch and lily appear, filling in and darkening on the negative plate, had been almost as heady as her first time with Tylia. This was *her* vision, *her* work—influenced by Man Ray for sure, but at the same time, emphatically personal. For something put together so quickly she thought it not bad, and she was hungry to use the camera again. But since that may not happen for a while, she has wrapped her glass negative in cotton and put it away. The whole enterprise feels fragile, like a fling that may not evolve into more.

The next day, when he's slept off his hangover, Man instructs her on printing some new images of Kiki. Eschewing his mistress's marvelous breasts, he has chosen to shoot her from the rear, and the coyness of this is just as erotic as her more revealing poses. In one, Kiki holds her arms in front of her body so that you only see her beautiful back, long and white, curving down to a deliciously rounded backside. In deference to Ingres, one of Man's favorite artists, her hair has been swept up and hidden under a scarf that is wound like a turban around her head. Her head is turned, so that you can just see the tip of her nose and a hint of lip. The pose reminds Berenice of waking up next to Tylia, admiring the curve of her shoulder and the sensual dip of her back. She smiles, wondering what Man would say if he knew her girlfriend was as beautiful as his.

"Lovely, isn't she?" Man says. "A pain in the ass, but still…"

Berenice nods. Truth be told, she's grown to like Kiki. If anything, she thinks Man should appreciate his muse more. His prints of Kiki are highly praised, and still he acts as if she's his personal albatross.

"Look," Berenice points at a print hanging from the washing line, "it's so symmetrical. Her back looks like a violin."

Man peers at the print, looking ready to laugh. But instead he goes quiet. "Yes," he says, "it does."

"You can see why everyone begs her to model."

Man unpins the print of Kiki from the line, adds it to the pile of other dry prints and, with the tip of his finger, traces the curve of Kiki's back. "Too bad if they do," he says thoughtfully. "She's all mine."

◆

The next day, when Berenice unlocks the door to the studio, Man rushes over, his hair sticking up. "Come, you must see what I've made!" His eyes are bloodshot and he smells rank, like the walkways by the Seine.

He grabs her coat and flings it over an armchair. "Come quickly, come, come!"

She follows him to the darkroom, laughing at his urgency. What could have happened to make him so agitated? He's usually finicky to a fault, insisting she hang her things up. He's taught her to keep the darkroom pristine, everything cleared away and wiped down.

And then she sees it. "Oh!" She puts a hand to her mouth.

"What do you think?"

"I think…my god, it's amazing."

"I knew it!" Man cries.

The print hangs from the washing line, in the same place as it did last night. But Man Ray has changed it. On top of Kiki's back he has superimposed two f-holes, like the holes on a violin, giving the illusion that Kiki's back is an instrument. How did he do it? Berenice left at nine; he must have been working through the night to get this right.

"André says photography is too grounded in realism to be truly surreal, but I think I've proven him wrong," he crows. "Can you imagine what he'll say when he sees this?"

"He'll be surprised," she says, feeling a lump form in her throat. *It was my idea*, she wants to say, *You stole my idea*. But it wasn't, really. She just noticed the violin shape of Kiki's back. Man Ray was the one who took the idea and made it into art.

Immediately, she can see it's a breakthrough. Man has done something bold. The image has a graphic simplicity that will catch people's attention. In its own way, it's as shocking as Duchamp's urinal—or the mustache and beard Marcel painted on the *Mona Lisa*. No wonder Man is pleased. Finally, he has done something to match his famous friend.

"I'm going to call it *Le Violon d'Ingres*," he says. When she doesn't respond, he prompts, "Get it?"

"Yes," she says. Like Ingres' *Odalisque*, it's a picture of a naked woman from the back. But "*violon d'Ingres*" is also a French phrase meaning hobby, or pastime. Is Man being clever, she wonders, or dismissing Kiki? Calling her a hobby, like playing cards or smoking a cigar?

Just then, the studio buzzer sounds. Berenice looks at Man, who shrugs. "Go, go," he says, so she runs into the hallway. She's so preoccupied with thoughts of *Le Violon* that she opens the front gate before asking who's there, and is surprised to find a stooped old man on the other side. There's no way he can be Man's friend or a client. His face is all angles and bones, and his clothes are threadbare, more patch than cloth.

"*Mam'zelle*," he says, addressing her in French, "if I could beg your indulgence. I'm looking for an opportunity to sell my photographs."

In a trembling hand, he holds out a postcard-sized print, a street scene, nicely composed and well printed, with a narrow lane winding through the middle of the frame. On one side of the lane is an abandoned wood building, on the other sits a fancy stone edifice. Old and new Paris, facing each other.

"I make documents for artists," he says. "Edgar Dégas has used my work as a study for a background in his painting." His milky eyes glint. This is clearly a point of pride.

Berenice is intrigued. The old guy seems like one of a kind, a real Paris character. There's no way Man will want to buy his work, but she's not in a mood to please Man right now. In fact, just the opposite. "Won't you please come in?" she says.

When Man Ray sees whom she's brought in, he shoots her an incredulous look. But when she explains the old man's business, his face changes. He smiles unctuously, and gives her a wink as if to say, *Let's have some fun with him.*

The old man's name is Eugène Atget. He lives down the street, he tells them, on the fifth floor of number seventeen, rue Campagne-Première. His voice is so raspy that it's hard to understand his French, but Berenice gathers he used to be an actor, and took up photography when he had a period of unemployment. "Then," he says, "photography became my passion." Now he goes out in the city every morning, capturing the old, disappearing Paris along with the new.

He opens his briefcase and takes out a dozen images. Expecting touristy views of Sacré-Coeur and Notre Dame, Berenice is shocked. Each image is as keenly observed and exquisitely detailed as the one he showed her at the door. A curving stone staircase, a fishmonger's store, a rag-and-bone man's house. He has captured them with clarity and thoughtfulness, in exact, elegant compositions, and there's a poignancy to the fact that he's documented such humble places. She'd thought the image he showed her at the door was a fluke—anyone can take one decent picture—but now she sees that it wasn't at all.

She picks up a picture of a tailor's shop window, and thinks of Ma in Contadino's. This shop is larger, with three grinning mannequins on display. Ornate buildings and trees are reflected in the glass, so that you get a sense not just of the shop but of the society around it. It's a complex, layered photograph, carefully wrought, with a touch of cheeky humor.

Man picks up a different print. "*Monsieur*, I must admire the way you've captured the *Epicerie Poubelle*," he says. "It's just as I remember it."

Atget's forehead crinkles. "Thank you, *monsieur*. But I have to inform you, that's not the *Epicerie Poubelle*. In fact, I've never heard of such a place. This is the *Café Grecque*."

"I think you'll find you're mistaken, *monsieur*. This is the *Poubelle*. I bought a salami sandwich there last week."

Atget picks up the photograph and peers at it. "No, I'm absolutely sure it's the *Grecque*. And over there is the *Hotel Montagne*."

Seeing what Man is doing, Berenice burns with indignation. She reaches forward and picks up the print. "He's right, Man, it's the *Grecque*. You must be mixing things up in your head."

Man bangs his hand on the table, with such force that the prints jump. "I know a place when I see it! I must say, it's extraordinary that the two of you are equally blind!"

Atget looks from one to the other of them, and his defeated slouch indicates that he's caught on to the game. "Well," he says wearily, "are you interested in buying any of my works? They're five francs each."

"I tell you what," Man waves a hand over the table, "why don't you leave these here overnight, and I'll decide which ones I want. Oh, don't look put out. You know where I live. I'm hardly going to steal them."

"All right." Atget puts two claw-like hands on the table and heaves himself up. As Berenice escorts him to the door, she hears him muttering under his breath.

"I'm sorry," she tells him at the gate, "he's American." Atget looks at her gravely and shrugs, and she watches as, briefcase in hand, he walks slowly down the street.

"That wasn't nice," she tells Man when she gets back. "You should pick on someone your own size."

"Oh, come," he laughs, "a crazy old man hawking picture postcards?"

"I think they're beautiful," she says sincerely.

He snorts. "They're mundane."

"I take it you're not going to buy any, then?"

"Of course not. Let the old fart stew in his juices, you can take them back tomorrow. That's what he gets for disturbing me at a critical moment."

He goes back to the darkroom, humming, and Berenice swallows, trying to rid herself of the sour taste Man's behavior has left. He's taught her so much about photography and his art is innovative. But he's a pig to Kiki, and now he's insulted a weak old man.

She looks again at Atget's prints. She does, honestly, think them exquisite—and besides that, something about the old man has moved her. His dedication, the patience he must have to do this work. At his age, carrying a heavy camera and tripod around the streets!

Life isn't kind to old men, she decides. Whereas young ones, like Man Ray, get to play their *violon d'Ingres* to their hearts' content.

THIRTEEN

The plate holder is in the camera. Berenice slides off the cover, counts off twenty seconds, slides it back in. The exposure should be right—she did a test shot earlier—but she tries posing Sylvia three more times, adding or taking away a second as the light dictates.

"Should I take off the coat?" Sylvia asks.

"No, it's wonderful. Just clasp your knee again—there, like that." The black coat, made of some kind of shiny new plastic, has a presence all its own, and as soon as Sylvia had turned up at the studio in it, Berenice knew how she wanted to shoot her. With a white scarf folded under the lapels, and her thick hair sticking up, the bookseller looked like a pilot about to fly directly to the moon.

"You could be Lindbergh," she tells Sylvia now.

Sylvia laughs. "Oh, darling. He's *far* prettier than I."

"Do you think he'll make it?"

"Couldn't say. Wouldn't like to be him, though, facing the pressure. Would you?"

Would she? Opening the shutter, Berenice goes into a reverie. She is slightly infatuated with Lindbergh, the handsome young mail pilot who has scraped together enough money to go up against the world's greatest flying aces. They call him the Lone Eagle, the Flying Idol. For months, ever since he announced his intention to compete for the Orteig Prize, she—like much of the world—has been obsessed. And since he took off from Roosevelt Field the previous morning, she has been running to the radio at every opportunity, almost too nervous to breathe.

"I'd like to be up there," she murmurs, "to know what it feels like."

"Not me," Sylvia says. "I can't find my way from Rambuteau to the Marais." She wriggles, making the stiff material of her coat crackle.

When the session is over, Sylvia stands and stretches her arms above her head. How like a man she looks, with her strong brow and jutting chin! Of course, she's a well-known lesbian—her partner, Adrienne Monnier, runs a French bookstore across the street from Sylvia's store, Shakespeare & Company. Berenice would like to talk to her about this, to ask how it feels to be so open. But the old Midwestern shame hangs on her. When she imagines the conversation, all she can see is Ma's aghast face.

Sylvia swings her arms, tipping her head from side to side. "I'm glad you could fit me in," she says. "Your portrait of Djuna was wonderful."

"Yours will be too," Berenice says. Shyly, she adds, "Thank you for putting my pictures in the bookstore. It's brought me a lot of business."

"You deserve it. Bring me prints when they're ready, all right?" So saying, Sylvia kisses her on the cheek, then starts down the stairs to the drawing room. Man Ray, who was half way up the stairs, steps aside and bows as she passes.

"Sylvia, you look ravishing."

"Thank you."

"I trust you had a good session?"

"We did. You're lucky to have Berenice, you know."

"I know. She's a gem."

When Man comes upstairs, he doesn't meet Berenice's eye. Instead he shuffles around the studio, fiddling with a tripod and moving it across the room. Is he annoyed? It certainly seems so from the way he's banging things around. *But I've done nothing wrong*, she thinks. *He's always said I could use the studio during his lunch hour.*

"I'm sorry, I thought you were going out for longer," she says.

"Me too," he turns, and his expression changes from irritated to glum. "But Cocteau canceled, so it was just me and Aragon. And all *he* wanted to talk about was the Party. I had to drink myself stupid to tolerate it."

"Ah." From the glazed look in his eyes, Bernice can see he's tipsy. As she begins packing up the camera, she feels his eyes on her. Of course this makes her self-conscious, and the camera wobbles and almost falls as she unscrews it from the tripod.

"Sorry…" she starts, but Man cuts her off.

"What a horrible coat Sylvia was wearing! She looked ugly. Couldn't you have brushed her hair?"

"I thought she looked fine."

Man paces around the room, looking agitated. Suddenly he stops and turns. "You're becoming all the rage with the Sapphic contingent!" he exclaims. "Tell me, do you sleep with them or just take their photos?"

Berenice freezes, the plate holders wobbling in her hand. His breath wafts toward her, an unpleasant mixture of table wine, onions and some kind of strong cheese. He must be very drunk, she realizes, that's when he's meanest. She's found the best thing to do in such situations is humor him.

"What if I do?" she says lightly. "*You* sleep with your models."

He lurches toward her, face flushed. "Ha! I knew it! You're a dark horse, aren't you? Diligent and serious, and then…" Suddenly he breaks into a grin. "Perhaps I could stay, one time when you're entertaining, and hide in the closet…?"

Berenice laughs, as if it's a joke. As if she's never seen the erotic photographs he keeps boxed up on a high shelf in the darkroom—naked women in leather collars, men with whips and ropes. Grabbing an arm, she steers him to the divan. "You're drunk, Man. Sleep it off. Ezra Pound is coming at four o'clock. You've got three hours to get yourself together."

"Maybe a little nap…" Falling back on the divan, he curls up in a fetal pose and promptly passes out.

Going downstairs, Berenice tries to shrug off Man's behavior, and his implication that her portraiture is a front for seduction. Implausible as it seems, she can't shake the idea that he must be jealous. On the surface this is ridiculous—it's so unwarranted—but she knows how his mind works. Before she started doing portraits, every notable writer and artist had to be "done" by Man Ray. His portraits were a Montparnasse feature. Lately, though, some people—especially women—have been asking to be "done" by Berenice. Now her photographs hang alongside his at Sylvia's store. Her reputation is spreading and as a result she has plenty of lunch-hour bookings for the next few weeks.

Maybe Man thinks she planned this all along. A wily, calculating person—someone like him—would have. But Berenice never meant to compete with him. Her entrée into portraiture had been purely accidental.

It had started when she ran into Djuna Barnes, her old New York roommate, on the rue Froidevaux. Djuna had branched into fiction, and her short story *A Night Among the Horses* had won praise. They went for coffee at *Le Select*, and when it emerged that Berenice was working for Man Ray and experimenting with photography, Djuna said, "Perfect! I'm having a story published soon, and the magazine has asked for an author photograph. I'd feel so comfortable with you behind the camera. You'll do it, won't you?"

Berenice shook her head. "I don't do portraits."

"Why?"

"I don't know, I just—" *Why?* It had occurred to her, of course, but she didn't want to encroach on Man Ray's territory. Surely, though, shooting a portrait or two wouldn't threaten him? His portraits were famous, and he had a clientele bigger than the jazz orchestra at *Les Ambassadeurs*. She looked at Djuna in her stylish cloche, with her enigmatic dark eyes. Why *shouldn't* she take a portrait?

"All right," she told Djuna. "But not for money. We're friends doing each other a favor. You get your portrait, I get experience."

The next day, Berenice found herself feeling fluttery. So far, her photography experiments had been limited to still lifes and street scenes—nothing that spoke back to her. She decided to practice for Djuna's session by taking a picture of herself.

The composition was simple: she wore a plain black jacket and white shirt, and the background was a white wall. But her new haircut—boyishly short, with a side-part and triangle of bangs—gave her face interesting lines. Self-conscious, she sat in Man's velvet chair, curling her hand over the shutter release cable. She exposed only one plate and it came out well. Man had recently shot a picture of her in pale make-up, chin resting in her hands, making her look like a china doll. Surprisingly, she preferred her own version, where she looked less pretty but more interesting.

The next day, Djuna arrived at the studio wearing a tweed jacket and a dramatic black cape and silver turban. At first, Berenice photographed her like that: the sophisticated writer, a woman of letters and layers. But then she had another idea. "You have a beautiful profile," she told Djuna, "let's do something with it." So they took off the turban and arranged her hair, and Berenice put a studio light behind her, highlighting Djuna's silhouette. It was unconventional, but she knew that if it worked she'd have something different, and special.

By this time, it was impossible not to let Man Ray know what she'd been doing. When he saw the portraits of Djuna, he looked at Berenice, his lowly assistant, with new respect. "Don't give your work away," he said. "Listen, I did it for years and it almost ruined me. These are good enough to sell." He looked around the darkroom, seeming to be making a calculation. "Tell you what,

I'll sell you paper and plates at cost. We can settle up at the end of each week."

"Deal," Berenice said, surprised. Man Ray kept you on your toes, for sure: you never knew when he'd ditch the pig and act like a human being.

Djuna thought the portraits wonderful too. As well as using one for her author portrait, she gave a print to Sylvia for the store. Sylvia hung it next to Man's portrait of Hemingway and soon other women were coming around, wanting "strong, real" portraits. That was the problem with Man's view, Berenice thought: he either glamorized or infantilized women. And of course, whenever he could, he got them naked.

So now, without intending it, she's a portrait photographer—a good one, too. She manages to put people at ease. A portrait is a psychological likeness and in her company her subjects often let their public masks slip a little. Jean Cocteau, Solita Solano, Jane Heap, James Joyce—the pictures keep coming out. Everything she couldn't achieve in sculpture—finding balance, having a distinctive style—has been startlingly easy to realize here.

That evening, after Pound's visit, Berenice approaches her boss in the studio. "Can we settle up for the week?"

He shakes his head. "I don't have any cash."

"That's all right. I owe you this week. Quite a lot, in fact."

Actually, she reflects as she's getting out the cash, *that's mostly the case these days*. It was nice of him to offer the use of his resources, but she's using so many supplies that she's always in his debt now. Which is embarrassing. She counts twenty-one francs into his hand. She can't pretend that what she's doing is a hobby any more. The axis between them has shifted.

Later, she takes a break and goes with Tylia to the Jockey Club. Kiki, who is on the bill, delights the crowd by singing a lewd sea shanty while teasingly removing her sailor suit. When she's down to a pair of blue bloomers, she extracts a large rubber fish and says, "Ooh, which of you naughty boys left this here for me?" The crowd goes wild, flinging flowers and cash onto the stage.

Berenice and Tylia order absinthe, and watch as the sugared water drips through the slotted spoons and clouds the clear green liquid below. After a few sips, the lights turn smudgy and Kiki's voice seems to come from far away. Sitting next to Tylia in her low-cut red dress, Berenice feels awestruck. Who'd have guessed that this "little girl from the Midwest" would be drinking absinthe with her girlfriend at *Le Jockey*?

Underneath, though, her heart is uneasy. She knows Tylia sleeps with other people from time to time. She has smelled, on occasion, an unapologetically male scent emanating from her lover. From the beginning, Tylia made it clear that their relationship did not preclude other, more temporary ones. It's a common enough arrangement in Montparnasse, but Berenice has no urge to follow it herself, and can't be fully at ease with it. Still, she tells herself that—for now, anyway—Tylia always comes back.

Before going to bed that night, Berenice scrutinizes the photographs she's pinned to her wall. After Man Ray treated old man Atget so badly, she went to his studio the next day and bought five prints, pretending she was fulfilling a request from Man. She looks at them now, appreciating the elegantly curving sidewalk in one, the window reflections in another. In one, dolls are ranged on a toyshop table, as fancily dressed as society ladies in the Jardin de Luxembourg.

What is art? It strikes her that nobody really knows—or rather, that everyone has a different opinion. To Man Ray, Atget's work is pedestrian, whereas to her it's the pure expression of an artistic eye. Sylvia thinks *her* portraits are art, and the avant-garde art world values Man Ray's rayographs but sees his portraits as inferior. Does it depend on the context, the creator's intention? Who is right?

She sighs: all she knows is that Atget's photography appeals to her, and that she strives for some kind of truth in her portraits.

When at last she falls into a fitful sleep, she dreams that Man Ray and Kiki are making love while she photographs them. The problem is the composition, because Man has shrunk to the size of a small boy. She has just closed the camera when Kiki reaches out, inviting her to join them…

She wakes to a groggy realization that she drank too much absinthe the previous night. But one thing is clear. She needs a mentor, one she can respect. Also, she wants to help Atget. She doesn't know why she didn't think of it before. She'll help him promote his work, and perhaps in turn he'll teach her what he knows…

An hour later, at the rue Campagne-Première, she walks past the studio and down the street to number seventeen. It's five steep flights up to Atget's apartment. The hallway paint is peeling, there are stains on the walls and a lingering smell of fish. Near the top, she stops for a moment, winded, to catch her breath. How does he do this every day, with his equipment, at his age?

At the top, she finds herself in front of a dull brown door, looking at a small bronze hand, his doorknocker. She raps and at first there's no response.

After a few moments, though, she hears shuffling. The door opens a crack and she sees a wisp of hair and a sunken, bird-like eye.

"*Qui est là?*"

"It's Berenice Abbott, Monsieur Atget. Do you remember me? I work down the street, with the photographer Man Ray."

"Ah, the arrogant gentleman who purchased my work." A chain is released; the door swings open. "Come in, *mam'zelle*."

Berenice follows his stooped form down a hallway, to the room she came to when she bought the prints. It's much the same as before, dark furniture silvered over with dust, books everywhere. A vinegary smell of darkroom chemicals. Last time, the old man had shown her his darkroom, a poorly ventilated galley off the kitchen, stuffed from floor to ceiling with boxes of negatives and prints.

"Well, *mam'zelle*, how can I help? Would you like to buy more prints?" Hopeful, he tilts toward her.

"I came…well, I was wondering if we could talk."

The old man blinks a couple of times. For a moment, Berenice thinks he might refuse. But then he bows deeply and waves at a chair. As she sinks into its depths, dust floats up and makes her cough. The shutters are almost drawn, but light streams from a crack, falling on his face as he sits opposite her, illuminating gray stubble and a dribble of something—egg yolk? jam?—caught in the hairs. She stares at the dribble, repelled and fascinated by it.

Atget leans forward, his bird eyes glittering, a faint smile on his face. "You came here to talk. But you're silent."

"I'm sorry, I can't think how to begin. But…I feel drawn to your work, *monsieur*."

"*Merci*." He bows his head. His few wisps of hair float upward like duck down. There's a large photograph on the mantle of a skinny old woman with freckles and dark eyes. His wife? The room bears traces of a female presence: a china doll, lace antimacassars. A half-finished needlepoint sitting on a table suggests that the lady of the house might be about to take her seat.

"Does your wife like photography too?"

"Madame Atget died last winter."

"Oh, I'm so sorry."

"Don't be," Atget says, "she was ill. It was a deliverance."

He's still in mourning, that's as clear as one of his photographs. "You must find comfort in your work," she says.

"It's all I have, now."

It's hard to know how to reply to this. She clears her throat. "Please know that I admire your pictures enormously."

He nods. "Do you take photographs yourself, Mademoiselle Abbott?"

"I do. I mean, I've just started."

"And why do you take them?"

She hesitates. "Because I want to create beauty, I think. To capture something evanescent, and give it a kind of immortality."

"Quite right. All photography is about loss. That is its truth. In that way, it is the saddest of all art forms."

Berenice breathes in, surprised. She has never thought about photography in quite these terms, but it makes sense. Photographs are an attempt to shore a thing up against its inevitable passing. The flower will shrivel, the building crumble, the person die. A photograph gives texture and depth to impermanence, although eventually, it too will fade...

At the same time, she finds this view depressing. "But don't you also think there's a joyousness? The way photography makes us look at the world as never before? To linger and appreciate?"

"Yes, *mademoiselle*, I suppose so." He dips his head. It's obvious that he hasn't experienced much joy lately.

The room goes quiet again. On an impulse, she blurts out, "Monsieur Atget, would you honor me by allowing me to take your portrait?"

"*Mademoiselle*, I take photographs. I do not appear in them."

"But you take pictures so that people will remember the old Paris. Do you not think that in the future, people might want to remember you?"

Atget gives her the look of someone whose dispiriting job is to open young eyes to the world's indifference. "You don't understand. My pictures have no lasting value. They are merely studies, *documents pour artistes*."

"I don't believe that. And how can you? They're your life's work." Indignant, she looks again at the picture of the stern woman on the mantle. "Do you think when you took Madame Atget's portrait, she thought it would have no importance? Or did it soothe her to think that, when she was gone, you would see her every day?"

A look like anger flashes across Atget's face. But then it's gone, replaced by something more indulgent. "All right, *mam'zelle*. I can see that you are a persistent young woman, and that if I want peace I will have to acquiesce.

Therefore, please tell me when I can oblige you."

His claw hands are folded in his lap. *If it weren't so cluttered and dusty I'd photograph him here,* Berenice thinks. But she'll have to move him. Already, she can picture him in profile against a light background—like Djuna, but obviously with a different tone.

"How about our studio, tomorrow at one?"

"I usually take lunch at noon, so—yes, one o'clock."

"Perfect!" She rises from the dusty chair, tempted to cross the room and embrace him. But then his chin catches the light, she sees the crusted food caught in his stubble, and she just smiles and bids him goodbye.

◆

At lunchtime the next day, Atget arrives at the door in a gray coat so large and thick that it looks as if he's been engulfed by a storm cloud. He follows her upstairs to the studio, the bones in his legs cracking as he climbs the wooden steps.

Faced with the task in front of her, Berenice is suddenly flustered. A man of Atget's age can't be rushed, and she's aware of how unpredictable Man is. He's supposed to be out for lunch, but what if he comes back early? The thought of him coming in drunk and ridiculing Atget is painful to contemplate.

She's already set up the Seneca on its big tripod. The days when she was afraid to use it are long gone; she now prefers it, for the increased definition its large plates yield. She's also set up a stool on which she plans to have Atget sit. She hopes he'll be able to manage the pose for the time it takes her to get two or three good exposures.

She motions him to the stool, and he perches there, just as she'd imagined, back bowed, head heavy on his neck. "Won't you take off your coat?" she asks.

"No, Mademoiselle Abbott."

Berenice looks up, surprised. It occurs her that he's ashamed of his old, worn clothes, and has borrowed this too-large coat to cover them up.

Well, she'll have to make it work. Certainly she's not going to make the old man uncomfortable.

She directs Atget into the pose she wants, then stoops to look through the lens. Even with the image upside down, she can see the portrait is strong, and actually, the coat works. The darkness of it makes the landscape of his face more prominent.

"Did you hear about Lindbergh, Monsieur Atget?"

He looks at her with rheumy eyes. "The American pilot?"

"Yes." She adjusts her focus, looking through the lens. "He landed safely. Isn't that grand? To think of America and Europe linked by air travel!"

"*Mais oui*. Though I can't imagine flying myself."

"No? It's one of my ambitions."

"Of which you must have many." He looks into the camera, eyebrows raised, mouth turned up in a smile. At that precise moment, she releases the shutter. Though she won't know until she develops the plate, she believes she's captured something, a rare moment of tenderness. Perfect for a man whose own photographs are so delicate.

"Now, would you mind turning to the side?" she asks. She adjusts the stool and places his right hand on his knee. In profile, the old man's back is stooped and his head pokes out of the coat like a turtle's. His cheekbones are prominent, the sunken cheeks beneath making him look about a hundred. A wisp of hair sticks out from the back of his head. She could smooth it down, but she likes the note of pathos it adds.

As she's taking the second plate out of the camera, Atget starts coughing, softly at first, then violently. He leans forward, doubling over and almost lurching off the stool.

"Monsieur Atget! Are you well?"

Another coughing fit overtakes him before he can answer, and Berenice rushes over. She hesitates, lest her touch embarrass him, but then reaches out, bracing his body against hers. Under the giant overcoat, his body feels as frail as a child's. She holds him until the coughing subsides.

At last Atget looks up, flushed. "Thank you, Mademoiselle Abbott. I hope I didn't alarm you. These fits sometimes overcome me. It's passed now, but I think I'd better go home. I'm a little depleted."

"Of course, you must go. I hope you'll allow me to escort you down the street?"

"That won't be necessary." He barks out another cough. "You must stay and develop those plates. I must say, you've piqued my interest. I'm curious to see them. Even an old man has his vanities."

"You'll see them first," Berenice promises.

She takes his arm and steadies him as he rises from the stool, then helps him negotiate his way down the stairs. When they reach the street door, she casts him an anxious glance, wondering if he's fit to be released into his own care. Should she insist on walking him to his door? She's still mulling it over when Atget gives her a toothy grin and pats her hand.

"Thank you for your attention, Mademoiselle Abbott. This has been an experience. To have someone your age appreciate my work—well, one day I think you'll understand how gratifying that is."

Berenice looks into his eyes. "I'll bring the prints to you soon."

"I'll expect you." He starts down the street, taking painfully slow steps, his body tipping from side to side. She watches until he reaches his own door. As he gets further away, she can no longer see the top of his bowed head. It is entirely swallowed up by the mass of his gray coat.

◆

"Where in hell is she?" Man Ray is pacing the studio, a scowl pasted on his face. The model is over an hour late. A new Fresnel spotlight sheds a pool of gold onto a *chaise longue* that has embraced its fair share of female flesh.

"Give it a few more minutes. She'll be here."

Bang, bang: the floorboards shake. "You think? I'm not so sure. Joubert had his eye on her the other night. So did Foujita. As for Gates, he was practically crawling down her dress."

"Wouldn't she tell you if she planned not to come?"

Man turns, his expression scornful. "Sometimes I don't know how you survive here, Berenice. You're ridiculously naïve." He wanders to the window, stares at his reflection, then wheels around. "Shit, that worm Joubert! I wonder how much he offered her. He's been taunting me ever since he bought that massive Deardorff. As if all the world's beauty could make up for his lousy technique!"

Berenice starts to laugh, but represses it when Man glares across at her. Still, she's amused. These men, these artists! They make such a show of mutual admiration, but underneath they're schoolboys, stealing crayons and throwing food at each other.

Then again, she can understand his disappointment. Serafina Selvaggia—*La Sirène*, as she's known—has been the talk of Montparnasse since she arrived from Naples. With her long neck, smoky eyes and triangular face, she has an enticing new look. Topping the package is her air of unattainability, which has brought out the men's competitive natures. Suddenly, all other models are no good. Berenice has heard about it *ad nauseam* from Tylia. "Imagine, Bertrand had the cheek to tell me my shoulders are uneven! And now he thinks Kiki too masculine. Well, I never heard him complain before!"

Of course, only two years ago Ty and Bron were the new girls, entrancing everyone with their wide-set eyes and coy smiles. So her pique is understandable, even if it makes for poor pillow talk.

They wait another twenty minutes, during which Man grows more agitated. At last, with an irate look, he says, "Look, she's not coming. There's only one thing for it. You'll model for me this morning."

"Me?" Instinctively, Berenice folds her arms across her chest.

"I know; it's far from ideal. But you've done it before. Come, be a sport. I need to see how the new light works."

Berenice looks over at the *chaise*. It's covered with a plain white sheet and she has a sudden memory of her visit, two years before, to a gynecologist. He was a cheerful, balding man with yellow-stained teeth and as his gloved hand was probing inside he'd talked about his children. "Can you imagine, my wife wouldn't rest until we had a fourth, and now she blames *me* for wearing her out! Oh, but they're amusing rascals. Are you planning any? No? If you'll permit me, *mademoiselle*, why not think about it? You'll be thankful when you're old—that is, if they don't turn to crime!"

Grimacing, she pushes the memory away. "All right. But I'm not undress- ing."

"Suit yourself."

"I will." He's looking her up and down, head tilted, nose wrinkled. What an ingrate! Anyone would think he was doing *her* the favor. Feeling sulky, she moves to the *chaise*. "How do you want me, then? Sitting, lying down?"

"On your back to begin with, knees bent. Your left arm is going to go up and around the top of the *chaise*, like this. Hey, shoes off! You'll dirty the sheet."

She pulls a face at his back—but she respects his rigor. His photographs have a style that few can match and it comes in part from this certainty and precision.

Lying on the *chaise* with her knees bent, Berenice stares at the ceiling, noticing how the sun has bleached all but one of the five mahogany beams. She's never had reason to look up here before, and it's surprising. She sees that the dark beam hugs the far wall, and that sun glances off an elaborate cobweb stretched between two of the lighter beams. She wonders if spiders like to sunbathe.

Man has her hold the pose while he exposes three frames. Then he directs her to recline with her torso swiveled one way, her hips another. He instructs her to put her arms behind her head and throw back her head, each hand clasping the opposite elbow. The pose makes her hips rise in a curve, her breasts strain against her shirt. She feels trivialized, but at the same time oddly titillated—it reminds her of the whores in Picasso's *Demoiselles d'Avignon*. With dismay, she realizes she is aroused.

"Arch your back more," Man says.

"My face is itching. I have to scratch."

"I'll do it for you." Frowning, he emerges from behind the camera and walks toward her. He's wearing his plain black pants and a creased blue shirt, and hasn't shaven in a few days. Berenice smells his body odor, sour and skunky, and then he's looming over her, his shirt ballooning off his chest.

"Where is it?"

"Above the left eyebrow."

"Here?"

"No, the other side. *My* left, not yours."

It's ridiculous, lying there as he scratches at her temple with a bitten-off nail. They *never* touch. Perhaps, when he was teaching her in the beginning, he might have taken her elbow once or twice, moving it to demonstrate how to swirl chemicals. But not since. Even when they work in the darkroom together, they're careful to give each other a wide berth. He knows better than to try anything.

But now his fingers linger, lightly touching her hairline—and then, instead of moving away, they move down her cheek with a light caress. Goosebumps rise on her arms, and she feels her pulse skip as she surveys his face, which wears a look of surprise. The repulsion between them has faded, giving way to something more slippery. They hold each other's gaze.

"Take off your clothes."

His voice is gruff, and its insistence irks her. Her first impulse is to tell him where to shove his camera, but something stops her. She realizes that his order was actually an entreaty, and that *she* has the power. This is intriguing. She wants to push it further, taunt him, make him squirm.

She stands and—holding his gaze—begins unbuttoning her shirt. It's like when children dare each other to climb higher or swim further. *Ten cents says you won't do it!* She carries on until the last button is undone and the shirt falls open. She shrugs it off, then unbuttons her skirt and shimmies out of it, letting it fall to the floor. Her brassiere is next, then her stockings and undergarment. There! She may not be *La Sirène*, but she has nothing to be ashamed of. Her skin is soft and white, her body firm. Her breasts are small but perfectly symmetrical, each tipped with a ruby nipple.

Man's eyes widen. Clearly he wasn't expecting much of a body to emerge from under her shapeless clothes. She reprises the pose from before, twisting at the hips and putting her arms behind her head, looking up at him. He's standing in front of her. She can't tell if he's about to go back behind the lens or rip off his clothes and join her on the *chaise*. If he did, what would she do? The morning has taken on a strange tone. Things are spiraling and morphing in front of her eyes.

He turns and walks to the camera.

At first she's surprised—and to her pique, deflated. His desire had made him weak. Now he has tipped the scale back toward himself.

But since showing this would make him insufferable, she leans further into the pose. It's warm in the studio, and the air on her skin feels silky. She arches her back, as he wanted, and there's the tiny pop of a joint cracking. She thinks she can see the spider curled in the corner of the web above, though it could be a play of light.

Man fiddles with the lamp while she holds the pose. It's difficult, her back throbs, but she stays there, suffering for art. She thinks of the photograph that so impressed her when she first came to the studio, of Kiki's torso zebra-striped with light. It feels as if, together, she and Man could create something that good.

"Damn," Man says, "the light's too strong."

"Just use the window," Berenice says. The morning light filtering through the shade has a creamy softness that will reflect well off her skin. It's what she would do in his place.

"Hm," Man glances at her, then at the window. After a moment, irritated, he snaps off the Fresnel light.

The last pose he wants is a simpler one in which Berenice lies on her belly, propping her head on her arms. She can feel the curve of her back and the soft swell of her butt rising behind her. Her breasts sway and settle, drawn by gravity.

"Look into the camera," Man says. "Imagine your lover is standing behind it. You want to speak, but are stricken dumb. Your eyes must do the work."

Berenice thinks of Tylia and a mixture of gratitude and pain wells up. How can one person make her so happy and so sad at the same time? Right now Ty has a new *copain*, a Russian composer named Vassili. She says he's teaching her the piano, but Berenice has seen Vassili. He's young and handsome, with Slavic cheekbones and stormy eyes. The other day she was walking past *La Rotonde* when she spotted him and Ty at a corner table, noses touching. She understands the attraction, but it shreds her heart.

Man clicks the shutter and Berenice flinches—she'd forgotten she was in the studio. She wishes Tylia were here, looking at her, seeing her ardent gaze. If she gives her lover a print of the image, will it show her the pain she's caused?

"Not bad," Man says. "Just one thing. Stay there—" He walks around the camera to the end of the *chaise*, kneels and puts his hands on either side of her head, like a priest giving benediction. For a moment she's confused—but then he strokes his hands down, smoothing her hair. After a few moments he sits back on his heels and surveys her, and she sees a reflection of herself in his eyes, pale and serious, her cap of dark hair now more even. She waits for Man to get up, but he hasn't finished. Still looking at her, he carefully puts a finger in his mouth and licks it, then uses it to arrange her bangs into a curve on her forehead.

Later, she'll realize it was pain, or anger. Whatever the cause, the moist touch of his finger lights up her nerve endings. It's as if a match has been struck. Need flares up, surrounded by a halo of recklessness. She looks at Man and can see he senses it too.

They move together wordlessly, mouths first, then his hands reaching for her breasts, pinching and bruising the soft flesh. And she, equally fierce, is tearing at his clothes, bracing and twisting as he grabs at her, her nails digging into his back. They can't stop, it seems. They're bodies scratching an itch, tussling and grunting like dogs in an alley. When he enters her, he bites her neck, making pain radiate through her. She feels a twisted satisfaction at being defiled in this way. *Look, Tylia! Now do you see how it feels?*

But then, as he grunts and thrusts, his head looming above her, the satisfaction fades. She is reminded that this is Man—her boss, the pig she hates. Memories flash: Gus in the tailor shop; Delon with his flabby hands. And she's disgusted—mostly at herself, though she saves some contempt for Man. Look at him! Sweat is popping on his forehead; his face is set in lines of grim resolve as he pumps away. She turns her head, gazing instead at the dark circle of the

Eastman Kodak's lens. Going limp, she closes her eyes and waits for him to finish the sordid business.

At last, with something between a grunt and a whimper, his release comes. She wants nothing more than to get up and wash—the idea of his fluid in her is dreadful. But even before she can push him off, he's withdrawing and rolling away, muttering to himself. Hastily, she pulls the sheet over her as he sits up, back toward her. He lets out a sigh and she realizes that what just transpired was meaningless for him too.

For a moment they just sit there, rigid, because in order to get up they would have to acknowledge what just happened.

"Well," he says at last, "I guess you like men after all."

"Don't flatter yourself."

"I can put the word out if you like." He starts to rise, but she catches his arm and pulls, so that he sits down again with a thump. He looks around, surprised and annoyed.

"If you *ever* mention this…" She can't help it, tears are stinging the backs of her eyes. All she wants is to wind the clock back twenty minutes. She lets go of his arm and folds her arms around her body, willing herself not to cry in front of him. That would be a new level of humiliation.

To her surprise, Man's face softens. "Relax, pusscat. It's not exactly flattering for me either."

"Can we forget about it?"

"Yes."

"Completely?"

"Fine." He walks over to the camera, removes the negative plate and stacks it with the other exposed ones, then picks up the pile and places it on her lap. "Here. Have these. My gift to you."

Berenice opens her mouth to speak, then closes it before she can point out that the images might be good—in particular the last plate, where she was tender and vulnerable. Unbelievably, Man is giving them to her. She must seize this crumb of generosity while it's available. He could change his mind in an instant and revert to his petty, mean self.

"I'll be in the darkroom." He nods at her clothes on the floor, then disappears downstairs. She's left sitting on the *chaise*, clutching the sheet in one hand and the negative plates in the other, grateful and stunned by his sudden show of decency.

FOURTEEN

The next couple of weeks go by in a blur. Man has been commissioned to shoot a new collection by dress designer Paul Poiret, and as a result there's a portfolio of fashion images to print as well as the ever-increasing backlog of Man Ray's portraits, and Berenice's own commissions too.

There's so much work that she ends up not printing the Atget portraits until the end of the following week. As she suspected, the profile is best. Getting the old man to sit on the stool was inspired. There's such pathos in the curve of his back, the droop of his head. That wisp of hair protruding from the back of his head, too, is heartbreaking. Thank goodness she had the sense not to smooth it down.

With the volume of work Man is giving her, though, she doesn't make good on her promise to get the prints to Atget. She leaves the studio after ten each night, when it's too late to disturb him, and begins work at ten, when he's already out on the streets.

Then, on Tuesday afternoon of the following week, comes an unexpected call.

Berenice is in the darkroom, printing a double exposure, when the telephone rings. At first she doesn't pay it any heed. But it keeps up, its harsh noise shattering her focus. So, after putting her print in the fix she stumbles into the light and takes the receiver from its cradle.

"Man Ray Studio. Berenice Abbott speaking."

"Ah, Berenice, what luck!" brays a brassy voice with an American accent. "I saw your portrait of Djuna Barnes. You're something! I said to myself, I must have her do me, *tout de suite*. When can you fit me in?"

"I'm sorry, who is this?"

"Oh lord, there I go again. It's Peggy, dear. Peggy Guggenheim."

Berenice sucks air in so sharply that she thinks she might have swallowed a fly. Miss Guggenheim! Even in wild Montparnasse, Peggy Guggenheim is notorious—as much for her sexual voracity as for her money and eccentricity. "She'll fuck anything with a pulse," it's said—and indeed, Berenice has seen her across the room once or twice at *Le Boeuf* or *Le Chat Noir*, ordering champagne and hungrily eying the catch of the day—a young man or, occasionally, a woman.

As for money, Peggy is rumored to be worth $400,000—a fortune she seems happy to throw around. For the past year, she has given Djuna Barnes a stipend of forty dollars a month. It's rumored that she's supporting the anarchist Emma Goldman.

Berenice finds herself saying, "Yes," "Fine," "Absolutely," and, when she puts the receiver down, it seems she's made an appointment for the following week. They're to meet at Miss Guggenheim's—this was non-negotiable and Berenice knew better than to argue. Peggy Guggenheim is connected to everyone notable in Montparnasse. She's slept with or given money to half of them, and the other half are blazingly jealous.

After the call, Berenice is so agitated that she can't go back to her darkroom work. Thoughts rush through her mind, colliding, sparking off each other. How much can she charge for the session? Who can she ask for tips? *And Man*, she thinks, *Man will be furious.* How will she explain to him that Peggy Guggenheim asked for *her*?

In the ensuing days, she tries to muster the courage to tell Man about the appointment. But whenever there's a quiet moment she loses her nerve, fearing his anger. It isn't until the fourth day when, tidying the studio, she can no longer bear it. "Peggy Guggenheim called the other day," she says.

"Oh?" Man raises an eyebrow. "Did she make an appointment?"

"She did."

"When is she coming in?"

"Actually," Berenice folds up a light-stand, trembling, "I'm going to her."

"*We're* going to her, you mean."

"No. She asked for me."

Man stands there for a moment, cables dangling from his hand, clearly confused. She watches as comprehension dawns, tightening his face into a mask. "You'll call back and rearrange the appointment," he says, "for here in the studio."

"I can't do that, Man. She asked for me, at her house."

"You—and who are you? Nothing, no one! You're my assistant—you work for the Man Ray Studio!" With a jerk of his hand, he whips the electric cable he's holding on the floor. It makes an impressive *snap!* six inches from her feet. "It's one thing to photograph your little friends. But Peggy Guggenheim… no! For someone like her, only a Man Ray will do."

"You mean someone with money? An heiress?" She paces the studio. "Well, I have a style too, and sometimes even American heiresses prefer it! And this one wants a Berenice Abbott!"

"Impossible. She made a mistake." He throws down the cable and storms out before she can answer.

For days after that, they work in near silence. Determined not to back down, Berenice walks around tight-lipped, hoping Man will relent and give her his blessing. Even if he doesn't, he's about to leave on a week's trip with Duchamp to the South of France, where the sun and sea might work their magic—or maybe Duchamp will sprinkle his special fairy dust. Things might not be the same when he gets back, but she thinks they will find a way to be civil.

She's not prepared for what comes next. On the day of the Guggenheim portrait, she climbs the stairs to the studio to find all the cameras gone. Man, who left the previous night, has either taken all five with him or moved them. In vain, she looks under the divan, in the closets—then gives up, kicking the doors in rage. *Bastard.* He has done this on purpose. She's worked herself crazy for him for two years and now, when she's succeeding, he has to sabotage it. *Pig. Merde embulante.* She has half a mind to go into the darkroom and rip up his prints, but that would just be stooping to his level.

And then an idea comes. What if—could she borrow a camera from old man Atget? He's just down the street, and has a view camera with eight-by-ten plates. She looks at the clock: it's seven-thirty. Her appointment with Peggy Guggenheim is for nine. If she runs, she might be able to do it.

In the darkroom she pulls out files and boxes until she finds the envelope with the Atget prints. Pulling them out, she sees they're as strong as she remembered. The profile pose doesn't flatter him, but Atget's own photographs are so honest that she thinks he might appreciate it. If not, there's always the more distinguished-looking frontal pose.

She puts on her coat, locks the door and runs down the street, envelope in one hand and a bag of negatives in the other. When she gets to Atget's building, she takes the five flights of stairs without catching her breath, and when she stops at the top her heart is pounding so fast she feels it might burst out of her chest.

He's not there.

Cursing, she bangs on the door with the bronze hand rapper, her lungs throbbing from the climb. *Rapraprap!* It's still early—surely he's not outdoors already? Probably he's sleeping. *Raprapraprap!* She stands there, knocking, calling, "Monsieur Atget? Monsieur Atget!" Eventually, she turns to go downstairs.

In the courtyard, a woman is polishing the brass plates of the mailboxes.

"Excuse me," Berenice asks, "do you know when Monsieur Atget will be back?"

The woman turns, revealing a port-wine mark on one side of her face. She looks at Berenice kindly. "Oh, it was you making that noise upstairs. I'm sorry, dear—I wanted to come up and tell you but my legs are bad, it's hard for me to take the stairs."

"Tell me what?" But she already knows, from the woman's face.

"I'm afraid the old man died."

Berenice takes a step back, almost tripping over a cobblestone. Her heart, which had slowed a bit, starts thumping again. "When?"

"About ten days ago. His friend, Monsieur Calmettes, came around and was worried when there was no answer. We unlocked his door and found him like this—" The woman opens her mouth and eyes wide, a child's depiction of death. "Still rigid, poor thing. Must have fallen, we thought, he had a bruise on the side of his face when Monsieur Calmettes lifted him up."

Berenice clutches the envelope and takes two more steps back, until she's up against the wall. She pictures the lonely end: Atget lying on the dust-caked rug, his breath coming out in rasps, remembering how, as an actor, he'd died on stage so many times. He must have thought, *This time it's real.* There's a pain in her chest, and her throat feels sore. *I promised him*, she thinks. *I said I'd bring his portrait.*

"Are you all right, dear?" the woman asks. "Do you need to sit? You look pale."

"I'm all right," Berenice says. She shakes her head, breathes out. "I have to go, I have somewhere to be. Only…" she looks at the woman, "could you tell me how to find this Monsieur Calmettes?"

◆

She's arranged to meet Tylia later at the *Rotonde*, but Ty doesn't show up. After sitting for an hour over a cheap *vin blanc*, Berenice walks down the Boulevard Raspail to Ty and Bron's apartment. But the lights are off; the sisters are out. She lingers a few minutes, looking up at the windows, then gives up and goes home.

At some ungodly hour of the morning, she's woken by a scraping sound at the door. She sits up, heart knocking, but relaxes when she hears a cry of "*Merde alors!*" It's Tylia, fumbling with the key from under the mat. Well, Berenice is damned if she's going to get up. She settles back down, face to the wall.

When Tylia finally makes it inside, she tiptoes lightly across the floor—as if being quiet could matter at this point. Berenice can tell, by the sound of her footfall, that Ty has been drinking, or worse—for she knows Tylia has fallen prey, lately, to the charms of cocaine. There's a rustle of fabric, the sound of a skirt shushing onto the floor. Then the sheet lifts and Tylia slides into the bed next to her.

"Are you awake, *chère*?"

"Hnnn."

"I'm sorry I didn't make it tonight. Foujita asked me to do an extra sitting. It was good money, you know."

Berenice feels a dull ache in her chest. Foujita, she knows, has been working on a new series with Trieze as his model. She can feel her pulse beating angrily in her wrist. "Who was he?" she asks.

"What? I told you, *petite*, Foujita. He's got a show coming up and is working around the clock."

"You're a bad liar, Ty."

"Who's lying?"

"You. Why did you even come here? And without so much as washing off the *Mouchoir de Monsieur*?" She rolls over to face Tylia. All she can see in the darkness is the outline of Tylia's cheekbone and a catchlight in her pupils, which are definitely dilated. "You know, it would be easier to bear if you didn't take me for a dupe." She sighs. "Do I bore you? Is there something I'm doing wrong?"

Tylia shakes her head, as if to say, *Must we, now?* But Berenice can't back down. She stares, unblinking, into Tylia's eyes.

"Okay," Tylia says at last, "You want this? The truth?"

"Always."

Tylia bites her lip. "It's like this: have you ever walked by the *Pâtisserie Foulard* in the morning?"

"Of course, all the time."

"…when they're putting out the pastries, and each one looks more delicious than the next?" Tylia's smile glimmers in the dark. "*Napoleons, éclairs, tartes au citron, réligieuses*. You look, and don't know how to choose. You want it all—but that's ridiculous! Then a thought occurs: I don't have to choose, because the same selection will be here tomorrow, and the next day, and the one after that! And each day they'll be fresh and just as good-looking. So I can have an *éclair* today and tomorrow come back for the *tarte au citron*."

A terrible heaviness settles over Berenice. *I lost someone today*, she wants to say. But instead she asks, "What am I?"

"What do you mean?"

"In your window—what am I? An *éclair*? A lemon tart? A *mousse au chocolat*?"

Tylia considers for a moment. "You, *ma petite*? You're a brioche. Not fancy or decadent, but something basic and good."

"Oh, Ty." Berenice doesn't want to give in—there's too much pain in her—but she can't help but soften. *What's wrong with being good?* she wants to ask. *Why isn't basic enough?* But she doesn't have to; she knows the answer already. Tylia needs novelty, and after a few days, even the most delectable brioche gets stale.

"*Minou*, let's not fight, shall we?" says Tylia.

"No," Berenice says, "fighting's a bore." And when Tylia holds out her arms, she moves into them and lets herself be held, stroked. She listens to the endearments being whispered, and pretends they mean something they don't.

◆

Two days later, she's tidying up the darkroom when she hears Man unlock the apartment door, whistling jauntily. As soon as he enters she's upon him, and his whistle peters out.

"That was a terrible thing you did."

He pretends to look wounded. "Well hello, Man Ray. How was your trip? Oh, hello Berenice. It was quite fine, thank you for asking."

"Shut up. You're not going to get out of this by fooling around."

"I don't know what you're talking about."

"Don't play dumb, Man. You took your cameras. You knew I had the most important job of my life, and you took all five."

"No. I went on a trip where I was photographing. You couldn't expect me to go without equipment, could you? I gave you the right to use my cameras when *I* didn't need them."

Slap, slap—it's as if he's slapping her across the face. Bludgeoning her, then rubbing salt in. "Is this what you want?" she asks. "To pretend nothing's wrong?"

"Nothing *is* wrong. Except you. You're in a tiresome mood."

She looks at him, incredulous. "*I'm* tiresome? Well, you're an asshole. And you know what? I've had it up to here with your *conneries*. I'm not working for you any more."

It comes out more quickly than she'd intended. She'd planned to deploy this move only after they'd explored other avenues. She'd also imagined Man Ray being cowed and apologizing, or at least being less of a boob and admitting he took the cameras out of spite. Her impulsivity surprises them both, it seems. Man looks shaken.

"You don't want to work for me any more?"

She shakes her head.

"But I've given you so much," he bleats. "Before this, you were nothing."

"Oh—and I suppose I haven't given you anything? All those nights I've stayed here 'til midnight, saving your ass when clients were clamoring for their portraits? Getting things perfect? The times I've *improved* your prints because you had some kind of creative blind spot?"

"Improve! Really? You'd know *nothing* about printing if I hadn't taught you!"

Has he forgotten the times she made suggestions and he took them? The times he hugged her in surprise for what she'd done? *Le Violon d'Ingres*? "Oh yes, the master!" She minces toward him, waving her hands in the air. "The genius, the artiste! Well I've got news for you, Man—you're not the only person in Paris who can take a photograph!"

Man stomps across the floor and they meet, furious, in the middle of the rug. His eyes are red-rimmed, their bottom edges sagging, but the expression in them is pure, liquid hate. "Get out," he says. "Come back at eight tomorrow to collect your things. If you're not here by eight-thirty they'll be out on the street."

"Don't waste your breath threatening me. I'll take them now, and we won't have to see each other again."

She brought two bags with her for this purpose—only part of her hoping she wouldn't need them—so she's prepared. In the darkroom she pulls her boxes of prints off the shelves, throwing them in the bags. Man follows, watching her every move, ready to pounce. Having him so near in this small space is abhorrent. Berenice flings her things willy-nilly into the bags, not caring if the corners of boxes get squashed. Tears wobble in the corners of her eyes.

"In case you were wondering, the shoot with Miss Guggenheim went beautifully," she says. "She was very understanding. We rented a camera. No one's ever taken a better portrait of her, she said."

"You're going to find it hard to get a business going, if that's what you're planning. You'll need equipment, supplies. I don't suppose you've been saving, have you?"

Berenice flinches: he's right. She'll have to go with her hand out to wealthy friends—possibly Miss Guggenheim. "And she's going to introduce me to her friends," she says. "She's a very gracious lady."

Man Ray follows her into the hall, fidgeting with his tie as she hoists a bag into her arms and tries to pull the strap of the other one over her shoulder.

"Do you need help with that?"

She blinks. "Are you crazy?"

"I just thought—you might need help."

"Goodbye, Man."

And then she's out on the street, clutching her bags, leaning against the wall, breathing gulps of the warm night air. *You did it,* she thinks, *you're free.* But the feeling of triumph is fleeting. *You've just lost all your security,* she tells herself. *How could you?*

She closes her eyes, feeling the breeze buffet her skin. Then, suspecting Man Ray might be watching from the window, she lurches down the street with her bags. People look her way, probably thinking she's had a lover's tiff and is carting off her belongings. *Well, it's something like that,* she thinks.

Around the corner, on the Boulevard Raspail, the truth of her predicament hits her with new, sickening force. She's left the studio of a famed photographer, where she had access to the best equipment. She's lost her salary and made an enemy of her former boss. Now, not only will he not help her, he'll take steps to block her where he can. She knows him: he's a grudge-holder. A bad loser.

But then come other thoughts. *I'll have my own cameras. I'll be able to shoot when I please.* This lessens the sting of her impetuousness a little. She'll make her studio a happy place, and take portraits that bring out her subjects in surprising, vivid ways.

Right now, it's hard to imagine how she'll get there. She only has a rudimentary Box Brownie and barely enough money to last out the month. But she suddenly knows that it *will* happen. This is what she wants. She won't be cowed by a *connard* who wants her to thank him for wiping the shit off his ass.

She walks down the Boulevard Raspail, staggering under her load. At the corner of rue Boissonarde, a man with a cigarette smirks, and she calls out, "Maybe you'd like to help?" In response he lifts his cigarette in a salute.

Rue Boissonarde, rue Victor Schoelcher. With each block, the bags get heavier, and hunger gnaws at her. Absent-mindedly, she wonders if she has enough money for a *cassoulet*.

As she's approaching the Place d'Enfer, something draws her attention. A small crowd has gathered in the park by the Trarieux monument, where it seems to be watching a spectacle unfold. People are shrieking, pointing. She gets a brief glimpse of a leg clad in an emerald stocking, some frilly white undergarments, and intuition tells her to go closer and inspect the goings-on.

She draws near, only to realize that the laughter has a mean, mocking edge. A fat man stumbles toward her, holding his sides, his mouth wet with spittle. "Take a look!" he chortles. "That whore should be in an asylum."

Berenice edges forward, feeling uneasy. Over the crowd's laughter she can hear a screeching voice giving a dissonant rendition of Mistinguett's hit, *Je Suis Née Dans le Faubourg Saint Denis*.

> C'est pare-e-e-eil tous les jo-o-o-urs
> quand les hommes me font des disco-o-o-o-ours
> et viennent me parler d'amo-o-o-o-o-our

She pushes through, elbowing people aside until she's in the front row, then bends and puts her bags on the ground. An enormous wave of pity sweeps over her, followed by burning anger at the crowd and its ugly *schadenfreude*.

The Baroness stands in front of the monument, stripped bare from the waist up. Something brown and sticky—mud, perhaps, or chocolate—has been smeared over her chest and breasts, and smooshed into it are feathers and twigs, so that it looks like an unruly bird's nest. From the waist down she wears a series of frilly petticoats, under which are the green stockings Berenice glimpsed before. There are black rings painted around her eyes, and her hair sticks out every which way—except on the left, where it's partially held in check by a tipsy silver tiara.

Berenice had heard that things weren't working out for Elsa in Berlin. Rumors swirled that the Baroness had been forced into prostitution, had remarried, had been put in a mental asylum. Once, Berenice got a vague letter asking her to send money. Not knowing quite what to believe, she had sent a small sum. Then the rumors had died down; she'd heard nothing more.

Now, as she watches, Elsa begins to climb the stepped levels of the monument's base, above the weeping figure of the widow and child, to where the noble worker, in his apron, leans against the central plinth. Looking down, she surveys the crowd beadily. "Does anyone want a *show*?" she cries.

There are whistles, hoots. In response, Elsa lifts her voluminous skirts and kicks up a leg, mimicking a Can-Can dancer. More whistles, catcalls—she does it again. The petticoats froth around her; green stockings flash. Something else, too—a dark triangle. *God.* She is not wearing underwear.

Before she's quite formulated a plan, Berenice has sprung forward and grabbed Elsa by the ankles, and is pulling her off the monument. Taken by surprise, Elsa loses her footing and slides down, improbably landing upright on her high-heeled pumps and looking into Berenice's eyes. Her face is a picture of confusion, as if she missed the rehearsal for this, the newest twist in her act.

Berenice turns to the crowd. "Show's over, everyone! Nothing to see!"

There's grumbling; a few choice curses are flung at her. But after a minute, when it's obvious she won't back down, the crowd starts to disperse. Perplexed, the Baroness raises an arm and waves people off, as if she's Marie Antoinette bidding her court goodbye.

When the last straggler has left, Berenice turns to Elsa. She sees, now, that her friend's face is haggard, her pupils so dilated that barely any iris is visible. The sight is eerie, as if she's looking at a ghost.

"Elsa, why didn't you tell me you were back from Berlin?"

"Elsa?" The Baroness blinks. "I'm Mistinguett!"

"All right then, Mistinguett—when did you get back?"

"Weeks, months, years," Elsa trills, "who knows?" She leans back against the plinth and yawns, revealing a set of blackened teeth.

Berenice takes her arm, gives it a little pull. "Okay, listen. I'm going to get you home. Where are you staying?"

"With the birds!"

"I see. And where do the birds live?"

"On the sun!"

Berenice sighs. She has no idea how she's going to manage to carry her own bags *and* keep Elsa from floating away on a cloud of cocaine-fueled rapture. But she'll have to do it, somehow. There's no way Elsa can be left alone.

After a minute, the Baroness begins to shiver. The drug might be wearing off, or she's just getting cold. How wasted she is, and pale! Looking at her bony shoulders, Berenice shivers too. *How?* she thinks. *How does a vibrant, inspired woman become a shadow of herself?*

"I was a poet, you know," Elsa sways in front of her. "I wrote."

"I know. You were wonderful."

Elsa reaches out then, her fingers brushing Berenice's hand, and Berenice remembers that other time, years ago at the party, when the Baroness reached out to touch her. When she was the ingénue, and Elsa the magnificent *grande dame*. "You're a sweet chickadee," Elsa drawls.

"Yes," Berenice says, "we're two sweet chickadees."

Ludovic Trarieux, the man to whom the monument is dedicated, was a fighter for human rights. Perhaps because of that, the sculptor has put an allegorical figure on the right-hand side. Justice wears flowing robes, and has a circlet around her head, but—perhaps referring to Trarieux's inability to get a fair trial for Captain Dreyfus—she leans wearily against the plinth, looking down, one hand supporting her head.

Berenice looks into the statue's downcast eyes, and wonders why it is so hard. Why do fierce spirits like Elsa's get crushed, why couldn't Man Ray treat her properly, why can't Tylia stop causing her pain? Justice looks back, her brow furrowed, her mouth despondently curled down.

Don't you dare give up, Berenice thinks. *If you droop, we all do.*

Taking off her coat, she lays it across Elsa's shoulders. "Come," she says, "follow me. Let's find you a place to stay."

PART FIVE

NEW YORK, 1929

Manhattan from Pier 11, East River, New York, 1936, by Berenice Abbott

FIFTEEN

The gallery brings to mind a mole's burrow. The walls are lined with dark gray velvet, and thick window shades have been drawn against the glare of the morning sun, leaving only spotlights for illumination. Photographs and paintings are hung salon-style, with every part of the walls adorned; there are even frames propped on the ground. If there's an organizing principle, Berenice can't make it out. Black-and-white photographs hang next to brightly painted landscapes, while delicate pen-and-ink drawings jostle with strident abstractions.

She gives her name to an assistant and wanders around, the Atget portfolio under her arm. Of course she's mostly interested in the photographs, though what she sees here doesn't reflect her taste for clarity and compelling subject matter. There are images of long, thin leaves, a close-up of ceramic bowls, some muddy pictures of cloud formations. The paintings are generally more interesting, though their overall quality is patchy. There's a watercolor of the Brooklyn Bridge she quite likes. It's painted in quick, rough strokes that convey a sense of the city's dynamism. But next to it is a painting she can't decipher at all. It looks like the body of a goat with a fried egg on top.

A rustle, and a deep cough, makes her turn.

"Miss Abbott."

"Mr. Stieglitz." He looks smaller and older than his image in the photographs she's seen of him. His thick thatch of brown hair is thinning, going gray at the edges, and his bushy mustache has turned completely white. Behind wired-rimmed glasses his eyes are intense, dark, with a hint of imperious anger. He pins her with his gaze as if trying to ferret out some nefarious purpose for her visit.

"I believe you have some work to show me. Follow me, please."

She blinks: so that's it. No *How do you do, How is Paris? I believe we both know so-and-so.* Just the barely softened order in his sonorous, German-accented voice, and another cough as he directs her to a small room off the gallery.

A large oak desk, a swivel chair behind it. Paintings all over the walls—one of a bleached goat's skull (what is it about this man and goats?) And there's a framed photograph that she recognizes as one of Stieglitz's own, of curving silver railroad tracks at dusk, with a train steaming forward. Soft-toned, atmospheric. Man Ray showed it to her years ago, and she seems to remember it had a pretentious title, *Guiding Hand* or *Hand of Man* or some such. She sniffs—in her opinion a picture should speak for itself, without needing to be imbued with mystical overtones.

Stieglitz moves around the desk and heaves himself into the chair, which creaks in protest. He caresses a paperweight on his desk, a black onyx cat, his blunt fingers moving in circles as if stroking a real animal. He says nothing, just wheezes slightly as she sits opposite, puts the portfolio on the desk and unties it.

"I've taken it upon myself, with limited funds, to rescue the career of Monsieur Eugene Atget," she says. "I see him as a pioneer of what I like to call poetic realism."

Looking curious now, Stieglitz leans over the desk. He picks up the first print, one of her favorites, a store window where four female mannequins parade in winter dresses and coats. She put it on top because she thinks it expresses the many sides of Atget: his impeccable sense of composition, his attention to detail and his humor, too.

Stieglitz doesn't speak, just stares intently at the image, giving no indication of his thoughts. After a couple of minutes, he gives a curt nod and turns to the next image. This silence, punctuated by nods, continues until he has turned over the last of the twenty prints. Then he looks up, his eyes fierce under their shaggy brows.

"Monsieur Atget is still alive?"

"No, he died two years ago. He was very old."

"Who owns these images then?"

"I do." Despite her determination not to be intimidated, she finds her fingertips trembling. "I bought them when he died. Otherwise they'd be gathering dust in an attic."

"You knew him?"

"A little. Not as well as I wished."

"Hmmph." Stieglitz pushes the portfolio forward, then drums his fingers on the desk. "So you're a dealer?"

"No, a photographer. I take portraits."

"Why didn't you bring your own work to show me?"

She breathes in, taken aback both by his rapid-fire questioning and by the assumption that any photographer, *all* photographers, must want to court his favor. "My studio in Paris is doing well," she says. "Monsieur Atget's work, on the other hand, is languishing."

Sunlight from the window reflects off Stieglitz's glasses, so that for a moment she can't see his eyes behind the two circles of light. "I see," he says in a rasping, insidious voice. "There was something between you and the old man."

What is he implying? Bemused and affronted, Berenice stares across the desk. She can see his eyes again, and they are flat, humorless. They remind her of the eyes of dead fish in the rue Mouffetard market stalls.

"Well, I've looked." Stieglitz huffs out a breath. "Now let me show you some work in my gallery. You'll learn something, I think. I'm going in a new direction now."

He pushes back from the desk and strides out of the room, leaving Berenice scrambling to pack up the portfolio. In the gallery, she finds Stieglitz in front of the painting resembling a goat and a fried egg, staring up as if contemplating a holy relic.

"Arthur Dove," he says without turning. "Such simplicity of form. You see, don't you? Everything non-essential stripped away, the image reduced to pure shape and color. Like Matisse, but pushed further! This is what our new American avant-garde can do."

"Ah," she says.

"And this—this is Marsden Hartley," he nods at a crudely-painted landscape of a canyon, done in reds and mauves, with trees in the foreground that look like sausages with broccoli on top. "He's painting our American landscape, New Mexico and Arizona—though he does it all from memory!"

He turns to look at her, and she peers again at the sausage trees, trying in vain to find something meaningful in them. The style recalls Cezanne to a certain extent, but with none of Cezanne's skill or complexity. "Nice colors," she says at last.

"I suppose you're wondering, what can photography do to approach this level of innovation?" Stieglitz booms. Berenice bites her lip. She wasn't wondering anything of the sort, but there doesn't seem any point in saying this—Stieglitz is going to give his lecture, whatever she says. "I've been asking that too," he says, "and I think I've found some answers." Taking her by the elbow, he steers her across the gallery, to the photographs of the long, thin leaves she noticed before.

"These are by Paul Strand," he says. "I've taken him on as a protégé. He was doing more traditional work, but then I told him to push himself. Now I think he's getting somewhere—there's an essence here. It's crude yet, but he's progressing. He's freed himself of his dependence on human subjects."

Berenice looks at the photographs. In one, the long leaves curl like ribbons; in the other, they spread out like fingers. They are decent compositions, printed with rich tones, but they don't excite her. They're leaves, and not very interesting ones. Why should a leaf be a more exalted subject than a person?

"He has some talent, though his work is derivative," Stieglitz says with a hint of disdain. "Everything *he* does, *I* have thought of before, even if I haven't made it yet."

Berenice looks down, frowning. The arrogance! If Stieglitz has taken on Strand as a protégé, why is he criticizing the young man? Plus, how can you call someone's work derivative of yours when you haven't yet realized the idea? Surely it's what gets made that counts. Even she realized that, years ago, with Man Ray and his *Violon d'Ingres*.

"And *these* are mine," Stieglitz says. He has come to a standstill in front of four small photographs of clouds—the muddy prints she noticed earlier. The prints have very little contrast, so that the gray clouds barely stand out from a dark sky. They're unusual, for sure, and the swirling pattern of clouds in one image is pretty, but other than that she can't see what's special about them. "I call these *Equivalents*," Stieglitz says, his voice rising with pride. "They're entirely new, I have transcended the literal. Each is equivalent, in my mind, to a musical symphony. They are revelations of man's place in the universe, documents of eternal relationship—perhaps even a philosophy."

Or maybe they're just clouds. Berenice leans in, looking at the images again, trying to see if she's missed something. No: the photographs are as dull and muddy as before. A pretentious use of the medium; a rich man's whimsy. If Stieglitz wasn't so dead serious, she might think it a joke. He is trying to elevate photography by twisting and contorting it every which way, making it ape painting or music. But why, when what it does best is be itself?

"It's a lot for you to take in, I know," Stieglitz says. "When you're used to seeing traditional work, it takes a while to adjust. The gallery arrangement is unusual. Still, I'm compelled to do it this way, that's why I called it the Intimate Gallery. With work this radical, it makes sense to put everything together around a theme."

"And the theme is…?"

Stieglitz looks surprised. "Spirituality, of course," he says. "Each of these artists is reaching for the ineffable. The subject matter is unimportant. It's the concept, the approach, the reaching for a higher consciousness. Some people tell me I have photographed God."

Luckily Berenice is now looking back at the Equivalents, or Stieglitz would surely have noticed her scorn. Ineffable spirituality, photographing God—what a crock! As for the absence of subject matter—nothing could be more different from her own approach. What *is* photography, if not a method for capturing and celebrating the subject in front of the lens? Why deny what the camera does best?

Stieglitz lets out a barking cough. She is tempted to whack him on the back—and try to knock some sense into him in the process—but refrains. Instead, she waits until the coughing has subsided, then turns, her expression carefully neutral.

"Thank you for showing me all this."

Stieglitz nods. "Your Monsieur Atget has a good eye. Of course, his is not the kind of work I'm showing at the moment, but I could perhaps see running a small show in the summer. Leave the portfolio with me overnight, and I'll consider it further."

Instinctively, Berenice hugs the portfolio to her chest. She desperately wants a show for Atget, but every bone in her body is telling her not to let Stieglitz have it. What if he disparaged Atget in front of viewers, as he did just now with Strand? Or stole Atget's ideas and claimed them as his own?

It's peculiar—before she came in to the gallery, she thought she'd do anything to get a show for Atget. But now she feels sure of her instincts.

"I'm afraid that won't be possible," she says. "I don't see his images here."

"Eh?" Stieglitz's eyes crinkle, first in confusion, then anger. His mouth purses, making the bushy white mustache arch like a perturbed caterpillar.

She'd hazard a guess he hasn't experienced much rejection in his life.

"No—I think they're too straightforward," she says, keeping her voice light. "No *ineffable* deities. Well, good day. It's glorious outside—not a cloud in the sky." And then, turning on her heel, she walks out of the door.

◆

After leaving the Intimate Gallery, Berenice wanders midtown, taking in the sights. The clatter and din of construction is all around, *bangbangbangbangbang*! It makes her nerves buzz like a telephone exchange at daybreak—but the signal they're carrying is not irritation, it's exhilaration.

A week ago, when she arrived from Paris, she hadn't been expecting this. Of course, she'd heard Manhattan was in the throes of a building boom, and that improvements in steel and elevator technology were allowing for much taller buildings. But nothing she'd heard prepared her for the development's scale and pace—or for the thrill she'd feel on seeing it.

Eight years can change a person and a city too. The New York of 1929 is radically different from the place she left in 1921. In midtown, glossy skyscrapers are rising, dwarfing genteel twenty-storey buildings that had themselves, a decade ago, seemed enormous. With construction crews of several hundreds, some of these giants are rising at the head-spinning rate of two floors a day. Some ascend to magnificent spires, others are flat-topped; some soar upward in straight lines while others rise in stepped tiers, like elongated wedding cakes. Like wedding cakes, too, they are festooned with decorations: crescents and fans, chevrons and sunbursts. Individually they are impressive; together they are breathtaking. *Here is ambition*, they say, *here is style*. They are modern, flashy and American to the core.

Now, as she walks along Fifty-seventh Street, sun reflects off glass and metal. It shines through gaps in the scaffolding, dappling the sidewalks below as overlapping sounds—*bangbang, clink-clink-clink*—come from above. The place has a syncopated rhythm all its own. It is a jazz poem in stone and steel.

She'd had no plans to come back and see this. Paris was home, she was settled there. But necessity had forced her hand.

Ever since buying Atget's archive from his friend and heir André Calmettes six years before, Berenice has been wearing herself out trying to sell the work. She'd thought to offset the storage and preservation costs by releasing selected Atget prints—but the sales haven't materialized. And now she's not only in debt, but saddled with tens of thousands of glass negatives and prints to preserve.

Three months earlier, a possible way forward had presented itself. A well-known publisher, Henri Jonquières, was interested in doing a book on Atget. But for reasons of prestige, Jonquières wanted an American co-publisher. Though it seemed unlikely she could secure one, it was the only offer she had. So Berenice brought a portfolio of the images to New York, and has been showing them around.

"Not our kind of thing," she has heard, and "It's just not likely to sell." That's the word from editors at Scribner, Henry Holt and Knopf, and she has to admit she can see why. New York at the moment feels assaultive and pushy, with everything pointing up and toward the future. Why would anyone be interested in pictures of Old Europe by a modest, dead old man?

Going to see Stieglitz was a last-ditch effort. His reputation preceded him—*arrogant, affected*—but he was too powerful a force in the photography world to ignore. She still remembers Man Ray's words about him from years ago: *If he likes you, he can make your career.* Hmph—well, so much for that. Rarely has anyone provoked such an antipathy in her as Stieglitz did just now. He could be the king of England and she wouldn't let him handle Atget's work.

At her hotel in the west Thirties, Berenice flops onto the bed with a sigh. Then it comes to her: why not make some photographs of New York? She's not a landscape or architectural photographer, and the only camera she has with her is her Kurt-Bentzin. Still, if she gets anything worthwhile she might be able to sell it to French magazines. France loves to look at America with a divided gaze, one eye admiring, the other contemptuous. She could pitch the story as *A City in Flux* or *America Grows Up*.

Energized by the prospect, she loads the camera and heads out, retracing her steps to the Fifties. Now that she's looking for pictures, every block serves up delights. She photographs fire escapes and railings, store signs, elevated railroad tracks. Inspired by Atget's elegant compositions, she works hard to arrange the elements just so.

It isn't easy. The roll film is slow and there are no swings or tilts on the camera. Even so, she's like a child unwrapping toys at Christmas. So much to see! One afternoon is too little, so she dedicates a second day to the task.

And so it is that, on Twenty-First Street the next day, she finds herself photographing a flophouse in the process of being demolished. Lovingly built, with arched windows and a mansard roof, the three-storey brick building is submitting to the wrecking ball like an aging boxer who knows he's been outmatched. Behind it, a brand-new office building rises, its gleaming white stone a rebuke to the crumbling wreck in the foreground. *Your time is past*, it could be saying. *We're in charge now.*

Berenice crouches low to the ground, angling her camera up so as to capture the base of the flophouse and the top of the office building. She's just framing the shot when the wrecking ball smashes into the third floor, making glass and brick shatter in a crash that sends shards raining down. Quickly she ducks, lest a wayward shard come flying her way. At the same time she pushes the shutter, conscious that her film isn't fast enough to freeze the falling glass (but maybe the blur will be interesting?)

When she looks up, there's a gaping, jagged-edged hole in the building, as if the boxer has been smashed in the mouth. It's sad to see a good old structure go. But there's also something thrilling about the destruction and pace of change. *It's all happening so fast*, she thinks. *Who cares, who's taking note?*

Suddenly, a ridiculous idea comes to her.

No, she thinks, her finger trembling on the shutter, *I can't.*

She focuses and takes another shot, trying to will the idea from her mind. But it clamors more insistently. A single question, hammering on her consciousness with the force of a wrecking ball. *Why not?* it says. *Why not come back?*

Because my past here almost destroyed me, she tells it. Lilian, the Village—those years now seem unmoored. Paris has given her stability and a reputation. She even has an assistant, Lood, who prints for her as she printed for the shit-smear, Man Ray.

It hadn't been easy. After she parted ways with the shit-smear, there were years of scraping by, borrowing and improvising. Equipment was expensive, she didn't have a studio—at times, she felt there was something deranged in her persistence. But eventually—helped by funds from Miss Guggenheim and others—she began to find her way. Her work was exhibited at *Gallerie Sulpice* and *Au Sacre du Printemps*, and there was a waiting list for portraits at her studio.

She thinks of her clients. For the past four years, the challenge of photographing a face has absorbed her. Technically and psychologically, it has been interesting. You can have the perfect pose, the perfect light, and still make a portrait that stinks. You have to be a mirror of sorts, adapting to people's styles, knowing their quirks. You have to coax your sitter to reveal himself, but still preserve some mystery for the viewer to ponder.

She has learned all this, and—if she might say so—achieved mastery. But isn't it true she's been bored recently? In many ways, she might have reached the end of the road with portraits. She's noticed a tendency to repeat herself. There are only so many ways you can place hands and feet, only so many variations in the range of human expression.

No, she thinks, *don't be an idiot.*

That night, a friend from Paris comes to take her dancing. Charley Bentley is an Englishman, a fanatical dancer and a flagrant homosexual. He arrives at her hotel in a tuxedo the color of old vellum, a silver bow tie glistening under his chin.

First they go downtown to a steakhouse in the old seaport. After eating watery soups and cheese sandwiches for a week, the juicy sirloin is almost too much for Berenice to bear, and she tears into it, abandoning all sense of manners.

"Well," says Charley, taken aback, "you're welcome."

"Terrific place." She glances around, taking in the dark wood walls with their gold-framed paintings. "Trust an Englishman to find somewhere that's been here centuries."

"Since the Dutch, actually," Bentley says. He waves his fork, speared with a broccoli floret, at her. "True, we like a place to have history. Back to William the Conquerer preferably, but over here one has to make do with what one can get."

"Yes," Berenice laughs, "it's a sad little country we have, isn't it?"

After dinner, he wants to take a taxi to the Savoy Ballroom, but she protests that she's stuffed and must first walk off her meal.

They head north on Water Street, looking east toward the boat slips. As they pass an old warehouse, Berenice makes a mental note to return and photograph it. *If I have time*, she thinks with a pang. She leaves for Paris in two days.

"Let's go look at the buildings on Wall Street," she says. She was there earlier, photographing people in the canyons between skyscrapers. She's curious to see the street deserted, the buildings left to enjoy their shadowy night lives.

At Wall Street they turn left, leaving behind the old brick buildings and their echoes of New Amsterdam. In front of them looms a huge, almost-finished skyscraper. There's an eeriness in the way its stone walls stop two thirds of the way up, giving way to steel girders that stretch into the night sky like beseeching arms.

"Bank of Manhattan Trust," Charley reads on the perimeter board as they get close. "What do you think, how many floors?"

"I don't know," Berenice looks up. "Fifty, at least."

"What's the highest building you've been in?"

She doesn't have to think. "The Eiffel Tower."

"Hm," Charley muses, "we can't beat that. But shall we try to get close?" He does a little dance step, ending with his arms outstretched.

She looks at him, baffled. "How?"

In response, he smiles and tips his head at a skyscraper on the corner of the next street. "I was thinking we'd go into that building there and go up on the roof."

"Don't be a boob, they won't let us in."

"Oh my dear, you'd be amazed what a British accent and an air of entitlement can do."

He takes her arm and they cross the street, veering right to the towering building, which turns out to be another bank headquarters. The name 'Equitable Trust' is carved into the stone frieze above the pillared doorway.

"Now," Charley whispers as they cross the threshold, "go and examine the flowers on the table. If the guard looks your way, be stern."

So Berenice goes to the middle of the lobby while Charley approaches the guard. She peers over the tops of purple orchids as the guard shakes his head, then laughs at something Charley says. They look her way, and she remembers to look haughty. Then Charley comes over, grabs her elbow and whispers, "Don't talk until we're in the elevator." He steers her past the guard into a gilded box, and as soon as the door slides shut, they look at each other and dissolve into giggles.

"What on earth did you say to him?"

"Elementary, my dear Watson. I told him it was our wedding anniversary and that I proposed to you on the Brooklyn Bridge. I hinted at an intimate connection between my aunt, Lady Nickelworth, and his boss, J.P. Morgan." Looking smug, Charley taps his pocket. "Oh, and I slipped him a fiver."

"You genius!" Springing forward, she falls on him and kisses his neck.

"Whoa!" Charley stiffens and pushes her away. "Take it easy. Remember, I'm not just a faggot, I'm an *English* faggot."

The elevator is beautiful, with inset mirrors, lighted ceiling panels and a door of polished brass. They watch, mesmerized, as the numbers of the floors tick away, all the way to forty-three. When the door glides open, they step out onto a thick beige carpet. They're in a hallway lined with gold-framed lithographs and sketches that resemble Renoirs and Manets. When she reads some of the signatures, Berenice realizes with a start that they *are* Renoirs and Manets.

"My lord," Charley says, "so this is where Impressionism comes to die."

She elbows him in the ribs. "What now, genius?"

"Well, according to my friend Lester, there should be a door down here." He leads her down the corridor, past painted ballerinas and bathing nudes. "Ah, here we are, door helpfully marked with the word ROOF. And open, as he said."

"I can't believe we're doing this," she says, even as she's following him through the door and up the stairs, her heart pulsing in her chest.

"Entitlement," he calls back. "I tell you, it's the ticket."

At the top of the stairs, he pushes open a heavy door and they're hit by a gust of frigid air. Above, gray clouds waft across a dark gray sky, as drab and monotonous as one of Stieglitz's *Equivalents*. Berenice gives a little snort. She steps onto the roof, wobbling on her heels, and then, looking around, falls silent.

In between two banks of clouds, a crescent moon sheds pale light on the water of New York harbor. The city stretches before her, as spangled and seductive as a flapper in sequins. They're on top of the world, it seems—as close as she's come to flying. She can see all the way to Queens on one side, New Jersey on the other.

"Oh my," she says, taking a few steps forward. "Oh."

She steps out further, heading to the edge of the rooftop. She feels dizzy with vertigo, but damned if she isn't going to look out from the edge at this city where ambition constantly drives everything up and up.

Breath held, she tiptoes toward the building's south edge. The lights of the Brooklyn Bridge stretch across the river like a spangled necklace, and, near it, cars speed across the longer, more workaday Williamsburg Bridge. She can see apartment buildings in Queens, their lights blazing, and the illuminated towers of the Singer and Woolworth towers. What an amazing city! So alive, full of energy and audacity and yearning. So young and restless, like a child in a hurry to grow up.

"It's like the whole goddamn city is on fire," she murmurs.

Charley comes up behind her. "Like your anniversary present, Lady Bentley?"

"Very much."

"Good. Because it's bloody cold up here."

Berenice takes another step forward until she's only a few inches shy of the chest-high parapet. There are construction lights on the Bank of Manhattan Trust Building, and on another partially built skyscraper, an Art Deco behemoth that is rising at the western end of Wall Street. Trinity Church is lit up too, floodlights illuminating its pillars and tall white spire.

Something comes over her then, in the midst of this crazy city, this hub of activity. A feeling of calm certainty, of knowing exactly what she must do.

She tilts forward. "My god," she says, "I'm going to do it."

Mugging horror, Charlie catches her by the waist. "Darling, no! You're too young!"

"Idiot," Berenice laughs. "I'm not going to jump. I'm going to…" but she stops, not wanting to say what she has decided. The decision to move back here is too young, too delicate. She must give it time to get properly rooted.

I'm going to do for New York what Atget did for Paris.

"To *what*?" Charley presses. "Tell me, dear one. I can't abide a secret."

"I'm going to…" she smiles. For all his sophistication, Charley is a child. She needs to redirect his attention, point at something bright and shiny he can run toward.

She looks out at the twinkling lights. The energy of the city crackles through her, making her demented with glee.

"I'm going to lose my mind," she says, "unless we go dancing *right now*."

SIXTEEN

LADIES OF THE AIR SET OFF FROM SANTA MONICA, reads the headline in the *New York Post*. Berenice stares, engrossed, at the photograph below the headline. It shows ten women standing under a biplane's wing, looking stylish in flying suits and aviator caps. Fascinated, she reads about how the first ever Women's Air Derby has been launched after years of complaints from women's pilot groups. "We can barnstorm, wing-walk and set speed records, so why can't we race?" one woman is quoted as saying.

Yes, she thinks, *yes*. This is what America does. France might be advanced in matters of sexual freedom, but here are American women on the leading edge of aviation. Leaving earth, carving paths above this new, young country. A country whose rapid pace of growth she is determined to document, in her own small way.

When she'd gotten back to Paris from New York, there'd been a thread of doubt woven into her resolve. She'd wondered if the City of Light would work its magic, dissolving the passion and certainty she'd felt in Manhattan. But in Paris she'd found herself dreaming of New York—of the sleek cars, the vertiginous buildings. For the first time, Paris felt staid, its glamor faded. She laughed off her friends' worries—it was a risk, yes, but she needed a new adventure. The urge to get back permeated her, as raw and insistent as an itch.

Of course, packing up had been difficult: she wasn't yet that detached. As she boxed up film and cameras, memories bubbled up of discussing the *Ballet Mécanique* with George Antheil, of gossiping about Winston Churchill with Martha Bibescu. The time Cocteau showed up with an entire wheel of Fourme D'Ambert and the neighbors gathered in the courtyard to dance.

Other than work, though, nothing bound her to Paris. Her affair with

Tylia had ended badly, two years before, when Kisling introduced Tylia to a painter from Kraków. For a while Ty had tried to please everyone, but more and more nights found her absent from Berenice, and preoccupied when she reappeared. In the end, Berenice had confronted her with the awful, needy threat she'd promised herself she'd never use. "I can't do this any more! Choose me or him!" And Ty had gone, leaving a hole that Berenice didn't even attempt to fill.

Back in New York, she devoted her first week to finding lodgings. On a recommendation from a friend she went to the Hotel des Artistes, an artists' cooperative in the West Sixties. Unlike the haphazard artists' coops she'd known in the Village, this one catered to the elite: Rudolph Valentino and Isadora Duncan had lived there. Given the success she'd achieved in Paris— and was sure to achieve here, soon—she felt it was suitable, and took an apartment on the spot.

In retrospect, that was hasty. She'd assumed her reputation would cross the Atlantic and commissions would flow in. When that didn't happen, she was faced with exorbitant living costs, and as a result, has had to quadruple her rates. One big problem is that the department stores here have portrait studios where, for a dollar, an uninspired hack will click a shutter and hand you your print the next day. It's been hard to convince people that she's doing something different, more subtle and artistic, for which they should fork over half their monthly paycheck.

Pursing her lips, she returns to the news story about women aviators. Humorist Will Rogers has dubbed their race 'The Powder Puff Derby,' a name that seems to have stuck despite the women's opposition. She sighs: these women deserve more than a silly name.

An hour later she's in Chinatown, standing on a lip of pavement jutting out from Canal Street. The otherworldliness of this part of town delights her. There are herbal emporiums, laundries, and shops selling strange, spiky fruits. Once, in a store here, she'd knelt to look at a box of shimmering gray-green lumps that she'd thought were dead frogs, and nearly jumped out of her skin when one of the creatures opened its eyes and blinked at her.

In the early morning light, the struts of the fire escapes glint white in the sun. She screws the hefty Century Universal onto the tripod, then opens its front side to reveal the shiny new Goertz Dagor lens. She bought the camera the month before and is still getting to grips with it. It's bigger and more complicated than her studio cameras. But the image quality is a world above her little Kurt-Bentzin, which she used for months to make 'notes' for future, more polished images.

She wants to capture the Manhattan Bridge rising from the neighborhood's chaotic clutter of shops. Examining the scene now, she sighs—a delivery truck has just pulled up in the middle of her frame. Finally it moves off, and she bends to look at the ground glass. What she sees is promising. The sun is lighting the tenements across the street and the sky in the distance is hazy, making the towering bridge appear mirage-like. She just needs to tilt the frame.

She straightens up, then finds herself jumping back in alarm as there's a prolonged screech and a truck barrels by, missing her by inches. The vehicle careens off, only just missing the tripod, and before she can curse, the driver leans from the window and, with a spray of spit, yells, "Put on a skirt, you crazy cunt!"

For the next few seconds, Berenice's heart pumps as if she'd run ten blocks. Did that just happen? She looks around for someone who might have witnessed it, but no one seems to have noticed. Only one person, a tall Chinaman, catches her eye from the doorway of a nearby butcher's—but he just breaks into a toothy grin.

Trembling, she crouches and waits to regain her calm, thinking, *So much for progress.* Beneath this glitteringly modern Manhattan there is still a bedrock of conservatism, a fossilized attitude that a woman in pants is the prelude to social collapse. *Well, have at it,* she thinks, *I'll wear my pants.* Skirts flutter; they don't allow her to climb a pedestal or scramble over rocks.

When her heartbeat is normal again, she bends to look at her shot. She sees now that the composition is all verticals and right angles, that it would be more dynamic if she photographed the bridge from an angle. Oh, well. She'll take a shot here, then explore the side streets.

"Hey, lady!" The man from the butcher shop is approaching in a blood-stained apron. "Lady. You want business deal?"

His shadow falls across the camera, and she feels herself stiffen. What now? "Are you talking to me?"

"You, yes, camera lady. You take picture of my wife for side of pork ribs? You want?"

She looks up, shading her eyes with a hand. He has an open face with high cheekbones, and surprisingly large eyes for his race. He's not bad looking, with a shock of black hair above his forehead. His wife might be photogenic.

It's an unusual offer, and for a moment she's tempted—but then she remembers how little time she has for her project, the changing city. And then, too, a darker possibility crosses her mind—what if he doesn't have a wife? Men outnumber women in Chinatown by six to one, and it's said they're like dogs in heat. *The neighborhood is a cesspit filled with sexual deviants*, she read in a recent editorial. Obviously there's an ugliness behind those words, but one should take care nonetheless. She remembers how he looked at her earlier, the leer hovering at the edges of his grin.

"No," she says, "I'm afraid I don't barter. Now give me room, please, I'm working." She looks at him pointedly, and when he doesn't move, waves her hands and says, "Go, scat!" This time he backs away looking crushed, and she feels a wave of guilt. What if he was genuine after all?

At seven that evening, dust-streaked and exhausted, she unlocks the door to her apartment. As soon as she's across the threshold she puts down her gear and sinks into a chair. Her mind wanders back through the day, pondering the ten plates she exposed. Will any of them work? The one she shot at South Street seemed promising, but only if she metered it correctly.

After a few moments, she retrieves the morning's *Post* from the side table. She didn't get further than the front-page story about the women aviators, and now she sees that Babe Ruth is the first player to hit five hundred home runs, and that the U.S. population has reached 120 million. She flips through, mostly looking at photographs—until, at the paper's middle spread, she stops and opens the paper wide.

Four big photographs, bold and dramatic. One, taken outside a steel mill, shows two tiny figures dwarfed by a row of enormous smoke stacks. The other three feature interiors of the mill, where great streams of molten steel cascade into huge vats and men are silhouetted against showers of sparks. The images are magnificent, like nothing she has seen before—they combine exquisite artistry with impressive technique. Berenice can't even imagine how they were drawn from such inky-dark environs.

PHOTOGRAPHER SHEDS LIGHT ON STEEL-MAKERS, says the headline—and, reading on, Berenice is floored to see that the mill is in Cleveland. Memories flood her: Ma and Hazel, Fredo. With a flutter of fear, Gus. Guilt pricks at her, because Ma doesn't yet know she's back in America. She keeps meaning to write, but work always seems to get in the way.

Cleveland. She has barely thought about it for years. But the sight of

194

the steel mill brings back a torrent of memories. Waiting for Ma outside the brick warehouse of Printz-Biederman, where, for a brief time, she worked as a pattern-cutter. Standing on Columbus Road, looking lakeward, seeing columns of black smoke rising from the factories in the Flats.

Ma is back there now. Berenice got a letter in Paris with a change of address, beneath which her mother had ambiguously scrawled, *Not that I'm expecting you to visit any time soon.* Was she encouraging Berenice to stay away or implying she was a bad daughter? As usual, it was unclear.

Perturbed, she pushes these thoughts away and scans the article, which is a gushing account of how an "intrepid" photographer was able to take "breathtaking" images inside a mill. How did he do it? She reads on, only to find that the photographer is not a he but a she. Her name is Margaret Bourke-White, and at twenty-five she is six years younger than Berenice.

A woman! There are so few professional women photographers, let alone fearless and talented ones. On the one hand, it's wonderful to see—but on the other, Miss Bourke-White has made a stunning entry onto *her* turf. It's immediately apparent that, though only twenty-five, she has already surpassed Berenice in skill and achievement.

For the next few hours, she finds it hard to settle. She flips through the rest of the paper, but keeps turning back to the spread in the middle, examining the photographs, wishing she could see the original prints. Remarkable! She makes herself a bologna sandwich—but after only two bites, can't eat any more. Instead, she paces up and down, thinking of all the questions she'd like to ask Miss Bourke-White.

Well, why not write her? she thinks. *Suggest a meeting. You have common interests.* She thinks of the women pilots lined up in front of the airplane. And it occurs to her that, were Miss Bourke-White receptive to a visit in Cleveland, she could kill two birds with one stone. The thought of having a professional reason to visit Cleveland makes the idea of seeing Ma more palatable.

Excited, she goes to the table and pens a letter. *Recently, I achieved some success in Paris with my photo-portraits of creative types,* she writes. *Now, like you, I am trying to portray the spirit of modernism, in my case through the dynamics of a changing city...*

She doesn't have an address. But she can send her letter to the *Cleveland Plain Dealer*, where the mill photographs were originally published, and ask for it to be forwarded. Satisfied, she writes another letter to the newspaper and folds the first inside it. She doesn't write to Ma yet. She'll wait for a reply from Miss Bourke-White first.

She's delighted when, five days later, a letter with a Cleveland date-stamp arrives. The handwriting is bold, assertive. *But of course we must meet*, writes Miss Bourke-White. *I'm surrounded by men here—useful for sure, but limiting. What a pleasure it will be to share notes with another gal!*

After another exchange of letters, a date is pinned down: August third at three. Berenice goes to Penn Station and books her train ticket.

And still, something keeps her from writing to Ma. As the time grows closer she decides it's too late, and that she'll simply arrive at Ma's as a surprise. She wants to see the true expression on Ma's face—whether it's anger, pleasure, or both—when she sees Berenice at the door.

◆

"You're not a spy from Kodak come to steal my secrets?" asks Margaret Bourke-White. Tall and slender, with curly dark hair and lips tinted cherry red, she could have stepped out of the pages of *Vogue*. She stands pouring water into a silver teapot, holding the kettle in one hand and, with the other, jiggling a strainer of tea that straddles the edge of the pot.

"A spy?" Berenice falters. She'd like to say something clever, but nothing comes to mind. She is conscious of her puffy eyes and train-rumpled clothes. She slept on the train and came direct from the station, not even stopping to brush her hair.

"Don't worry, I'm teasing. But actually, since my pictures were published I *have* been getting all kinds of letters. It's as if I'd baked a prize cake—people think they're entitled to the recipe." Miss Bourke-White puts the lid on the pot and places it on a lacquer tray, along with a silver creamer and sugar bowl. A diamond on her ring finger catches the light and, seeing Berenice observe it, she grins. "Oh no, I'm not married any more. I just keep it on to stop men from being pests." So saying, she edges past Berenice, leaving a trail of perfume in the air.

Clutching her case, Berenice follows her hostess down the hall. She can't help but notice what beautiful things Miss Bourke-White has in her living room. A soft white rug, a Chesterfield sofa, two pink velvet chairs with seashell-shaped backs. She's drawn to a framed photograph on the wall that shows a woman with a camera standing on the rooftop of a building, silhouetted against the sky. The woman wears an aviator cap and one of her arms is bent and raised, as if conducting an orchestra.

"Do you like it?" Miss Bourke-White puts the tray on the table and comes to join her. "My friend Ralph took it, he has an eye for drama. I told him not to waste film, but he would, and it came out so beautifully that I had to put it up. A bit vain, I suppose."

"So it *is* you," Berenice looks again, appreciating how the photographer cast his subject as an impresario bending the world to her vision. "What were you shooting that day, Miss Bourke-White?"

"Oh, Margaret, please—we're cohorts, aren't we? We were just larking around, shooting factories. Nothing as dramatic as the skyscraper shots you sent me in your letter. You must be intrepid!"

"Not really, I get awful vertigo. But I do it anyway."

"That's right—can't let it stand in one's way! I was a fearful child, actually, but Mother taught me to overcome it. She had me draw pictures of the monsters under my bed. We'd give them names, hobbies, favorite foods. Soon enough they came to seem like friends."

"How amazing." A wave of jealousy runs through Berenice, to think that this woman had a mother both finely attuned to her problems and creative enough to solve them. She's so poised, too, and elegantly attired in a dark pencil skirt and cream shirt with a soft scoop of fabric at the neck.

"How do you take your tea?" Margaret is walking back to the coffee table. "Milk? Sugar?"

"A little milk." Putting her case down, Berenice sits on one of the seashell chairs, which surprises her by swiveling. "Oh!"

"Should've warned you, sorry." Margaret laughs, then hands her a teacup. "It's a Paul Follot. Rather an extravagance, I fear."

They talk about Margaret's work, and her unlikely affinity with the steel mills. Her father was an industrial manufacturer, she says, and accompanying him on factory tours inspired her. Even so, it took many months before she accomplished the technical breakthroughs that enabled her photographs. She shows Berenice the originals, which are breathtaking, with shimmering highlights and deep, velvety blacks. Looking at them, you can almost feel the oppressive heat and hear the clanking machinery.

"I couldn't have done it without my friend Beme—Al Bemis, that is," Margaret is saying. "He manages the equipment at Wolf & Sons, and he let me borrow all kinds of things. Then he introduced me to lighting people from Hollywood, and to salesmen who set me up with special printing paper."

"Oh," Berenice feels another tug of jealousy. She doesn't have friends who work in camera stores and are hooked up to a network of helpful salesmen.

"Beme kept saying we were doing something entirely new, no one had done it before," Margaret goes on. "He was right. The varnish blistered off the cameras, my clothes were soaked in sweat. So much film wasted. But we did it in the end."

"Remarkable," Berenice says. She can't help making the obvious comparison: what has she done so far? Her Paris portraits were skillful but hardly groundbreaking. And her New York work has barely begun.

She opens her case and takes out her portfolio, showing Margaret some of her portraits from Paris. Jean Cocteau, Isamu Noguchi. James Joyce and Coco Chanel.

"But you're marvelous!" Margaret exclaims. "Such wonderful light in Joyce's eyes, and how imposing Chanel is! What was she like?"

"I can't say I warmed to her. She was tough. Though I do give her credit for saving us from corsets." They chuckle in unison. Margaret's laugh is staccato, like machine gun fire—*hahaha*! Encouraged, Berenice pulls out her New York material and hands over prints from Wall Street, the docks, and the Williamsburg Bridge.

Margaret studies each print, then looks up, eyes alight. "Such strong work. What's your plan for it?"

"It's going to be an extended survey. There are changes happening in every borough. Not just the construction, though that's a big part. But it's everything. Jazz, politics, the whole pace and texture of the place. I want to record the transition. It'll be called *Changing New York*." She sits back, nervous. Margaret is a photographer, with a gimlet eye; her reaction to this will be a bellwether.

Margaret arches an eyebrow. "I thought so. You're the real thing. But you'd better take care."

"Why?"

"You and I are a new breed, sister. Having a portrait studio in Paris is one thing—women are good with people. But now you're being more ambitious. You're taking on the boys, and they'll try to shoot you down. Don't be daunted. Keep telling yourself there's no progress without risk."

"Right," Berenice says. Put like that, it sounds big and important. She's embarrassed to tell Margaret that this risk-taker might not be able to pay her rent next month; that she can't afford the new camera she so desperately needs.

She drains her teacup and looks at Margaret on the buttoned sofa, so *soignée* in her cream shirt and silk stockings. In less than an hour she'll be with Ma on the wrong side of town, and the thought makes her droop. She has a fierce desire put down roots in Margaret's living room.

As if intuiting her thoughts, Margaret stands and takes her empty teacup. "My dear, I could chat all night, but I have a party to get to. Perhaps we can meet in New York next time. I'm moving there in January."

"Oh!" Berenice perks up. "Why?"

"You know Henry Luce, the owner of *Time*? He saw my pictures and offered me the position of staff photographer at his new magazine, *Fortune*. Risky, of course—" Margaret ushers Berenice out of the room. "One never knows if these new ventures will last. But it works with my interests. I'll be traveling, visiting industrial sites all over the country. And he's paying me very well, thank you."

At this, Berenice feels a pain in her chest, as if her heart has twisted around on itself. The jealousy she's been holding at bay gushes out, green and bilious, and she's glad Margaret can't see her face, which must be ugly with it. How can this woman be so privileged by birth, so loved, *and* fall so neatly on her two tone Oxford-clad feet? And at only twenty-five! *It's not fair*, a voice whispers. Yet she knows the photographs of the steel mills are extraordinary, better than anything she's accomplished yet. *Be happy another woman is succeeding,* she tells herself. *It means it can be done.*

They've reached the front door. Berenice looks at Margaret. "We'll see, anyway," Margaret says. "If it doesn't work out, you can always call me *Miss Fortune*." She smirks at her joke. "But I envy what you're doing. Your independence."

Yes, it's blissful, Berenice thinks, *if only you knew. Heating up my can of soup on the sterno because I don't have money to eat downstairs. Sneaking into the Dakota, pushing my business card under apartment doors. A life of glamor and adventure.*

Affecting nonchalance, she puts a hand against the wall. "Do you think *Fortune* might have anything for me?"

"Oh, goodness, I didn't even think of that! I can ask." As Margaret moves to open the door, Berenice wonders if she'll follow through, or if the offer will be shucked off as soon as the door closes. How wonderful if she did, if they became fast friends. But there's no telling. People can be duplicitous.

"Goodbye then," Margaret reaches out a hand. "See you in New York."

"In New York." Berenice takes the proffered hand and, looking at Margaret, feels a confusing mix of emotions. On one hand she admires the other woman, who has chosen to do rigorous work rather than wallow in the fripperies of her class. On the other hand, she wishes Margaret weren't *quite* so glamorous and skillful.

Margaret's apartment building is on a hill overlooking downtown. Walking downhill, Berenice sees, silhouetted against a coral blaze of setting sun, a skyline with buildings she doesn't recognize. A new railroad complex is being built, and a tower as tall as a Manhattan skyscraper looms over Public Square. Cleveland has changed. The landscape of her childhood is being overwritten.

It isn't until she crosses Public Square that she starts to feels nervous. Ontario Street has been torn up, its buildings razed; batch trucks and concrete mixers fill the streets. In the once fine park, weeds poke from cracks in the path and the iron benches are populated with the humped bodies of derelicts. Ma can't be living near here, surely? Turning onto Euclid Avenue, she passes a vacant office building with boarded-up windows. Streetlamps flicker, illuminating potholes and trash.

"Hey, lady!" A man floats into a doorway. "Got a light?" He holds out a damp cigarette, his smile suggesting more than the need for a match. Berenice shakes her head and hurries on.

When she finally reaches the address on her postcard, she can only stare at the building in dismay. The window frames are crooked and the front door is ajar, an open invitation to thieves. She walks into a hallway that must have been imposing once, but is now a mess of water-stained wallpaper and crumbling plaster. There's an odor of dusty carpets and urine. The smell of failed lives.

Ma will have moved, Berenice thinks. And sure enough, when the door to 5C opens, the thin sliver of eye seems to belong to a shriveled, older woman. But as the door opens an inch more, she sees that this *is* Ma. How withered she is! She's bent over, her hair grown wispy, her face bloated. A stranger would put her at seventy, not fifty-seven.

Ma stares back, her eyes flickering with surprise and, for a moment, something that might be pleasure. But then a hardness takes over.

"Come in, then."

"Thank you." As she steps across the threshold, Berenice has to struggle not to grimace. Cracks run down from the ceiling, splitting the gray walls and exposing patches of wooden lath work. A limp blue curtain separates an iron bed from a kitchen area with empty bottles on the countertops. It pains Berenice to see the grimy windows, the stained curtains. Even at her lowest ebb, Ma used to keep her home clean.

"Well," Ma looks down at her suitcase, "I guess you're staying. You'll have to make yourself a bed there." She tips her head at a tattered sofa. "I'm too old to share."

"That's fine. It's only overnight."

"Of course it is."

Berenice chafes at her mother's tone, then stops, because in a sense, she thinks, she deserves it. She flew the coop. *It was your life or mine*, she thinks.

"The stairs must tire you," she says. "What about a place on a lower floor?"

"This is good enough for me." Ma shuffles over to a table and, with a grunt, eases herself into a chair.

Berenice sets her case down. At the table, she sits opposite Ma. There's an awkward silence and to fill it, she says, "I brought you something from Paris." She opens her suitcase and pulls out a bag from *Le Printemps*, immediately realizing that it would have made a better gift for Margaret.

Ma takes the bag and pulls out the soft, tissue-wrapped package. She unwraps the tissue, revealing a green silk scarf with a design of peacocks. Her stiff hands don't seem to know what to do with it.

"Can I tie it for you?" Taking the scarf, Berenice wraps it around her mother's head, knotting it at the nape of her neck. It's difficult to touch the crepey skin at the back of her neck, her bony shoulders. Ma just sits there, neither yielding or resisting.

"That's pretty," Berenice says when she's done. Ma lifts a hand, touching the silk with her fingers. She feels around her head, patting it here and there as if re-acquainting herself with an old sensation.

Berenice waits for a thank-you, but it doesn't come. Ma's eyes have clouded over. She has gone somewhere faraway.

◆

For dinner, Berenice goes to buy groceries, then takes them back to the apartment. Despite the late hour she manages to procure some onions, carrots and a boiling fowl. She also buys a pot of peach jam and a loaf of Irish soda bread.

Cooking proves tricky. The sink in Ma's apartment is blocked and there isn't a carving knife or pot big enough for the fowl. Berenice has to wash the vegetables in the bathroom down the hall, then saw the bird apart with a steak knife and put it in two pots. In Ma's kitchen drawer, the few utensils are encrusted with dried food barnacles. It's hard to touch them without shuddering.

As they eat the soup with the bread and jam, Ma grows chatty.

"Your cousin Martha did well for herself," she says. "Married a factory manager, got a big house in Fairfax. Five kids and still going."

"Oh, I'm glad."

"Why?" her mother spits. "You never liked her."

"No, but she wanted a big family. All those dolls she played with. I don't need to begrudge her, do I?"

Ma chews on a piece of meat, then opens her mouth and, with surprising finesse, spits a bone into her hand. "Earl lived to see three of his grandchildren. After he went, Martha took Ruby in. Said she didn't want her mother being alone." This last sentence is said so flatly that Berenice can't tell how much of a rebuke it's meant to be.

"Have you seen Hazel?" When she was last living in New York, her sister had made contact with Ma. The two of them had exchanged letters and had a few visits. Hazel had also written to Berenice saying, *I hope we meet some day.* She'd become a social worker, she wrote, and there was no shortage of work.

Her mother purses her lips, shakes her head. "Hazel moved to Detroit. Took up with a man for a while, but it didn't come to anything." Her eyes narrow. "Hold on a minute. This might interest you."

It takes an age for Ma to get up from the table, walk to the other side of the room and retrieve the object from her closet. When she comes back, she's holding a scrap of yellowing newsprint that she hands to Berenice.

The article, from the *Cleveland Plain Dealer* of 12 June 1926, is headlined *Four Unsolved Murders in the Flats*. Berenice holds it to the light, scanning the column, her heartbeat quickening as she looks for a name. When she finds it, her eyes flick so fast over the type that, on a first read, she can barely take it in.

The paragraph on Gus's death is eight lines at most. That's all it takes, because the story is entirely unexceptional. According to the police record, his death was the consequence of a barroom fight in which he was beaten and left to bleed out. *This kind of brutality is the unfortunate, all too frequent result of the loose morality reigning in the area known as the Flats*, the article opines.

Berenice lowers the paper, her hand trembling. *This might interest you*, her mother had said. How many emotions were tied up in those four words! Ma was right: she is interested. Blood courses through her, pulsing in her wrists and temples. There's a grim sense of satisfaction. She's glad he suffered, happy to think of him squirming on the sidewalk. But there is, too, an odd sense of regret. Now she'll never face him as an adult. He won't see that despite him, she has flourished.

Whatever Ma feels about the murder, it isn't revealed by her expression, and Berenice has no desire to dig further. She hands the slip of paper back, though she'd just as soon hold it to the candle flame.

"Do you think Hazel would like to hear from me?" she asks.

"Maybe. But don't expect much. It's been two years since I heard from her."

It's not especially cold in the apartment, but Berenice shivers. "Ma…" she begins.

"What?"

"Why…why did Pa want Hazel, not me?"

Ma shrugs. "You were a baby."

"But what about when I was older? Did he ever…come look for me? Or write? Like he promised he would?"

For the first time since Berenice arrived, Ma looks at her with a softened expression. "I'm sorry, Bernice. He never did deliver on half his promises."

"What was he like…at his best? Do you remember?"

"Of course." A faint smile plays over Ma's lips. "He had a spark. Devilishly handsome and knew about the world. But he was a dreamer—lots of big ideas, no patience. Something better was always around the corner." Her face turns sour. "Turned out to be like that with women too."

"There were good times, though? Before?"

"Of course." Abruptly, Ma gets up from the table, limping away to the kitchen, signaling that the conversation is over.

That night, huddled under a moth-eaten blanket on the lumpy sofa, with Ma's sawing snores breaking the silence, Berenice lies thinking. How much of her temperament comes from Pa? *He was a dreamer—lots of big ideas, no patience.* She has just left her life in Paris on a whim, following a 'big idea' to New York. Has she inherited the curse of never being satisfied?

Not for the first time, she has doubts about the path she's chosen. Was it foolish to leave Paris, the place where she'd felt most free? Should she have tested the water first, not uprooted herself completely? Oh, she could go back, but it wouldn't be the same. She'd be creeping back with her tail between her legs.

She thinks of Paris in the fall—of open café windows, and the suck and pop of wine bottles being uncorked. People laughing, revitalized by summers out of town. Leaves turning color, and the comforting warmth of a *crêpe* at *Chez Emilie.*

And then she has to clench her face to keep tears from falling. She thinks of her friends gathering without her, sharing drinks at *Select* and *Le Boeuf.* Her studio on the rue Servandoni, occupied by a painter or writer—or perhaps redecorated and turned into a chic young couple's apartment.

But people need roots, she thinks. Maybe part of growing up is coming to grips with where you're from. In Paris, it often seemed to her that the expatriates were more fiercely patriotic than anyone. Joyce, Fitzgerald, Hemingway—they left their countries because they needed distance to see them clearly, but in the end they were drawn back. The pull was primal. They reached a point where they had to grow in native soil.

What now? she wonders. *Can I really reinvent myself?*

She burrows more deeply under the blanket. Turning on her side, she tries to block her nose against the sofa's smell—a mixture of creosote and damp boots—and summon oblivion. The sooner she goes to sleep, the sooner she can get back to New York.

SEVENTEEN

Everyone is looking at Wall Street today after yesterday's concentrated selling, a voice on the radio intones. *At closing yesterday, the Dow Jones Industrial Average had fallen by four point six percent. Leading economists are split on whether it's a temporary dip or the start of a larger decline.* Clearly bemused, the voice goes on, *Well, if* those *fellas don't know, I'm not sure* who *does...*

Berenice spoons coffee into the filter cone, but her hands flutter and grounds spill on the table. She wipes them off, chiding herself as her hand sweeps the cool marble surface. The water is boiling and she shuts off the heat, then pours water into her filter. She remembers how Claudine, in Madame Archambault's flower shop, *tsk-tsk*ed when she first saw Berenice make coffee. *Il faut gonfler les semoules*, she'd said sternly. *You have to let the coffee grounds swell.* Ever since, Berenice has observed the rule, appreciating her rich, dark brew.

Sitting at the table with her coffee, she goes over her plan for the day. It's Thursday, her day for photographing the city, but in place of her usual excitement she is weighed down by anxiety. She's three weeks late with the rent, and the managers will be onto her soon. Just last week her neighbor, a tenant of ten years' standing, was forced out for lack of funds. She'd seen him sitting on a box in his apartment, surrounded by walls bearing pale squares where his paintings had once hung.

Something will come along, she tells herself, *it always does*. But the mantra now seems shaky, founded less on evidence than on blind—and probably foolish—optimism.

A few hours later, in the East Village, she heads down to the Bowery. She's not far from places she went to with Lil—the Oak Tavern, for one—and the memories are a dull ache in her side.

Today, there are two storefronts she wants to photograph. One is a hardware store with boxes of tools laid out on the sidewalk, the other a pawn shop whose windows are loaded with candlesticks, banjos, vases and guns. To her, they symbolize two sides of the same coin: American abundance bestowed on the one hand and on the other, taken away.

As she walks along Houston Street, she notices that the East Village is unusually subdued. Normally the streets are busy with handcart vendors, street musicians and bums hustling for change. But today, men hurry by with their hats pulled low and even the bums are somber.

What will happen if the economy goes down? The thought is awful, but is it better to bury one's head in the sand? That's what everyone's been doing for the last year or so, it seems—borrowing money and buying shares, trusting the market not to fail. "It's called buying on margin," a friend told Berenice, "for every dollar you put down, you can borrow nine more!" Berenice had considered investing her few dollars, but found the frenzy too bizarre. It didn't seem right to go to a diner and be handed stock tips by the waitress along with your fries.

On the Bowery, she's setting up her equipment when a man hurrying by accidentally knocks her tripod over.

"Watch it!" she cries as the tripod clatters to the sidewalk.

"Sorry, miss." He turns back, distracted, to help her. The corners of his shirt collar are frayed and he's hatless.

"What's the hurry, anyway?" she asks.

He grimaces. "I'm going to take all my money outta the bank."

"Fleeing the country?" she teases.

The man straightens, looking her full in the face. "Guess you haven't heard. There's a run on the banks—Dow's in freefall. Stocks are dropping faster than a whore's underpants. Miss, if you've invested, go get your money. Don't put it off." He touches a finger to his oiled hair. "Good day."

As Berenice watches him darting down the street, queasiness stirs in her gut. Surely he was exaggerating. If what he said is true—that the Dow is plunging—the country will face a catastrophe.

She shoots the two storefronts, but can't find her rhythm. She's too distracted to look properly. But it's four hours until the afternoon editions of the papers come out, so she might as well work. She moves on to a butcher shop with signs for *Leg of Mutton, Fancy Broilers, Smoked Tongue!* It's no good, she can't settle. She packs up her equipment and heads to the El.

At home, with a mug of tea in hand, she paces the floor while listening to the radio. The news is mixed. The market has fallen by almost ten percent, and there's been panicked selling. But a group of leading bankers has pledged a reserve of money, authorizing the president of the stock exchange to start buying stocks. This vote of confidence is effective, it seems. The panic has died down and the market has stabilized.

It's better than she feared. Relieved, she spends the evening developing negatives while listening to the jazz on *Fleischmann's Yeast Hour*.

The next day, Friday, is peaceful. Berenice stays in her studio, printing negatives from *Changing New York* and designing a new business card. The market remains stable. The crisis seems to have passed.

On Saturday, Djuna Barnes—who's in New York to see her publisher—drops by, bearing a pair of lobsters that she has somehow acquired. They have a hell of a time cooking the creatures on Berenice's sterno heater. After sharing a bottle of wine and laughing at their incompetence, they finally sit down to a messy but delicious meal of lobster, tomatoes and creamed corn.

"I was scared last week," Berenice says. "Getting work here has been hard. A market collapse would destroy me."

"Oh," Djuna waves a lobster claw in the air, carelessly dripping butter on her skirt, "it was a hiccup. America can't fail." Easy enough for her to say. She's heading back to Paris in a few days—and, too, her career is soaring. *The Ladies Almanack*—a book she published pseudonymously, satirizing lesbian life in Paris—was a surprise hit, and then her novel *Ryder* made the *New York Times* bestseller list.

"Have you seen Thelma?" she asks now. Though her tone is neutral, Berenice isn't fooled. She knows Djuna is sick at heart. Last year, the mercurial Thelma Wood—Djuna's lover for eight years—moved to the West Village with another woman. It was a huge blow for Djuna, who'd been wild about Thelma and had put effort into molding her as an artist. Then again, their relationship had always been volatile. Friends in Paris had joked that, if feeling cold, you could always go to Thelma and Djuna's and huddle under the sparks.

"I'm afraid not," she says. "I've been very boring since I got back."

"I wonder if she's all right. I may go see. People say she's drinking like a fish."

"Do you want her back?"

"God, no," Djuna laughs, then quickly raises her wineglass and drains it, shaking her head. But when she sets it down and looks across at Berenice, her expression is pained. "Well, sometimes. The truth is life was never dull with her. But we fought—oh god, how we fought! I always wanted her for myself, but she wanted me *and* the rest of humanity."

"I know," Berenice sighs, feeling a tug under her heart. She's tempted to throw Djuna's question back at her—*Have you seen Tylia?*—but resists. She doesn't want to hear about how Djuna saw Ty dancing on the table at *Le Boeuf*—or, worse, found her glassy-eyed on the sidewalk. With an effort, she pushes the thoughts away.

Djuna seems to have intuited them anyway. "Why do we go after these difficult women?" she bursts out. "Wouldn't it be easier if we fell in love with each other?"

Berenice raises an eyebrow, Djuna pouts, and then they both burst out laughing. If they were going to be together it would have happened by now; they've had their chances. Djuna goes for troubled, high-voltage women, and Berenice—well, she hasn't been with enough women to know if she has a type. All she knows is that after Ty, she has no more appetite for drama.

"I don't have time, anyway," she says. "New York is my lover now. We understand each other. We have passion, but also trust."

"And plenty of erections," Djuna adds. Berenice, who had taken a sip of wine, starts coughing and almost spits it out, and they end the evening on a note of hilarity that sustains her all the way through Sunday.

Then on Monday, it comes to a crashing halt.

Over the weekend, people across the country have had time to think about the previous week in the stock market. They've read the newspapers, listened to broadcasts—and on reflection, have decided they're not convinced by Friday's rally. Monday starts with a run on the banks that no one, not even the most powerful moneyman, can stop. By the end of trading, the Dow has fallen by over twelve percent. The next day, Tuesday, is worse. Over sixteen million shares are sold, a volume so unprecedented that the ticker-tape machines in the stock exchange seize up.

It feels like an earthquake. The ground is shifting and can't be stopped. Each news bulletin is worse than the last. The small brokerages—the ones that had lent money at a ninety percent margin—start to announce bankruptcy first. Then, like falling dominoes, small banks follow suit. People line up outside buildings to get their money, only to find they've lost every penny. The mood turns ugly and windows are broken.

Berenice sits in her apartment, unable to do anything except listen to radio broadcasts and read newspaper articles with a creeping sense of fear. The news is wildly inconsistent, unable to keep pace with the rapid developments. The *Washington Post* carries a front-page story in which business leaders assert that the American economy is strong. But the *Post* predicts further chaos— and on Wednesday morning, NBC reports that a leading stockbroker has been found hanging from a doorframe in his Park Avenue apartment. If the economy were really about to recover, wouldn't he have held on?

That evening at the Hotel des Artistes, a group of residents gathers in the ground floor restaurant for a meeting that feels like a wake. One fellow, an aging actor, has lost his life savings; another had been painting a mural in the headquarters of a bank that has gone belly-up. Berenice listens, feeling lucky she had no money to lose. But luck is relative. She's in trouble. Her portrait business is non-existent and she hasn't sold any Atget prints. At this point she probably couldn't give them away. For the first time in years, she's facing the prospect of not being able to support herself.

The next day, tight-lipped, she arranges her cameras in front of her on the table. Her big studio camera might fetch a good price, but it's the camera she uses for portraits, which might be her only chance for income. The Century Universal is valuable, but if she sells it she won't have anything to use for her new work. In the end, she decides on her Kurt-Bentzin. It's small but has been well looked after, and she has three lenses for it.

At City Camera, the salesman looks the package over and shakes his head. "Another time, I would have given you fifteen dollars for this outfit. But we've got orders from the management. There's a freeze on buying."

She droops. "How about taking it on consignment?"

"No point. No one's buying; it would just sit here. You might as well use it yourself."

The same thing happens in the pawnshop, and in the clothing store where she takes the jeweled hat she bought on the rue de Rivoli. Everyone compliments her taste. No one has money to buy right now.

The following week, she sits amid packing crates in her studio and waits for the moving van. Unlike her neighbor, she hasn't been in the Hotel des Artistes long enough for the walls to tell her story—but even so she feels embarrassed.

She has found a small place in the west Thirties, a fourth-floor walk-up with a half-bathroom big enough to use as a darkroom. It's a step down, for sure—yet it's better than the compromises she's seen others make. Half of New York is moving, it seems, people picking up and shunting themselves along, like a game of musical chairs. From Park Avenue to Madison, from Madison to Lexington, from Lexington perhaps to Chelsea or—god forbid—Brooklyn. There must be a lot of mansions going empty these days.

She sits on a packing crate, looking at the beautiful room that is no longer hers, the shifting squares of light falling from the high windows onto the now bare floors. And, too, she thinks of her bright, spacious studio on the rue Servandoni, close to the Jardin de Luxembourg. People would come for their portraits and wander over to the tall windows, lingering to admire the gorgeous view over Saint-Sulpice. "Lucky you," they'd say, "you came out on top with this place."

The rue Servandoni, the Hotel des Artistes. And now—but best not to think about it. *Something will come along,* she tells herself. *It always does.*

EIGHTEEN

By summer, President Hoover is inspiring little trust. The jobless rate is soaring; new figures show more than three million unemployed. In New York, men stand on street corners in neat suits and ties, selling apples for five cents apiece.

Berenice's fortunes are, if not as dismal as those of the apple-sellers, nothing to brag about. She has scant savings, unreliable income and an overhead she can't afford. Though still in her apartment in the west Thirties, she's just hanging on, with stress-related stomachaches that she can't buy medicine for. Dinner one night is a sad plate of sardines on toast, accompanied by water. She's finishing it when the telephone rings.

"Berenice Abbott, you're a hard woman to track down," says a pleased-sounding voice. "How *are* you?"

"Miss Bourke-White!"

"*Margaret*, please. Had the darnedest time finding your number. Called the one you gave me, but it was kaput. Had to use all my snooping powers."

"I'm so sorry. I moved. I gave my old building the new number, but I suppose—"

"Are you all right?" Margaret interjects. "This damn economy!" Her voice, coming through miles of telephone cable, is warm and kind. It's the most welcome sound Berenice has heard in months.

"Surviving," Berenice says. She grips the telephone more forcefully. "You?"

"Oh, don't worry about me," Margaret says. "I'm jake."

Of course you are, Berenice thinks, remembering Margaret's charmed life. *And that's just as well, because I need all my energy to worry about myself.*

"Anyway, look," Margaret goes on, "I didn't just call to gab. I might have some work for you. Hank Luce wants to assign you a few portraits for *Fortune*."

"Oh!" Berenice almost knocks over the vase on her telephone table. "So the magazine's going forward?"

"Yes, believe it or not. Crazy, huh, at a time like this? But Luce is determined. His parents were missionaries, and he has the same kind of zeal."

"Does he want to see my work?"

"No. Well yes, of course, at some point. But he trusts me, and I told him you were the elephant's eyebrows. He wants to give you two or three portraits as a trial. If he likes those, there'll be more." There's a pause, then Margaret adds, "Of course, I said I didn't know if you'd be interested. After photographing Joyce and Chanel, you might have better things to do than getting mug shots of businessmen."

"I don't!" Berenice blurts, then catches herself. "What I mean is, I'm very focused on my New York work. But I think I can spare time."

"Swell! I'll have Briton Hadden call you. He's Hank's business partner and the managing editor. He'll give you the details. And sister, don't sell yourself short. Make sure you don't take a penny less than fifty per print."

"I won't," Berenice says, her heart knocking against her ribs. Two months' rent, from one print! And more to come! She feels absurdly grateful to Margaret, conscious of being in her debt. "You must come over soon," she says. "I make an excellent dirty martini."

"How wonderful. But I'll have to take a rain check. Luce has got me running around all over the place. Maine one day, Texas the next. Speaking of which, I must dash—I'm heading out to California to photograph the Douglas Aircraft Company. Mr. Douglas himself has promised to give me a spin in his new prototype!"

"Have fun," Berenice says, a second before hearing the click on the other end. She shakes her head, amused by Margaret's escapades, and—if she's honest—crazy jealous. How does Margaret do it? She'd kill to be among the first people to take a spin in the new Douglas airplane.

After putting down the telephone, she makes a cup of tea and sits at the kitchen table. Then she puts her face in her hands and has a good cry, from sheer relief. Margaret's offer has appeared at just the right time, and it's a blessed deliverance. She'd managed to sell a few images of skyscrapers to a French magazine last month, but since then, nothing. If this hadn't come along, she might have been facing a move to an even shabbier apartment.

When her tears have dried, she stares at the dregs in her teacup. Margaret has come through, she is a good egg. Whether she mentioned it casually to Henry Luce one time, or lobbied hard for Berenice, either way she came through. Given how anxious everyone is now, that is a big point in her favor.

Would Berenice have done the same? She won't know, she supposes, until life gives her the means and opportunity to reach back and help someone else.

◆

The next day she leaves her apartment dressed in her best charcoal-gray suit, tripod slung across one shoulder, camera in a canvas bag on the other. She is going to photograph Carleton Morris, the director of National Life Insurance, a self-made millionaire. It's her first assignment for *Fortune*.

Two blocks north, an encampment of shacks—a Hooverville—has been set up in an empty lot. It has about twenty structures jerry-rigged out of old doors, packing crates and sheets of galvanized tin. Two grubby children sit near the fence, lethargically poking sticks into a puddle.

They're everywhere now, these places. Some of her neighbors petitioned for this one to be removed, citing disease and crime, but Berenice didn't sign. These people had suffered enough, she felt—plus, she was conscious of being only a few hundred dollars away from such a place herself. Besides, she finds the encampment intriguing. She stops now to admire how people have hung curtains and put out flowerpots. Such a potent mix of optimism and despair! Some day, when she gets up the nerve, she might walk in and ask to make some photographs.

Around the corner, men stand four-deep in a line, hats pulled down, waiting for the lodging house to open and serve its free lunch. The program started a few months ago and every day the line gets longer.

Fourteen blocks away is a different city. The windows of Tiffany and Bonwit Teller are shined to perfection. Stylish men and women stroll by as if they'd never heard of a Depression.

In the National Life tower, an elevator glides her smoothly to the nineteenth floor. She waits in a reception that looks like a gentlemen's club, its walls adorned with antique rifles and paintings of battle scenes. After a few minutes, a secretary bustles over.

"Mr. Morris is very busy this morning. He's asked that you take no more than twenty minutes."

"Oh!" Berenice looks at her in disbelief. It will take at least five minutes to set up her camera, another five to focus and meter the light. Twenty minutes! In Paris, her shoots could last for hours and she only did one a day, in order to get to know her subject. In twenty minutes, she'll barely be able to say hello. But she needs this job. So she follows the woman down the hall.

"Miss Abbott," the woman says, giving her a little push into an office twice the size of Berenice's apartment. It boasts the same dark, heavy furnishings as the reception, and through the large windows you can see down to Wall Street and across the Hudson to New Jersey. You can see Grand Central Terminal and the new Chrysler tower, whose Nirosta steel spire sparkles like a sharpened dagger in the sun.

Berenice walks to a mahogany desk that could shelter a Hooverville family and shakes the hand of Carleton Morris—who might like his classical art, but is no oil painting himself. Small and doughy, with tufts of greying hair, he has a bulbous nose decorated with a cockroach-sized wart, and deep-set eyes. This is going to be a challenge.

"Miss Abbott."

"Mr. Morris."

"Let's have at it, then. I don't have much time."

"I'm afraid it's going to take me a few minutes to set up."

"Hmph! I leave at twelve-thirty. Better step on the gas."

Right. She starts to unpack her equipment, and is about to engage him in conversation when he barks out, "Cutter! I don't care! Pull him out of the meeting if you have to!" Flinching, Berenice looks up to see he's holding a telephone receiver a few inches from his mouth. Apparently, small talk is not a part of his repertoire.

Sure enough, when she starts trying to photograph him, he won't converse. He sits like the proverbial sack of potatoes, answering her questions in terse monosyllables. After a few minutes, he waves her away as if she's a fly. She holds her tongue, but bristles. She's used to being treated as an artist not the hired help.

Three days later, when she photographs steel magnate Henry Voss in his Fifth-Avenue mansion, things aren't much better. In his sixties like Morris, Voss is also overweight and homely, with one eye distinctly smaller than the other. Yet he's terribly vain and keeps calling a maid to brush his hair and pat his forehead with powder. Between the maid's ministrations and Mrs. Voss's interruptions, Berenice can barely get five frames exposed.

When the prints come out, she winces. Any semi-competent photographer could have taken them. It's not just that Morris and Voss look entitled: they look *boring*. For her, nothing could be worse. Maybe she could have done better if she'd had more time with each, but she'll never know.

Henry Luce's secretary calls a week later, saying that the *Fortune* editor would like to talk to her. Berenice braces herself, knowing she's got it coming.

"I don't understand," Luce says. There's weariness under his bite, as though she's a child who's flunked her best subject. "I was told you were number one for portraits."

"I'm sorry," she says. "If I hadn't had to send them, I wouldn't. You're right and I have no defense, other than that Mr. Morris and Mr. Voss didn't give me the time I needed." Her knees wobble, and she sits down. "They seemed to think that sitting for a portrait was worth about as much as getting their nose hairs trimmed."

On the other end, Luce guffaws. "Ha! Guess I could have warned you about Morris. Tyrannical old boor, we're striking him from the first issue. Tell you what, though, if I get you another meeting with Voss, can you promise you won't screw up?"

"Yes I can, absolutely."

"What makes you sure?"

"The knowledge that if I do, you won't hire me again. And I need this work. Without it, I'll be eating beans all winter."

"Hm," Luce pauses. "Hunger is a good motivator, I guess. Consider this a second chance, then, Miss Abbott. And you're right—if you fail, there *won't* be a third."

Three days later, Berenice shows up at the Voss mansion with a silver globe pendant hanging between her breasts. The necklace is antique, she struck a deal with a pawnbroker to borrow it for the day. As she stands in front of Voss, moving some objects on his desk aside, she bends so that the necklace swings forward and catches the light. At first she thinks he hasn't noticed, but as she pulls away he puts a heavy hand on her arm.

"Where did you get that necklace?"

"This? Oh, it was a gift. It's rather heavy but I don't think it's worth much."

"Nonsense! That's a Hunneker, nineteenth-century German. You can recognize it by the filigree work. He was a master silversmith. Whoever gave you that thinks highly of you, young lady."

"Really? I had no idea."

"Yes indeed. There were very few of these made, the labor was intensive. I believe it's modeled on the globe in Vermeer's painting *The Astronomer*."

"Goodness, imagine that! I've always loved globes. I keep one at home—just a cheap Rand McNally, but I like to spin it and think of places I might visit."

From there, the wheels are greased. He takes her to his gallery, a converted attic room filled with antique globes from all over. There, he pours her three fingers of malt whiskey and shows her his most prized possession, a French globe that was once owned by Verrazzano. "See that space where the western United States should be?" he says. "Not even dreamt of!" When Mrs. Voss comes to ask about a household matter, he tells her to decide for herself and not bother him again.

The portrait she shoots shows Voss in his attic with his globes all around. She has positioned him so that his big, spherical head protrudes from a sea of orbs. A prominent vein in his temple could be a river, snaking down the side of his head with tributaries flowing to his ear and cheek.

Thank god for public libraries, where biographies of notable New Yorkers in the Social Register have lists of their hobbies.

The following week, Luce tells her she's exceeded his expectations. "I won't even ask how you persuaded him to sit that way. All I want to know is, can you give me more work like that?"

"Definitely."

"Are you still hungry, Miss Abbott?"

"I'm ravenous."

"That's the spirit. Keep it up. I'll have Briton call you later this week."

NINETEEN

Though soon to be a gallery, Julien Levy's ground-floor space on Fifty-Seventh and Madison is currently unfinished. Wires dangle from the ceiling; the walls are raw plasterboard. Even so, you can see its potential. The space is large and well lit, and its position on the ground floor of Madison Avenue will ensure business from Manhattan's most elite customers.

Levy stands by a window, lost in contemplation of the swirling snow outside. He doesn't seem to notice Berenice until she's almost next to him, then he turns and embraces her warmly. Despite the dust he's wearing a three-piece suit with a pink handkerchief in its breast pocket, and smells as if he's showered in cologne.

"Berenice! You look wonderful."

"Not next to you, Julien. But what a terrific place!"

"Isn't it? Gloriously cheap, too. Brokers are giving away real estate these days. See that?" He points to the Fuller Building, a skyscraper down the block on Madison Avenue. "Opened last year and still half empty. You've got to pity the owners."

"Yes. Though I'm more inclined to pity the men in the breadlines."

Levy cocks his head and smiles. "Still the same Berenice, I see."

"In most ways."

"Hm, well. Let's go to my club, shall we? It's not too far."

As they walk along Fifty-Seventh Street, she congratulates him on having the courage to open a gallery now. Despite President Hoover's assurances, there have been no signs of economic recovery—in fact, quite the opposite. The jobless rate has soared to twenty percent, and homelessness is endemic. Of course, the cold weather has made everything worse. Recently, there has been a rash of food riots, desperate people smashing store windows, grabbing everything they can.

For her part, Berenice has been scraping by. Hank Luce continues to assign her portraits for *Fortune* and out of this has sprung other, sporadic work for *The Saturday Evening Post* and *Vanity Fair*. She continues to work on *Changing New York*, and thinks she has at least thirty images that are worth showing. She would dearly love to have them up in a gallery, to draw attention to the project and attract some funding.

She first found out about Levy's return to New York in a gossipy letter from her old patron, Peggy Guggenheim. Levy had inherited money, Peggy wrote, and was intending to open a photography gallery. It was amazing news, especially at a time like this. Other than Stieglitz's Intimate Place, there are no serious galleries in New York that show photography.

Now, walking beside Levy, she notices that he has changed since she met him in Paris. Though he still has the same shark-like intensity, he also seems more settled and resolute. Can she trust him? He was tight with Man Ray and is friends with Stieglitz. But he's sharp, and that—along with the buoyancy conferred by an inheritance—will serve him well as an art dealer.

"What do you have in mind for your new place?" she asks.

"Ah, I'm glad you asked. It's going to be a different kind of gallery. Unique, fashionable, a little bit dangerous. With a concentration on photography."

"Amen to that!"

"Let's hope so. I'm going to bring over the Dadaists and surrealists. Moholy-Nagy, Man Ray. And painters, too—Ernst, Dali. It will be a place for people who are open-minded. Like 291 in its heyday."

At the mention of Stieglitz's first gallery, Berenice's smile drops. "So you're emulating Stieglitz?"

"Of course! The man's a genius. Anybody hoping to shake up the art world would be a fool not to look at what he's done. Though I'll take it further—I'll show films, and have surrealist happenings."

"Interesting," Berenice represses the urge to repeat what a friend once called surrealism, *Freud and Goya having a wet dream together.* They've reached his club, and he shepherds her through the front door, into a dark lobby where a porter looks at her as if he's just sucked on a lemon. Levy takes her elbow and steers her down a corridor lined with paintings—bewigged men, hounds at their sides. "This land was sold to the club by the Duchess of Marlborough," he whispers. "Pierpont Morgan founded the place."

He's smug now, on home turf—but she won't be intimidated by old money and privilege. When they're sitting with coffee in a small back parlor, she gets down to business.

"So tell me, will you be representing traditional photography in your gallery?"

Levy glances at the leather case leaning against her chair. "It depends."

"On what?"

"Whether it has artistic merit, of course, but also if I think it can sell. Do you want to show me what you have?"

She has brought a selection of Atget images, and a collection of her own. Levy scrutinizes them, holding some up, asking questions here and there. He admires her image of the Manhattan Bridge, then falls silent when he comes to an Atget.

"I know it's not avant-garde," she says, "but trust me, people will take you more seriously if you anchor the shocking shows with a solid collection of realist work."

Levy considers. "How much are you looking to sell these Atget prints for?"

"Fifteen dollars apiece." It's the price that, on the way over, she decided to start from. She needs an infusion of cash, because she's almost out of film and chemicals. But, too, she thinks the Atget prints are worth it. Especially given the unpaid work she's put into their preservation.

"I see. And your own prints?"

"The same."

Levy rubs his face with a hand. "No, it's too steep. If I buy from you at fifteen dollars a print, I have to sell for thirty. People will never pay that much for a photograph. Maybe before the Crash. But now it's back to *Oh, photography, horsefeathers! I could do that myself.*"

"And if you drop your prices, they'll believe that more," Berenice says. "Isn't it your job, as a dealer, to educate the public? Guide taste? If *you* believe in a person's work, they will too."

"True. The question is, *do* I believe in it?"

The air between them grows still. To fill the space, she reaches out and begins to gather up the prints. It's a gamble, she knows, but she had to start negotiating high. He's starting a new gallery and needs inventory, so chances are he'll be willing to buy *something.* The question is whether he feels strongly enough about her work, or Atget's, to pay anywhere near her price. And so far, he's keeping his cards hidden.

"I'll leave you to think about it," she says.

"Wait," Levy reaches out, catching her arm. "Let me look at that one again."

It's Atget's picture of the toy store with dolls outside. Some of the dolls' arms have been arranged to look as if they are reaching for something, but their expressions are blank, their glass eyes impenetrable.

Levy leans in. "This one is uncanny."

"Isn't it?" Berenice takes the print from him, tucking it into her case. "Well, Julien, think about it. You know where to reach me."

◆

The following Thursday, at the bottom of the foundation pit of the Rockefeller construction site, it is *cold*. Not just cold, but frigid—the kind of weather that makes you think of ice-hole fishing. Berenice's fingers are almost too frozen click the shutter, but she can't leave yet. The light is so clear today, and water running down the foundation rock has frozen, in places, into gleaming twenty-foot-long icicles. From here she can see some of the work crews above, tiny figures silhouetted against the sky. The scene feels timeless, monumental.

And, too, it has taken her so long to get here, down to the tough backbone of the city, the brown-gray schist on which Manhattan is built. There have been weeks of coming back, chatting with the foreman, bringing chocolate for his daughters. Showing him images, making herself a nuisance. She had to do it, because there was no way she could leave this site out of *Changing New York*. It's too symbolic. The fact that Rockefeller is persisting with his ambitious plan in this economy says something about American grit and resolve.

She positions herself at the side of the pit that will anchor the RCA building, the grand centerpiece of the complex. Gently, she tilts the tripod platform up so that the camera is at a forty-five degree angle. She's decided to fill the bottom two-thirds of the frame with rock and icicles, the top third with the base of the building. The idea is to convey the might and toughness anchoring New York's biggest skyscrapers.

Forty minutes later, she's rubbing her arms and stamping her feet, wondering if the Rockefeller complex will be built around her frozen body. Her ears are tingling; her fingertips are almost completely numb. She's exposed three plates, but can't be sure if they've worked, because her film—

already slow—has seized up with the cold.

She's beginning to pack up when she hears footsteps crunching toward her. Two men are approaching, their thick boots striking the ground in unison. Both tall, one likely in his thirties, the other younger, the older man with close-set eyes and a cleft chin.

Straightening up, she tries to get her numb face to smile. To keep warm, she swings her arms back and forth.

The men come closer, and the older one nods. "Get something?"

"I don't know. I hope so."

"Who ya working for?"

"Myself, right now."

She can tell he doesn't believe her—indeed, even to her it doesn't seem plausible. Taking an even slightly objective view, she'd have to say that what she's doing now looks pretty nuts.

"We thought you were a man. Didn't we, Pete?" He turns to the younger man, who smirks and nods.

"Ah," She breathes out a scrolling white plume that, for a moment, obscures the men. "A lot of people make that mistake."

"A man could sure use the work."

Oh, she thinks with a thud, *so we're here.* Her steaming breath dissipates, revealing the older man's thin lips and mean glare. Squaring her shoulders, she says, "I'm not taking work from anyone. And no one's supporting me. I have to do it myself."

"That's what all you bitches say."

Like the wind, it comes out of nowhere: *slap.* The denigration, the malice. Yet at the same time, she's not shocked. The papers have recently been carrying editorials against working women, imploring them to step down and give their jobs to men. Even unmarried women aren't exempt, it seems. If truly patriotic *they* would get married, stay home and have babies.

Berenice looks down. Anything she says now will likely make things worse, so she bends to the camera, fumbling with the catches to check they're tight. The men stand by, watching. Out of the corner of her eye she can see their breath swirling in front of her. After a moment they move off, then a pebble comes caroming over the ground, almost hitting the leg of her tripod. She hears the rumble of a retreating laugh.

And now her face is completely numb, though whether from cold or outrage is hard to tell. If the threat of hypothermia weren't so strong, she'd linger until she could be sure they'd left the pit. But she can't. She has to get herself out of this blasted place before it freezes over.

At the ladder, she adjusts her equipment. The camera box rests on her back, its strap tight around her chest. As with the descent, she has to hold her tripod in one hand and grip the ladder edge with the other, tilting to the right to maintain her balance. Creeping up, she can't bear to look down. She's dimly aware of men peering over the edge at her, apparently amused by her inchworm-like progress.

But when she gets to the top, an arm with a gloved hand appears, reaching out like Michelangelo's hand of God. She hands it the tripod, which disappears over the edge. She's about to grasp the other side of the ladder when the hand reappears, and with gratitude she takes it, allowing herself to be hauled over the rim. Then she's standing on solid ground on the edge of the chasm, doubled-over, coughing as her savior looks on.

"You're tough," he says, and her breath catches—it's the man who called her *bitch*. Something has changed, though. His voice is conciliatory. She straightens and looks at him, and he puts his palms out in a gesture of contrition. Behind him, half a dozen men huddle around a riveters' fire.

"I'm sorry for down there," he says, "Like to make it up."

"You already did," she says. "You helped me out of the pit."

"The boys and I were thinking you might like a hoist. Get a shot from a crane."

"Really?" Despite the numbness, she feels a surge of excitement. She's been itching to get on a crane for weeks. Is he having her on? His squinty eyes radiate sincerity. He does, genuinely, seem to be offering an olive branch.

"Name's Tom Dwyer," he says, "I operate crane number five."

"Can you hold steady enough for me to get a clear shot? There'd be no point otherwise."

"Think so."

She looks at the men behind him, a couple of whom are watching the exchange. "Dwyer's the best we got," one says.

"All right, then," she says, "I'd like that."

First, though, she must warm up. The men bring her to the fire and give her sugared tea in a mug. She turns, warming herself all around, her extremities gradually thawing. Her throat is so frozen that when she first sips the tea she can't tell if it's hot or cold—but as it slips to her stomach, she feels a delicious heat spread through her, radiating to the tips of her fingers and toes.

At the crane, the men lower the boom with its giant hook and attach the box lift, a flat piece of steel with railings on three sides and, on the other, a chain-link gate. They help her step in, and hand in her equipment before latching the gate. They bring rope so she can tie the tripod legs to the railings, and wait until she's screwed the camera to the platform. "Not gonna go up high," says Dwyer. "Wind's fierce. But we'll get you to the tenth floor at least."

And then she's alone, staring at the skeleton of the building rising on the northwest edge of the site. What a behemoth! Steel beams cross each other, forming an enormous grid that's slashed by diagonals of ropes and pulleys, and in the middle, an open-sided elevator shaft that extends to the highest floor, carrying tin boxes of men up high. If she clears the first few floors and points her camera straight, she'll get something unique, like a modernist painting, all straight lines and diagonals. But instead of being abstract it will document something magnificently man-made.

Behind her, an engine rumbles. The crane has come alive. There's a jitter of nerves and her stomach pulses, releasing a wave of anxiety. But she's excited. She grips the railings as the lift bumps off the ground, then tightens her grip as it sways lightly before stabilizing under her. Cold air buffets her face and she's rising, the ground is falling away and it's as if she's in a hot air balloon. And she laughs, because although she's always dreamed of soaring over fields and streams, this man-made landscape is better. It feels like the heart, the red-hot center of it all.

Up they go, then further, until she can see the foundations of the next building, and beyond that the white confection of St. Patrick's Cathedral, whose neo-gothic spires stand out like lacy tusks.

And then the box creaks to a halt, swaying under her. Turning, she looks into what must be the tenth or eleventh floor, a beehive of steel cubes and diagonal struts. It's blisteringly cold, but that doesn't matter any more because this is the shot she'd imagined, but better. It is gloriously rich, a geometric delight. No one has photographed the city like this before, to her knowledge; no one has seen a building's skeleton as art. If she can get it in focus, she'll have created an enduring image.

She plants her feet firmly on the floor of the lift, checks her balance, then takes an exploratory step to the right, so that she can reach the lens.

She's just figuring out her exposure when there's a crack, followed by a jolt that sends her lunging back to the rails. *What the…*her heart is in her throat, punching a fevered beat. The box lift lurches and tilts, and all she can do is clutch the rails and wait for it to subside. Oh! The building is approaching, receding; the sight stirs a wave of nausea. She squeezes her eyes shut and, clinging on, tries to forget she's a hundred feet in the air.

The box swings out, swings back, slows. After a minute or so it comes back to center. When it is only tipping gently, she dares to open her eyes and loosen her death-grip on the rails. Seeing the building's scaffolding vertically aligned with the lift, she feels relief so strong she could cry.

She has just begun to relax when there's another crack and jolt, and again she's thrown against the rails. This time, the tilting is so bad that the only thing to do is cower in the corner of the box, one arm clamped around the rails, the other shielding her head. *Jesus Jesus fucking Jesus help.* Thankfully the tripod is lashed down, the camera seems safe. She waits, but the insanity continues, the floor rising up, swinging back. It's like the roughest sea crossing, but without any sense of heft under one's feet. The boom swings left to right, the lift torquing so rapidly that there's only one conclusion to draw. She's being shamed, taught a lesson. *You uppity women. You bitches.*

By the time the boom creaks to a stop and the box-lift lowers, it seems she's been up there for a lifetime. Probably it was only five minutes, but without doubt they were the longest of her life. She's had time to plan her last will, ponder her legacy. She's had time to imagine Dwyer strung on a gallows, pleading for his life.

She is shaking uncontrollably as the men run to help her. Even so she waves them off, unties the tripod and hoists the thing over her shoulder, camera and all. She's tempted to swing it at them, to see those complacent faces smashed by wood and metal, but that would be a waste of a good camera. Instead, she musters her dignity and steps out of the lift, trying not to wobble as her feet meet the ground.

"Sorry," says Dwyer, "windy up there."

"Like hell," she says. Giving him a stony glance, she telegraphs that she sees down to the tar pit of his soul. "Like hell, you piece of shit." And she walks off, grasping the tripod to her chest.

◆

Julien Levy calls the next day.

"I've thought about what we discussed," he says, "and I've decided. I'd like to put on a show of the Atget work some time next year."

"You would?" She looks out of the window at the bare tree branches, frowning but feeling vindicated. He's seen the value of the work, which is only right—and perhaps, in an odd way, this is the universe squaring things after her affront at the Rockefeller site the day before.

"Yes. It's different from the other work I'll be showing, but I agree with you. It will give the gallery *gravitas*."

"Well, Julien, this is good news."

"Yes." He clears his throat. "One other thing."

"What's that?"

"I'd like to purchase a portion of the archive from you. But for a different price. I've talked about it with some other dealers, and I think I have a good sense of what the work is worth."

"Really? Who are these dealers?"

"A few people." His voice wavers—he's a bad liar. She has an idea who's behind his waffle, though: Stieglitz. Two years before, when she showed the Atget prints to Stieglitz, the maestro recognized their worth. And he was mad when she wouldn't let him show them.

"What are you proposing?" she asks.

"I'm willing to buy two hundred negatives and three hundred prints from you at two dollars apiece. Also, I know from Man Ray that your printing skills are excellent. If new prints need to be made, I'm prepared to pay you two dollars per print."

"Two dollars!" she sputters. It's an outrage, the work is worth ten times more. At the same time, her mind whirs, doing calculations. A thousand dollars! It could support her for a year if she really eked it out.

"A thousand. It's a nice amount of cash," Levy says, as if reading her mind.

"Not if they're worth a good deal more."

"Eleven hundred, then—but that's my final offer. If you don't want it, take them somewhere else. It won't break my heart. I'm just trying to help out."

"Right," she says. "Like those people who offer to occupy empty offices for free, *just trying to help* the poor owners of the building."

There's a silence on the other end.

"It's not what you wanted," Levy finally says. "I understand. But if you *do* sell them to me, I'll do something else for you."

"What's that?"

"I'll present a solo show of your New York images."

At this, Berenice takes a sharp breath through her nostrils. *Bastard, bastard.* He has her attention now. No one else has offered her a show of any kind—let alone a solo show in an exciting new gallery.

"When?" she asks.

"Next year. When you've had time to build up the work and get yourself some better equipment. For which, I'm guessing a thousand dollars would come in handy?"

Bastard. Skunk. Sonofabitch. She has been outplayed. There's a soft exhalation on the other end and she imagines him licking his lips, metaphorically if not literally. She'd make a resolution similar to the one she made at Stieglitz's gallery—that Levy would never get the Atget work—if it weren't for the fact that she so desperately needs the exposure for herself. And the money.

"I'll think about it," she says.

"Do that," his voice drips with satisfaction. "You know where to reach me."

TWENTY

The Atget show opens in the spring of 1932. Levy has gone overboard with publicity, advertising in top society magazines. As a result, the gallery is full of craggy-faced men and elegant women, whose diamond necklaces and fur coats provide something of a secondary show. *Just as well old man Atget is dead,* Berenice thinks with a smile; *this attention might give him a stroke.*

But as she looks around, she sees that almost nobody is looking at the photographs. Instead people stand in groups, urgently discussing a single subject. Because there is only one subject today, in New York and across the world. A subject big enough that it has eclipsed the economic news.

At eight o'clock the previous evening, Charles Lindbergh's baby son was kidnapped. His whereabouts are still a mystery and the whole world is aflame with speculation. No one can believe that this has happened to the storied aviator and his wife, America's golden couple. Recently, the two had been flying together, charting routes for commercial airlines, launching a new age of air travel. They were skilled and glamorous, seemingly untouchable.

"...a ladder on the property," she overhears, and, "...helper on the inside, they think." A matron, double chin wobbling, warbles over a champagne flute, "Well, *I'm* not surprised. I don't trust my staff one bit!" Others purse their lips and nod, and Berenice bristles at how quickly the servant class has been vilified.

For her, the shock is compounded by another more personal loss. Simply-mounted, in thin black frames, the Atget prints look fine on the wall—but of the forty-five photographs on show, none belong to her. They are the property of the Julien Levy Gallery now. Other than her own images, they are the closest things she has to children. And now, like children, they have passed out of her hands, to be launched on their journey—not kidnapped, but appropriated at a criminally low price. She hopes Levy will steward them well through the art world's capricious currents.

"Berenice!" She turns to see Jane Heap, an editor whose portrait she shot in Paris. As masculine as most of the men in the room, Jane is dressed in a white tuxedo jacket and a black bow tie, with a Cossack-style fur hat set at an angle.

"Jane!" They embrace, kissing on both cheeks.

"I'm only in New York for a week, but I thought I'd come see what Julien is up to. When I heard the name Atget, I thought you must be behind it."

"Far behind, I fear. I sold some works to Julien. He's done the rest."

"He's a lucky boy."

"Yes. Though I'm not sure he knows it."

They look at the nearest photograph, of a sweeping marble staircase with an ornate wrought-iron banister. It is simple but artfully composed, leading the eye from the bottom left of the frame up a sensuous curve to the top.

"Quite a day," Jane remarks.

Berenice nods. "It feels personal, doesn't it? As if a family member has been taken. And yet there's part of me that's excited to see how the story develops, as if it were a movie. Is that terrible?"

"*Au contraire, chérie*. It *is* a movie. The question is, who's directing—Frank Capra or Alfred Hitchcock?"

Later, when Jane leaves the gallery with a pretty young woman in tow, Berenice has to smile—the woman can reel them in—though she also wonders if Jane realizes the danger. Since the Crash, America has re-discovered its puritanical roots. Social conservatives and soapbox moralists have risen like phoenixes from the ashes of the collapsed economy, and people are listening. Priests now sermonize—in all seriousness—that the Crash was divine retribution for the turpitude of the Twenties. The old freedoms are gone—the pansy clubs, so cheerful and popular, have vanished. Berenice has even heard of men being rounded up and taken to fruitcake factories upstate, where rumors have it they will be zapped with electricity or—god help them—lobotomized.

Luckily, her own activity in that area has tapered off. Once or twice, she has been reckless enough to leave a bar or party with someone, but mostly she doesn't take the risk. How could it be worth it? Sometimes, thinking about the early days with Tylia, she's beset by a loneliness so raw and piercing that she has to moan, not knowing if she will ever love that way again. But she tries to forget about it, and channels her energies into her work instead.

Later in the evening, she's standing by Atget's picture of the Passage du Pont Neuf when Alfred Stieglitz approaches her. She hasn't seen him since she took the work to show him at An Intimate Gallery, and he looks older, with deep wrinkles around his eyes. But the eyes themselves haven't changed. They're still black, with a hint of imperious anger.

"Good evening, Miss Abbott."

"Mr. Stieglitz. How nice to see you."

"You had a hand in this exhibit, I heard."

"Somewhat. The work is exquisite, don't you think?"

Stieglitz directs his eyes to the photograph on the wall, which he seems to regard with a mixture of disdain and hostility. "For period illustration, it serves well enough," he says.

Berenice feels the sting, as she was supposed to. Squaring her shoulders, she faces him. "Strange you should say that. You see, for me, Atget is the preeminent photographer of his generation. A consummate artist, yet compassionate too."

"Compassion?" Stieglitz raises an eyebrow. "That has no bearing on art."

"Really? We're so different. You see, *I* see compassion as the starting point for all significant works of art."

"Hmmph." Stieglitz peers at her, then apparently decides not to pursue the matter. "What of your work? Julien tells me you're making a study of New York."

"I am." She feels a flash of irritation toward Julien for gabbing about her work, and girds herself for the scorn Stieglitz is about to pour on her, for her work's triteness and lack of spirituality.

She's not prepared for what he says next.

"I've been making some photographs of the city myself. The skyscrapers, the construction. The spirit of modernity—such possibility! I like to think of my photographs as grasping the essence of the age."

He smiles, and Berenice feels a shiver of unease. She has seen Stieglitz's earlier images of the city, when he was in pictorialist mode: hazy reflections in puddles and soft puffs of smoke floating across tall buildings. *Those* don't scare her. But if it's true, as people have told her, that Stieglitz has abandoned his pictorialist aesthetic for a more modernist look, then wouldn't his images compete with hers? She's so disturbed by this that she can't speak—which Stieglitz clearly senses, because he gives her a haughty nod and drifts back into the crowd.

Curse the man! Was he put on earth to make her life difficult? She's heard he's about to launch a new, bigger gallery, which will be a perfect place for him to showcase his work. She looks at the wall, at Atget's photograph of a street in the *Troisième*, and sighs. Life in Paris was so much easier.

At the end of the evening, when only a dozen or so people are still milling around the gallery, she approaches Levy.

"Julien, congratulations, you did a swell job. This was a knockout opening."

"I'm not sure. We got the crowd, but no sales. Not a single wallet opened. Everyone was too obsessed with Lindbergh."

"Really? Well don't worry, the reviews will be great."

"I can't eat reviews." He looks at her, his brow furrowed under smooth brown hair. "I hope I didn't make a mistake buying this work from you, Berenice. I need sell-out shows, that's what makes a gallery's reputation. Not to mention that I was expecting a return on my investment."

"Give it a few days," she says. She can feel a hole in her stocking, just above the heel, that wasn't there when she left home—and suddenly she feels weary. "You haven't forgotten the other part of our deal?"

"Of course not. I said I'll give you a show and I will. I keep my promises."

From the corner of her eye, Berenice catches sight of Stieglitz's nimbus of white hair. He's leaning in to examine Atget's photograph of a women's lingerie shop. The sight produces anxiety. "When, Julien?"

"Next year."

"I want it to be in the beginning of the year."

"Really!" He leans against a radiator and laughs. "Well, my dear, don't stand around—you'd better get to work! A show at the Levy Gallery is an occasion, you know!"

The laughter, and his loud voice, cause a few people to turn and look. Berenice sees Stieglitz regarding them with interest from beneath his bushy brows, and thinks she sees him and Levy exchange a smile.

Flooded with irritation, she turns to Julien. "I assure you," she tells him, "I do nothing *but* work." And with a nod, she turns and leaves the gallery.

◆

A week later, she goes to photograph the director of a map-making company. The offices are in Chelsea, rather insalubriously jammed between a plumbing-supplies store and a meatpacking facility.

She's now done more than twenty assignments for Luce, and thanks her lucky stars for the day she decided to write to Maggie Bourke-White. The *Fortune* relationship almost nosedived, but since re-photographing Henry Voss with his globes, she's figured out how to handle these stuffy businessmen. The key is to come at them like a British nanny, with a base of esteem peppered over with bossiness. Because, as powerful as these men are, deep down they're all little boys waiting to be told what to do.

But when she's shown into the office of Roderick Gedney, of Gedney & Sons, his warm smile disarms her. He looks no older than thirty, and is photogenic, with an arresting combination of blue eyes, clipped dark beard and leathery face. Moreover, he seems to treat her as a human being. He has his secretary bring in coffee while he tells her about his grandfather, an Irish immigrant who started making maps as an addition to his printing business.

"It took forever back then—no aerial photography, of course. The labeling conventions were hit or miss. When I started out here, road maps that existed for New York State made no distinction between paved and unpaved roads. A guy could take his girl out for a country drive and find himself in the middle of a field full of cows."

"I guess that could work out, with the right girl," Berenice says. She can't help but stare at the walls behind Gedney, which are covered in framed maps of New York and Connecticut.

"I see you're looking at our map of the Adirondacks. Fine, isn't it? Made history, that one. The highways were unnumbered there until '26. We numbered 'em, put the signs up, then Albany took the system over. I drove the roads myself, supervising. Not to be too grand, but it kind of makes you feel like you have a claim on the place."

"I can see that," Berenice says. The idea of traveling an open road, organizing and mapping, seems thrilling. Claim, tame and name: isn't that what American history has been about?

Even after she has set up her equipment and has started to pose him, Gedney continues the conversation.

"Have you traveled much in the United States, Miss Abbott?"

"Not really."

"Then you've missed out. It's a grand place, this country of ours. There are so many climates, from arid desert to lush tropics. And all different terrains."

"What's your favorite?"

"That's a hard one. The Florida Everglades are unique, and I adore the ruggedness of coastal Maine. But if I had to choose one place, I'd pick the Grand Canyon. You can't match it for majesty. Experiencing a sunset in the inner canyon is about as close to a religious experience as I've come."

"Could you hold that pose for a minute? Look at the window. That's it…"

She likes the expression in his eyes, their spark and enthusiasm. Posed under the map of upstate New York, he looks like a boy scout who's happened into a suit and beard. She doesn't mess with the set-up much, she knows a good portrait when she sees one. For once, someone has made her job easy.

"Would you like to see our printing press?" he asks, and although it has no part in her assignment she finds that yes, she would. Gedney takes her to the other end of the building, where machines hiss and clank, spitting maps of Connecticut into a series of wire trays. The maps are wet, and Berenice is fascinated by the slick wiggles of drying ink. They're at once delicate and authoritative, like tattooed skin or a musical score.

"This must keep you and your father busy," she says.

"Well, one of us—my father died two years ago. Don't worry," he swoops in to save her, "I was the product of a second marriage, he was elderly when he had me. He got the son he wanted. But it meant he left me in charge pretty young."

"I admire you, Mr. Gedney," she says sincerely. "You must have many talents."

"Right back at you, Miss Abbott."

And so, when the next day brings a note from Gedney inviting her to dinner that night, she surprises herself by saying yes. A decent dinner with good conversation—she's been starving for it. If he's after more than that—well then, she'll put him straight. Intriguingly, he has instructed her to "dress for adventure," and after deliberating, she chooses a khaki skirt, flat shoes and a crisp white shirt.

At five o'clock, Rod, as he asks her to call him ("Roderick sounds like my great uncle") picks her up in his Stutz coupe, a gorgeous long-bodied car with leather seats. She eases into place beside him, thrilled by the soft leather and polished mahogany dashboard. She has never touched a car this luxurious.

"Should I be worried?" she shouts as they head north through Harlem. "Are we going to end up in a field full of cows?"

"Perhaps!" he shouts back. "Do you mind?"

"Not really!"

"I didn't think so! You seem like a girl who can hold her own."

In fact, though, they end up in the Pocantico Hills, a wooded area outside Sleepy Hollow, where Washington Irving's headless horseman famously galloped. A frisky spring breeze buffets them. After parking the car by a trailhead, Rod takes a picnic hamper from the trunk and swings it in his hand.

"I can't take you to the Grand Canyon, but at least I can show you some of your own state."

They hike up to a vantage point where you can see the Hudson River scrolling into the distance, all the way down to the city and up to the valley that bears its name. It's a view Berenice has never seen despite her years in New York, and she finds it lovely. Shimmering, the river winds through the valley like a scarf shot through with silver thread. Lifting her head, she closes her eyes and lets the cool air kiss her skin.

"Imagine coming here with your Wappinger tribe in the sixteenth century," Rod says behind her. "No one for miles around, and everything you could want within a mile. Good soil, deer and elk to hunt, fish practically jumping out of the river. Edible plants. And the view."

Berenice opens her eyes and, shading them with a hand, looks at the view. "Then we came and took it all from them," she remarks.

"True. Although unless your ancestors were Dutch, you needn't blame yourself much. It was the wars with the Dutch that finished off a lot of the Wappinger tribes."

She turns to him, admiring. "How do you know so much?"

"I read."

"I suppose you know which plants are edible, too."

"Of course." Grinning, he sprints off and plucks something from a nearby bush. When he returns to her side, he's holding a sprig of leaves with a clump of purple berries. "Elder," he says. "Delicious *and* medicinal. The Indians used the berries to treat everything from colds to paralysis."

Tentatively, she takes a few berries from the bunch. They taste sharp and intense, like concentrated blueberries.

"Well, aren't you just a regular Natty Bumpo?" she says.

Inside the picnic hamper there's a plaid blanket, a baked lobster, a jar of potato salad, dill pickles, and a chilled bottle of champagne. The lid of the hamper is cleverly arranged with china plates, wine glasses, cloth napkins and silverware.

"Thank goodness—I think it survived," Rod says. "I was worried. I had my housekeeper chill everything this morning."

"Fancy. I rather thought you'd be shooting us some wild duck and roasting them over an open fire."

"Ah yes. Well, confession: I'm a lousy shot. And anyway, why live rough if you don't have to?"

Why indeed. Looking out at the sunset over the Hudson, with a plate of lobster and potato salad beside her and a glass of fizzing champagne in hand, Berenice wonders if the moneyed classes know how good they have it. Of all the meals she's had in her life, this must be one of the most lovely. If it's undercut with a little guilt—that she's eating lobster while people around the block from her building are shivering in their cardboard shacks—she doesn't let the feeling take over. Tomorrow, no doubt, she'll be back to her Campbell's soup.

When the champagne bottle is drained, the two of them lie on the blanket, looking at the stars. Rod tells her about his ambition to travel through China, and his dream of mapping Alaska. She tells him about the overwhelming scale of *Changing New York*.

"There's so much to photograph! It's a subject crying out for attention, but no one has done it yet."

"So, Miss Abbott, you're a pioneer."

"Maybe." She tips her head to look at him. "It's just what I'm driven to do."

"I think you're very brave."

"You do?"

"Sure. You could follow someone else's path along the water, but you're headed up into the mountains instead."

She isn't surprised when he takes her hand—it's that kind of moment— but she's shocked by her own lack of urge to pull away. His hand is warm, solid, and although the gesture is intimate, it doesn't seem to preface any kind of monkey business. It's just a sign of fellowship. He's an unusual man, she decides—gentle and thoughtful, yet too masculine for a homosexual. She can't quite make him out.

They lie there holding hands, and she feels stupidly grateful. She's been lonely since leaving the Hotel des Artistes. Very few friends have come to visit her in her shabby walk-up, mostly because she's been too embarrassed to invite them. Plus, everyone is working hard to survive.

After a few minutes, Rod pulls his hand away and begins pointing out constellations. Of course he knows all the names, and she enjoys hearing the Latin words roll off his tongue. *Cepheus. Camelopardalis.*

When he drops her back at her apartment, he seems suddenly nervous. "Do you think we might see each other again?" he asks.

"I'd like that."

"You would?" His body relaxes. "Swell."

"Swell," she echoes.

"Berenice—" he says earnestly, and she leans toward him, prepared to hazard a friendly kiss. But instead he lifts his right hand off the wheel and extends it to her, and they shake, with what seems like strange formality after their intimacy in the hills.

"Good night, then."

"Good night."

Intrigued, she watches from the stoop as the Stutz roars around the corner.

TWENTY-ONE

After that, it seems easy to slip into a pattern where she and Rod see each other once a week, at least. They roam all over the city, eating dumplings in Chinatown and knishes on the Lower East Side. They visit Nellie Bly's grave in the Bronx and see the Marx Brothers' film *Animal Crackers*, which is lightweight and ludicrous, a perfect antidote to the times. Leaving the theater, she and Rod keep repeating, "Ever since I met you, I've swept you off my feet."

One night they go to the Savoy Ballroom, where, with some effort, Berenice manages to turn one of Rod's two left feet into an acceptable right. Afterward they drive back to her apartment, and on a whim she pulls him in and closes the door.

They've known each other for three months now, but still, there has been nothing more than the occasional peck on the cheek. He seems to see her as an older sister, someone to run around with and have fun—which suits her fine. At times, she imagines what would happen if he *did* make a move, and though mostly she sees herself rebuffing him, there are times when another door opens. She imagines the feel of his beard on her face, his hands on her breasts—and it makes her feel warm and confused.

"Hold on," she says, "let me get the mail." But as soon as she unlocks the mailbox, she wishes she hadn't. For there they are, stiff as soldiers: today's thick envelopes from the Upper East Side. They've been coming in a stream, thirty-four so far, all rejections. Her expectations for these last three are low.

Inside the apartment, she smiles at Rod's earnest attempts to compliment the room. She's past noticing her surroundings any more, but with him standing there in his English suit, she sees the place afresh. God, but those curvy beige lines on the wallpaper are hideous! And there's a water stain on the floor near the radiator that seems to be spreading more every day, turning the wood almost black.

"I'll get some water," she says.

"You're not going to open those?" He nods, and she realizes she still has the letters clamped under her arm. She puts them on the table.

"No. I know what they say."

"Really? I'm finding out a lot tonight. You're not only an ace dancer but a psychic too. Sure you won't? They look like invitations to swell parties."

"Death notices, more like."

"What do you mean?"

She looks at him, unsure for a moment whether to share this less-than-flattering side of her life. But his warm smile disarms her, and she spills the story of how she went to see Hardinge Scholle, director of the Museum of the City of New York. "Scholle likes my work, but doesn't have money to support it at the moment. He suggested I appeal directly to the museum's trustees. Perhaps my letter sounded cheeky, or they felt ambushed—I don't know, but they've all rejected me. And it's damaged my reputation with Scholle, too. Now I smell of failure."

Rod comes to the table, where he stops in front of her and takes both her hands. "You don't know that all of them have rejected you."

"The numbers aren't on my side."

"Why not open these now, while I'm here? If it's good news, I can celebrate with you. If it's bad, you won't have to bear it alone."

"Oh, honey," she says, "you're sweet."

"I mean it. I'd like to support you in this. What are friends for, if not to be around for hard times?"

He's still holding her right hand, and when she tries to slip away he holds on, forcing an answer. "All right," she says, "but I'm getting whisky for this."

A few minutes later they sit side by side, the letters in front of them, then bring their tumblers together, clink, and take slugs. Berenice tries to decide which letter looks worst, but they're all of a piece: the embossed home addresses, the sweeping cursive of her name.

"Here goes," she says, slicing open a letter. She holds it to one side for a moment, then puts it in front of Rod. "See? It's as I thought. Mrs. Abeling thinks the museum already has a fine collection of photographs of New York City."

"Well, I know nothing about art, but clearly Mrs. Abeling is a horse's ass," he says, making her laugh out loud. He was right, it's better to have company for this. They lift their glasses, clink, drink again. She feels the burn of the whisky in her throat, the warmth as it slides to her stomach.

"Want me to open the next one?" Rod asks, and she nods—why not? He takes the letter-opener and slices through paper, then takes out the letter. "Mr. Jeremiah Payne admires your ambition. However, he advises that you apply for funds to institutions rather than individuals."

"Because naturally, I haven't done that already." Under the table, Berenice's hand trembles. She can't help feeling each new rejection as a fresh wound. "Oh, what's the use?" she says, beginning to rise. "The last one will be the same."

"No," Rod catches her elbow and pulls her back. "Remember what was at the bottom of Pandora's box. Let's finish what we started, okay? Take a big slug for this one, all right? Dutch courage." He brings his glass to hers. This time, the whisky has a sour taste that makes her lips pucker. At the same time, she's feeling the effects of the previous two glugs—an all-over loosening, as if she's made of soft wax.

"Shall I do it?" Rod asks, and she nods. His large, slim hands slit the envelope precisely, and as he draws the letter out, she closes her eyes. Though she's almost certain what it says, there's a thread of hope—just as there has been for the other thirty-six. She waits, not daring to breathe, as Rod reads it.

"Berenice," he says gently, "my dear. I'm afraid it's a no."

No. She sees them then, a portrait gallery of wealthy New Yorkers, like the men she shoots for *Fortune.* All pointing, laughing. *How could you think we'd support you?* And then the remark of Man Ray's comes to her: *You're still just a little girl from the Midwest.*

She opens her eyes. "I've made a perfect fool of myself."

"No. How could you think that?"

"I have," she says. "You don't know. God." She puts her face in her hands, feeling tears gathering in the corners of her eyes. How humiliating—and now on top of everything, she's about to cry in front of Rod!

"Berenice," he says, "my dear. Berenice." He puts an arm around her and draws her to him, kissing the crown of her head. "You're going to be all right, do you hear me? This doesn't mean anything. It's a few stuffed shirts who wouldn't know art if they tripped over it on the street."

Her nose is in his shirt, just below the collar. "Do you think so?"

"Of course. Of course." He lifts a hand to brush hair from her eye, then kisses her forehead, her eyebrow, the bridge of her nose. It seems like a benediction, a mark of faith. She holds her breath as he goes on, softly kissing her closed eyelid, then her cheekbone. "May I?" he murmurs.

By way of an answer, she tilts her face up and their lips meet—his are warm, tasting of butterscotch and whisky. His beard rubs her face and it's as she imagined, scratchy but soft, not entirely unpleasant.

Tentatively, she parts his lips with her tongue and explores his mouth, the uneven teeth, the ridges of his upper palate, the wet recesses of his cheeks. That isn't unpleasant either. Beneath her chest she can feel his heart beating, so fast that it seems as if it might take flight. As the kiss goes on he gets bolder, reaching deep with his tongue, his hands gripping the back of her head—and she's pulled along, excited by his ardor.

When at last they detach, he looks at her in wonder. "I thought you weren't attracted to me."

"And *I* thought you weren't attracted to *me*."

"Oh, Berenice," he shakes his head, "I've wanted you since the first day we met."

Something about this is more intoxicating than the whisky. It's flattering, of course, but it's not just that—she finds his old-fashioned restraint arousing. It makes her feel wolfish, as if she could devour him, whiskers and all.

She looks into his sapphire eyes. "I have to tell you something. You see, in the past—" she pauses and sighs, unable to say it. "I'm thirty-four."

"I'm twenty-eight. So?"

"So?" Berenice echoes. The room suddenly feels hot, her clothes an encumbrance. Rising, she pulls him from the table and leads him to the bed, where she practically shoves him down. And then, for a while, they're too busy kissing and unbuttoning to talk.

"Are you sure?" he asks when they're naked, and she nods—for she is, at that moment, sure as could be. When he enters her, she almost cries—not from pain, but surprise. This is unlike those hurried, desultory nights she endured with men in Paris. It is a proper coupling, born of affection and respect.

In the morning, things are less clear-cut. She lies in bed, aching and unsure, wondering if she's just destroyed their friendship. He *is*, by now, a dear friend—but is he more? He was last night, for sure—but how much was that about easing her distress?

At least Rod isn't there to witness her confusion. He went home, saying that he should get in before his housekeeper. But if he's not there in person, his essence lingers. She can smell his cologne on the sheets, feel the depression where he lay. She can feel where his beard rasped against her skin, leaving it raw...

She gets up feeling muddled, and goes about her day out of sorts. Developing film in the darkroom, she drifts in and out of thoughts, some of which involve the hollows and curves of Tylia's soft body. She thinks about Rod's beard and mouth, how they resemble a certain part of the female anatomy. And then she feels so embarrassed that she has to hide her head in her hands.

In the afternoon, she tries to make some prints of the Seaport, but finds herself too distracted to do it properly. She's half-napping at five when there's a knock at the door, making her jump: Rod? Her first impulse is to cower and hide. But as she wraps her arms around her head, the knocking turns to pounding—surely he wouldn't do that. She goes to the door and lifts the porthole cover.

"Who is it?"

"Package, ma'am."

It does, indeed, seem to be a deliveryman holding a box.

"I don't think that's for me."

"Are you Berenice Abbott?"

"Yes."

"Then it's for you, lady."

He must be about forty, heavyset. Cautiously, she opens the door. The man's face is the color of a baked ham and he has raised veins on his temples. The sweat gilding his forehead says he has no business climbing four flights of stairs.

"What is it?"

"Damned if I know. Sign here."

She digs a couple of quarters out of her purse and gives them to him, takes the box and closes the door. At the kitchen table, she slips a knife blade between the lid of the box and its underside. Inside is a leather case with the name *Weston Electric* stamped into the leather, and she breathes in sharply—could it be? She has coveted one of these ever since they came on the market the year before. Gently, she eases off the cover and there it is, with its three dials: the Model 617, the most advanced exposure meter in the world. So elegant and detailed—such an improvement on her battered old Avo!

She's so overcome that it takes a minute before she sees the note underneath.

Drawing it out, she feels the heavyweight paper and sees the sloping letters of his handwriting.

May this help you sketch with light, though perhaps not as much light as you've brought me. Waiting for your call. Thinking about you—R.

Her fingers tremble and the note flutters in the light. For a moment she feels abashed, like a kept woman. Is he trying to bind her to him with fancy gifts? But then she looks at the note again: *Waiting for your call.* No. He's not assuming anything. He just wants to show that he understands her, and knows she'd rather have this than a dozen boxes of roses.

"Oh, Rod," she says, "you dolt." In her hand, the light meter is solid and heavy as a rock. She can't wait to take it out to the streets.

TWENTY-TWO

"What about moving the skyscrapers there?" Berenice says. She points to a wall near the back of the gallery. For some reason, Julien hasn't assigned any of the photographs to it although it's the best wall in the place, the longest and tallest.

He shakes his head. "I have a surprise for over there."

"What is it?"

"If I told you it wouldn't be a surprise, would it?" He studiously avoids her gaze. "You'll have to trust me."

"How mysterious," she says, thinking, *How irritating*. What does he have up his sleeve? Perhaps he's gotten a billboard-sized blow-up made of one of her prints, or had her name printed in giant letters? She hopes he understands how much there is riding for her on this, her first solo show in New York. She's been driving herself crazy for the last few months, putting in eighteen-hour days in order to make her prints as perfect as possible.

They continue to work, moving photographs around until they find an arrangement that makes sense. By the time Berenice leaves the gallery it's nine o'clock and she's famished. It isn't until she's in bed, on the way to falling asleep, that she remembers Julien's evasiveness about the big wall. She falls asleep imagining a photograph of her face floating over her picture of the city lit up at night, the two of them merging so that her dark eyes are filled with the lights from a dozen tiny windows…

And then, impossible as it seems, it is the day of the opening. The morning drags, full of boring but necessary business like leg-shaving. By contrast the afternoon flies, as if she's caught in a river whooshing her forward. Her stomach feels weak. She hasn't eaten all day, for nerves. Who will come, what will they say? Will critics be there, and if so, what will they write?

"Wow," Rod says when she opens the door at six o'clock. "You'll steal attention from the photographs."

"Don't be silly," she replies—though she *is* quite proud of what she's put together. It took two hours to get ready. She's bathed and scented, and is wearing a fitted green dress over a flattening bra and hose. The dress is high-necked in front and lower in the back; its skirt hugs her hips and ends above her ankles. Her hair is finger-waved against her head. She has never felt so feminine in her life.

"I'm serious," Rod holds her by one hand at arm's length so that she can do a pirouette. "You're a vision."

"You're not so bad, either." He's wearing a black tuxedo with satin lapels, and a bow tie that matches his sapphire eyes. With the show to prepare, she's barely seen him in weeks, and as usual after an absence, she takes her emotional temperature. *Am I happy? Glad to see him?* Pretty much, she decides. For sure, the relationship doesn't have the passion she knew with Tylia, but it has something else: a lived-in quality that she likes.

She wobbles out of the door on her heels and Rod takes her arm. He has hired a driver for the evening, and it feels odd to step into a black DeSoto instead of his Stutz, sitting in the back instead of up front. The leather seat is slippery and Rod puts his arm around her, holding her close so that her dress doesn't send her sliding into the door.

"Don't be nervous," he says.

"I'm not," she says. "I actually feel quite poised."

But when they arrive at the gallery, she gets such an intense rush of panic that she can hardly breathe. The opening has only just started and already there's a crush of people, so many bodies that the artwork is barely visible. There are tuxedoes, fur jackets, dresses with gold lamé collars and chiffon cap sleeves. Voices are raised, people laughing and shouting to be heard. Briefly, Berenice closes her eyes and opens them again to check she's not hallucinating. Is it possible—can all these people be here for her?

Julien greets them at the door, looking sleek and smug as a fox. When he sees Rod's arm slung across her shoulder he regards Berenice with interest, a question hovering in his eyes. She ignores it and introduces Rod as her good friend, enjoying the perplexed look on Julien's face.

"How's it looking, Julien? Who's here so far?"

"A few collectors, a lot of newspapermen. Some major artists. Edward Hopper. Aaron Douglas. Alfred Stieglitz."

"Oh," Berenice takes a deep breath in. The names are impressive, but she can't help but droop at the mention of Stieglitz. She can see him to the left, hands behind his back, leaning forward to peer at her close-up of the George Washington Bridge. Detestable man! He's probably thinking that *he* had the idea first, but hasn't gotten around to executing it.

"Come," Rod squeezes her arm, "let's get you a drink."

"A drink, yes. See you later, Julien." And she allows herself to be propelled further into the room.

That's when she gets the sense that something is off. People's voices are high with excitement, their body language too eager. It's as if there's a movie star in the room, or a gangster. And this energy is being directed at someone—or something—across the room. Whereas she, the photographer, might as well be invisible.

And then she sees the big wall, and feels the blood drain from her face.

"What—" she begins, then stops. Her heels tip, almost capsizing her. Thank heavens for Rod's arm.

The wall has been painted red, and four huge paintings have been mounted on it. She can only see half of one and a few details of others, but it's enough. The garish colors, the otherworldly backgrounds and dissonant objects... she has seen this style of work before, in Paris. Surrealism! It's painting's new sensation, the bastard child of Dada and Freud, in which dream-like fantasia is painted in hyper-real style.

And now she feels as if she's in a dream herself—or a nightmare. How can Julien have sprung this on her? Or have thought it made sense to put her photographs in the same room as these gaudy, attention-sucking works?

"What *are* those?" Rod asks. "I thought it was your show."

"So did I." She stands on tiptoe, craning to get a view of the artist—and when she sees him, her body goes rigid. It's the young Spaniard, Dalí. The most flamboyant and outrageous of the surrealist bunch.

Dalí! Around Paris, he was known for his crazy antics. Once he pissed into a hostess's fireplace; another time, he presented a museum curator with a dead mouse in a box. Breton had thought him promising, though she recalls overhearing him tell Man Ray that the Spaniard was "a sick little fuck. Told me that as a child, he'd blind frogs and see how long they could live."

She turns to Rod. "I need to ask Julien something. Go get us some drinks and meet me back here, will you?"

Back at the door she bears down on Julien, trying to control her fury. "Julien, why didn't you tell me?"

"Huh?" He blinks. "You mean about the paintings? Ah, yes—well, I would have, but I didn't want to get your hopes up. It almost didn't come off."

She blinks. "You thought I'd be *glad*?"

"Of course! It's a coup. Think what this association does for you! He's the talk of Paris, and this is the first time his work has been seen over here. While people are waiting to see his work, they'll be looking at yours!"

Berenice looks at him, speechless: is he really suggesting she's there to pick up the crumbs from Dalí's audience? "But…" she stammers, "I don't want to be associated with surrealism."

"Come," he slings an arm across her shoulder, leading her away from the door, "you're so serious all the time! Art can't be all purity and worthiness. People want to be seduced, given a show. You've got to draw them in with some razzle-dazzle before you bludgeon them with solemnity."

"You think my work is solemn?" She sucks in a breath. "You think it's boring?"

"Don't put words in my mouth. You've made real strides and I'm happy to have your show here. It's just that I was talking with Alfred—"

"Stieglitz?" Roughly, she pushes his arm off her shoulder.

"Yes, Stieglitz. He's wanted to bring the surrealists over for a few years, but since he's only showing American art these days, he couldn't do it himself. He put me in touch with them, and then I got this chance with Dalí and seized it."

It is all, suddenly, very predictable. Stieglitz hates her; he is threatened by her work. He can't even let her have a show on her own.

"But I was here yesterday," she says in a small voice. "You could have told me."

"I'm sorry. The paintings only came in from New Jersey last night. It was touch and go the whole way."

They have moved far enough into the room that she can see half of one of the paintings, in which two pocket watches, rendered as flaccid as laundry, flop over a tree and a box. And there is a glimpse of another painting in which a naked woman's torso seems to be disemboweled and bleeding, except that instead of inner organs she has luxuriant red roses. Both painted with masterful technique, they could be Renaissance icons—except, of course, for their bizarre subject matter. What chance does her work have against this riot of color and sensationalism? How can she begin to hold her own?

And then she sees Dalí himself, in the middle of a group of people, smiling and preening, holding something that, as she looks more closely, appears to be a raw cauliflower. There are reporters all around, avidly listening and scribbling as a woman translates his *bon mots* into English. Someone must have asked if he paints from life, for the woman says, "Mr. Dalí does the opposite. He paints a portrait and the subject then grows to resemble it." Laughter rings out, and Berenice is amazed that they can be taken in by this facile showmanship. *Is this what art is now*, she wonders, *a dog-and-pony show? Should I go to the other side of the room and dance the Charleston?* But it's no use. Even if she were willing to play the game, she doesn't have the charisma to pull it off.

Perplexed, she looks around for Rod but doesn't see him. He must be in the crush of people at the bar. She needs him, badly, to replenish her reserves of self-esteem, but if *that's* not possible, she should at least get away from Julien. "Excuse me," she tells him, "I'm going to see what's happening over there."

She's moving across the room when she's intercepted by a man who looks vaguely familiar. "Berenice! Do you remember me?"

"I'm sorry, I don't…"

"Holger Cahill," he says. "We met at the apartment on MacDougal Street."

Now she remembers the oval face, the green eyes. And something else comes back to her. "That ghastly psyching party! But you didn't have a mustache then."

"And you weren't a photographer. What happened to the sculpture?"

"I turned out to be better at sculpting with light." Still unnerved by her conversation with Julien, she scrutinizes his kind face. "Tell me, what do you think of these paintings?"

Cahill glances at the red wall. "They intrigue me," he says, "which doesn't mean I like them. I would never have put them in the same room as your photographs."

"Thank you." She clasps his hand, remembering how he offered to consider her for Sloan's group. What a compliment that was! It makes her wonder what would have happened if she'd stayed in New York. Perhaps she would never have touched a camera!

"Cahill!" Rod is suddenly there, a drink in either hand.

"Gedney! What brings you here?" It turns out they have mutual friends, and they're soon chatting about an acquaintance in Dobbs Ferry. After a while, Berenice drifts over to her photographs. If she's going to listen in on a conversation, it might as well be one about her work.

She's standing by her photograph of a rope-seller's shop when she sees Alfred Stieglitz weaving across the room, making his way to her. For a moment she's tempted to dart away, but then she chides herself. Better to stand tall and face him with dignity.

He stops in front of her, his mustache quivering. "Miss Abbott. You look different this evening. Quite—" he pauses, considering his words, "elegant."

"Thank you. I made an effort for what I *thought* was going to be my first solo show."

Stieglitz blinks from behind his glasses, then bares his yellowing teeth in a little smile. "Julien didn't mention the Dalís?"

"No. Strange, isn't it? I understand you were the one who suggested he bring the work over."

"I might have put him in touch with some people. We're dealers with similar interests—we often converse." He looks over her shoulder, at the photograph of the rope shop. "European artists are doing all the exciting work. The past doesn't hold them. They're constantly remaking the world."

"Yet you've dedicated your new gallery to American art," she says tartly. "A strange choice for someone who thinks it's so stagnant."

She faces him, hoping he can't detect the frantic beat of her heart. Stieglitz's neck tightens and his nostrils flare, like a bull who's seen the matador's cloak. In a tone bright with anger he says, "The artists I represent have worked in Europe. They have been influenced by styles over there. They're taking that influence and creating a new American art that is bold, daring—there is nothing safe about it, nothing at all!" And with that, he turns and walks away.

Berenice's heart is still pounding when Rod approaches, holding her drink. "Oops! Looks like you need this."

"Bless you." She takes the glass and drains it, even though it's cheap white wine that burns her throat.

Just then, a high-pitched *ting!* reverberates around the room. Julien is standing on a platform near the Dalí paintings, tapping a spoon against a glass. People's heads swivel and the chatter dies down.

"I must say, it's an honor to see you all," the gallerist begins. "As the owner here, I constantly strive to provoke and innovate. That's why I decided to contrast Berenice Abbott's simple black and white photography with Salvador

Dalí's inventive surrealism. Ladies and gentlemen, I must inform you that you are here at a historic moment. It's the first time paintings from the surrealist movement have been seen on our shores. The Julien Levy Gallery has brought you the wave of the future."

Applause breaks out, and people murmur appreciatively. Julien holds up his hands for silence. "And now, I'd like to invite each of the artists up here to say a few words, beginning with Miss Abbott."

Berenice clutches Rod's arm, alarmed. At no time in the last few months has Julien mentioned making a speech at the opening. How can he put this on her now? Of course, he can't know how deeply she dreads public speaking, but even so…she glances at Rod, who must see the terror in her eyes because he gives her a smile that says, *you can do this.*

Shaky on her heels, she makes her way to the platform where Julien is standing. He reaches out a hand to help her up and she takes it, giving him a withering look. But he doesn't seem to notice. "Don't take too long," he whispers before retreating.

Berenice looks at the crowd, wobbling, wishing there was something to hold onto. The sea of faces makes her feel dizzy, and there's a ringing in her ears. She sees Stieglitz hovering at the crowd's edge, a craggy vulture looking for his next piece of prey.

"In 1929 I came back to New York from Paris," she says, and her voice emerges as a squeak, making a woman titter. Dismayed, Berenice glances at Rod, who gives her a nod. "What I saw was a subject crying out to be photographed"—ah, better, her voice is more normal—"a uniquely *American* scene." At this she glances at Stieglitz, who looks back levelly, his arms crossed. "I saw this with fresh eyes and wanted to convey my excitement—not, you understand, by using fancy techniques or bestowing grand titles on my work, but by using the camera to do what it does best, show our world straightforwardly, at the same time capturing its gloriously modern feel—"

A hand on her arm: Julien is on the platform, nodding at her. "Thank you Berenice! I'm sure we all appreciate your sweet tribute to our city." He claps, and people around the room join in.

Berenice stays frozen in place, because it seems impossible that Julien is dispatching her so quickly. Does he not understand what she's put into this work, the struggle? Did he just imply that the work was sappy?

She turns and leans toward him. "I have more to say."

"No," he says, taking her elbow with a strained smile, "you don't." Turning to the audience, he shouts, "And without further ado—Mr. Dalí!" Excited murmurs rise from the crowd. From her perch on the platform, Berenice sees reporters draw notebooks and pencils from their pockets.

When she doesn't move, Julien gives her a little push, forcing her off the platform. She has to stagger to regain her balance. No one notices, it seems, because all eyes are turned, watching Dalí bound toward the platform. *You're still just a little girl from the Midwest.* Tears well in her eyes, and as she weaves through faceless bodies toward Rod, it seems to her that she's moving through dark water toward a buoy, the brightest and most upright thing in the room.

Still reeling, she experiences Dalí's speech mostly as a dumb show. It's easy enough to read the body language, though—the artist's sweeping gestures, his ebullience, the adulation of the crowd. Dalí takes some papers from his pocket and starts to read—evidently *he* was expecting to give a speech. It must be English because the translator is nowhere in sight. People strain to decipher his accent, smiling indulgently, as if he's a child reciting a memorized poem.

When it's done, and the crowd is surging around Dalí, she looks up at Rod. "Take me home, would you?"

"Now?" He looks perturbed. "Don't you have to talk to your public?"

"This isn't my public. I'd rather be with you."

He seems to hesitate a moment, then puts an arm across her shoulder. "Okay. You're right, let's get you home."

Outside, their driver is leaning against the car with his jacket off, smoking. "Good time?" he asks in an over-familiar way, but when Rod glares he straightens up and discards his cigarette in the gutter.

They glide across Fifty-Seventh and down Fifth Avenue, and then, as if by magic, they're in a pool of brightness that could be daylight. Berenice looks out, then flinches when she sees that they're passing the Rockefeller Center. Enormous floodlights beam white rays into the air, illuminating the rising buildings where men are working through the night. When she sees the tilting cranes, she feels a wave of nausea as she remembers her jolting ride in the lift box. She thinks of her terror, and the men's sneers.

And then exhaustion seeps through her, so dark and thick that she goes limp against the seat. *I'm tired,* she thinks. *Tired of fighting for my right to love, to create. Tired of the art world's fickleness...*

She looks at Rod's illuminated profile, at the well-proportioned nose above the bristle of his mustache and beard. He squeezes her hand, and she feels absurdly grateful for his presence.

"Tonight wasn't much of an evening, was it?"

"No, but—" He shakes his head, "after everything…"

"Do you think we should get married?" she asks. Her heart is beating rapidly. This isn't what she'd expected to say. But somehow, at this moment, it seems right. She needs support, a partner to help her navigate life's currents. She needs to take control of her life. If those aren't the most romantic motives, so what? Romance hasn't served her so well in the past.

In the bright light, Rod's expression seems exquisitely pained. "I'd like that more than anything. But are you sure, Berenice? You're not just saying it because—"

"No, I'm not. You're decent and good, and you believe in me. We ought to be happy, don't you think?"

"I—do," Rod says. "God, I do." Now his face lights up. "My love, we'll be more than happy! We'll be blissful!"

He gathers her to him, peppers her hair with kisses, then brings his mouth to hers. At first the kiss is light, as if he can't believe his luck—and for a moment, Berenice feels a tug of disappointment. They are getting married, for god's sake—she wants passion and vigor, she wants to be swept up and tossed about by a huge, hungry force! A feeling like despair rises in her as she wonders if she's making a mistake. But she pushes it down and kisses him harder, forcing him to return the pressure. They are getting married: she *will* be happy.

TWENTY-THREE

Light floods through the windows of the apartment, highlighting dusty surfaces and making the living area look shabbier than usual. It's as if she's being rebuked for her absence. Surveying the scene, Berenice sighs. She didn't do the dishes before she left, and the kitchen sink holds an array of unpleasantness, from greasy plates to mugs rimmed with coffee scum.

She's been sleeping at Rod's more often lately, for the obvious reason that the surroundings are ten times more pleasant. It doesn't bother her that the housekeeper, Mrs. Linnet, is mildly scandalized by the arrangement, or that Rod's parents stare balefully from their framed positions over the mantelpiece. She and Rod may not be legally married, but at thirty-four and twenty-eight respectively, she thinks they've earned the right to please themselves.

And oh, it is so nice to have one's dinner cooked and waiting in the evening, with polished cutlery and someone else doing the dishes! Not to mention the pure bliss of waking on freshly washed sheets, or taking a bath in a private five-foot tub which she doesn't have to clean first!

There was a time when she would have disdained such things. Back in the Village and in Paris, living poorly was a sign of authenticity. Heating and feather pillows were for the weak. And perhaps there's reason in this, because there *is* something numbing about life on the Upper East Side. Silk slippers! Chocolate truffles! It's as if she's a French goose being fattened for *foie gras,* and all she has to do is eat until she's too stuffed to move.

She crosses over to her dining table and flips through the pile of letters from the mailbox. Most are the usual nonsense, bills, bank circulars, advertisements. RCA would like her to purchase a radio in installments for the astoundingly low price of two dollars per month! She's about to toss it all down when a letter catches her eye—it's from Julien Levy. Surprised, she pulls it from the pile.

Since her show at the gallery, she's had little contact with Levy. He seems to blame her that the prints didn't sell, even though *he* was the one who rendered them all but invisible. Of course, there was plenty of ink spilled on Dalí's debut: he was a genius, a visionary. Only one review mentioned that *also on show were some photographs of New York by Miss. B. Abbett, who spoke briefly about her love for the city, but failed to bring any Spanish verve to her presentation.*

She slits open the envelope and three items fall out: a small note, a letter and a newspaper clipping. The note is written in Julien's tight cursive: *This arrived a few weeks after your show. I meant to forward it, but got distracted. Apologies for the delay, but perhaps this late notice will offer some cheer, even if it is from the provinces.*

The letter is on printed stationery from the *Springfield Republican*, a newspaper in western Massachusetts. It is typewritten and the key printing the letter *O* is misaligned, so that the lowercase *o* seems to bounce like a ball above the other letters. It is dated two weeks after her opening.

Dear Miss Abbott, it reads. *It is always a source of great joy when my work as an art critic for this paper takes me beyond our borders—especially if it brings me to New York, where recently I happened upon your exhibition. While you have no doubt been inundated with reviews from eminent papers, I thought you might like to read this regional consideration. As you will see, your work inspired me to write at length. Sincerely, Elizabeth McCausland.*

Curious, she unfolds the page of newsprint. The article is indeed long, covering two-thirds of a page, and includes a reprint of one of her images, taken from the walkway of the Manhattan Bridge.

Berenice Abbott studied with Man Ray in Paris—yet her style could not be more different, Miss McCausland begins. *Eschewing her mentor's overblown dramatics, labored stylizations and lacquered surfaces, she has brought the medium back down to earth.*

She sits up straighter. This critic seems to know what she's talking about. She writes of Berenice's *genuinely honest respect for her medium…she has taken a big theme and approached it modestly*. The critic implies that this kind of approach is far preferable to *the more pretentious, self-conscious sort of art* that has become fashionable—for example, *the shadow of a fork falling across a table, or a dark sky with scudding clouds meant to represent a spiritual state…*

Reading that line, Berenice sputters with laughter. *A dark sky with scudding clouds*—it's a clear dig at Stieglitz. If a New York critic had written that, she'd be ostracized. Maybe that's why Miss McCausland stays in Springfield, so she can lob her grenades from a distance.

After reading the review over a second time, Berenice feels energized for the first time in weeks. She must have breakfast! In the pantry she finds an old packet of Ritz crackers and a jar of Skippy peanut butter. It's better than nothing. She makes herself some peanut butter crackers and a pot of coffee and sits at the table, where she re-reads the note that came along with the review. *While you have no doubt been inundated with reviews from eminent papers…*Ha, well, the perceptive art critic got that wrong. But she called Berenice's show *a source of great joy,* and said it inspired her. She should be thanked for this.

Dear Miss McCausland, Berenice writes, *I am indebted to you for sending your eloquent review of my work. Indeed, I had not seen your article or been told about it, and now I am very glad to have that situation rectified. Quite frankly, your review is the first truly astute assessment of my work that has appeared in this country. You seem to have a natural understanding for photography. You write that I have 'a clear passion for the subject,' and you couldn't be more right: I have a fantastic passion for New York, one that is far from being sated. To convey that, and for you to understand that the work goes beyond illustration, is satisfying…*

She continues for another paragraph, admitting that the show didn't get the kind of attention she'd expected, and that *I am obliged to do a rather uninteresting sort of commercial work to make money. However, I am hoping some institution will eventually recognize my New York project. Self-doubt hovers, but as Mrs. Roosevelt says, we must strive to realize our dreams…*

She stops then, surprised—she has gone on for two whole pages. She'll end here, on a positive note. Writing the letter has lifted her spirits—she has reminded herself of her purpose. Satisfied, she signs with a flourish and folds the paper into an envelope.

A few days later, when she opens her mailbox, she's delighted to see a letter postmarked from Springfield, Massachusetts. The art critic! Unable to restrain herself, she tears the envelope open in the lobby and begins reading as she's walking upstairs.

Unlike its predecessor, this letter is handwritten, and seems to have been penned in haste. The loops of the lower-case *b* don't meet the stems, the cross-lines of the *t* and *f* are long swipes of ink. The paper is beautiful, though—a thin, Japanese-style sheet with deckled edges and an embossed monogram,

EMC, composed of swooping, crossed letters that take up almost a quarter of the page.

You wrote that you have a fantastic passion for photographing New York. I have a passion for a number of things, too, for all kinds of things with capital letters. Life, America, Nature, Man. I want to take it all in, to bask in the intricacy and richness of our new, young country.

What a miraculous place it is! Don't you feel it? (But I sense you do, from your photographs.) My own response is to write and write, then write some more: as well as art criticism, my scribbling includes some social commentary and a lot of rather poor poetry. In my spare time I am also an amateur letterpress printer—I printed the monogram on the letter you are now holding—which is a secondary sort of art, I fear, yet gives me the satisfaction of executing a good design…

Berenice smiles. What a generous spirit! *Life, America, Nature, Man*—the words make her arms prick with goosebumps. Before even beginning the third paragraph, she is composing responses in her mind. *My dear Miss McCausland, you should not denigrate your creative efforts by calling them 'poor poetry' and 'secondary art.' One is never the best judge of one's own work…*

She stops herself in order to read on. The third paragraph expresses sympathy for her financial plight. *I am so sorry to read about the reception of your show. I had no idea. I must implore you not to give up hope, for your work is genuine and true, and such work cannot but be recognized in time.*

A lump rises to Berenice's throat, and she stops to lean against the wall of the corridor. How well they seem to know each other, after only three letters! She feels as if she could unravel the letter's scrawl into a thread that, if tweaked, would tug directly at its author's heart. How is that possible? That she can feel so connected to someone she has never met?

Before too long, letters are hurtling every few days between Springfield and West Thirty-Seventh Street. They discuss everything from the Soviet famine to Roosevelt's programs, but always circle back to art—its genesis, its relationship to commerce, its power in the world.

One evening, after a day in which none of her ideas has led anywhere, Berenice takes refuge in paper and pen and finds herself launching into a fulsome diatribe against Stieglitz. *Those piercing eyes that say 'you must be intimidated,' the severe lines of his mustache—what a ghastly, bottled-up person Stieglitz is!*, she writes. *Do you know he took a photograph in 1923 of a castrated horse and called it 'Spiritual America,' as if to imply that our country is devoid of depth? If he has such contempt for his adopted country, I wonder he doesn't go back home. I'm tempted to make my own photograph of the same subject and title it 'Mr. Stieglitz,' for he is indeed a horse's ass...*

She seals up the letter and mails it, only wondering later if it might have been impolitic to express herself so freely. For a few days, she worries that Miss McCausland will see her as a blabbermouth and stop writing. But then the reply comes: *Oh, how you made me laugh with your Stieglitz description! Indeed, I feel your frustration, but I would urge you to look at all his work before dismissing it. Some of his earlier portraits are quite fine...*

Never! Berenice writes back mischievously, *not until hell freezes over! I can't forgive him for championing the aesthetic of pictorialism, which in my opinion has been the biggest blight on photography...*And they're off again, arguing about realism and symbolism, purity and artifice.

As she's photographing the city, these exchanges give her confidence in her own point of view. Sometimes, she takes one of Miss McCausland's letters with her, folding it into a pocket as a kind of talisman. *There is something classical about your work*, Miss McCausland writes. *I am trying to put my finger on it...I think it is because of the objectivity with which you approach your subjects. However, I don't mean to imply that the work lacks sensitivity. There is objectivity but also nuance, and this is what makes it so satisfying...*

*Something classical...finely-honed...*What is the woman like who penned those words? Berenice imagines the reporter played by Joan Crawford in *Dance, Fools, Dance*—tall, languid, brilliant. She sits at a beaten-up desk, a cigarette poised between glossy red lips, her fingers flying across the typewriter to keep pace with her thoughts. When men try to flirt with her, she bats them away like flies.

Please let me know when you are coming to New York next, Berenice writes. *I should so like to continue our conversation in person.* A few days later, a response comes from Massachusetts: *I was about to suggest the same thing! As it happens, I will be there on 21 May for an opening at the Museum of Modern Art. Might we meet for coffee the following morning?*

Berenice takes a breath. Three weeks! She must get out and shoot new work, something meaningful. The thought of the two of them sitting together, discussing art and photography, makes her spine tingle. *The 22nd would be wonderful*, she responds. *Let's meet at the Automat on Fifty-Seventh Street— a favorite haunt of mine. My studio is not too far away, and if you have time, I would love for you to see my new work...*

"We don't have to go," Rod says later that day. "Allen and Evelyn will survive."

"But I want to meet your friends."

"I'm afraid you'll find them boring."

"If *you* like them, they can't be so bad." She kisses the top of his head, enjoying the clean smell of his hair. "Anyway, I should meet your best man before the wedding, don't you think?"

She has heard a lot about Allen Salter, who was at Harvard at the same time as Rod. Allen was the one who persuaded him not to sell the map business after his father died. A graduate of Harvard's business school, he now works for Shell Oil. He has been loyal to Rod, and she is determined to like him for this.

But when they walk into the Fifth Avenue apartment a few hours later, she feels an urge to flee. The place is huge, with dark paneled walls and sofas the size of Cadillacs. There are five couples, and all the women are in figure-hugging evening gowns. She looks anxiously at her calf-length ready-to-wear dress.

"Berenice!" A woman who must be Evelyn swoops down on her, blonde, big-boned, in a blue evening gown. She looks Berenice up and down, and her smile seems to freeze as she takes in Berenice's age, her hair and get-up. Then she laughs. "Well! Rod has been so *mysterious* about you! We were beginning to think he'd conjured you from his imagination!"

"Oh, he's not that imaginative," Berenice says. She means it as a joke at her own expense—no one could imagine a person so weird and singular—but she realizes, too late, that it sounds like an insult to Rod. Evelyn gives her a confused half-smile.

"Evelyn, meet Berenice," Rod says stiffly. "Berenice, this is Allen's wife Evelyn."

"All right, thank you—you can go now!" Evelyn swats at Rod's arm, then threads her own through Berenice's. "We ladies will get acquainted. We'll make sure to interrogate Berenice until we know *everything*."

As Evelyn is leading her away, Berenice flashes an anxious look over her shoulder at Rod. He holds his palms up helplessly, and she has no choice but to let herself be guided toward the grand piano, where the wives stand in a huddle. There are two brunettes and a redhead, all of whom are bone-thin and a good three inches taller than Berenice. As Evelyn thrusts her forward, Berenice feels as if she's a veal calf being prodded up a ramp to the slaughterhouse.

Actually, though, the women—Charity, Audrey and Irene—are barely interested in her. Once they've determined that she is no one, really, they turn away and start debating the relative merits of summering on Long Island and Martha's Vineyard. Evelyn gets drawn in too, and there's much disputing about the quality of beaches and staff.

Finally the redhead, Audrey, turns to Berenice. "Where will you be buying?"

"Buying?" It takes her a moment to understand, then she blinks. Will Rod want a summer house? "Oh, we won't. I'm very attached to the city."

"Even in summer?"

"Especially then. The hotter and stickier the better. It brings out something in people, I think—their grit. We all have to survive together."

"How rugged," Audrey says coolly.

Now Charity, the tallest of them, leans forward. "That will change when you have children," she informs Berenice. "You'll be desperate to escape. You should visit us on the Vineyard, try it on for size. You'll love it. Except," she leans forward, lowering her voice, "that in the last few years, it's become a haven for well-to-do Negroes."

Berenice almost laughs, but then, seeing that Charity is serious, stifles the urge. She thinks about the Savoy Ballroom, where she has danced, so many times, with Negroes to a band whose members display twenty different skin tones.

"Charity!" Audrey laughs. "You'll be cutting eyeholes in sheets next."

"No I won't!" Charity juts out her chin. "I went to that lecture by Oscar Micheaux, didn't I? I just think…well, that they should stay in their communities and we in ours, and that way, everyone can be comfortable." Berenice looks at her chiseled face with its cool green eyes, but there's no hint of irony there. Apparently, Charity doesn't live up to her name.

At dinner, things are not much better. She is seated between Allen, the host, and Floyd, Charity's husband. Allen manages to ask a few questions about her work before Floyd monopolizes him, talking over her head about boxing and the new line of Packards. When the conversation turns to national matters, it centers on the merging of small banks with larger ones, and involves economic terms with which she's unfamiliar.

"But will the small banks' customers get their money back?" she asks at one point. This—and not the price-specie flow mechanism—seems to her to be the salient point.

Floyd, who has a pencil mustache and receding hair, chews a bite of beef

Wellington and swallows. "Probably," he says. "But it's going to take a while to get the banks insured under the new federal regulations."

"If you want to make a mess of a system, just hand it to the government!" Allen puts in.

"But it must be better for the government to take over now," Berenice says. "The banks have had their turn for three years, and I don't see that they've done anything."

"Now, see, that's the problem," Floyd sighs. "Bankers have become the bogeyman in the public's mind. No one sees how we've been like beavers, plugging the holes in the dam for years."

"But didn't *you* make those holes? No one asked for loans on a ninety-percent margin. That was the banks' doing—something you dangled like a carrot in front of hardworking people."

Floyd's hands freeze around his knife and fork, and a muscle under his eye twitches. Allen looks stunned for a moment—then bursts out laughing.

"Looks like she's got you there, Barnes. Didn't get such tough questioning from the feds, did you?"

Later, after dessert and coffee, Evelyn pulls her aside. "I'm sorry we didn't get to chat. I didn't even see your ring! Show me now."

"Oh, it's not fancy," Berenice holds up her hand with the ring, a simple opal set in rose gold. It was a compromise. She hadn't wanted a ring at all, but Rod had insisted.

"Sweet." Evelyn takes Berenice's hand to get a better look, but seems to be inspecting the hand's rough skin and bitten nails rather than the ring. She leans in, speaking quietly. "Between the two of us—you're a bit older than Roderick, aren't you?"

"A little bit."

"I thought so." Still holding Berenice's hand, Evelyn leads her over to a recess in the living room wall. "May I speak frankly, my dear?"

"Of course."

Evelyn leans in, her large face looming over Berenice. "Well, I can see that Roderick is charmed, right now, by your bohemian lifestyle, which is very colorful and enticing. But trust me, at heart he's a conventional man. He wants a wife and mother for his children." Coolly, she scrutinizes Berenice's face. "So if *you* want *him*, you should prepare to make some changes. Or—" she smiles falsely, "you could keep up the drinking and dancing, and in a few years, you'll be left with what? A funny little haircut and a divorce."

Berenice feels numb. Courtesy demands that she not berate the hostess, so instead she pulls her hand away. "Thank you," she says, trying to suppress her trembling as she walks to the lavishly appointed powder room, where she closes the door and leans against the wall. Hot tears gather at the corners of her eyes, and after a moment one escapes and rolls down her cheek, wobbling at the edge of her jaw before falling with a *plash!* on to her ready-to-wear collar.

In the mirror, a face with swollen eyes stares back. Insecurity pricks at her. Evelyn is right, she is out of place here. A failure in art and love. What is she doing, thinking she can be part of this world? That she can live among normal people?

Prepare to make some changes. She and Rod have told each other that marriage won't change them. They'll both keep working, and will travel together. She believed it when they said it, but now it strikes her as naïve. Why won't she be like other women, exhausted by her children? Or what if she can't conceive and Rod resents her for it?

In the car on the way home, Rod touches a hand to her knee. "Tell me the truth. You hated them, didn't you?"

"Well," she begins—and then it tumbles out in a rush. "Oh Rod, I never want to be like those women! They have everything and are still unhappy. And narrow-minded! They looked at me as if I'd just crawled from under a rock! Why didn't you tell me it was fancy? I felt like a fool in this dress."

He laughs. "If you don't want to be like them, why care about your outfit? Just be yourself."

"But they made me feel shabby. I'm still a woman, I have pride." She hates the way she sounds, petulant and needy. "Promise me we won't be like them."

He sighs. "I don't like that loudmouth Barnes and his wife, but Allen and Evelyn are solid. I owe them. They've been like an older brother and sister to me."

Really? she wants to say. *Because your 'sister' more or less told me I was a freak.* Instead, she says, "I won't change my hair."

He turns to look at her. "What's eating you, Berenice? Nobody's asking you to change your hair."

"And I don't want to stop dancing."

"We won't. Is there anything else you don't want to do?"

"A lot. I'll make a list." She leans back on the seat and closes her eyes, trying to relax. But for once, the purring of the Stutz's engine fails to soothe her. All she can hear, as the wheels circle over the macadam of the streets, is a whispering refrain. *Funny little haircut, divorce, funny haircut, divorce...*

◆

A few days later, she walks up Eighth Avenue for her appointment with Elizabeth McCausland. The morning is not auspicious. Rain pummels her umbrella and cars send sheets of water arcing over the sidewalk. Every cab is taken. Still, Berenice manages to arrive at the Automat a little early. That was her plan, to be settled and ready for this meeting she has been so excited about and so nervous, too. In her letters she has been free and unguarded; she has poured out her heart. What if she and Elizabeth don't have that kind of electric connection in person? Or—potentially more of a problem—if they do?

She shakes the rain off her umbrella, then briefly surveys the food in the little windows, considering a slice of cherry pie, then deciding against it. Before getting her coffee she lingers, enjoying watching other patrons in front of the tiny windows, each one deliberating, then putting a nickel or two in a slot and opening a glass door to extract a dish. *I must bring the camera here*, she thinks, surprised the thought hasn't occurred before. She doesn't typically shoot interiors, but something about the Automat—the combination of commerce, technology and speed—seems quintessentially American.

Once she has her coffee, she makes her way to a table not far from the door and hooks her umbrella to the back of the seat. She sips her coffee, eyeing the restaurant door as it swings open, admitting a blast of cold air and a tall woman with auburn hair and shapely legs under a red gabardine coat. Berenice straightens, but the woman's smile is aimed beyond her, at a man sitting further back. She hurries to his table, her red coat flinging off bright diamonds of water.

Rain beats against the windows and shivers through trees. A man walks by with a turned-out umbrella, making Berenice feel glad she's inside. She clasps her hands in her lap, feeling an unfamiliar sensation as, instead of finding the hard edges of her engagement ring, her fingers meet flesh. Why did she take it off? She's not really sure—except, perhaps, that the most recent letters from Massachusetts have had a thrillingly flirtatious tone. *If only we could make time elastic*, Elizabeth wrote last week, *and squeeze or expand it as necessary. In that case, I would compress every second standing between the present and our meeting next week...*

Just then the door swings open and a woman shuffles in, her face doughy and red under a gray fedora. She is wearing a shapeless brown wool coat and a lumpy necklace that draws attention to her rather thick neck. Looking around, she spots Berenice and gives a little wave.

Berenice raises her coffee mug and nods, feeling confused. Is there some mistake? This woman looks nothing like Joan Crawford; she might be someone's frumpy spinster aunt. She watches as the woman does an awkward pantomime, signaling she'll get herself coffee, then fiddles with the coffee spigot, splashing liquid onto her thumb, grimacing and shaking it off.

Observing this, Berenice feels guilty. She'd like to think that she sees beyond people's surfaces. But Elizabeth's appearance is a genuine shock. Her voice on the page is so elegant and incisive. It gives off a sense that its author is, if not beautiful, at least in control of her limbs.

The woman approaches the table, breaking into a wide smile that makes her reddened cheeks swell. "How wonderful to meet you," she says, putting her mug down so clumsily that coffee sloshes onto the formica. Rather than apologize, she grasps Berenice's hand and shakes it fervently, and Berenice has to suppress a laugh. She looks into Elizabeth's eyes, which are large and gray. The light dancing in them gives her pudding face an animation that wasn't apparent from across the room.

Elizabeth thumps herself into the chair opposite. "I'm not taking you away from work, I hope."

"Oh," Berenice waves a hand in the air, "I can't do much when it's raining like this." Not true—she could be in the darkroom or making calls. But she's unnerved, and doesn't want to look as if this meeting has been almost all she's thought about since Monday. She pulls a paper napkin from the holder and blots the spilled coffee. "You were reviewing the African Negro Art exhibition at the Modern?"

"Yes! I just came from there. The press preview was packed."

"How was the show?"

"Extraordinary. Such wonderful life force in the objects." Elizabeth pins her with a gaze full of its own intense force. "You know, seeing those masks and sculptures, I understood Picasso's preoccupation with African art. The immediacy, the dynamism—it makes our Western fare look pallid. Oh!" she looks stricken, "How tactless. I didn't mean you, of course. Your photographs are so real, so blazingly honest. And exciting—my word. I feel as if I'm on top of the skyscrapers with you."

Berenice smiles. "Thank you. But really, can I call myself an artist? There are those who'd say I'm just documenting the city."

"Nonsense! There's no 'just' about it. Photography's invention freed painting to be non-figurative. Just because it's a mass activity doesn't mean it can't be art too. If anything, the opposite."

"Exactly!" Berenice leans forward. "It makes me so mad when people try to turn photography into painting. As if that's the only way to legitimize it as art."

"I know, I know, the abstract photographers annoy me too. I feel that a good photograph isn't just beautiful to look at. It should be aesthetically strong, but have social relevance too. A finger on the pulse of its times. Your images have that. And if that's not art, I don't know what is."

"Oh—well, thanks again." Berenice leans back, succumbing to the flattery. It feels delicious, warm, like having a towel draped over her after swimming in a frigid ocean. "And what of you?" she asks. "Are you still writing poetry?"

"A little." Now it's Elizabeth's turn to look down. "Though not progressing, I fear. One has to try, though, doesn't one? I attempt to express something that seems so utterly beyond words, and at best, what I come up is a pale reflection of the impression in my mind. Then I look at a Picasso or a Dickinson and wonder why I'm bothering."

"I think we all feel like that," Berenice says. "Even Picasso. I bet he looks at his work and says, *It's not bad, but it's certainly no Picasso.*"

Elizabeth throws her head back and lets out a big, braying chortle. "Oh, not you, surely!" she says. "You're not telling me the well is dry? That your fantastic passion for New York is beginning to ebb?"

"No, I don't think so! It's the opposite. I've bitten off more than I can chew. I want to do the thing properly, you see. I'm trying to do justice to people's ideas of New York, but then I want to surprise them. And myself."

"That's what I love about your work! The ambition. Better to soar high and fail than stay earthbound, don't you think?" Elizabeth takes a sip of coffee and smacks her lips. "Personally I've always wanted to write a huge ode to America—the gaudy, messy glory of it all." She leans forward, and Berenice can see a tiny version of herself reflected in Elizabeth's eyes—small and dark, her bangs hanging severely across one half of her head. She has the odd feeling that she can see beyond the reflection, to the crystalline purity of this woman's mind. She's gradually adjusting to the shock of Elizabeth's physical form, responding to the clarity of her thought and expression. Slowly, the Elizabeth of the letters and the woman in front of her are merging.

"Would your American ode have a political slant?" she asks. She has done a little digging on Liz, enough to know that she has fierce political convictions. A few years ago she published a pamphlet called *The Blue Menace,* an account of the New Bedford textile strikes that morphed into a spirited attack on anti-liberal government policies.

"I think so," Liz says. "It's unavoidable, isn't it? Even in photography. Take your pictures of skyscrapers. When I look at them I see dazzle and glory, but I also sense a question about the relentless, phallic thrust of capitalism, the way it's worshipped in this country. It's in the angles, the quality of the light. I see how the buildings and the spaces between them are a new American landscape—as inexorable, in their way, as the vast canyons of the West."

"Goodness," Berenice blinks, embarrassed to think that she hasn't conceived of her work in these terms before. "I see you're not just eloquent on the page." She smiles. "And how would you describe this place?"

Liz looks around. "An artful combination of luxury and accessibility. A castle of aspiration. You see that in the décor—the stained glass and carved ceilings—as well as in the shining jewel cases of food. And yet, the message is that any man with a couple of nickels can be a king, a manipulator of his own destiny. He stands, as if before Ali Baba's cave, whispers, 'Open Sesame!' and a ham sandwich or apple dumpling is his for the taking."

"You're something!" Berenice bursts out before she can stop herself. In the next moment, she feels herself blush to the roots of her hair. "I mean, you have a way with words. It's a gift. I struggle to be even half-way articulate."

"Well, I could never take images like yours."

"You see them clearly."

"If I didn't I'd be out of a job, wouldn't I?" Liz teases. Then she turns serious. "Honestly though, it's been a joy. I rarely have such a strong reaction to work. If you ask me, there aren't five photographers in America of your caliber."

They glance at each other then, and something passes between them. A tiny acknowledgment, a shiver of recognition. *I see you,* the look says. In its wake, Berenice finds her heart pounding and her face growing hot. Liz's confidence—the way she fully inhabits her intellect and doesn't apologize for it—is appealing. *Thank goodness I'm not physically attracted to her or I'd be in trouble,* Berenice thinks. It's a relief to know that she can go back to Rod this evening with a clear conscience.

Liz leans forward. "What are you thinking?" she asks.

Berenice looks around, avoiding her companion's gaze. An inarticulate longing wells up, pooling, threatening to spill itself all over the table. If only she could merge Elizabeth's mind with Rod's social ease and physique! The thought hovers, teasing, making her ashamed. Then her eye catches a bank of windows under the lighted sign *Pies*.

"I was thinking I'm positively famished," she says. "Would you care to split a piece of pie?"

TWENTY-FOUR

Mrs. Linnet has learned to make coffee the Parisian way, strong and dark. Sipping it one morning, Berenice reflects that Rod's housekeeper has become more accepting of her. Just yesterday, she'd found a pair of neatly darned stockings draped over the chair in Rod's dressing room. She remembered throwing them in a corner, meaning to get to them sometime herself. They were back, repaired, almost before she'd realized they were gone.

"Is this the day your writer friend is coming?" Rod asks.

"Yes." Flustered, Berenice looks down at her scrambled eggs to hide the blush creeping up from her throat—because, although she has told Rod about Elizabeth, she hasn't revealed the full extent of their friendship. Rod knows that Liz has helped Berenice professionally, but doesn't know about the books and gifts the two of them have exchanged. He doesn't know about the late-night telephone calls that can go on for hours, or the fervid tone of Liz's last letter. *How good it was to hear your voice last night, after longing for it all week!* He doesn't know that after reading this, Berenice felt as if an electric current was lighting up every nerve in her body.

"Remind me what the two of you are doing today."

"She's going to be shadowing me as I shoot in some different locations. Then she'll write a profile of me for *Parnassus*."

"Never heard of it."

"It's an art journal."

"That must be why," Rod grins. Looking thoughtful, he adds, "Should we add her to the guest list for the wedding?"

"No," Berenice says quickly, "the two of us aren't close." The lie leaves her with a bad taste, but it would be worse to tell the truth and have to explain herself. For the truth is that her friend doesn't know about the upcoming wedding; she's never even heard of Rod. As far as Liz is concerned, Berenice lives by herself in a walk-up apartment on West Thirty-Seventh Street. In fact, Berenice needs to leave now and get over there, because Liz is due to arrive in less than forty minutes.

Why hasn't Berenice told her, in all these months? The time is long past when she could say that the subject was irrelevant. In their late night conversations, she and Liz have grown intimate, discussing everything from their family histories to their deepest fears. She's had opportunities to slip in references to Rod ("My fiancé thinks…." or "Rod and I plan to…") but somehow, she hasn't. And Liz hasn't spoken about her romantic life either. For all Berenice knows, she could prefer men. (If that's the case, though, she certainly injects passion into her female friendships.)

It's better they don't talk about it, Berenice thinks. As long as they stay silent on the subject, she's not doing anything wrong. At times she thinks that her relationship with Liz is a perfect, clear pool, and that introducing Rod would muddy it. At other times, she thinks the pool is already muddy—because along with their friendship, she has been allowing Liz to help her professionally. So is she stringing Liz along, indulging in a flirtation to further her career? Or is it a coincidence that Liz is well connected?

Soon after their first meeting in the Automat, Liz had written to say that a friend, Alvin Johnson, was looking for someone to teach photography at the New School. *The school was founded on progressive principles—especially the idea that people learn best by doing,* she wrote. *The students are mature men and women who come to study at night. Johnson has scored some 'firsts'—the first ever courses on cinema, modern dance and creative writing—and would now like to offer the first college course in photography. I told him I knew just the person to teach it, if that person was game.*

You're kind to think of me, Berenice wrote back, *it sounds like an intriguing opportunity.* She didn't tell Elizabeth—or Johnson, when she met him— that the thought of speaking to a room full of students terrified her. She'd figure that out later, because the idea of teaching the first college course in photography was thrilling. How satisfying it would be to mold photographers for generations to come! And, she thought, it would give her a prominent position, which could only help in the advancement of her own work.

And indeed, it did seem that as soon as her appointment was announced, other opportunities began to flow. First she got a phone call from Hardinge Scholle, who'd seen the news in the *Times* and wondered if she might have time for a fall exhibition at the Museum of the City of New York? Not long after, she bumped into Holger Cahill at an opening, and he told her he'd been tasked with setting up the Federal Art Project, one of Roosevelt's New Deal programs. "We'll be paying artists a weekly salary to create works of social importance," he told her. "Your project could fit. Will you apply?" *I think you're my good luck charm,* Berenice wrote to Liz. *Since I met you, it seems my career has been on the up and up.*

She crosses to the other side of the table and kisses Rod on the cheek. "I have to go."

"Will you be back for dinner?"

"No. I should buy Elizabeth dinner, don't you think, after she's devoted a whole day to trailing me around?"

"Of course. Well, look—why don't we all go? I could make a reservation at Lucio's."

Berenice's heart does a little skip. "Oh, darling, that's kind. But we'll be tired and dirty—I expect we'll just go to a diner. Anyway, she'll probably want to grill me for her article."

"Right," he looks disappointed. "Let's have dinner at Lucio's tomorrow, then, the two of us. We really need to discuss the seating plan." He surveys her face. "You look awfully nice for a day of traipsing around the city. Are you wearing lipstick?"

"Just a touch," she says. She leans down, kisses him again, then quickly leaves before he can start talking about flower arrangements.

Outside, she buttons her coat and, seeing the midtown traffic at a standstill, starts at a brisk pace to walk the twenty-six blocks between Rod's apartment building and her own. As she trots along the sidewalk, she has the odd sensation that she's hurrying to a tryst—but how can that be? Nothing has been declared, nothing promised in her relationship with Liz. And yet…there's a feeling she gets when she's talking to her friend, or reading one of her letters…

Luckily, there's still the barrier of the physical to overcome, although even that, lately, has been seeming less significant. She now thinks of Liz's round face with fondness, and sees a nurturing softness in her portly form. It doesn't stir her to fits of passion, true—but neither did Rod at first, even though he was, by any objective standard, good-looking. So maybe physical attraction is less important than people think.

As she turns and walks down West Thirty-Seventh Street, she sees a figure in a green coat standing at the bottom of her stoop. An immense tide of happiness washes over her, and she runs the last hundred yards, arriving rumpled and out of breath.

"Sorry! I was on an errand."

"Please, I got here early! I've been appreciating the light on the buildings."

"I like your coat. Is it new?"

Liz nods. "I bought it yesterday at Bloomingdale's."

"What a good choice. It suits your eyes."

As Liz's face flushes, Berenice notices that the coat—a long, slimming one made of nubby green material—is not the only difference about her friend. Liz's short hair has been fashionably cut and feathered around her broad face, and the face itself looks softer, more feminine, adorned with touches of lipstick and rouge. Evidently she has made an effort to look her best, just as Berenice has worn a skirt suit and put on lipstick. *Did she do it for me?* The thought is both worrying and exciting.

"Come upstairs—I'll get my equipment. It won't take long. But perhaps you'd like a cup of tea?"

"Thank you, but I just had breakfast."

"Or you might want to powder your nose."

Something has shifted between them. Their attention to dress has raised the stakes, making them formal with each other. *Powder your nose*—when has she ever said that? When they get upstairs, Liz paces the room, making pat comments about the weather. This is not how they are with each other. It's as if a beloved symphony has been transposed into a minor key.

Their smart dress is ironic, too, given that her plan for today is to visit slums. She wants to show Liz that she's developing more of a conscience, and sees potential for photography to address social ills. Liz thinks artists should be in a constant dialogue with current affairs, and Berenice wants to prove she's evolving in that area. Because she *is*, she thinks. She's beginning to feel that she has focused her project too much on New York's grandeur. People should know there is ugliness too; that crushing poverty is part of the current moment in this dynamic city.

Down on the street, with her equipment piled around them, she turns to her friend. "I'd had an idea to photograph in Harlem, but—well, what do you think? Your new coat could get dirty."

"Nonsense!" Liz's eyes are shining. "I'd dirty ten coats if necessary."

"All right, let's get a taxi."

"Let's!"

In the taxi, she is acutely aware of Liz's hand on the seat between them, and of her smell, a mixture of sandalwood and freshly laundered cotton. At one point the taxi swings around a corner and the two of them collide, Berenice's arm making contact with the soft, ample protrusion of Liz's breast. She skitters back across the seat, heart racing, not daring to lift her eyes. The atmosphere feels to her like the air before a storm, heavy and vibrant with possibility. But who knows what Liz is thinking?

After what seems like both the longest and shortest ride of her life, the taxi drops them between Tenth and Eleventh Avenues on One Hundred and Thirty-Seventh Street. It's a neighborhood where crumbling factories share space with dilapidated five- and six-storey buildings. The road is lined with cobblestones, pocked with sunken potholes filled with oily water. Above the roofline, a chimney belches black smoke into the air.

Oh, Berenice thinks as they get out, *what have I done?* She has been to bad neighborhoods before, but they have always been well populated. This place is eerily deserted. As the cab bumps away down the street, it seems to her that her confidence is inside it, rolling away. She sneaks a peek at Liz's Oxford shoes, wondering whether, if it came to it, the two of them could pick up and run.

But she shouldn't be so feeble. Steeling herself, she points to a spot on the opposite corner. "Over there looks best for capturing the light. I'll do a long shot and then maybe"—*if we don't get killed first*—"some details."

"Lovely." Already, Liz has pulled a notebook from her bag and is scribbling, looking fascinated by the surroundings. Her insouciance has a calming effect on Berenice. They cross the street and stop on the corner, and she sets up the Century Universal.

And then, looking at the ground glass, Berenice feels a thrill—because the scene is beautiful in the way that squalor, rendered in black and white, can be picturesque. The cobblestones and faded signs offer an appealing textural element, and the old tenements seem to be buckling, almost pleading for the wrecker's ball.

As she's checking the light meter, Liz taps her on the shoulder. "May I go into reporter mode?"

"I should think so. That's what you're here for."

"All right," Liz clears her throat. "So, Miss Abbott, why was it important to you to come here today?"

Because I wanted to impress you, Berenice thinks. *Because you've woken me up.* But she says, "Every city is an experiment where some people rise and others fall. As a photographer of New York City, it would be irresponsible of me not to include such places. Just as a soaring bridge is a symbol of progress, this slum indicates how far we still must go to address the needs of all New Yorkers."

Pleased with this self-serving eloquence, she raises her left hand to the shutter, and as she does so, something twinkles. Her engagement ring! *Damn me*, she thinks. She glances at Liz, who's nodding her big head as she scribbles—has she noticed? Surely not, or there would have been a shift in mood, if not a question. Can she slip it off now? But where would she put it? She dare not place it in her pocket; it could fall out. She could hide it in her camera bag...but then Liz glances over and smiles, and Berenice smiles back, hastily covering her left hand with her right. Finding the opal, she twists the ring around on her finger so that it's facing inward. That will have to do for now.

In any case, they have worse problems. Lumbering up the street toward them are two huge men with skin as dark as coal. One of them is swinging something that, as he comes closer, she makes out—*Christ*—as a crowbar. The other one seems to have a hammer strapped to his overalls. As they advance up the street, Berenice grows jittery. The Century Universal alone is worth hundreds.

"We're being approached," she murmurs.

Liz squints down the street. As the men come closer, she strides forward with her right hand outstretched.

"Good morning, gentlemen. Elizabeth McCausland, writer."

Her hand trembles in the space between them, the sun bleaching it an anemic white. The men regard it warily, as if it's just fallen from the sky. There's a silence, in which Berenice is acutely aware of her fluttering heartbeat and the crowbar's silver glow. Time seems to waver, elongate. Then one man steps forward and grips Liz's hand.

"Ulysses Evans."

The other man shifts the crowbar from right hand to left, then steps forward too. "Dexter Davis."

"A pleasure, Dexter, Ulysses. And this is my friend Berenice Abbott. She's photographing this street as part of a major study of New York City—which, trust me, will be famous one day. We'd appreciate your advice..." and just like that, Liz is off, charming the men, cracking jokes that make them smile. She finds out that they are heading to a demolition site to try to pick up work—but yes, they can go back and see if Ulysses' wife will allow a photograph with the kids.

Berenice looks on, awed by Liz's confidence. She knew her friend had intellectual powers, but this ability to transcend social barriers shows another side of her. Never in an age could Berenice be so relaxed. Once again, Liz has astonished her.

When the men have gone off to find Ulysses' wife, she can't help laughing from relief. "My goodness, you were magnificent. I was so sure they meant us harm! How did you do it?"

"Nothing special. I just assume the best, and people usually prove me right."

"What a good person you are. I'm suspicious of everyone."

"I hope I didn't overstep my role. Would you *like* to photograph the family?"

"Very much. If you don't think it's a ruse?"

Liz considers. "No. But if you're nervous…"

"I am. But let's do it anyway."

In fact, she needn't have worried. Ulysses turns out to be a gentle giant whose wife, Sarah, welcomes them with a smile. When Liz explains the project Sarah nods, seeming to intuitively understand it. Their four young children sit and stare, unabashed, as Liz asks questions about schools, neighbors, and crime.

When they've finished talking, Berenice takes a portrait of Sarah holding the baby, the other children clustered around her. She takes one of the children on the stoop—and then, as the faded lace curtain in the window flaps in the wind, she gets an idea. She has them move inside and poses them between the curtain and the glass, then shoots from outside as they talk. The curtain and peeling paint provide context; the window creates a frame-within-a-frame. She has captured something here, she thinks—a portrait that conveys the derelict conditions but also presents the family with dignity.

Walking away from the apartment, Berenice feels jubilant. She can't believe that just an hour before, she had thought this place sinister. She's in a state of disbelief, giddy and elated at what they've achieved.

"They were so generous!" she says. "I've always been shy about approaching strangers, but you were so brave! Just asking them, flat out."

"They saw we were serious," Liz says. "It's about the way you come at people."

"I know, and you did it just right! Oh Liz, this could be just the beginning! I've been concentrating so much on buildings, but what's a city without its people? I could devote a whole section of the project to people and how they live!" She grins at Liz. "How would you feel about another adventure? I've had it in mind for a long time to go to one of the Hoovervilles in Central Park. I didn't dare on my own, but with you next to me…"

"Yes," Liz says quickly, "I think we should."

"The squalor wouldn't upset you?"

"It would," Liz says, "but that's the point, isn't it? To show those people that we see them and won't look away?"

Berenice looks at Liz then, and suddenly the street falls away and all that matters is that they are together, here in this moment. Liz's face is glowing, her eyes have a glint that is admiring, and at the same time so full of its own ebullience, that Berenice can hardly breathe. And it seems they're both aware of the moment's significance, because they hold each other's gaze for longer than necessary, and she can see that Liz is flushed and trembling too.

On Amsterdam Avenue, they manage to hail a cab. Normally Berenice would ride with her equipment on the back seat, but now she asks the driver to place it in the trunk. As she and Liz settle themselves in the cab, her heart knocks against her ribs and the air seems to be pulsing. *Do something*, she thinks, *say something to her!* But she can see the driver's eyes looking at her in the rearview mirror—and when she stares, he just flashes a grin. It's infuriating. She wants to absorb Liz, envelop her—to know, one way or another, if her feelings are reciprocated. But all she can do is sit there, her body crying out as the blocks pass by.

Soon, they're crossing Eighty-Sixth Street and she knows they're nearly there, and that she'll burst if she doesn't do something. Carefully, without looking down, she glides her right hand across the seat until it reaches the nubby weave of Liz's coat, then stealthily lifts it and puts it into Liz's lap. She hears an intake of breath on the other side of the car, but dares not look across. She's sick with nerves. What if she's misread the signals? But after a moment, she feels her hand being covered and grasped, forcefully, by another. *Yes!* The grip says. *Yes, I'm ready for this adventure too!*

272

The taxi leaves them on the curb at Seventy-Ninth and Central Park West, across from the Natural History Museum. They stand there for a moment, dazed—then Liz looks at her. "Are we dreaming?"

"Maybe. But let's not wake up." She thinks of Rod that morning, asking if she was wearing make-up. *Let's not wake up, because if we do I'll have to deal with him, when all I want is to be next to you.*

Just then, a bus stops in front of them, hurtling so close that they have to step back. Instinctively, Berenice reaches for the camera and hugs it to her, and then they're back on earth—yet something has changed. A force has been set into motion, a genie loosed from a bottle. At some point in the future they will touch again, and the anticipation of this is delicious.

Now, though, they're on a mission. Loaded down with equipment, they move toward the park's periphery wall and enter Central Park.

They're heading to a site north of Belvedere Castle, where a reservoir was drained a few years before. The idea was to create a great lawn, but then the Crash came and plans were suspended, leaving room for encampments. Berenice isn't sure what to expect. Over the last few years the papers have reported raids, lawsuits, and other attempts to rid the park of its human inhabitants. But public opinion has been on the side of the Hoovervillers. A judge even gave each resident two dollars out of his own pocket after refusing to sign their eviction orders.

As they approach the former reservoir, she's surprised at what she sees. As in the Hooverville near her apartment, the shacks are crude, made of canvas and old doors and boards nailed together. But they're tidy, and some look like actual houses with windows and chimneys. Thin lines of smoke twist into the sky. One dwelling even sports a flagpole flying a tablecloth-sized American flag.

There's not much activity on this cold morning, but Berenice sees a man heating something on a distant fire. She should stop here and take a long shot, for context. But their success in Harlem has fired her up. She wants to taste that success again, and have the triumph of pulling off a meaningful portrait. And she wants to feel the charged intimacy of working closely with Liz, continuing their thrilling seduction.

"I'd like to talk to that man," she says.

So they walk over the bumpy earth, past a dozen or so dwellings to where the man is sitting. His shack is makeshift but large. On one of its walls is a faded advertisement for Baby Ruth bars, in which can just be made out a scrap of peeled-back wrapper and some lettering—*Candy rich in dextr*—as well as the lumpy silhouette of the bar itself.

As they approach, the man looks up. He's wearing a newsboy cap turned backward, and might be forty. He has crow's-feet and a jaw peppered with gray stubble. He's not bad looking, if thin—but there's a sense of hostility in his crouch. It touches off Berenice's wariness, and for a moment she falters. But then she remembers her misplaced fear over in Harlem and walks up to the fire.

"Hello there. My name is Berenice Abbott, and I'm doing a photographic project on New York City. This is my friend Elizabeth McCausland. We were wondering if you might be able to spare us some time."

"Miss Abbott is on the brink of a breakthrough," Liz adds, her voice sounding more credible than Berenice's shaky treble. "Her photographs will be shown in museums and magazines, and the world will get to see what your life is like. You'll be part of an important historical record, Mr...?"

For a moment, the man doesn't respond. He stirs the fire with a bent poker, until a few sparks fly from it, then says, "Yeah? How much you payin' folks for bein' in this important historical record?"

Berenice glances at Liz. She has no idea what the rules are for this. She can already see the photograph—she'll place him near the Baby Ruth advertisement—but is it ethical to pay for it?

Luckily, Liz is prepared. "We can't pay you," she says. "But if you'd like, after we've taken the photograph we could take you to Broadway for a meal."

"Hnh."

"And you could have this," Berenice pipes up. She holds out a worn pack of Wrigley's gum fished from her coat pocket. "I'm sorry it's so little. But I promise, we only want to convey the truth. When people see your photograph, it will wake them up to what's happening here in our city."

"Hnh," the man says again, and goes back to stirring the fire. After a moment, he looks up. "Okay."

"Really?" Berenice is taken off guard. Nothing in the man's demeanor had indicated a desire to cooperate. "Thank you! Would you mind sitting over here by the wall?"

"There?"

"Yes, by the advertisement. Excuse me, it will take me a minute to get set up. In the meantime, Miss McCausland will ask you some questions." She looks at Liz, who has already taken out her notebook, and who gives her a kittenish smile. *How in tune we are,* she thinks. *How she understands me!*

As she sets up her equipment, she sees that the man is reticent and that Liz is working hard to draw him out. This makes her think he might only sit for one shot. She frames it to include the fire, the skyscrapers in the background and the haphazard shack with the Baby Ruth advertisement. It's a good composition, but in the end it will come down to that hair-trigger judgment—the moment of freezing time.

Luckily, the man has a natural air of gloom that serves her well. When it comes time to click the shutter, she asks him to lean back and not smile, and presto! If her instincts are right, it should be there, a portrait of privation, adversity in a thousand shades of gray.

"That's it?" he says. "You done?"

"I think so," says Liz, "unless there's something else we should see?"

"How 'bout the inside of the shack? So's people see how we live?"

Liz cocks her head, then comes over to where Berenice is standing. "What do you think? Would there be enough light for a picture?"

"I don't know. Possibly. And it would show something people never see."

Turning back to the man, Liz nods. "Thank you. We'll come."

The man breaks into an odd, lopsided smile. Berenice doesn't like him, she decides—but that doesn't matter. He's destitute, and you don't have to like your subjects to make a good photograph.

She folds up the tripod with the camera on top, then picks it up and follows him and Liz around the corner. When they get to the shack's front door, the man opens it and then, as if to prove that distress is no excuse for poor chivalry, bows and gestures them inside. Liz goes first, stepping gingerly, and Berenice follows, the camera wobbling on her shoulder. The man comes close behind her—too close, she thinks. She can hear the wheeze in his breath as he exhales.

Still, it isn't until she gets across the threshold that she knows they've made a mistake. The smell inside is foul, and nailed to the near wall are some filthy, blood-spattered things that look like squirrels' tails. A curtain is drawn across the window, and in the dimness, she can just make out a pot-bellied stove and an apple crate table.

A thud behind her makes her jump, and she turns. The man has closed the door, shutting out most of the light.

"What—" she begins, "I won't be able to…" but before she can go further, something stirs in the shadows. A person, an animal? No, it's too big to be an animal. It's rising from a cot and is coming…

"Well whaddaya know," it says. "What's this, Clarence?"

"Company," the other man says behind her. "Come to see how we live."

The big man lets out a grunt. As he crosses the shaft of light cast by the single small window, Berenice can see that he's not only tall but broad, and has a swagger to him. He's certainly the leader of the two. A chill runs through her, making hairs on her neck stand up. The man's bald scalp glimmers white, revealing the lumps and dips in its construction. He wears a dirty vest and torn pants, and gives off a rank, fecal smell.

"How kind," he says. "Well here we are in the Plaza Hotel of Hardlucksville. Does it give you a thrill, ladies? A tingle down below?"

Berenice's heart is juddering faster than she thought possible. In front of her, Liz seems to be paralyzed. How could she not be? The threat is now clear, though its magnitude is yet to be determined.

She steps forward, trying to stand in such a way that the camera shields Liz. "Look, I don't know you but we're on the same side," she says. "We're here to help you, to show people how hard it is to survive—" she casts a glance at the squirrels' tails, "so you'll get the help you need."

"The help we need!" the big man exclaims. He steps forward, looming over her. "So you're going to wave your wand and get us clean clothes and running water, are you, and hot food? Find us jobs and lodgings?" He breaks into a leer. "Or should we take what we can get now?"

As he turns towards Liz, she's reminded of something, though she can't think what. Then it comes to her: Gus. She thinks of Fredo, the necklace, the bottle. Could she swing the camera at this man now, as she swung the bottle at Gus? A well-aimed blow could knock him out, but then there's the other man, and who knows what weapons they might have hidden about the place.

She puts her left hand up in front of her. "Please," she says. "We'll give you all the money we have. Other things, too—our watches, coats. The camera, if you want it—just don't touch us, please."

"What's this?" The man squints down at her hand, then picks it up and raises it to his face. Too late, Berenice realizes that her engagement ring is still on her finger, turned inward so that the opal directly faces him. "Well," he says, "looky here, Clarence. Broad's engaged. And I was so sure the two of them were bulldaggers."

Berenice pulls her hand back sharply, making both men laugh. Next to her, Liz seems to wilt and close up. To know that she has caused her friend this pain makes Berenice feel like the worst woman alive.

Things move quickly after that. Clarence takes the camera from her, and the big man pulls out a hunting knife and instructs her to take off her engagement ring, her watch, her dragonfly brooch. Her mind slows to an almost catatonic state as she focuses on the blade's dull silver, following instructions to remove her coat and shoes. From the corner of her eye she can see Liz moving jerkily, being similarly divested by Clarence.

"Thank you, ladies," the big man says finally. "You've been very helpful." He speaks slowly, carefully. "Now we're going to let you out, and you'll walk directly to Fifth Avenue and not speak to anyone for the rest of the day. Do you understand? Or should I make it clearer?" So saying, he jabs the point of the knife into the loose flesh of Berenice's throat, where it digs into her skin. For an awful moment, she fears losing control of her bladder.

"We un—we un-un…"

"You what?"

"We un—derstand."

"Good. And remember," he puts his face close to hers, "I could have done worse. I've been compassionate. You may not be so lucky next time." With that, the two of them are pushed out of the door and left there, shoeless and trembling.

How do they get out of the park? She has no idea except that they are teetering, stumbling toward the east side, and stones are pressing into her feet, ripping the bottoms of her stockings. "Are you all right?" she calls to Liz at one point, but there's no answer. She's not sure if she expected one. Liz is moving forward with single-minded purpose, her eyes glazed over, deaf to the world. She doesn't stop until they get outside the park, and there, under the canopy of a large elm, she sits on a bench and seems to collapse in on herself, a punctured balloon.

"Liz," Berenice says miserably, "Elizabeth…" She moves to the bench, but Liz shakes her head and holds up a hand. She looks almost afraid. There are two patches of red on her otherwise ashen face, and a feathery tuft of hair sticks up in a point on one side, like a tufted owl's ear.

Berenice goes to the other end of the bench, where five feet of wooden slats and two iron armrests separate her from Liz. She perches on the edge and leans forward. "It was all my fault," she says. "I won't ever forgive myself. Of course I'll pay for a replacement watch, and for your lovely new coat…"

In response, Liz looks up at her with an expression so offended and outraged that it takes Berenice's breath away. Without breaking eye contact, she says, "You're engaged."

"Yes." Berenice can't meet her eye.

"You didn't think to tell me?"

"It's not like that. I just thought—" *What?* What did she think? "I thought—until today, that is—that we were just friends." Saying the words, she realizes how flimsy and pathetic they sound, and how disingenuous. If they were just friends, why didn't she tell Liz about Rod? And why have the letters between them shaken her to the core, weaving a spell of language that has grown into so much more?

Sighing, she tries again. "Oh, Liz. I've had to struggle so much, and I thought I didn't have the energy to struggle in my work *and* my personal life. And the work—well, the work is so important." She dares look up then, and the disappointment on Liz's face rips at her heart.

For a moment, Liz doesn't speak. Then, in a voice edged with contempt, she says, "I thought you were brave."

"I guess I'm not. Not in everything."

"Are you in love with him?"

"I—I feel a great affection for him."

"May I know his name?" It is said with weariness, edged with curiosity. She has a right to both, of course.

"Roderick Gedney," Berenice says. "But Elizabeth, believe me—" She tails off as again, Liz holds up a hand.

"Enough," she says. "I don't want to hear. We'll go to the police station now, then I'll go home. I'd like our correspondence to end. Of course I'll honor my commitment to write the article for *Parnassus*. I think there's enough material from Harlem."

"Yes," Berenice says. Every cell in her body is protesting, telling her to reach out and take Liz in her arms. But she can't. She deserves contempt; she must take the punishment she's earned.

There's a brief pause, then Liz says, "I may not get the chance to say this later, so I'll say it now—I wish you luck, Berenice. You're a rare talent. I hope—I hope you go on working for a long time to come." Her tone is wistful, and it opens a pit of wretchedness so deep that Berenice thinks she might never crawl out of it. This closing down, the ending of their association, is worse to her than what just happened in the shack. Worst of all is knowing that she did it to herself. What an idiot she has been, thinking she could keep her relationship with Liz a secret, picking at it like a delicious side dish! Of course it had to end badly, like this, with the woman she loves about to shut her out for good.

"Oh Elizabeth—" she begins. But it's too late. Liz has risen and is walking toward Fifth Avenue. Her feet in their ripped stockings move unsteadily over the hexagonal paving stones as she trudges on, the back of her dress flapping in the wind.

TWENTY-FIVE

"You're quite the talk of the town," Rod says. "Major exhibition one week, wedding a week later. What will you follow that with, darling? A run on Broadway?"

"Not likely," Berenice says. She's sitting in front of the mirror in Rod's bedroom, applying makeup. There's nothing she can do about her nose, which occupies far too much territory in the middle of her face, but she has painted her lips a vibrant scarlet and her hair is oiled. Her dress, too, is striking— a cranberry-colored silk sheath with a plunging neckline and sleeves made of foamy black lace. She didn't think she could get away with it—but Rod, who came to Worth's with her, pressed her to buy it. He also insisted on the fancy garnet brooch and matching earrings.

She looks into the mirror, beyond her reflection to where he is sitting on the bed, suave in a tuxedo, his right hand moving in circles as he polishes a shoe. In the last few months he has lost his boyishness; there's an air of assurance about him now. By contrast, she feels increasingly unsure of everything. There's no doubt about it. He has taken charge, and she has fallen into a child-like passivity.

It started after the incident in Central Park. The police had taken her and Liz to the park to look for the men, but there were so many delays—from filing their report to finding shoes for themselves in the precinct's lost property office—that by the time they got to the shack, nothing was left but a few boards and the ashes of a recent fire. The men had absconded, melted into the city. "It's pretty hopeless," the officer admitted. "They'll probably hawk one item, then take a train outta here and sell the rest."

When they were finally done, it was four in the afternoon and they were exhausted. Berenice had hoped to talk, but Liz bade her farewell on the steps and hurried away, almost tripping in her eagerness to depart. Watching her broad figure disappear around the corner of Seventy-Ninth Street, Berenice felt a deadening sense of dejection. At once, she started penning an imaginary letter explaining her actions. Perhaps if she could phrase it just right, with enough sincerity, she could earn herself a second chance.

But that letter, when she wrote it later, went unanswered, and Liz's telephone number has been changed. Like the men in the shack she has melted away, leaving a chasm into which Berenice at first wept bitter tears, then began throwing as much work as possible.

Luckily, she had her exhibition at the Museum of the City of New York to prepare for. She busied herself taking photographs in Brooklyn, in Murray Hill and midtown. Of course she could barely pick up a camera without Liz's words bubbling up—*there is objectivity in the work but also nuance, and that is what makes it so satisfying*—but after a while, the pain this caused became routine, an accessory she packed along with her light meter and spirit level.

In the meantime Rod coddled her, making her stay in bed while he brought her toast and broth. He bought her a new engagement ring— "A proper one this time, with a diamond"—and a brand new Century Universal. He supervised her shooting schedule, and sent a driver to shadow her—insisting that she not go to Harlem, even though she pointed out that no one had attacked them there. She felt too tired to argue, and there was something comforting about letting someone else make the decisions. He brought her pictures of wedding flowers and dresses, and she nodded. She had no opinion, so why not accede to his?

"We'd better go," he says now. "Bad idea to be late for your own opening. Though—" he glances at her cleavage, "I could ravish you right now." Berenice smiles weakly. They have fallen into a new pattern with sex, too—Rod taking charge while she lies there, trying to register some feeling. Mostly she feels as if she's floating above, watching herself go through the motions. Rod, who has noticed the change, attributes it to delayed shock over the attack. "It's all right," he keeps reassuring her, "you're safe, I promise. I'll never let another man harm you again."

In the car, he puts an arm around her shoulder. "I've hardly seen you in the last month," he says. "It's selfish, but I'm looking forward to this opening being over so that we can be married."

"I'm sorry," Berenice says, "I've been distracted."

"Oh, I wasn't trying to make you feel guilty. You needed to throw yourself into it. And you'll rise to the occasion next weekend, I'm sure."

"I'm glad you think so." Berenice isn't so sure, herself, about her ability to rally for the wedding. Whenever she thinks about it, a mild dread bubbles up. The whole idea of the day brings back memories of performing. There will be an audience familiar with the play, the characters, the costumes. Her part is clear-cut: she must sparkle, shed a tear or two, look dazed at her luck. And it *is* luck, by any measure. Rod is smart and kind, not to mention wealthy and good-looking. He's offering her the lead role in an ongoing story that everyone understands, one that will cause no discomfort, ruffle no feathers. If she'd imagined a different narrative, one with greater danger and more reward, she can only blame herself for the loss. It had been hers to take; she hadn't had the courage to reach out and seize it.

"I'm looking forward to it all being over," she says.

"Amen to that," Rod squeezes her arm. "We'll tell people we're sorry, but we're indisposed. If they don't get the hint, they can go to hell."

Tonight, however, no one is going to hell. When they reach the museum, cars are lined up outside, disgorging passengers in evening dress. People are climbing the marble steps to the museum's new building, with its red brick wings and imposing portico. The sky behind the building is indigo, with scraps of dark cloud whisked across it like brushstrokes.

Inside, laughter and chatter reverberate off the walls. The exhibition is not large—forty-six prints hang in the special exhibitions gallery—but it gives the impression of scope and depth, mostly because of its bold presentation. Some images are no bigger than a paperback; others have been blown up to billboard proportions, so that they feel like environments into which one could step and disappear.

"Wow," says Rod as they enter the room, "this is something."

"You like it?" She hadn't let him see it before now, almost as if the exhibition were the bride that must be kept from him, virginal.

"I'm speechless. I had no idea...how do *you* feel?"

How *does* she feel? Gratified, of course, that Scholle believed in her, and that the public is getting to see work she's labored over for five years. Proud of how far she's brought the project without any financial support. But intensely melancholy, too, because the person she most wants to see this new work is absent. What would Liz say about her portraits of peddlers on the Lower East Side, or her forays into Brooklyn to photograph immigrant churches? Would she think the images artistic *and* socially responsible?

"Speechless too, I see," Rod says. "Well, let me take a good look at everything." He takes a few steps forward, gazing at the walls.

"Berenice!" Scholle hurries over, stoop-shouldered, his broad face perspiring. "You're here in the nick of time. Edmund Morgensen wants meet you before he leaves. Come," he winks, "you never know what could happen."

"Oh. Yes." Berenice follows him, trying to compose her face to look pleasant. It's touching that, even after their debacle with the museum trustees, Scholle is still working to match her with potential patrons. She must be gracious, even though sometimes she feels like telling these people to staple their mouths shut.

For the next hour, she is ushered to meet various members of the city's elite. The ones who are amateur photographers ask for recommendations on film and lenses. Others want to tell anecdotes about the subjects of her images: Grandfather Ellard lived in this building; cousin Harold had a hand in designing that one. She listens and nods, agreeing that one should live above the tenth floor if possible and that the new Waldorf Astoria is an improvement on its predecessor.

At one point, from the corner of her eye, she sees Julien Levy enter with Alfred Stieglitz. The sight makes her anxious, especially when she sees Stieglitz tilt forward to examine her shot looking south from the Salmon Tower. In its angle and composition, and the use of shadow, that photograph bears a passing similarity to some images Stieglitz showed last year at his gallery. Of course, the two of them have entirely different approaches and aesthetics, but to a layperson, that might not be apparent. She wonders if Stieglitz himself sees the differences, or only the overlaps. And—much as she hates herself for the thought—she wonders if he admires the work.

She doesn't have time to dwell on this, though, because in the next moment, Rod is at her side with Holger Cahill.

"Holger!" She steps forward to clasp his hands. "It's good of you to come."

"Berenice! You look as good as the photographs."

"If only."

"He has a great interest in your work," Rod says, "don't you, Holger? Won't you spill the beans?"

Berenice glances at Rod, who's bouncing on the balls of his feet, grinning as if the Giants just scored a touchdown. "What's going on?"

"You'll have to keep it under your hat for a while," says Holger in a low voice. "The announcement won't be made for two weeks—but I want you to know that the committee at the Federal Art Project has approved your grant application in full. We're going to fund you to continue with *Changing New York*."

"Huh?" She can only stare, dumbfounded. Her application had been submitted so long ago, and the names of the agencies changed around so much, that she'd almost forgotten about it. She'd certainly abandoned hope. It had seemed like just another funding request that was doomed to fail.

"Do you know what this means?" Rod says. "You'll get a monthly salary *and* a budget for staff and equipment. For years."

"You'll be able to expand *Changing New York* into a comprehensive survey," Holger says. Looking amused, he adds, "Rod asked if it would affect your family planning. I told him not to worry. The contract is for thirty hours a week, so you'll have time," he raises an eyebrow, "for other activities."

"We'll have a nurse," Rod says. "She can bring the baby to you. You'd want to do that, darling, wouldn't you? Your own nursing?"

"Discreetly, of course," Holger adds.

Berenice looks from one man to the other. Feelings pierce her like pieces of shrapnel: shock, disbelief. Elation. On the one hand, she's overcome with gratitude that her vision, and mission, has finally been funded. On the other hand, she's horrified that the men have determined her childbearing schedule. And that they're discussing the use of her breasts in public.

Holger pats her arm. "It'll become more real soon," he says. "In the meantime, you should look around for assistants and figure out a plan for the work. Your title will be Project Supervisor, and our office will be at your disposal. The FAP will help with anything we can."

And that's when it sinks in: this is real, she has funding. Gratitude and vindication flood her, warming her through. "Thank you, Holger," she says. "Thanks for believing in me."

"There were others involved," he says, "but you're welcome. And now I must go. I have a dinner with the Society of Scribes and Illuminators."

After he takes off, Rod pulls her close and kisses her cheek. "Well, Mrs. Gedney, how about that! It's turning out to be quite an evening."

"It is."

"I'm going to get us champagne. Don't go anywhere; I'll be back in a minute."

The next hour passes in a blur. People are introduced to her; there are conversations and handshakes, congratulations. She talks with a reporter from the *New York Sun*, and poses for a photograph under her image of the De Peyster statue. People hand her glasses of champagne and she drinks, bubbles fizzing and popping in her mouth. It's a good crowd; there must be over a hundred people. She listens to herself holding forth about wooden buildings in the Bronx, and the structural complexities of the Manhattan Bridge.

And then, in a rare quiet moment, Alfred Stieglitz is in front of her. He's wearing a black cape that enfolds him like a bat's wings, and he doesn't look well. His cheeks are sagging, his eyeballs are an unhealthy shade of yellow. "May we—*hrghh*—speak privately for a moment?" he asks.

"All right." She takes a step closer to him, but Stieglitz waves her off.

"No, not here. Come with me—*hrrh*—down the hall. Need to say something…" Before she can respond he takes off, the cape swaying behind him, his heels clicking on the marble floor. Irritated but intrigued, she follows.

They end up in a corridor off the lobby, around a corner, where a landscape painting hangs under a light. Stieglitz positions himself in front of the painting, then folds the wings of his cape around him. With his bushy eyebrows and stern gaze he looks like an owl, or a high court judge about to deliver a verdict. For a moment, she thinks he must be about to congratulate her, and begins to smile. Then he wheezes, a strange rasp with a little whistle on top, and looks at her so stonily that her smile freezes.

"I'm sorry you're not well," she says.

He stares at her through his glasses. "My physical condition is—*hrrgh*—irrelevant. The thing we must discuss is your photography. Specifically your images of midtown, which are—*urggh*—blatant imitations of my own work."

"Excuse me?" She can hardly believe her ears, and for a moment has the urge to take his shoulders and give them a fierce shake, however unwell he might be. The arrogance! "How can you say that? I started working on this project in 1929, before photographing the changing city was even the flicker of an idea in your mind. And my project encompasses the city, whereas *yours*," she gives a dry laugh, "is shot entirely from the windows at your gallery and apartment."

He tilts his head. "That may be. But your image of Fortieth Street was shot this year, and it is entirely derivative of my earlier works. The angle of the light, the shadows on the buildings…"

"Are you crazy?" she cries out. "Light and shadows? Do you think you own the sky?" She pauses, wondering whether to use the word *delusional*—then settles for something else, perhaps worse. "I think you're jealous. *I* have a museum show, whereas *you* have to show your second-rate work in your own gallery." She faces him, determined not to back down.

Stieglitz's skin has turned ashen; his eyes say that, if he could, he would incinerate her. "You are a rude, untalented, inconsequential *woman*," he spits out. "Just wait. I'm going to bury you…" He takes a step forward, almost as if to make good on the threat—then stops suddenly, clutching at his chest. For a moment he's frozen like that, eyebrows raised, lips parted—then blind terror flashes across his face, and her contempt shifts abruptly to alarm.

Gripping his chest again, Stieglitz comes toward her, waving his hands and trying to speak. "*Heh—heh*—help me." He staggers forward, arms outstretched, and then is tipping toward her, falling, crumpling, and she is staggering back from the weight of him, only just managing not to tip over and fall herself. He is tall but thankfully not heavy; under the cape his body feels skeletal. Somehow, she supports him and lowers him to the floor, where he lies on his stomach in a puddle of black cape, face mashed against the marble. He is unconscious but breathing.

Fuck, she thinks, catching her breath. Her heart bangs against her ribs, pumping furiously. Of all the people Stieglitz could have collapsed against, of all the places it could have happened, and he's with her! *What the hell was he thinking, coming at me like that? Coming here at all?* Even when seriously ill, it seems, he still needed to come and berate her. But his venom missed its mark tonight; it hit him instead.

She looks down at him. The side of his face is beaded with sweat and he's shuddering, taking labored breaths. A terrible thought comes to her mind—*What if I leave him here?* He's clearly not going to get up any time soon, and perhaps not at all. The corridor is at an angle to the lobby; his body wouldn't be visible. *He could have come here for air and collapsed, fallen to his knees…*

Trembling, she pushes herself up from the ground. And then she is standing, looking down on him. His glasses are askew on his nose, his lips are dry and pale. White hair wisps across his face like strands of cotton candy.

Go on, Berenice, she wills herself, *walk away. You owe him nothing.*

Tentatively, she takes a step away from his prone body. *Good girl. Keep going.*

And then she thinks of his last, ironic words—*I'm going to bury you*—and stops. She thinks of the fear in his eyes as he came teetering toward her.

Quickly, she casts a glance toward the lobby—no one is passing. *Fuck.* Should she run for help? Just then, Stieglitz's breathing becomes more urgent, with a sound that sends a chill through her. He's struggling, his chest rising and falling with deep, labored heaves.

And she knows what to do—of course she does. There isn't much time. She sinks to her knees and puts two hands around the cape and under his chest, then tries to lift him and turn him onto his back. It won't work, she realizes. She'll need to support his head, to make sure it doesn't fall to the floor with a crack. Inching forward, she puts her right hand on the back of his head, marveling at how small it feels under the soft white hair. She uses her left hand and knees to nudge his body onto its side. Once she has levered it up, it's relatively easy to push him down onto his back. His body flops down, landing with a *thwok!* on the marble. But his head is safe. She draws her hand from under it, lowering it carefully to the marble as she does so.

He's still gasping for breath, and she gets to work. With her fingers knit together, she pushes down on his chest. *One two three four five six seven...* After Lil died, she looked up resuscitation in library books, desperate to see what she could have done differently. She read the details over and over, so many times that they might as well be tattooed on her heart. The preferred method: thirty compressions, two rescue breaths. Hard, fast pumps in the middle of the chest; head tilted back for the rescue breaths. *When administered correctly, cardiopulmonary resuscitation can triple a person's chances of survival...*

...twenty-seven, twenty-eight, twenty-nine, thirty... She bends down, pushes his glasses up on his nose, lowers her mouth. His mustache is wiry, uncomfortable on her lips, and his breath is cool and sour. No matter: she pinches his nose, gives the two breaths, then readies her hands to push again. *One two three four five six...*

She's at twenty-one when she hears heels clicking across the marble of the lobby. "Help!" she cries out, "down here! Help me!"

The footsteps stop, start again—then around the corner comes a young couple she doesn't recognize. It doesn't matter. "Call an ambulance!" she cries. "Get help! He's having a heart attack!"

For a moment, the young man and woman hang there, gape-mouthed, then the man pulls away and runs. Berenice continues pumping, doing rescue breaths—her actions now pared-down, pure. The museum around her melts away, and nothing exists but the transfer of air from one pair of lungs to another, the pressure of her hands on his chest. *Fifteen, sixteen, seventeen, eighteen...*

Footsteps; faces peering. A crowd in the lobby; the couple's panic must have rippled through the room. Scholle at the entrance to the corridor, arms akimbo, trying to calm the crowd. *Ladies and gentleman, we have things under control! The ambulance is on the way!* Rod materializing at her side, trying to take over. She elbows him in the chest—*No!* She's in a place where she can't stop. It's as if she and Stieglitz have become conjoined, a single entity—their rhythms match, she is transferring her life force to him.

Finally, a siren sounds outside and two medics run in with a stretcher. She sits back and watches, feeling emptied-out and sick. Stieglitz's mouth is red from her lipstick; there are flecks of crimson on his mustache hairs too. The medics fit him with an oxygen mask, which sits like a beak on his sunken-in face. They lift him onto the stretcher.

As the stretcher passes her, Berenice looks down at the man who has directed so much of photography's course—and made her own life so difficult. His forehead is wrinkled; his eyes are creased in pain. What is happening in his brain now? In some well of consciousness, is he feeling alone and scared? Much as they hate each other, she doesn't wish this on him. He's not a monster, he deserves compassion.

"Darling, are you all right?" Rod is behind her, touching her shoulder, trying to take her arm. "You must be worn out."

She can't face his ministrations now. "Don't make a fuss. I need some air." She staggers down the corridor, blinking as she reaches the lobby. With Stieglitz's removal, attention has shifted, and no one registers her as she emerges from the corridor. Instead, there's the excited babble of people whispering, comparing notes. *Of course...in New Mexico...who knows...? Pretty new assistant...not the first time...*

Berenice walks forward, conscious of Rod hovering behind her. And then she stops dead—for she has seen something, or thinks she did. Behind a group of people, a figure in a black crocheted evening dress. Short feathered hair; eyes the color of silver smoke. Her breath quickens, but before she can get a better look, two people push in front of her, obscuring her view. She stands on tiptoe, trying to peer around their heads, but by the time she gets a clear view, the woman has vanished. Where did she go to? Or was it a mirage?

"You should get a medal," Rod says behind her.

"No!" She turns, flashing him a warning glance. "It can't be made public. Can you go and tell Scholle to shut down the press? Find me in a minute. I need to do something…" Without waiting for an answer she stumbles off, weaving through groups in the lobby, hobbling, the thin soles of her shoes slapping against the marble—*thwap, thwap!* A man reaches out trying to ask a question, and she waves him off. Eyes follow her; she must look a fright, with wild hair and smudged lips. It doesn't matter; none of it matters.

Finally, she reaches the edge of the crowd. Left, right: she scans for a black dress—by the doors, the cloakroom—but there's nothing. Crestfallen, she looks back into the crowd. No crocheted black dress, no feathered hair. All she sees are men in tuxedos, women in jewel-colored dresses. A bald head reflecting the ceiling chandelier.

Where to? She runs down a corridor to the ladies' room, then bursts through the swing door. "Anyone here? Elizabeth?" Only one stall is occupied; visible under the door are two black lace-up shoes. "Is there a problem?" an elderly voice warbles, and Berenice sags. "No. I'm looking for someone, that's all."

Panting, she hurries back to the lobby and, skirting the crowd, runs to the double doors, pushes them open and steps into the night. Humid air enfolds her, bringing with it smells of cut grass and diesel. A bus careens down Fifth Avenue, almost empty; beyond it, Central Park bristles in the dark. But there is no one on the entrance steps; no one in the covered walkways lining the courtyard. In the window of a neighboring building, someone pulls curtains together. The city is winding down its day.

Did she imagine it? Stress can do things to the body. Or there could be a simpler explanation. It could have been a woman who resembled Liz. But then why would she disappear?

She can't go back inside yet. The thought of listening to the Stieglitz gossip and having Rod all over her is unbearable. The entrance steps feel cool and inviting. She sinks onto the lowest one. The adrenalin surge that has carried her through the last half-hour is wearing off and she is drained now. Mostly, though, she feels crushing sadness, a sense that she should have been on the bus that passed a minute ago. Forlorn, she lets out a moan.

It's an unusually clear night for the city; some constellations are visible. She can make out the Big Dipper and Polaris, though anything else is beyond her. Rod, of course, would know. A crescent moon hangs low, the merest shaving of light. But between these points of brightness, the sky has the blackness of a void—a darkness that could suck you in, obliterate you.

Behind her, a rustling, some footsteps. Someone stops and, with a creak of bone, sits on the step. There's another rustle, a soft exhalation—as if the person is carrying something weighty but fragile.

"So, Berenice Abbott," a voice says, "are you thinking of photographing the moon?"

And then, goosebumps cover her skin and her pulse is everywhere. The air is alive, permeated with a magic that didn't exist a few seconds ago. She hardly dares move, lest the enchantment vanish.

"That was a good thing you did, back there," the voice goes on. "You showed compassion."

"How do you know it was me?"

"I saw your face across the room. The expression, your make-up. Don't ask me how, but I knew. Don't worry, I won't tell."

At this, Berenice dares to steal a glance at the form next to her, solid and curvy in the crocheted dress. Lit by muted light from surrounding windows, Liz's face is a faint oval. But Berenice can make out the broad cheeks, smudges of nostril, a shine of iris.

"Why did you come?" she asks. "If you didn't—"

"I wanted to see the show," Liz says. "To see your new work. I felt sure it would be wonderful, and I was right."

Her voice is firm, as if she's practiced the line—but there's a shake at its edge, a tremor of disingenuousness. This sets off a corresponding tremor—fearful, hopeful—in Berenice. "And me?" she asks. "What were you going to do if you saw me?"

"I don't know. Run away," Liz says with a laugh. "Or maybe congratulate you on the exhibit and your upcoming marriage. I hadn't really thought that far. I dressed discreetly, to blend in. Then I was leaving and saw the crisis, and it upended the story I'd been telling myself about you. That you were cold, opportunistic."

"That I'd been using you for my work," Berenice murmurs.

"Yes. And I came out and saw you sitting here, and it seemed cowardly not to congratulate you. The new work moved me, I wanted to tell you that. I thought it would be petty not to. You know, because of our—misunderstanding."

The new work moved me. And if she's moved by the work...Berenice's heart is thumping so madly that it seems to be blocking her airways. She's afraid of what will come out of her mouth next, afraid she'll miss the mark, botch it somehow. There's a sliver of hope, thin as the moon, and if she can use the right words it might grow bigger and brighter.

"I owe so much to you. I couldn't have done it without your help," she says quietly. "Every intelligent thought I've had about the work has been inspired by you. When I pick up my camera, it's your voice I hear. You're in my blood, Liz. I'm a better artist when you're near me—a better person, too. And that's the person I want to be."

Next to her, a sharp intake of breath. It feels to Berenice as if the air is vibrating, stretching with a tension that could snap at any moment. She waits for Liz to leave, to run down the steps as she did at the police precinct. For a moment, she wishes she could press a shutter and freeze them in this moment.

"What—" Liz begins, her voice so soft that Berenice almost doesn't hear. She clears her throat and starts again. "What about your fiancé? Does he inspire similar feelings?" Her tone has only the barest hint of bitterness, and Berenice hangs her head, knowing she deserves worse.

"I've been such an idiot, Liz. I told myself I could make a decent job of being his wife. I thought friendship was a reasonable foundation for a marriage. And maybe it would be. But oh, my love—it's nothing like I feel for you! And now I think that he doesn't deserve that. I don't want to lie to him. Or anyone."

She dares lift her head. Even in the darkness, she can tell Liz is flushing, that her body is taut. Within this tension floats a second chance, as filmy and tenuous as a soap bubble. She must reach out—gently, tenderly—and see if she can touch it without breaking the fragile membrane. Because she knows, absolutely, that she wants to. Respectability, material comfort—it doesn't matter any more. She's interested in another kind of richness.

Slowly, lest the ripples it causes are startling, she moves her hand through the warm air and places it on top of Liz's. Like she did in the taxi, but if possible, more tentatively.

And, just as slowly, Liz takes her hand and threads her fingers through the gaps in Berenice's, so that the two hands are knit in her lap. It is at once deeply calming and erotic, like sinking into a steamy, scented tub. A sigh shudders through Berenice, and then something splashes on her skin. A tear has fallen from Liz's face. Tiny shockwaves shiver through her hand as Liz's body convulses with silent sobs.

She pushes herself across the step until the gap between them is closed. Then she raises her free hand and lifts Liz's chin, tilting it until she's staring directly into the gray eyes. "It's going to be all right," she says. "Do you hear? Everything will be fine. Listen—" her voice falters for a second, "you make me brave. And I won't be the first person to break off a wedding."

She moves her face toward Liz's—and when the gray eyes blink in shock she smiles back, telegraphing *I don't care! Let the whole world see!* By some miracle, Liz doesn't pull back, and they move together—slowly, so slowly—until their lips meet in a tremble of softness and warmth. At first the kiss is hesitant, almost chaste, but then, as they move closer, there is urgency, and moisture, and the intense happiness of this is almost too much for Berenice.

In the back of her mind is the knowledge that her life has just become harder. There will be no wedding, no social acceptance. Instead there will be prejudice and struggle. But she doesn't care. She tastes saltiness on her lips—her tears or Liz's, it isn't clear—and drinks it in. She doesn't deserve this, she knows. It seems outrageous that she could ever be this happy.

PART SIX

NEW YORK & OHIO, 1951

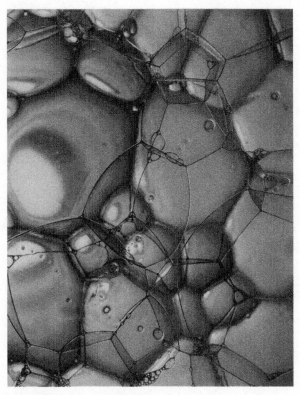

Soap bubbles, 1946, by Berenice Abbott

TWENTY-SIX

"Damn," Berenice says, "damn, damn." She waves her fingers in the air to cool the burn, but it keeps throbbing.

"Ice?" asks Pat.

Berenice shakes her head. "It's not bad. Let's push on."

Cradling her hand, she walks to her desk and picks up the textbook on electromagnetics. Just then, her assistant jumps up and shakes her own finger. "Shit!" Pat exclaims. "I can't believe I did that!" For a moment they look at each other in dismay, then Berenice laughs.

"I guess we should invest in a couple of pairs of gloves," she says. "Or alternatively, not do hot experiments."

They're trying to visualize a sound wave, which is the most complicated process she has attempted yet. It's done by playing music through a sort of glass flute called a Rubens tube. One end of this tube is connected to a propane canister, the other faces a stereo speaker. First you open the gas valve and light the gas leaking through the tube's twenty flute-holes, which creates a line of tiny flames. Then, when you send sound through the tube, the differing sound wave pressures make the flames rise and fall in concert with the music. It's a thrilling sight. When Berenice saw it demonstrated weeks before at New York University, she wanted to jump to her feet and applaud.

But it isn't working as a photograph—yet. The flames move too quickly and are hard to manipulate, even when she plays them lugubrious music. And she and her assistant are fast losing sensation in their fingers.

She sighs. "I'm shooting at the highest possible speed, but there'll still be blur."

"Maybe that's not so bad. It could give a sense of movement."

"No," Berenice says, "too sloppy. I'm beginning to suspect it might only work as a movie." It's hot in the studio. Having the Rubens tube in the Supersight has created a furnace-like effect. Her shirt is sticking to her chest under her arms, and her forehead is moist. She juts out her bottom lip and puffs upward, blowing her bangs off her forehead. "I've changed my mind, dear— let's call it a day and re-try tomorrow."

"Should I come early, before you teach? I could make contact prints."

"No," Berenice looks at her young assistant, whose keenness reminds her of herself at twenty-three. "Get some rest, come at noon. God knows, you've earned it."

When Pat has gone, she moves across the studio, carefully avoiding her light rigs and the Supersight. She's tired and cross. They've been working on this image for two days and it's still not coming out. She has to return the Rubens tube to the lab at NYU by the end of the week. If she can't get her shot tomorrow, she'll have to call it quits.

Whenever she can't get good results, she becomes irritable. Unfortunately, with scientific photography, this happens more often than not. Taking scientific phenomena and turning them into art is the hardest thing she's ever done. It's harder than capturing a person's essence in a portrait, harder than combining light, framing and composition to make a decent picture of a skyscraper. Perhaps because of this, her few successes have given her an almost giddy joy. So that's how it is with this project. The lows are lower, the highs higher. Which, it turns out, is enough to keep her hooked.

At her desk, she sees something that gives her encouragement. She made the print a few weeks ago, having gotten the idea when she was soaking in a bubble bath one day, idly watching light reflect bubbles onto the facing tiles. The reflections danced and undulated, playing out little dramas, flirting and clashing with each other. With sudden clarity, she saw that some bubbles were not at all round, but instead formed interesting trapezoids and polyhedrons. She watched, entranced, until her fingertips were pruned into waved ridges.

That image had failed too, at first. The lighting was near impossible and even without hot lights on them the bubbles kept popping, spattering soap on the lens. She only started making headway after happening on an article about Man Ray's famous Rayographs, which made her realize that a camera-less print could work here too. She'd had to laugh. Man was a bastard, but he'd had some good ideas.

There's a knock at the door and Liz peers carefully around it. They live in a converted perfume factory on Commerce Street in the West Village, with Berenice's studio and their rooms in the front of the building. Liz keeps a room down the hall that she uses as an office and library.

She steps in and over a snaggle of lighting cables, wincing as she lifts a foot. Her rheumatoid arthritis has been flaring up lately. "Still no luck?"

"How can you tell?"

"Your posture. And stillness. You'd be bouncing around all over if you'd had good results."

"Oh, my love," Berenice says, "you know me too well."

Liz *tsks*. "I'm sorry it's not going better. Listen, do you want to come to this thing with me tonight? A Stevenson fundraiser?"

"No, I'm worn out. I'll just rest." This is a bit disingenuous, but Berenice can't get beyond her own woes at the moment. And really, she's not in the mood to spend time with Liz's political buddies, who are sadly still convinced that Stevenson has a chance against Eisenhower.

"All right," Liz says, "but don't sit here being glum."

"I'm always glum when I can't find an answer."

"I know. But you get so wrapped up in the problem that you forget what you've done right." She comes up to Berenice. "You're brilliant, Bea—and I'm not just saying that because I love you. For goodness' sake, you invented a camera! You'll figure this out." She reaches a hand to Berenice's face, and Berenice closes her eyes, leaning in to the warm skin. The touch is at once soothing and reinvigorating—it spurs her to continue working. How miraculous that Liz always knows what she needs!

"I'd stay," Liz murmurs, "but I promised Alex."

"Go," Berenice pats her on the shoulder, though she'd like to continue the intimacy. How far they've come! Not open with the world, perhaps, but gloriously open with each other, and as entwined physically as they are intellectually.

She watches as Liz steps carefully back to the door. Before Liz can leave, she says, "Have fun tonight, Butchy."

Liz looks up, grinning. *Butchy and Sassy*—a bum had shouted it one day as they were walking down Lafayette Street. They could have been offended, but they decided to laugh. After that, Berenice had started calling Liz Butchy, and it stuck as their private nickname. It suits her, with her muscular shoulders and broad face.

Left alone, she contemplates Liz's words. It's true, she did invent a camera. She glances at the huge Projection-Supersight, which looks for all the world like some kind of H.G. Wells time machine, five feet tall and black as tar. It is, she believes, the first super-high definition camera in existence. Unlike a normal camera, it works by putting the subject *behind* the lens, then projecting the image onto a wall, where she pins a sheet of film to record it. In this way she can produce a poster-sized negative with every tiny detail as sharp as a knife. She can shoot a picture of a fish that shows the lacy lines on its scales, or show each pore and follicle in a human hand.

And yet, she thinks, *no one gives a damn.* A few years ago she had approached camera companies with her patent for the Supersight, only to be sent packing, blueprints in hand. Giants like Kodak and Agfa were the only ones capable of funding something that ambitious—but they only cared about the mass-market. That's where the money was. It was infuriating; she took them gold and they acted as if she was peddling horse manure.

Her science photographs have been met with indifference, too. She's caught between two camps: scientists don't appreciate her artistry, and fine-art curators find the work too clinical. Though their lack of vision is depressing, she feels sure it can't persist—it's just a matter of waiting for the world to catch up to her.

She glances at the Rubens tube, and Liz's words reverberate through her mind. *You'll figure this out...* All of a sudden she realizes that the answer might not lie in changing the music going into the tube. The rubber tube feeding the gas in to the tube is half an inch wide. If she puts an adjustable clamp on it, she could control the flow and likely get a more elegant line of flame.

"You couldn't have thought of that before?" she murmurs. But she knows it's the way. Sometimes you have to let go, letting your subconscious worry away at a problem. Then, when you're least expecting it, there's a ring on the doorbell and here is your answer, looking as cool as if it had made a formal appointment.

Now, does she have anything that could serve as a clamp? She looks around, evaluating her scrap materials. Ah! She grabs a piece of copper wire. Then, feeling cautiously optimistic, she hurries over to the tube.

◆

"We see very differently from a camera," Berenice says. "*Our* vision is flexible, imaginative. It is influenced by our personal psychology and, of course, our memories. At times, the mind even alters what we see."

"How so?" asks a student. His name is… Howard? Harold? She can't remember, probably because his work is so bland. She thinks of him as Mr. First, because he is always first with comments and questions.

"Say you're photographing a skyscraper," she paces to the window, then turns to the twelve students. The way their faces are raised to her—open and wide-eyed, like baby birds waiting for a worm from Mother—gives her a quiver of pride. It has taken a while, but after seventeen years at the New School she has finally relaxed into her role as teacher, guru and nurturer. "When you look up at that skyscraper through the camera lens, the outer walls converge as they go skyward—that's perspective," she says. "Our mind, however, knows those walls are straight. So when *we* look up, it presents us with parallel lines. It makes a physiological correction based on what we know."

"So you'd adjust the camera's tilts and swings to get a true shot?" asks another male student.

"But what is 'true'?" A soft voice from the back of the room—Ah, a woman! With relief, Berenice turns to look. It's Rosa Jaworski. An odd girl, with a glittering, ferret-like intensity, but she takes gorgeous pictures of working-class Poles.

"Good question," she says. "The discrepancy between the two visions gives us a choice. I could choose the camera's perspective and get a shot that disconcerts the viewer, because it's not how we see. That could be dramatic. Or I could adjust the tilts and swings for a more conventional shot."

"But, Miss Abbott—" Mr. First again, sounding uneasy. "Aren't you an advocate of straight photography?"

She looks at him and thinks, *Harvey*. That's his name. She can't help smiling. Truth be told, she has a soft spot for all her students, even the hopeless ones.

"Yes, Harvey, I am," she says. "But I don't consider it 'crooked' to produce an image that reflects a state of psychological realism. That might be the truest image of all. And now," she looks through the window at the downtown buildings smudged against an indigo sky, "that's enough for today, I think. The night is lovely. Go enjoy it."

A few minutes later, as she begins the fifteen-minute walk from the New School to Commerce Street, she contemplates Rosa's words. *What is true?* One way or another, the question has dogged her for years.

Is it foolish to assume one can pin the concept down? With *Changing*

New York she'd tried, most of all, to expose the wondrous fluidity of a city in transition. She wanted to lay the place bare (in her own particular style, of course). Is that truth? Now, with her science photographs, she's making visible hidden forces like magnetism and sound frequency, to reveal their beauty. The aesthetic is hers, but the forces and entities belong to nature. Is *that* truth?

On Seventh Avenue, she pauses briefly to admire a sleek Chrysler whose hood ornament is styled to look like a flying bird. Ah, the human desire for flight! She feels it still, an ache in her solar plexus, a longing to rise up and escape the banal bonds of gravity. One of her recent Supersight images is of a detached goose's wing, spread to show all the tiny, intricate vanes in the feather.

Her interest in science had begun in 1939, that fateful year when Europe was gearing up to confront Germany. It was also the year Holger Cahill called her in for a meeting about her grant from the Federal Art Project and explained that, with war looming, the government would be making cutbacks. The FAP was an obvious target because, in the public's eyes, it supported Communist radicals. "Your actions there haven't helped, you know," he said, which made her want to laugh, or cry. So she belonged to the Photo League—so what? Granted, some of the League's members were card-carrying Commies, but that didn't mean they spent their meetings singing the Internationale or plotting to overthrow the government.

"I need this, Holger," she'd told him. "I've barely even started on my third section, *People and How They Live*." But it was already too late; she could tell by his eyes. She was given three months to wrap up the project.

She turns onto Grove Street, feeling the familiar anger bubble up as she remembers how she was treated: the repossession of her FAP car, the hasty removal of her files from the midtown office. After that, she'd been lost for a while. *Changing New York* had been her life for ten years. Without it, she barely knew who she was. She sank into what she supposed, now, was depression. If not for her teaching and Liz, it would have been worse. As it was, she stopped taking photographs for a few months, gave up dancing and going to clubs. Instead, she huddled in bed reading novels by Sartre and Camus, fancying herself very authentic.

And then Liz had dragged her—kicking and screaming—to the World's Fair.

She smiles, remembering this—for yes, odd as it seems now, she'd been reluctant to go. Frankly, she expected it to be all gaudiness and blather. The papers had been touting silly exhibits like the General Motors transparent car and Elektro, a seven-foot robot that could smoke. On top of that, the whole thing seemed profoundly tone-deaf given what was happening in Europe. Hitler was trampling the continent liked a crazed bull, and the clueless Americans were celebrating science and commerce.

But as it turned out, the fair was a triumph. A former ash dump in Queens had been transformed into a candy-colored utopia, a place to come and forget about the news for a day. There were flashy exhibits, yes—but there were others too, less silly and more substantive. Glass tubes of cool white fluorescent light! A "facsimile" machine that could take a letter or drawing and send it around the world!

She saw something else, too. As exciting as the scientific processes were, the photographs illustrating them were woefully inferior. Badly composed, insufficiently lit, shoddily printed—it was as if the scientists *wanted* their work to be ignored. You had to squint to make anything out, and even then, they were often more obfuscating than enlightening.

I could take this on, she'd thought. It was the first time she'd felt her pulse in months. The feeling was similar to the one she'd had in 1929, when she returned from Paris and walked the streets of New York: euphoria, dread, disbelief. *It would be like a flea attacking a giant*, she thought. But the thought of stepping onto virgin territory was exhilarating.

She'd try, she decided. What was the point of staying safe and comfortable? If she failed, at least she would have made a valiant attempt.

If she failed… She gets in the elevator at Commerce Street and leans against the wall. Has she failed? She's been chipping away at this science photography for over a decade and the recognition has been scant to non-existent. The only exception was the year she worked as photo editor for *Science Illustrated*, where she'd enjoyed some authority and had fun photographing beetles and brains. But the work was limiting, and she left when the magazine was sold to a pair of idiots. Since then, it's been like pushing a boulder uphill.

She sighs. *Believe in yourself, Bea*, she thinks, *you're doing something worthwhile*. It's something that's never been done before. If only because no one else has been obstinate enough to try.

◆

A few weeks later, Pat calls her to the telephone. "It's your sister," she whispers, her hand over the mouthpiece.

Berenice feels her stomach tighten, as it does every time Hazel calls. She always expects it to be *the* call, the one in which they face Ma's inability to live alone. For a brief moment she's tempted to ask Pat to take a message—but she can't, that would be too cowardly.

Her older sister had moved back to Cleveland three years before, and located their mother. Ma has arthritis and lapses of memory, and her liver must be pickled by now, but still, she hangs on. Say what you want about the Abbott women, they are survivors.

She takes the receiver from Pat, then girds herself against the telephone table. "Hazel?"

"Bernice," Hazel says. "Ma isn't doing well."

Berenice sits down heavily on the chair by the table. She feels the familiar tangle of guilt and anger, sympathy and resentment that the thought of Ma brings up.

"She called me last week—I knew it must be bad. I took her to the doctor, and he says she has emphysema now as well as the cirrhosis. I guess she's been smoking a lot these past few years, as well as drinking."

"I—" Berenice struggles with what to say. The idea of Ma being incapacitated is unthinkable. She's the one who grew up with Ma, and by rights should be looking out for her—but how could she? She could hardly bring Ma to New York to live with her and Liz; neither could she upend her life and move to Ohio, for however long it took for Ma's stubborn organs to give out. "What do we do?" she asks.

"I don't know. She refused to come stay with me. So I set her up there as best I could. Got her some new sheets, cushions. Tried to make the place look cheerful."

Gratitude floods Berenice. "Thank you," she says. "I'll send some money."

"She'll like that," Hazel says drily. They both know what will happen to any money Ma receives.

"Do you think I should come?"

On the other end of the line, there's a soft sigh. "You have to decide for yourself, Bernice. I know things weren't easy between the two of you."

There's no resentment in Hazel's tone, it seems, only weariness. As a social worker, she must be used to situations like this. Judging by their phone calls, she is an intelligent woman who focuses on the practical. But they haven't talked at length, because of the cost—or maybe they have too much to say and are afraid to start.

"Will you check on her in a few days, and let me know if she's worse?" Berenice asks.

"Yes, I can do that."

"Thank you." Before putting down the receiver, Berenice pauses. "Look after yourself, Hazel."

"You too, Bernice."

Berenice replaces the receiver. It's disturbing to think of Ma huffing up the stairs to her apartment with stiff limbs and labored breath. She wonders why, in her desperation, Ma turned to the daughter she barely knows. Was she trying to make Berenice feel guilty? Or was it merely that Hazel is local?

A vague memory surfaces then, of her chubby hands being laced with string, and having to keep still as Hazel untangled it. They'd been playing cat's cradle, but Berenice's fingers were clumsy. She can't have been more than four. Her sister's ability to transform the string into bridges and diamonds had seemed almost magical.

Looking across the room, she sighs. Much as she dreads a visit to Cleveland, she'll have to do it. Ma is her blood, her past. If the end is coming—and it seems to be—then Berenice can't delay the visit much longer.

TWENTY-SEVEN

Beaumont Newhall is sitting in a corner of the Charcoal Grill Room, sipping a Bloody Mary and looking every bit the tweedy professor. When she spots him, Berenice's spirits lift. She's always glad to see Beaumont. He was the first head of photography at the Museum of Modern Art, and as such, was discerning and courteous. They became friends, and she'd been disappointed five years ago when he decided to move up to Rochester. He's now directing the museum at the former mansion of George Eastman, Kodak's founder.

He stands as she approaches, his large frame towering over her as he kisses her cheek. "Berenice! You look good. How are you?"

"Well," she answers. "You?"

"Oh, you know. Rochester's like the Arctic Circle. But I'm digging in and doing a lot of work."

"Good for you."

"Let's order you a drink, shall we? And some food?"

A few minutes later, when she's three sips into her own Bloody Mary and they've dispensed with small talk, he leans forward. "Listen, I have a surprise, and I think you'll be happy. I had dinner the other day with an old friend, Sam Kittredge. He's an editor at Doubleday and Co."

"Oh?" The walls are mirrored, and just beyond him she can see a small reflection of her face—pale, red-lipped, intrigued.

"Yes. He came to the house and I happened to have some of your proofs around. Sam liked them. Wanted to meet you, actually. Said he'd consider doing a book."

Berenice puts down her Bloody Mary, suddenly acutely conscious of its peppery aftertaste. "You mean the Supersight work?" She thinks of the proofs she sent Beaumont: her fish head, the bubbles. A close-up of Pat's ear. It has been difficult to get the work published and as a result few people have seen it.

"Yes. I know you're selective about who sees them, but I felt I could trust Sam. He's a bit of a scientist *manqué*. He remembered the fish photo from *Science Illustrated*. Captivating, he called it. Of course I told him how dedicated you've been to this Supersight work."

Berenice's throat has constricted. She doesn't trust herself to speak. Is it possible that now, without her having to go after it, someone wants to publish her Supersight photographs?

She holds up her Bloody Mary, her hand a little shaky. "Well. We might have to switch to champagne."

"There's just one thing," Beaumont says, and she thinks, *Ah, the 'thing.'* There always is one. "Sam is a top-shelf editor," Beaumont continues. "He does beautiful books and he wants them to be prestigious. He's asked that you get an exhibition at MoMA to coincide with the book's publication."

She'd been taking a sip of Bloody Mary and she sputters and almost spits it out. Getting an exhibition at MoMA would be wonderful, of course, but it's not as if she can rap on the door of the country's premier photography gallery and ask to be put on the schedule. She's no fan of Edward Steichen, the blueblood who took over from Beaumont. He's a former pictorialist who worked closely with Stieglitz for years, then became a slick advertising photographer. In her view, it's a travesty that he was given the top job at MoMA.

"Do you think I have a chance with Steichen?"

Beaumont sighs. "Ed can be short-sighted. But you have such a strong body of work. I think even he should be able to see that."

"Does it have to be MoMA?"

"I'm afraid so. Sam was emphatic. Listen, I can make sure Steichen agrees to see you, and I'll press your case. Then you'll have to charm him."

"Not my strong suit."

"Oh, come. I'm sure if you put your mind to it, you can do it. Should I set up the appointment?"

She pauses. "Yes."

"Good."

They look at each other then, with a wry smile that acknowledges what they're both thinking. If Beaumont had still been head of photography at

MoMA, she would have been a shoo-in. Beaumont is down-to-earth, a realist and champion of documentary photography. She and he see eye to eye.

Steichen, on the other hand…getting him appointed at MoMA had been one of Stieglitz's last power plays before dying, three years before, from a final heart attack. That was Stieglitz all over. If he couldn't have the job himself, he was going to make sure his proxy got it. He died without knowing her part in saving him from his first heart attack, which was fine with her. She was going to earn his respect through her work, or not at all.

Now she looks at Beaumont, who is deftly dissecting an almond-encrusted trout. "Beaumont? May I ask you something?"

"Of course."

"Did Stieglitz try to sabotage you when you were at MoMA? Is that partly why you left?"

Beaumont looks up. He is prematurely balding and the top of his head is a shiny, furrowed dome. "Sabotage? No. But I can't say he made life easier. I must say, it was clever of him to donate so much work to the museum in its early days. It gave him a certain—access."

"Are things better up in Rochester?"

He mulls this over. "It's early days, but I think so. Kodak more or less owns the town, but it's a decent company. The people at Eastman House are very professional." Now he looks over at her. "Funny, isn't it, that we can't seem to agree on what kind of photography should hang in museums? One would have thought we could be civil, have a decent discussion. But instead, we're like children scrambling for toys in a sandbox."

"Because there aren't enough toys to go round."

"I'm not sure I agree. There could be. You'd think someone like Steichen, in his position, could widen his perspective. Give a nod to pictorialism here, a nod to documentary there, another nod to abstraction. Include it all. But no, in his mind there's a hierarchy, and 'straight' photography is on the bottom."

"That doesn't augur well for my meeting with him."

"No," Beaumont says. "Well, I'll help you however I can. But I'm not someone he listens to that closely."

Walking away from the restaurant, slightly tipsy after two Bloody Marys, Berenice contemplates having to win over Edward Steichen. A blueblood, the producer of slick commercial work, this is the man she must impress. She must bow down to him, cede to his authority, do her little dance and dazzle him with her artistry. She must leave him breathless and convinced.

It's a hard assignment, but she won't be daunted. She's known tougher.

◆

From the Charcoal Grill Room, she goes to meet Liz at the doctor's office. Liz hadn't wanted her to come, but Berenice had insisted. If there's more bad news, Liz shouldn't have to bear it on her own.

She walks east on Fifty-Second Street, past the '21' Club and a couple of weathered juke joints. In the Forties—already it seems an age away—she and Liz had frequented some of these clubs. She remembers seeing Thelonius Monk, in his sharkskin suit and fluffy knit cap, play at the Three Deuces. The idiosyncratic twists and syncopations, those dissonant chords—his music inspired her to reach for similar flair with her science photography.

When she gets to Dr. Vinson's office, Liz is in the waiting room, looking stoic in her burgundy suit. She's reading a copy of *McCall's*, but when she sees Berenice, she puts the magazine down.

"You needn't have come. I'm fine."

"Too bad, I'm here."

"Yes," Liz sighs, and Berenice sees she's too drained to argue.

"Not a good day?" she asks.

"It's not bad, just some pain in my hips. The worst thing is that I had to miss the De Kooning preview. It's so aggravating."

Berenice smiles. How Liz-like, to put an art opening above her own health. She decides not to tell Liz about Beaumont. Let them deal with the doctor first. If she shares her news now, Liz would be so fluttery that she wouldn't be able to concentrate.

"Miss McCausland," the receptionist calls. Instinctively, Berenice rises too, only to be frowned at. "Just Miss McCausland, ma'am."

"I'm her—" Berenice starts, then falters and sits down again. She can't say it, even now. The cowardice makes her feel like a traitor.

Liz pats her arm. "It's all right, Bea. I'll be fine. Just wait for me here."

And so, marooned in the stuffy waiting room, Berenice examines the diamond pattern in the textured wallpaper, tapping her fingers on the wooden chair arms until she senses a woman opposite staring at her. Then she picks up the copy of *McCall's* and tries to guess what Liz was looking at. She very much doubts Liz was reading *How to Make a Little White Jacket* or *Eight Fabulous Recipes for the Smiling Strawberry*. She could have been taking in Eleanor Roosevelt's latest column or losing herself in a short story. But if Berenice had to guess, she'd say Liz was studying John Gunther's interview with presidential hopeful Eisenhower. She would have committed quotes to memory, ready to bring them out later to prove a point.

Oh, Elizabeth McCausland, she thinks, *you're a fine specimen.* Sixteen years together, and her admiration for the woman has only increased. It maddens her that other people think Liz's writing too florid, or political, and that she has been passed over for jobs at the major newspapers. Thinking of this, Berenice shakes her head—what a lot of rejection they've been through together, one way and another! But they've gotten through it, and they'll get through this medical business too. Rheumatoid arthritis doesn't scare her.

After twenty minutes or so, Liz emerges from the doctor's room looking pale. Berenice rises and goes to her.

"Are you all right?"

"Yes. He drew blood, though, and I'm feeling a bit light-headed. Can we take a taxi home?"

At home, Berenice settles Liz in bed with a cup of tea and her current read, a brick-like biography of Trotsky. She sits on the edge of the bed, her weight pulling the sheet tight over Liz's legs.

"Now, are you going to tell me what happened?"

"What do you mean?"

"Why did Dr. Vinson need to test your blood so soon after your last visit?"

Liz sighs. "I told you, Bea. He was worried I might be getting anemic."

"But anemia isn't part of rheumatoid arthritis, is it?"

"No. But he thought I looked pale, and I told him I'd been getting tired, so he wanted to check." Liz smiles wanly. "I'm lucky he's thorough. Now, dear girl, let me rest, will you? Otherwise there's no way I'm going to get my piece on Guston finished."

Berenice nods, but doesn't feel satisfied. Liz wears deception badly. She's definitely keeping something to herself—but now isn't the time to probe. Butchy is right, she needs rest, not nagging.

She starts to walk out, then stops. "Oh! I almost forgot. I have news. Beaumont has a friend who wants to publish a book of my Supersight work."

"What?" A light comes into Liz's eyes and she scrambles to push herself up. "But that's wonderful! My goodness! Why didn't you tell me before?"

"It's wonderful, yes. But there's a condition. I have to talk Ed Steichen into giving me a show at MoMA, to coincide with the book's release."

Liz's face puckers. She knows what this means.

"Exactly," says Berenice. "I've got some work to do."

"Oh, but we can do it, Bea! We'll talk to John Marin. He's friendly with Steichen. And do you remember my friend Nora Beacham from the editorial board of *Art News*? She knows Mrs. Steichen. I'll see what I can find out from her." Liz is sitting up straight, eyes shining. "A book! I can't believe it! When do you meet with Steichen? We must start calling around…"

She looks so animated that Berenice has to laugh. "Whoa, girl," she says. "You have to rest, remember? There'll be plenty of time for this later."

"You're right," Liz settles back onto the pillow, her face pink and excited. "Oh, but it's such good news! A book *and* a show! The best thing to happen in ages!"

Don't count on it, Berenice almost says. But she stops herself, not wanting to dim Liz's excitement. She hasn't seen Liz this energized in a while, and it's lovely to see. Bittersweet, too, because it makes her realize how much the illness has been stealing this side of her beloved away.

Heartened, she casts a fond smile at the bed. "Sleep, now, darling," she says. "I'll be in the next room, plotting how to conquer the art world."

TWENTY-EIGHT

As she's shown into his office, Edward Steichen rises and walks around his desk. He's tall and angular, all pointed features and jutting elbows. When he shakes her hand, he turns his head away slightly, with that patrician haughtiness that wealthy Easterners do so well.

"Miss Abbott. Good to see you."

"Mr. Steichen." She doesn't thank him for making time to see her. That would position her as a supplicant, rather than an equal.

"Do sit down. Could I get you some coffee?"

"That would be nice, thank you."

He pushes a button on his telephone and almost immediately the young woman who showed Berenice in appears at the door. She is slim and serious, with cropped brown hair and green eyes magnified by cat's-eye glasses.

"Ah, Jean. Coffee for both of us, please."

"Yes, sir." The girl disappears.

As Steichen sits down, Berenice looks around. On the walls are photographs by Paul Strand, Gertrude Kasebier, and, of course, Stieglitz. Always Stieglitz. He's represented here by *Spiritual America*, his image of the hindquarters of a castrated horse. She remembers when the photograph was first published. People cooed at his audacity with the title, but she'd thought it a cheap trick.

"Well," Steichen stretches back in his chair, putting his hands behind his head, "Beaumont tells me you've been doing some extraordinary things."

"Beaumont has been very supportive."

"Yes—a good egg, isn't he, Beaumont? I'm so grateful for his work here. He did what was needed to get this department off the ground. Of course, I've been able to expand on his vision since my tenure began."

The hair on the back of Berenice's neck prickles, and she shifts awkwardly in her seat. She can't believe that, with a straight face, Steichen can imply that he knows more about photography than Beaumont Newhall. The arrogance! Luckily, the girl comes back with the coffee tray just then, providing a distraction before Berenice can say something she'll regret. For a minute or so, she and Steichen are engaged in the business of pouring and stirring.

"I expect you'll want to know about my process," she says after taking a sip. "I invented the Supersight-Projection camera almost a decade ago, after I became frustrated with the lack of sharpness in my lenses. I wanted to get more definition into my pictures."

She's conscious of the irony of saying this to Steichen, a man whose reputation was made on his blurred, moody landscapes. But Steichen doesn't seem put out.

"How resourceful," he says. "Why don't we put the prints over here, so the coffee won't get in the way?"

She moves over to the table he's indicating, then opens her portfolio and takes out four prints, laying them side-by-side. The fish head, the bubbles. A grain of corn that has sprouted on both ends. A close-up of an eye that belongs to her friend, the poet Muriel Rukeyser.

Steichen picks up the image of the fish head, carefully handling it by its corners. He looks at it closely, frowning, peering at the oily scales and the jelly-like eye.

"What kind of fish is this?"

"A salmon trout."

"Mmh, thought so. My sister and I used to catch fellas like this in Lake Michigan."

How sweet, Berenice thinks. She waits for Steichen to give some indication of how he rates the image aesthetically, but he just lays it down and picks up the eye and eyebrow.

"What made you do this one?"

"The same impulse that made me do the fish. A desire to see more, and see it clearly. The eye, I suppose, is a symbol of that, a referrent. It engenders a certain self-consciousness on the part of the viewer, a visceral awareness." To her ears, this is pretentious piffle. But it is the kind of idea one must spout to a Steichen.

"It reminds me of Man Ray's eye."

"Really?" She almost sputters it, aghast. To her, the two images have nothing in common beyond both being photographs of eyes. Everything about the Man Ray image is fake, from the glass tears to the impossibly long eyelashes. He used a mannequin, for goodness' sake! And he cropped the image tightly as a response to being left by Lee Miller, or so she heard. It was one of a series of photographs in which he focused on women's body parts, sometimes chopping them up and sticking them onto objects like metronomes.

Steichen has taken another image out of the portfolio. "This is pretty. What is it?"

"What do you think?"

"I don't know. It looks like a lady's powder puff. Or a sand dollar."

"It's penicillin mold."

He blinks and moves the print closer to his face. "Amazing."

"There's so much more I want to do with this. I have ideas every day. But sixteen-by-twenty-inch sheet film doesn't come cheap."

"I heard you worked for *Science Illustrated* for a few years," Steichen gives her a condescending smile. *Don't mention it*, Beaumont had advised about the magazine. *It will make you seem like an illustrator.*

"No, not that long. Just under a year."

"But in your mind, what you're doing is art?"

Ah, here they are, she thinks, *the blinders*. She's heard it before. What she's doing is too straightforward to be art. Maybe if she called her image of the fish head *Sensual America* she'd stand more chance of getting Steichen on board.

"It is, yes," she says. With a deep breath, she launches in. "You see, in my opinion ours is a serious age that requires precise chronicling. People are tired of pretty, inconsequential pictures. They want something substantial to chew on. Beauty for its own sake is pleasant but forgettable—whereas an image of a fish's scales can be beautiful but also spark one's intellectual curiosity. I believe my images speak volumes about our world. They dissect it, demystify it. If I can be so bold, I think this is the kind of thing Michelangelo was doing when he sketched muscles with such fine delineation. It's what Daumier was doing when he took his sketchbook into laundries and third-class railway carriages. It's even what prehistoric man was doing, when he painted buffalo and deer on the walls of his cave with such astonishing precision."

A little out of breath, she stops. She has stated her case, she feels, and made good points. But probably she shouldn't have said "pretty, inconsequential pictures." Steichen, after all, has staked his career on such pictures.

She watches him, thinking, *That's it, then. In a moment he'll make an excuse about a meeting he has to get to. He'll promise to be in touch, but the call won't come. And I'll be the idiot, waiting and hoping.*

Steichen has put down the image of penicillin mold. He paces in front of her, frowning, his hands knit behind his back. Then he wheels around. "I like them!" he announces.

"You…"

"I do! I think you're doing something bold. The subjects are unusual, and the tonal ranges you've achieved are extraordinary. One sees the influence of past masters, but also something fresh. A medium pushed to its limits."

"You…" Apparently, she is stuck on that one word. She tries to get another out, but it can't get past the lump in her gullet.

"I can see a spring show," Steichen is saying. "Three rooms, I'd say. Do you think you could come up with fifty good prints in six months' time?"

She looks at him gape-mouthed, incapable of mustering either the insouciance or elation she knows she should be displaying at this moment. But she does manage to squeak out another word. "Yes."

"Well," Steichen is collecting up her prints, ushering them back in the portfolio. He folds it and hands it to her. "Thank you for bringing this to me. I'll need to take it to the director, of course, but typically that's a formality. Jean will be in touch."

Berenice takes the portfolio from him. It's a relief to have something solid in her hands, to anchor her to the moment. And what an odd moment it is, full of spiraling emotions. Elation because she has a show; gratitude to Beaumont and Steichen. And confusion, because Steichen might not be a philistine after all—which means there might be other things she's been wrong about.

At last, collecting herself, she faces him squarely. "Thank you, Mr. Steichen, thank you. I'm thrilled you like the work." She pauses—he is standing under Stieglitz's photograph, and the lonely penis of the castrated horse is pointing directly at his head. "You won't regret it, I promise," she says, at last feeling the proper confidence. "This is going to be one hell of a show."

◆

When Liz walks into the studio later she stops abruptly, wobbling on her heels.

"What's happened? Is something going on?"

"Yes," Berenice says, "something is going on."

In the hours after she met with Steichen, she was a ball of nerves. Unable to sit still or focus, she decided to channel her energy into preparing a celebratory meal. She cleared the studio, putting away the tubes, tanks and other paraphernalia, and throwing colorful cloths over the Supersight and a table. Then she went shopping. She's never been much of a cook, but she found a recipe for crab cakes with potato salad that looked doable. Also, she bought flowers and a bottle of Moët & Chandon. Never before has she blown a weeks' worth of teaching salary on a single meal. It felt exciting and dangerous, like whooshing down a slide.

"We're celebrating," she says now. "Steichen's giving me a show."

"What?" In an instant, Liz's face turns from bafflement to wonder. "Really?"

"Really. He called the work extraordinary." She looks at Liz, feeling pride well up. "He liked it."

"He's giving you…"

"…a show, yes. In spring, he said." Now she can let it out—a laugh full of joy and relief.

Liz takes a step forward, then another, until she's in front of Berenice. She knows what this means. At last, Berenice has been unquestionably accepted into the world of art photography. After a show at MoMA, nobody will be able to dismiss her as 'just' a documentarian.

"Oh, darling. I'm so happy for you."

"It's your accomplishment too. You made me believe in myself."

They are about to embrace when the telephone rings. Berenice puts a hand on Liz's arm. "It's all right, we won't answer." But the shrill cry of the telephone has brought the outside world in, and they move apart, self-conscious. Berenice walks to the dinner table—which, she has to admit, looks good. In addition to the red cloth Pat found, she has set it with champagne flutes and their best, un-chipped plates. The flowers she bought, white lilies, fan out from a steel film-developing tank. The air is rich with their perfume.

In the corner of the room, the telephone's harsh jangle goes on. The caller is not giving up, and Berenice's curiosity tweaks at her. Could it be something to do with MoMA—has Beaumont spread the news? "I'll just take it," she tells Liz. Gesturing toward the table, she says, "Go ahead. Take some food while it's fresh."

When she picks up the phone, the voice on the other end only has to say one word. "Bernice?"

"Oh! Hazel."

"Yes, it's me. I'm sorry to call so late. But it's been a hectic day, and I wanted you to know…"

"I'm listening." She feels her heartbeat quicken, her pulse throb in her temple above the telephone receiver.

"Ma fell down the stairs this morning. A neighbor called, and I rushed there and got her to the doctor. There were no broken bones, thank heavens, but she's badly bruised and shaken up. And along with the other problems—well, the doctor said she shouldn't be living alone."

"Oh!" Berenice feels guilt creeping from her stomach, because she should have been to Cleveland by now. Several times over the past months she has been on the point of planning a trip, but something always came up. There was an article to write, a class to prepare. That's what she'd told herself, anyway.

She looks across the room at Liz, who is holding her champagne flute, her face tinged with concern. She has filled Berenice's flute too, and the pale liquid is effervescing, bubbles fizzing into the air and exploding with wet pops.

"I've brought her to live with me," Hazel says, and Berenice's heart does a flip-flop of gratitude and relief. "I'm pretty sure it's her time, Bernice. If you're going to come, you shouldn't put it off."

"Of course." Berenice says. Quickly, she runs the week's schedule through her head. "I'll come tomorrow. I'll have to find a substitute to teach my classes, but—I'll do it. Can you put me up for a few nights?"

"Sure, I've got a sofa you can sleep on."

She gives Berenice the address and directions from the train station, and Berenice writes it down, all the while imagining things she doesn't want to think about. Ma falling, tumbling down a flight of dirty stairs. The awful thump of her body on each tread, her skirt dragging behind, and no one there to help her. By the time she puts down the phone, she has lost her appetite.

"Oh, my dear. Do you want me to come with you?" Liz asks later, as they're lying in bed. "I'd stay in a hotel. Your family wouldn't have to know."

Berenice reaches over, finding Liz's hand in the dark and giving it a squeeze. "No, love. But thank you. It means the world that you offered."

"When will you leave?"

"Tomorrow afternoon. Frank Oberhaus has agreed to teach my Wednesday and Thursday classes. I'll take the three o'clock train."

They're silent for a moment and in the velvety darkness Berenice can hear the rumble of traffic on Seventh Avenue. The pendulum clock in the studio marks off the seconds with loud clicks, each one a grain of life disintegrating, disappearing. How many seconds remain for Ma? How many before her own life runs out?

Liz turns to her. "Is there anything you need me to do? Do you want me to keep an eye on the studio? Give directions to Pat?"

Berenice rolls over to face her companion. In the darkness, she can just see the whites of Liz's eyes. Dearest Liz, who has been her support and comrade for almost two decades; Liz, whose zest for life remains undimmed despite her health problems. How lucky they are, despite everything.

"I need you to hold me," she says.

In response, Liz opens her arms and Berenice moves into them, nuzzling her face against Liz's neck. She can feel Liz's breasts against her own, and Liz's hot breath on her shoulder, but rather than stirring any desire, tonight these sensations simply give her a feeling of comfort. Mother, sister, lover, friend: they are this to each other, and more. If the best thing she ever did was to get herself out of Ohio, the second best must be that she opened her heart to this extraordinary woman. To let oneself to be loved; to love in return. Whatever judgment is cast against them, this is one thing she can never regret.

TWENTY-NINE

Outside the house, Berenice stops to glance at the address again. She appears to be in the right place, but Hazel's home is not at all what she expected. For one thing, the house is in a new suburb of Cleveland—a place that, until a few years ago, was scrubby marshland. The land has been neatly divided, each property fenced off with a small yard, trees planted with military precision along the sidewalk. Hazel's house is one of the smaller ones, but it radiates cheer. Its metal siding, painted bright blue and yellow, looks like something out of a children's book. There are box hedges at the front of the property, lace curtains at the windows. One of the windows flickers with light. There must be a television in there.

It's early evening, and the streetlamps are glowing orange. The wind has been rising steadily; it whistles through the young trees, making leaves shiver. Berenice feels exhaustion settling over her like a shroud. There was an unscheduled stop outside Pittsburgh to fix an engine problem and, on getting off the train in Cleveland, she found herself trying to hail a taxi in a rainstorm along with half of Manhattan, or so it seemed. As a result she is damp all over and chilled to the bone.

Almost as soon as she presses the buzzer, a light flicks on in the hallway and a silhouette approaches. Then a woman who must be Hazel peers through the patterned glass panel, her face and shirt forming a kaleidoscope. When she opens the door, Berenice sees she has Ma's strong features, with a prominent nose and long, wide lips. She is in her mid fifties now, and is tall and imposing, like Ma in her prime.

"Bernice?"

"Hazel?"

Her sister steps aside, holding the door open. "My goodness, you look half-drowned." She reaches out and takes the carpetbag. "Oh, your hands are cold. Come, let me take your coat! Should I draw you a bath?"

"Maybe later."

"Let's have some tea, then. Ma's sleeping. I was just watching *You Bet Your Life*."

She strides down the hallway and Berenice follows her to a kitchen that looks as if it came from the World's Fair. The sink unit incorporates some kind of under-sink washing machine, and the counters bristle with other machines—toaster, blender, stand mixer. Beyond is the living room and she can hear strains of the television show Hazel was watching. *Well, Rosemary, you're up to one hundred and forty-five dollars. Whaddaya think, all or nothing?*

She watches this woman, her older sister, bustle around. As Hazel reaches to take a teapot from the shelf, she tips her head and furrows her brow, the expression so familiar that Berenice could almost be looking at herself.

"Do you live here alone?" she asks. "I mean…"

"…without a man? Yes. I saved for years to buy this house. Do you know Lustron homes? When I bought this plot, it came with a choice of models. I ordered one, then they came with all the pieces and built it in a day."

"How modern."

Hazel shrugs. "It suits me. I like new things. Come, let's take our tea in the living room. The fire's on and it's warmer."

The fire in the living room consists of an electric hearth made from fiberglass shaped to resemble red bricks and coals. Hazel goes to the television console and turns down the volume, leaving the picture flickering in the corner. Berenice is shocked to see that the game show's host is Groucho Marx, her old favorite. Groucho! She knew his career hit a lull in the Forties, but didn't know it had fallen this low. Instinctively, she thinks of huddling with Rod in the Loew's Sheridan, watching *Animal Crackers* when their relationship was new and fragile. *Ever since I met you, I've swept you off my feet.* The memory makes her smile. Dear Rod. He's married to a writer now; they have three children. She's glad she doesn't have to feel guilty any more.

Hazel sits on a Barcalounger, and Berenice takes the winged chair opposite. They sip their tea, suddenly cautious and formal.

"How's your photography going?"

"Very well. And your social work?"

"We're busy. Most of our clients are migrants from the South, who are finding Cleveland no easier than where they came from."

"Sounds challenging."

"It is, but I like to feel useful. What about you? When I visited Ma the first time, she showed me a clipping from the *Plain Dealer*. They printed five of your photographs. It didn't surprise me. You had an eye, even as a baby."

"I did?"

"Sure. I remember when you were four, you collected scrap wood from the alley and made your own little table. You screamed for hours when Ma threw it out."

Berenice doesn't remember the table. She shakes her head. "Sounds like I was a brat."

"No, just independent. You never married, did you?"

"No," Berenice feels herself blush. "But…well, I have someone."

"Good for you. It's been a while for me. But I'm not complaining. I have my health and house, and I like my own company. If I ever…"

Just then, there's the tinkling of a bell from down the hall. Berenice flinches. She'd almost forgotten why she'd come.

"That's her," Hazel says, "it's how she calls me." They look blankly at each other for a moment, then Hazel says, "Let me go first."

Left alone, Berenice leans back in her chair, taking comfort in its wings as she looks around at Hazel's living room. On either side of the television console are built-in shelves, one side stacked neatly with books, the other containing a collection of precisely spaced horse figurines. On the wall, a clock with a spiky gold surround ticks off the seconds.

Before she has time to notice more, Hazel appears in the doorway holding a cup of tea. "She's all right, just thirsty. I've told her you're here. Why don't you bring this to her?"

Berenice shrinks back in her chair, then chides herself and stands up. She came to be helpful, after all. She moves toward Hazel and takes the teacup and saucer, following the tilt of Hazel's head down a corridor. The cup wobbles in the saucer, sending a splash of amber liquid over the rim.

At the end of the corridor, a door gapes open. She approaches it warily. "Ma?" The shades are drawn; the room is dim. "Ma, it's Bernice."

She has to blink before she can make out the bed across the room, and the hump of her mother's body, half under the covers and half propped on pillows.

The room smells cloyingly sweet. Ma's eyes are closed. She looks shrunken and child-like except that her face is gaunt, the skin pulled tightly across the bones. Is it possible that her skull itself has shrunk? Transparent wisps of hair straggle over the pillow, and Berenice can't help but remember Ma brushing her hair when she was younger, the brown tresses that fell to her waist.

"Ma, I brought your tea." At this, her mother's eyes open halfway, revealing lizard-like slits of iris and pupil.

"Ber—nie?" It comes out as a rasp, nails on sandpaper.

"Yes, it's me." One of Ma's arms is on top of the blanket, and Berenice can't believe how thin it is, how ropy with raised veins. The sight sends a ripple of compassion through her, even as it repels her.

She sits on the chair by the bed. "Are you thirsty?" Her mother doesn't answer, but looks longingly at the tea. It's obvious there's no way she can hold the cup, and so after a moment Berenice takes the teaspoon and fills it, then brings it to Ma's lips and dribbles the warm tea into her mouth. As the liquid coats her tongue, Ma's eyes close and she looks serene, almost beatific. Then, as Berenice withdraws the spoon, her eyes snap open with a question: *More?*

All told, it takes almost half an hour to spoon the tea into Ma. Some of it dribbles down her chin, and Berenice has to take a napkin from the bedside table and wipe it off. A few drops seep into the collar of Ma's salmon-colored nightshirt. The old woman looks into Berenice's eyes all the while, her gratitude so obvious and pathetic that Berenice can't bear to hold her gaze. She wonders if Ma spoon-fed her like this when she was an infant, or breast-fed her. It's hard to imagine.

Just as they're finishing, Hazel comes to the doorway. She glances at the two of them in the dim light, a tableau that must look like a Renaissance pietà. For a moment, she watches with a smile. Then she bustles in.

"She'll be needing the bedpan. I'll show you where it is." Alarmed, Berenice looks at her sister. "Oh, no need to worry, she's good about it," Hazel says. Retrieving the bedpan, she waves it in the air. "Ma! Time for your you-know-what!"

Berenice watches as, briskly, Hazel goes to the bed and folds the sheets and blanket down, then rolls Ma onto her side, pulls up the nightshirt and places the copper pan under her. As she empties her bladder, Ma's eyes close and she sighs deeply. When it's done, Hazel removes the sloshing pan, covers it with the lid and puts it on the floor, then rolls Ma onto her back and takes the bedpan out of the room. Berenice looks away, embarrassed. But when she looks back, she sees Ma giving her a toothy grin.

In a few moments, Hazel comes back. "Well, now you have the thrust of it. She's eating a bit, not much. Soft-boiled eggs are good, cheddar grits have worked. If you—" She stops, because Ma is holding a hand in the air.

"Ber—nie," Ma begins, but before she can go on, a fit of coughing overtakes her, and Hazel has to lean her forward and thump her on the back. Ma coughs more, a wet bark with a gravelly undertone. Once she has coughed it out, she lifts a trembling hand, pointing to a battered suitcase leaning against the wall.

"The suitcase?" Hazel looks puzzled. "No, Ma. We emptied it when you got here, remember?"

Ma shakes her head. She screws up her eyes, as if summoning the effort to speak, then points again. "In-side," she rasps.

Hazel looks at Berenice, raises her eyebrows and shrugs. She lifts the case and lays it on the end of the bed, then opens it. Inside, there is a stained gingham lining, but the case is empty. Hazel and Berenice peer into it, inspecting the corners: nothing.

"She must be confused," Hazel says. "Ew, this case stinks. I'm going to get it out of here." She freezes as Ma lets out an anguished moan.

"Wait!" Taking the case from Hazel, Berenice puts it back on the end of the bed. "Look, Ma! We're not taking it." She runs her hands over its dirty outside, feeling for a hidden compartment: nothing. Opening it, she looks inside again. No magic has occurred, the case is still empty. Is Hazel right, is Ma out of her senses? Berenice is about to give up when she notices an elasticated gingham pocket in the lid of the case.

"Here, Ma? Is this what you meant?"

Ma's eyes light up. "In-side!"

Sure enough, when Berenice puts her hand into the pocket, her fingers meet something stiff. She draws out an envelope, yellowed with age and brittle. On the front, her name, *Bernice*, is written in a shaky hand. Inside the envelope there is no letter, just a photograph mounted on stiff card.

She draws it out. It is a studio portrait, of the formal kind typical in the early years of the century. A man sits on an armchair in front of a backdrop painted with mountains and clouds, with rubber plants and ferns spread around him. He is handsome, with black whiskers and wavy, dark hair that falls across a high forehead. He wears a suit that is too tight, his flesh straining against the fabric, and one of his arms is wrapped around the waist of a chubby child who stands by his side. The child, who must be about five, rests her face against his cheek, not seeming to mind the bristles. She's dressed in white, with a dark belt, and has her hair in lopsided braids.

Berenice looks at the photograph and her throat tightens. Aesthetically speaking, it's not a good image. The composition is poor, and Pa looks as if he has leaves growing out of his head. But the photographer is not entirely incompetent. He has captured an emotion, pure and real—tenderness between a father and daughter.

Hazel looks over Berenice's shoulder. "Huh. I've never seen it."

"It's not you, then?"

"No, definitely not. I'd remember."

Berenice turns the cardboard over. On the back, there is only a stamp from the photographer's studio: *Philip Bainbridge & Son, 162 Lake Street, Cleveland,* and a date, *14th June, 1902.* She scours her memory. She was four in 1902.

"Didn't Ma and Pa separate that year?"

"That's right," Hazel says. "He left in July."

July. So he might have known he was leaving when the photograph was taken. But how did the photograph get into Ma's possession? And why did her father bring just her, not Hazel, to the photographer's studio?

She looks over at the bed, but Ma's eyes have closed and she is grunting softly in sleep. So there's no chance to ask her these questions, or others—like how long she has been keeping this to give to Berenice.

Evidently, though, it was important to her. Berenice looks at the photograph again, perplexed but thankful. Her memories of her father have been doubly erased, overwritten at first by childish fantasy, later by bitterness. But now here he is in thousands of silver halide crystals, fixed on paper, with an animating intelligence in his eyes, a careful flourish in the way his whiskers are cut. Photographs can lie, but she thinks this one reflects something true. Pa loved her. Before he left, she was loved.

◆

Later, she sits at the kitchen dinette as Hazel puts together a tuna casserole. The photograph is on the table between them, a three-by-five inch window into the past.

"You and he look alike," Hazel observes.

"Yes," Berenice inspects the similarities: wide-set eyes, long nose, receding chin. "And you look more like her."

"Funny, isn't it? I wonder how things might have gone if he'd taken you instead of me."

"I've often wondered that." They look at each other then, wary. They're on dangerous ground, veering close to buried resentments. "How did it feel?" Berenice asks. "Did you want to go with him?"

Hazel shakes her head. "I didn't want to leave you and Ma." She lifts a can of mushroom soup and pours it over some noodles in a pan. "But he promised me things. He'd brought a doll with him, and it had a lovely blue silk dress and braids of real hair. I thought there'd be more like that. And he told me that Ma couldn't afford to feed the two of us, so I'd be doing you a favor by leaving. He'd worked it all out. He knew what to say." She laughs. "I didn't expect to be moving from place to place, barely eating some days."

"Whereas I would have loved going on the road."

"I know," Hazel says. "The two of you had more in common. I bet he would have taken you if he'd thought he could handle a four year old."

"Why did he even take *you*?"

"Who knows?" Hazel shrugs. "Maybe to punish Ma." She stirs the soup-pasta mix, growing thoughtful. "Or maybe he knew how Ma would turn and wanted to protect one of us."

"But she might *not* have turned that way if he'd treated her better!" Berenice's voice comes out loud and angry, making Hazel look up in surprise. In response, she sags in her chair. She's too tired to work this out. Which came first, the chicken or the egg—Ma's depression or Pa's mistreatment? In retrospect it seems absurd, this gothic drama that afflicted their family. The fuss that split her and Hazel apart.

And now here's the photograph, turning things upside down again, seeming to prove Pa's good intentions—and Ma's too, to an extent, because she'd needed to get the image to Berenice. Through the tunnel of time, Berenice can look at her parents and see that they weren't malevolent, just flawed. The ground crumbled under them; they couldn't stop the slide. She and Hazel just happened to be in the way.

◆

She stays at Hazel's house for seven nights. On the day after she arrives, Ma's condition worsens. She no longer has the strength to reach for the bell and her mouth can't form even simple words. Mostly she sleeps, but when awake she looks at them with wide eyes, as bewildered as a newborn foal.

Each night, Berenice and Hazel take turns keeping watch. Ma sleeps on her back, open-mouthed. Her chest heaves with the effort of breathing, and the breaths rasp and catch in her throat. Her forehead looks waxy, like tallow.

When will she die? They attend to her needs diligently, but it's obvious they're waiting for the inevitable. During the day, while Hazel is at work, Berenice sits by the bed and reads a novel she found on Hazel's bookshelf, a pulp thriller set on Nantucket. At other times she talks to Ma, telling her stories about Paris and New York. Occasionally, after not moving in what seems like hours, Ma's face will twitch and her tongue will start making ticking sounds. *Tick-tick! Tick-tick-tick!* It happens in the middle of the night, just as Berenice has finally dozed, waking her. *Tick-tick-tick!* The sound is eerie, disturbing. She wonders if Hazel, too, has fantasies of putting a pillow over Ma's head and ending it.

"Go for a walk," Hazel says on the fourth day, "you need to get out of the house." So Berenice goes into the misty morning air and walks, feeling giddily freed but also out of place. The houses here hunker on their geometric plots, fronted by driveways so neat you could serve dinner on them. They don't seem real. She misses New York's grime and exuberance, and her heart longs to be with Butchy.

And then on the sixth day, when she's staring out of the kitchen window as she washes dishes, Berenice feels a chill, as if a cool wind has whispered through the house. She draws her hands out of the sink and wipes them, then hurries down the corridor, to where the door to the second bedroom is ajar.

At first when she peers in, everything looks normal. Ma is in her usual position on her back, mouth open. But something is off. As Berenice draws close, her nostrils pick up an unmistakable smell and she looks down to see a puddling stain on the sheet between her mother's legs. Breathing through her mouth, she puts two fingers on Ma's throat to confirm what she already knows.

She leans against the bedpost, biting her lip. Not since Lilian has she seen a dead body, and she'd forgotten about the terrifying vacancy, the blankness in a corpse's eyes. As she moves her hand to close Ma's eyelids, she feels the awful, heavy finality of this passing. There is no more chance to make amends. She might have paid for Ma to visit New York; Liz could have been her friend from down the hall. The three of them might have splurged on a meal at Delmonico's.

But in the next moment she's chiding herself: whom is she kidding? Ma was no fool. She must have had suspicions when Berenice broke off her engagement to Rod. If she'd ever come to New York, if she'd met Liz, Ma would have known. She would have greeted the realization with a smile, but not the kind that makes you smile back. Her smile would have had judgment in it, and rejection. It would have telegraphed *I knew there was something wrong with that girl*.

◆

The funeral is a pathetic affair. They bury her in a cemetery on the edge of town next to a General Mills factory. Machinery drones in the background and a billboard at the periphery advertises Sugar Jets cereal. As the priest mumbles his benediction, a vinegary smell wafts across the grounds and Berenice and Hazel have to hold handkerchiefs to their noses.

When it's over, Berenice picks up her carpetbag. She is heading straight to the station. It occurs to her that she is fleeing Ma as soon as possible, even after death. But it can't be helped. She has work to get back to; her colleagues can't teach her New School classes indefinitely.

Hazel walks with her, and they sit on a bench on the platform until the train comes. Mostly they're silent, because the platitudes people reach for at such times—*she had a good life, she didn't suffer*—are so patently untrue that to say them would be insulting each other's intelligence.

When it's time for Berenice to leave, Hazel looks at her with a faint smile. "Thank you, Bernice. Let's try to be in touch more, shall we? Maybe I could get to New York next spring to see your exhibition."

Berenice blinks, thinking of Steichen and MoMA. Over the last week, she's mostly put the show out of her mind, though there were times, sitting at Ma's bedside, when she allowed herself the luxury of ruminating over it. And she couldn't help telling Hazel about it one night, even though it wasn't finalized.

"I'd like that," she says now. "But you know, you'll have to learn to call me Berenice."

Hazel shakes her head and smiles. "Berenice—so cosmopolitan! But it suits you, I think. You've made it your own."

They embrace then, and Berenice feels her sister's natural restraint give way to a cautious warmth. Five days ago they had started out stiff and shy, but they've come to know each other more. She admires Hazel's independence, her common sense. And Hazel seems to admire her, for her creativity and drive.

And so, after all, this trip has yielded something. A sister; a friend. A thread connecting her to family and past.

THIRTY

Back at Commerce Street, Liz is waiting for her with tomato soup and buttered bread. Solicitous, she sits Berenice at the table and serves her, then takes a place beside her.

"How was it?"

"Pretty ghastly. Hazel and I were the only mourners."

"I'm so sorry."

"Me too. But it's over now. And I've got so much to catch up on."

She flips through the stack of mail that Liz has collected on the table for her. There are all manner of letters from the administration at the New School, catalogs from camera companies, personal correspondence from one or two friends. But what she hoped for most—a letter from MoMA—is absent.

"What's this?" She fingers a thick, creamy envelope. Embossed in its top left corner is a stylized logo of a man and a giant leaf, and beneath it are the words *Aspen Institute for Humanistic Studies*.

"It's an invitation to a photography conference," Liz says. "I got one too."

"In Aspen?" Berenice says with a chuckle. "Why not Tibet?" She slides her index finger under the envelope flap, rips it open. "I've never even heard of the Aspen Institute for Humanistic Studies."

"It's new. A Chicago philanthropist set it up last year as a place for artists and intellectuals to gather and think. All very lofty."

"And very nice for people who have the money to get there," Berenice says. She pulls out the invitation, looks at the cost of attendance and laughs. "Which, as far as I know, doesn't include us." Scraping the last of the soup from her bowl, she asks casually, "Nothing from MoMA?"

"No. I assure you, I was looking like a hawk."

"No phone messages either?" She eyes the scraps of paper she checked when she first came in, some scrawled on in Liz's looping hand, others carefully written by Pat.

"No, my dear. We were both vigilant. When Pat went out on errands, I came here and worked in the studio. But," Liz pauses, "I do have something good to tell. Two things, actually." Looking up, Berenice sees her beaming with the excitement of suppressed news.

"What is it?"

"You know those blood tests Dr. Vinson did? It turns out it *was* anemia. He's been giving me vitamin injections, and I feel so much better!"

"Oh, Butchy!" Berenice blinks, realizing that she's been so wrapped up in her own concerns that she hadn't paid attention to Liz's appearance. Indeed Liz *does* appear better, her eyes brighter, the color restored to her cheeks. "That's wonderful! But what about the rheumatoid arthritis?"

Liz laughs. "I still have that. He's a doctor, not a miracle worker. But I'm not greedy. If the stiffness wears off by midday, and I'm not in too much pain and can work, I'll be happy enough."

Knowing how debilitating the morning pain can be, Berenice feels a wave of tenderness for her brave *inamorata*. "Yes, my love. And what's the second thing?"

"Something swell," Liz says. She looks at Berenice, bubbling with pride. "I got the contract and advance to write the Inness book."

"You didn't!" Berenice drops her soup spoon against the dish, where it makes a bright little clink.

"I know—can you believe it? After all those years of taking it to publishers, and no one showing interest. Having me believe that a book on an early American painter was a lost cause."

"Oh, Butchy, that's wonderful!" A flush of triumph—someone has seen Liz's potential. "A book is just what you need right now. You'll be able to spend more time at home instead of running around to galleries."

"So we both have books, *and* you have a show," Liz shakes her head. "Who'd have thought? So many good things."

"We have to drink to this!" Pushing back her chair, Berenice gets up to rummage in the drinks cabinet. She's greeted by a sad assortment of neglected bottles: crème-de-menthe, an old and sticky Pernod. But there's a bottle of blended malt whisky, and it's half full.

"I'll get glasses," Liz goes to the kitchen, coming back with a pair of tumblers that makes Berenice laugh. Back in the late Thirties, they'd been at a winter party where someone dared the host, a Russian abstract painter and former Olympic swimmer, to dive into the Hudson. With drinks in hand, all the guests had trooped tipsily to the nearest pier and watched as the painter stripped to his shorts and, still admirably muscular, prepared to dive. He launched himself, arcing through the night sky, cutting across the reflected lights of New Jersey and making only a mild splash as his body knifed into the water. Then, nothing. Everyone watched, hilarity turning to concern, then panic as the water remained dark and still. Until at last, the painter's head broke the surface and he pumped his fist, crying, "This is nothing! Try the Volga!" In their drunken relief, people screamed and embraced strangers, a few even jumped in. It was an exhilarating moment. Berenice and Liz made off soon after, with their ridged, heavy-bottomed glasses in hand.

"Oh, Butchy," Berenice says now, "these are perfect. We're taking the plunge, aren't we?" She pours two fingers of whiskey into both glasses, and they solemnly raise and clink.

"To success," Liz says.

"To success," Berenice echoes. She knocks back the glass, tipping some of the whisky to the back of her throat, where it feels hot and alive. Another sip coats her tongue with its warmth, and this time she gets notes of malt and caramel too, as the distiller surely intended. The sweetness slides to her stomach, then diffuses through her body so thoroughly that even the roots of her hair tingle.

She raises her glass again. "To my mother. Who never understood me."

"Your mother," Liz says. Berenice puts the glass to her lips and drains its contents. And then, with a visceral jolt, it hits her: Ma is gone. Gone. At last she can release the guilt that has weighed her down for so long. She did what she could to make Ma's last days as comfortable as possible. Now she's free, a kite with its strings cut, at liberty to flaunt her colors.

She lifts her glass. "Let's have another."

◆

The price for this drinking is a colossal hangover the next day. Berenice wakes with heavy-lidded eyes, her head feeling like a swollen, overripe melon. Sprawled next to her, Liz looks similarly indisposed. It was only half a bottle, but they've been out of the habit of drinking. Also, it must be admitted that they're not as young as they used to be.

She's puttering around the kitchen, looking for a lemon to squeeze into water, when the telephone rings. "Go away," Berenice mutters, but it doesn't. The ringing continues, its urgency seeming to increase although the length and volume of rings don't change.

She stumbles across the studio, narrowly avoiding tripping on a box of insect specimens that appears out of nowhere.

"Berenice, it's Beaumont."

"Oh, Beaumont!" A burp bubbles up from her stomach and she lets it out, then puts her hand over her mouth and giggles. "Sorry! I've been meaning to call you. Just got back from Ohio last night."

"Are you all right?"

"Perfect—why?"

"You sound a bit rough."

"Nah, no—just a little whisky last night."

"Oh." He's silent, and she senses him weighing something. "I'm sorry about your mother."

"S'allright. She was sick."

"I know." Another silence.

"What is it, Beaumont?"

More silence; a heavy sigh. "Berenice, listen, I have some bad news. I hate this timing, but…the show's not going forward."

"What show?" She tries to remember Beaumont's exhibition schedule up at George Eastman House. He was putting together a show of Walker Evans' work, she recalls, and something about the Civil War.

On the other end of the line, Beaumont sighs. "My dear, I'm talking about the MoMA show. *Your* MoMA show. Steichen has pulled the plug."

She almost laughs. "Come on, Beaumont, that's not funny."

"Bea, I'm afraid it's no joke. He called me yesterday evening. Said he'd made a mistake in his scheduling, thought there was a slot in the spring when there wasn't. Asked me to break it to you." His quiet tone sobers her. He wouldn't persist with a joke this long. It's true, then. She has lost her show at MoMA.

"But Beaumont, he can't—we had an agreement!"

"In his mind, there was nothing set in stone."

"He promised me! How can he go back on his word?"

"I know, I know. It's awful."

"And isn't he man enough to tell me himself? Why the heck are *you* doing his dirty work?"

"Good question. Cowardice, I think. But also, since I was the one who brought you to his attention, he probably thought I could let you down more gently."

"Gently!" Berenice shrieks, so livid that a pigeon sitting on the windowbox outside the window flinches. "Gently! How do you tell someone *gently* that you're ruining their life?"

"Oh, Berenice. I know it's a blow. But it's not that bad. Listen, we'll do an exhibition up here. We're renovating the stables and the poultry house into new galleries, they'll be opening next year. You could inaugurate the space. And maybe Sam could be convinced to do the book."

Berenice sits on the chair by the telephone table. If Beaumont's offer was supposed to calm her, it has done the opposite. A show in a henhouse, in the frozen north of Rochester, instead of at MoMA! "No," she says. "Oh, I didn't mean no to your offer—just *no*, he can't do this. He gave me his word."

"I'm afraid he can."

"What if I make a stink? Go to the papers?"

"Do you have anything in writing from him?"

She pauses, considers. "No."

"Then I wouldn't advise it. It will be your word against his, and you'll come off looking bitter. Delusional, even. It won't help you in the long run."

She bites on a hangnail, tearing it from the corner of her thumb as she sinks into the back of the chair. "So that's it? We let it go?"

"Yes. Berenice, believe me, I lobbied for you as hard as I could. But Steichen had anticipated all my arguments. He's even talked himself into a reassessment of the images."

"Oh? How?"

"Are you sure you want to know?"

"Damn straight!"

Beaumont sighs. "Well, he said that when he'd had a chance to think further, he'd decided they weren't art. Not enough transcendence of the subject matter. It was too straightforward, too documentary."

Berenice can't speak. This hurts her more than anything else, the casual dismissal of the imagery into which she has channeled everything she knows. All her passion, her aesthetic beliefs. No one has photographed objects in such intricate detail, no one! For Christ's sake, she invented a camera!

"Berenice? Are you going to be all right? I hate to do this over the phone."

"It's all right. I'll be okay."

"Are you sure? Is Liz there with you?"

"She's here."

"All right," Beaumont exhales, sounding relieved. "I'll check in with you later, okay? And remember, this doesn't define you. It's a tiny moment in a long, distinguished career."

"Right," Berenice says. She replaces the receiver in its cradle, but seems unable to move beyond that. Numb, she stares at her reflection in the mirror above the telephone table. A puffy, uncomprehending face stares back.

There's a sound, and Liz appears at the bedroom door, curling her hand around the frame. She looks a fright, her hair sticking up on one side and her lipstick—apparently not removed last night—smudged around her lips. But she's smiling, blissfully unaware and apparently not alert enough to read Berenice's mood.

She blinks and yawns, revealing flashes of silver at the back of her mouth. "Can you believe, I dreamed I was directing Stevenson's presidential campaign!" she says. Her brow furrows. "I must write it all down before I forget."

THIRTY-ONE

On the fifth day of her self-imposed exile, Berenice lies staring at a fly on the ceiling light. The fly extends its two front legs, rubs them together. Then it settles, still as a blob on the glass cover of the light.

It occurs to her that the common housefly is a maligned creature. Too few people realize its ingenuity, its magnificent construction. This one is large, and she seems to be able to see it with Supersight. She can make out the domes of its compound eyes, the multiple joints in its legs. Its thorax is a soft gold, almost bee-like. Gossamer wings spread from it.

The fly walks forward, and she marvels at how its legs seem to oppose each other, some slanting forward while others move back. Why? Is it connected with the suction the fly needs to stay on the ceiling?

"Bea," Liz's voice at the door breaks into her thought, "Bea, I really think you should get up."

She doesn't answer. It's a new tactic, this silence. She has found it works better than trying to argue. Faced with silence, even the most persistent interlocutor will eventually give up. She waits for Liz to get tired, let out a sigh and go, as she's done countless times already today.

But Liz doesn't go. Instead she takes a few steps into the room. "All right, you've made your point. Pat's in a state and as for me, I'm half worried to death. It's been five days, Bea. This is ridiculous—it's selfish. And you're starting to smell."

Berenice knows better than to take the bait. Liz wants nothing more than for her to rise up in righteous indignation, crying, *Selfish? My world has disintegrated and you're calling me selfish?* That, at least, would be doing something, responding. Instead, she just looks at Liz with limpid eyes, feeling confident that Liz is exaggerating—though it's true there's an odor, like sour milk. Even in her torpor she has noticed that.

"You're not the first person to have been turned down for a museum exhibition," Liz is saying. "What does it matter? You've had so many setbacks and rejections, and you've always rallied and come back stronger. There's no reason for this, no reason at all! I won't stand for it, Bea, I tell you!"

In response, Berenice turns her back and pulls the coverlet over her head.

It comes, then—the soft sigh, the retreating footsteps. There's some murmuring outside the door that sounds like Liz and Pat conferring, then the room goes quiet. At last. But, oh—even when she's alone, people won't leave her in peace. They come around, nodding and murmuring like the goddamned ghosts of Christmas Past. Tylia and her Polish painter; a sad-eyed Rod. Man Ray, saying she'll never make it on her own as a photographer. Steichen telling her she has not transcended her subject matter.

She closes her ears, shutting out their yammering as best she can. It's infuriating, all a person wants to do is be quiet. Is that too much to ask?

Time passes, the light outside the window changes. And changes again. Flies buzz. At some point—it could be an hour later, or a day—there's a knock at the bedroom door. She's vaguely aware of the door opening a few moments later, of footsteps on the parquet. Then someone sits on the edge of the bed, tipping the mattress. She frowns. A smell of citrusy shaving cologne, so it can't be Liz. But she doesn't look to see who it is.

"Hello, Berenice."

When she doesn't answer he doesn't press, but just stays there, sitting. His body, tall and lanky, blocks light from the window, changing the pattern of shadow that falls across her. He emanates calm. It's as if he's saying, *You don't scare me. I'll sit here for as long as it takes.*

Eventually she raises her head. "You shouldn't have come, Beaumont. It's not going to make any difference."

He raises his eyebrows. "You can tell the future as well, can you?"

"As well as what?"

"As well as being the most maddeningly gifted person I know. Or perhaps that should be the most giftedly maddening."

A tiny laugh bubbles in her stomach, but Berenice suppresses it. She curls up. "I appreciate what you're trying to do. But I need some time to myself."

"I understand you've already had that. Are you planning to go into hibernation? If so, I'm surprised. The Berenice Abbott I know wouldn't let a little setback knock her flat."

At first, she tries to burrow more deeply into the bedding. But then pique gets the better of her, and she can't help herself. Pushing up on her elbows, she faces him. "See, this is what I find annoying. Everyone keeps telling me it's a *little setback*. But it's not. What if you'd been promised your job in Rochester, then they called a week later to say it was a big mistake? And casually added that you know nothing about photography?" She glares at his soft, kind eyes. "Do you think you'd see that as a *little setback?* Or would you be mad as hell?"

"You betcha." Beaumont meets her gaze evenly. "So…fight."

"Fight?" She grimaces. "How? You told me Steichen wouldn't reconsider. And I can't go up against an institution as powerful as MoMA. You said it yourself, people will think I'm delusional."

"I know I did. But there are other ways. What I mean is, don't let them have the last word. State your case. Tell them what you believe in."

"How should I do that? Commandeer a television station? Stand in Times Square with a megaphone?"

Abruptly, Beaumont gets up from the bed and strides to the window. He puts his hands on the windowsill, leans forward and looks out. Backlit by the sun, he is almost a silhouette. She can only just see the ruck in the shoulder of his jacket, the tufts of hair on either side of his head. He is thrumming his fingers on the sill, and she thinks, *That's it, I've alienated him too.*

But when he turns, his expression is inscrutable. "I have an offer for you," he says, "but I'm not sure you deserve it."

"I'm sure I *don't*. But you can try."

"You've heard about the photography conference in Aspen?"

She snorts. "I got the invitation. It went in the trash. Who the hell will go? A few wealthy hobbyists and some overpaid hacks."

"On the contrary, I hear everyone is going. Ansel Adams has signed up, so have Margaret Bourke-White and Edward Weston. Steichen will be there. The heads of all the major camera companies."

"And…?"

"And I've been asked to program events on the second day. I'd like to invite you to be the keynote speaker." She looks at him, dumbfounded. Beaumont returns to the bed. His rear end occupies the same indentation as before, as if the bedding were a saddle molded to his form. "Think of it. All expenses paid.

The conference will fly you out and cover accommodation. Nothing else will be scheduled during your speech, so you'll get full attendance. And it's not like a magazine article, you won't have an editor breathing down your neck. You'll be able to say what you like."

Berenice looks at him, at the large head that seems too big for his slim body. "I'm no public speaker," she says softly. "No. I don't know." She closes her eyes, trying to imagine it, a full auditorium, all eyes looking at the podium where she, dressed in a suit, stands awkwardly in front of a microphone. She opens her eyes, perturbed. "Have you thought about this, really? You could ask anyone."

He smiles. "I know."

"It's not just a pity prize?"

"Oh please, give me credit. Have I ever said I pity you?"

Berenice doesn't answer. She thinks, again, of the scene at Aspen. An audience made up of executives and curators. The top practitioners of her field. And Steichen, sitting where she can disembowel him with a glance.

Beaumont leans down, pats her hand. "I can see you're thinking about it. Think some more. I'm going to a meeting now. I'll stop in to see you later." He gives her a quick peck on the cheek, then straightens up. "Not to be picky, but it would be nice if you bathed by then."

◆

Afternoon shades into evening, and Beaumont doesn't return. Berenice wonders if she dreamed the whole encounter. Or if Beaumont's loyalties have been turned and he's now part of a conspiracy to drive her insane. That would be effective—send a person she trusts to mess with her mind. She's seen movies where the CIA used the tactic to great effect.

But she's rambling, obsessing. Seeing shadows where none exist. No doubt, such things can happen to someone who stays in bed for five days, barely eating or drinking. The body is forced to draw on its reserves, one's physiology literally changes. But Beaumont was here, she's sure. She remembers his weight on the bed, his silhouette. And he made her an offer. A very interesting one.

After Beaumont left, she shocked Liz and Pat by announcing that she was getting up. She has bathed, washed her hair, brushed her teeth. While she did that, Liz snuck in and changed the sheets, shook out the rug. She opened the window and aired the room. Then, when Berenice was reinstalled on clean sheets, Liz brought her a tray with toast, scrambled eggs and a banana. Invalid food, bland and soft. For someone whose stomach has to be coaxed gently back to use.

She is still weak. And, despite her change of course, she hasn't conceded anything yet. Because actually, she's not sure if she wants to meet the world on its terms. What has the world done for *her* lately? Where have her efforts at establishing a new photographic realism gotten her? In the last few days, the idea of turning into an eccentric recluse has become appealing. She could be like Baroness Elsa. Wearing animals around her neck and postage stamps on her cheeks.

So she doesn't know what she'll tell Beaumont. Nevertheless, she's grateful to him for jolting her back to life.

Just then, Liz sticks her head around the corner of the door. If possible, she looks even more flushed and excited than she did when Berenice got out of bed. "Bea, are you ready for company? Beaumont is here."

"I'm ready."

"I'll send him in."

The door closes behind her, and Berenice can hear shuffling on the other side. Someone coughs, a sound like a small dog's bark.

Then the door opens, and Beaumont walks in. He wears slacks and a sport jacket, and holds aloft a bunch of flowers—tulips, irises, daffodils. But he isn't alone. Behind him comes his wife, Nancy, then someone else. Berenice squints and then, disbelieving, slumps back on the pillows. It's Hippolyte Havel, her friend and surrogate father from her early Village days! Where on earth did they dig him up? His wild hair has turned completely white, making him look like a disheveled, careworn Einstein. She remembers how, after Lil's death, he coaxed her back to life, bringing her art supplies and goulash and dragging her to parties. She has always wanted to thank him for that.

Beaumont and Nancy move further into the room, and so does Hippolyte, and she sees that behind them are some of her colleagues from the New School, and students—Mr. First in the lead, as is only fitting. Dark little Rosa Jaworski hovers behind him, looking vaguely uncomfortable in a purple turtleneck.

Beaumont, Nancy and Hippolyte come to stand in front of the bed, and she sees that each of them is holding something: a photograph. One of *her* photographs.

She looks at them, shaking her head. Liz and Beaumont must have cooked this up between them; no wonder Liz looked flushed.

It's hard to talk. When her voice comes out, it sounds gruffer and more accusatory than she intended. "What's this? The Gift of the Magi?"

"Something like that," Beaumont grins. "We decided to throw you a party."

"Like the old parties," Hippolyte says. "Remember?"

"Oh, I remember."

"We each picked our favorite Abbott," says Nancy. "I chose this one." She holds up a print of *Night View*, the image Berenice shot from the top of the Empire State Building. What an effort it had been to get it! There was only one day in the year when it was possible: 20 December, when dusk fell before the myriad office lights were extinguished. She'd had a scant half hour to make it work—to get those constellations of window lights twinkling from the depths.

"Mine's this," Beaumont offers her a Supersight photograph of a bird's wing, the large sheet of film rendering each feather's vanes and barbs with impeccable clarity. She isn't surprised; the choice says everything about Beaumont's love of documentary realism. But it's thrilling that he picked the wing, an emblem of her lifelong obsession with flight.

"As for me, it could only be this one," Hippolyte says. He thrusts forward her American gangster portrait of Jean Cocteau wearing a fedora and trench coat, pointing a toy gun at the camera. Berenice smiles. The anarchist spirit is still alive in Hippolyte.

"And *I* picked out something for you to wear." Liz moves forward, holding a dress Berenice has never seen before. It's the color of blood, made of a silky material. It has a full skirt and a V-shaped neckline that plunges to a gathered waist. The sleeves have tassels hanging off them, each of which ends in a shiny red bead.

She looks at the faces in the room. Every one of them is turned toward her, expectant. It's a critical moment, a pivot. It feels as if what she does now will determine not just the next couple of hours, but the rest of her life.

She looks at Liz, at Hippolyte, Beaumont and Nancy. And, weak as she is, she knows what must happen next.

"Well, what are you waiting for?" she says. "Someone put some music on. Let's dance!"

THIRTY-TWO

From behind, Berenice can tell that the woman's outfit is expensive. Sable jacket, white linen dress, kidskin gloves. The whole ensemble is topped by a jaunty little Robin Hood hat. Though normally disdainful of high fashion, Berenice finds herself pleased by the woman's glamor, and the smart suits of the businessmen around them. It fits the importance of the day.

She has dressed up, too. She's wearing her brown skirt suit with the peplum jacket, a hummingbird brooch pinned to one lapel. On her feet are the new maroon and white pumps that Liz insisted on buying her. She has buffed her nails and brushed her hair until it shines, and has applied lipstick, kissed a Kleenex and peered at her reflection, examining it as carefully as if she were about to collect a prize.

And it *does* feel as if she has won something, or come into money, or been turned into a movie star for the day. Here at the airport, she has been catapulted into a brilliant future-scape. Lights gleam, floors and countertops shine like glass. The stewardesses, almost identical in starched blue uniforms and pillbox hats, are sleek and polished. Even the porters have a glow, as if burnished by the important enterprise they're part of. Surveying it all makes her feel light, as if she's already in the air.

Liz nudges her, bringing her back to earth. "Nervous?"

She looks down, nods. "I think there's a battalion of butterflies in my stomach."

"Good. They'll keep the plane aloft."

Berenice smiles, but there isn't time to say more, because the stewardess—whose name badge says *Marilyn* under a pair of gold wings—is calling her forward.

"Good morning, ma'am. Chicago?"

"Yes. Then on to Denver." She hands over the ticket.

Marilyn glances at the printed card, then says with a practiced smile, "Welcome, Miss Abbott. Is it your first time with us?"

"Yes. Actually—" trembling, "it's my first flight."

"Is that so? Well, you're in for an adventure!" Marilyn rubber-stamps the ticket, then hands it back to her. "Don't worry, there's nothing to it. You'll give your suitcase to that porter, then go to gate four. There's an hour until the flight. Your friend can stay with you until then." She leans forward, smiling, and whispers, "The best view of the runways is from gate two."

"Thank you." Berenice moves off feeling dazed, the stamped ticket in her hand proof that it has started, this process of air travel. It's something she's wanted for so long, and so fervently, that she can barely believe it's happening. In an hour she'll be rising, soaring, shooting forward at unimaginable speed. She'll feel the exhilarating rush, the sight of everything becoming smaller and, at the same time, expanding to a magnificent breadth beneath her.

As they're reaching the porter, Liz pulls her arm back. "Sure you won't put anything else in the suitcase?"

"No, Butchy, I need these books. It's two long flights and a train ride."

Liz shudders. "I hate to think of you traveling so many hours."

"It'll be beautiful," Berenice says. She knows Liz is anxious, and knows exactly why. They both read the same article on the risks of air travel. The most common danger, and therefore most worrying, is turbulence-related whiplash. But there are other horrors too, from random mid-air collisions to temporary hearing loss. *Even on an otherwise uneventful flight, passengers can expect to be vomiting from time to time*, the article stated. So much for the glamor of life in the air.

"I wish you were coming," she says as they're walking to gate two. They couldn't afford it, of course. As a keynote speaker Berenice is getting her flights and hotel paid for, but none of Liz's editors had wanted to send a writer, and without that commission, the trip isn't possible. It is probably for the best, though. She's been ill lately, and the turbulence would play havoc with her arthritis.

At gate two, they watch airplanes glide across the tarmac, graceful as dancers doing warm-up exercises. After a couple of minutes there's a thundering sound, the building vibrates, and Berenice grabs Liz's hand and clutches it to her chest as a plane descends, swooping over buildings, tilting one way and the other, going out over the water and turning, its wings almost vertical before it straightens up and comes in to land. It's a stratocruiser, a Boeing 377, bigger than the Douglas DC-6 in which she'll be flying to Chicago. One of Pan Am's clippers, it must have come in from Europe. She's seen the advertisements, the *Maxim's of Paris* menus and private staterooms. To think, you could reach New York from Paris in eleven hours instead of the eight days it took her by ship in 1929!

As the plane approaches, it seems to hang in the air for a moment, wings and snub nose wobbling. Then it descends rapidly, hurtling toward the ground with breathtaking speed. They watch as the plane's wheels touch down, bounce, touch again—then join the applause breaking out at the gate. Berenice hadn't even noticed other people watching, so fixated was she on the scene out of the window. But now it feels as if they've been through an edge-of-the-seat experience together—like sports fans rooting for their team.

She could watch planes land all day, but it's her turn to board. At the gate, she faces Liz. She looks at the downy flesh of Liz's cheek, wanting to touch her lips to it. But they're in public, so instead she takes her beloved's hand and gives it a hard squeeze, hoping it expresses what she's too choked up to say.

Liz smiles bravely. "You'll telephone when you get there?"

"I will. I'll call from Chicago too, if I can."

"Don't forget your Dramamine."

"No. And don't *you* forget your pills."

"I won't." Carefully, Liz scans her face. "You'll be fine, Bea. You will. I'm so excited for you."

And then they're engulfing each other in a mighty hug, Liz's arms crushing hers to her side, holding her as if she is a jewel that will have to be prized away. "Take photographs for me."

"Of course." With her nose nestled in Butchy's hair, she whispers, "I love you." Then she walks to the stewardess, shows her ticket, and makes her way down the steps to the tarmac. At the last possible moment she looks back and sees Liz in the window, lumpy in her beige wool coat, waving a handkerchief. The sight makes her heart swell, and she waves back with all her might.

Onboard the DC-6, she finds her seat, a good one near the wing. It's wide and deep, with an ashtray embedded in the armrest. The interior of the plane looks homey, with orange curtains across the windows and wooden shelves that hold pillows and blankets. A businessman with oiled hair sits next to her; he has unfolded a copy of the *Wall Street Journal* and is reading it intently. Well, she supposes that's better than having a talker constantly prodding her elbow.

"Postcards?" A stewardess extends her arm over the newspaper, handing Berenice two cards. "Some passengers like to write to friends while on board."

"Thank you." One card shows the airplane flying through a cobalt sky, while the other has a picture of a steward carving prime rib. The colors are lurid, but Liz will be amused by them. She tucks them in a pocket; she'll write when she has more to describe.

Fragrant smoke wafts toward her; a man across the aisle has lit a pipe. It's Granger, a tobacco she likes. Leaning back, she breathes its full, spicy odor as the plane's engines start up, a gentle whir that builds to a roar and a steady vibration that pulses through her entire body.

As they glide backward, her neighbor folds his paper and glances at her. "Nervous?"

"A little."

"Don't worry." He smiles, revealing deep dimples that make him look suddenly boyish. "I'd breathe, though. It helps."

"Yes," she laughs. Perhaps he won't be such bad company. Glancing out of the window, she can see the airport buildings, the low terminal and the shining tower where the controllers sit, directing the comings and goings. The engines' roar intensifies, making conversation impossible, but she turns and grins at her neighbor. She feels eager, like a child in a giant tire about to be pushed down a hill.

A turn, a jerk, and then the plane is rushing forward, shaking like bejesus, and she grips the armrests as the shelf over her head rattles in its socket.

It is going to happen. She is going to fly.

With a shudder, the wheels leave the ground.

EPILOGUE

It's almost time. Berenice sits in her parlor, a plaid blanket over her legs. Atticus is dozing on the rug at her feet, one of his ears turned part inside out, like a hat with an upturned brim. Outside the window, the sun steals over the lake in a blaze of crimson and orange, a diva making her entrance. A pair of ducks flies over the water, swooping low, as graceful in the air as they are clumsy on land. *The eggs must have hatched by now*, she thinks, imagining the flimsy ducklings testing their lungs and webbed feet. Yesterday she'd tried to take the lake path, but her body wouldn't cooperate. A mere twenty steps and she was done in, obliged to lean on her cane for a few moments before shuffling her way back up the path.

The girl, Lindsay, will be here soon. They're making an early start in order to reach New York by mid-afternoon, which will give her a chance to rest. It was good of them to send a driver; she doesn't do well any more with taxis and public transport. There's too much walking; too many fast-moving, frantic people. Crowds used to excite her, but that was decades ago. Now they just make her jumpy and querulous.

Such a betrayal, this physical collapse. Abilities are being removed from her one by one, like those darned green bottles on the wall. Her body is a symphony of pain, but it's no Bach or Beethoven—more like one of those discordant rackets that passes for music these days. Yesterday her chest felt as if her heart and lungs were on strings, being jerked by a sadistic puppet master. Death doesn't frighten her any more—still, at ninety-one she lingers, having a strong urge to last out the century. *Her* century, the twentieth.

She puts her hands on the chair arms, beginning the long process of hauling herself up. Atticus opens an eye, sniffs, then opens the other. When he sees what she's doing he lets out a strangled whine and sits up, eying her with suspicion. Something's up, he knows—he's not a complete dope. Ever since she started packing yesterday he's been moping around, being tragic. The doggy version of Garbo.

"Come, now," she says, "it's only three days. Kimberly will be here to feed and walk you, and probably give you all kinds of treats. You know I'd take you if I could."

In response, Atticus sniffs her foot, then gives her shin a soft butt with his forehead, almost sending her tumbling back into the chair. "Cut it out," she warns. He is her second red setter. The first, Edison, who she bought to quell her grief after Liz passed, died after a good life of eighteen years. When Edison died, she found she couldn't bear to be without a dog. Perhaps it was unfair to choose a second setter, since she can't resist the inevitable comparisons. Where Edison was gentle and intelligent—as if Elizabeth's spirit had passed to him—Atticus is overwrought, needy. All in all, he provides too much drama for an old woman. Still, he's only five; maybe he has to mature and, as the kids say, 'find his zen.'

She hobbles out of the parlor, casting a cursory glance at the wall of images that embody some of her greatest hits. There are her Paris friends and sitters: luminous Djuna Barnes, Jane Heap, and James Joyce with his pirate's eye patch. Next to them is an image of midtown Manhattan shot from the Fuller Building, and near the door are a few of her science photographs—patterns of water waves, a silvery ball bouncing into the distance. All her shifting interests, their lack of unity posing something of a career liability. What was she, exactly? People never could pin her down.

In the kitchen, she puts the kettle on for tea. Atticus is a nervous nuisance, circling her until she sits down, whereupon he flops at her feet. Her pills sit in the middle of the table, boxes and brown cylinders of different heights and widths that, clustered together, are like a tiny city. She opens them one by one, carefully tipping out the morning's dosage, the same combination she put in her sorter box for the trip. Blue, orange, purple—apparently it takes bright colors to ease the ills of old age.

And then, inevitably, she thinks of those last months when she'd bring the evening's dosage to Liz. Never as patient a nurse as she wanted to be, she would hold out the pills and the water, her mind flashing through her day's work as Liz struggled to muster a smile and swallow all the tablets and capsules.

So many fancy drugs and in the end, not a damn one could save her. Why? Because, while having a minor impact on her rheumatoid arthritis, the Predni-this and Oxy-that were giving her a cocktail of side effects—including the liver failure that ultimately killed her.

Medicine: a zero sum game, more often than not. And that's if you're lucky. Her own orange pills sometimes give her hallucinations, which can be pleasant at times—especially when Liz appears. Last night, she could have sworn she saw a barn owl on top of the stove, regarding her stonily. When she closed her eyes and opened them again, it was gone.

The sound of a car pulling up outside; a door slamming. A minute later, there's a knock and the creak of the screen door. Atticus sits up and sniffs, proving himself alert though unwilling to investigate. What a shirker! Fortunately the town of Blanchard is safe.

"Miss Abbott?" a voice calls, "It's Lindsay!"

"In the kitchen!" she shouts back.

A few soft steps, and the girl appears. Not a girl, of course, but a woman—one has to be careful with the terms these days. And yet, to Berenice, Lindsay seems gloriously, luminously young, with her unblemished face and swinging blonde hair, her slim legs encased in tight jeans. She's a Barnard graduate. They have only spoken briefly, but she seems serious and intelligent. Atticus loved her, of course—but then, he's a pushover for anyone under seventy.

"Take your time, Miss Abbott. Hey, Atticus!" Lindsay bends to tickle him under the chin. Berenice wobbles up from the table.

"No, I'm ready. If you don't mind, dear, my suitcase is up in my bedroom. And there's a smaller bag on the hall table."

"Of course. I'll put them in the car."

She bustles away, leaving Berenice to take a last look around at the sunlight on the kitchen counter and the maples outside the window. The pottery mugs on their hooks under the china cabinet. And Atticus. Of course she plans to be back, but at her age you don't know, any day could be the last. And she wants to remember the kitchen like this, with the lingering smell of tea and the single fork in the drying rack, its tines catching the light.

On the porch she breathes in cool air, observing the glint of silvery dew on the lawn. Then, steeling herself against Atticus's frenzied whines and scratchings at the door, she grips her cane and makes her way to Lindsay's car, a surprisingly jazzy vintage Camaro with frills of rust around its wheel arches.

They don't speak until they've navigated through Blanchard and are on route fifteen. Then Lindsay turns to her.

"Miss Abbott, would you mind if I ask a few questions?"

"Call me Berenice. And certainly, fire away."

Lindsay slows the car, caught behind an Ocean Spray truck with a dirt-streaked picture of a juice bottle in a cranberry bog. "I've always wondered about your science photographs. They're so different from what you did before."

"One has to move with the times."

"That's true, I guess," Lindsay chuckles. "Did you enjoy working at M.I.T.?"

"Yes, dear. But that was only a small part of what I did with my science photography. Before M.I.T., I spent years struggling to make the pictures on my own. No one else was interested for a long time."

"What changed?"

Berenice blinks—do schools not teach history any more? Trying not to be too tart, she answers, "In 1957, the Soviets sent the Sputnik satellite up. It was what your generation would call a reality check. We'd spirited the Nazi rocket genius Wehrner von Braun out of Germany, and he was supposed to win the space race for us. Then when Russia got there first, there was a fear the world would see it as a victory for Communism. Suddenly, science programs sprouted up like mushrooms."

"And that's when you got your job?"

"Yes, M.I.T. pretty much hired me on the spot." *And fired me too*, she thinks bitterly—the Physical Science Study Committee used her talents for a decade, then tossed her out. It didn't matter; she was done with cities by then. Done with employment. She'd already burned so many bridges. After her speech in Aspen she hadn't had a show or a magazine assignment for years. That was when she moved up to Maine.

"It's an amazing career," Lindsay says. "You've gone from horses and buggies to the space age, haven't you? What luck!"

Berenice smiles. Of course, without benefit of intimacy or hindsight, her life can be viewed as a string of glittering successes. Few people know how she struggled, the recognition she craved arriving only in the last two decades. It's gratifying, of course—but what she couldn't have done with the accolades and income when she was younger, when she and Liz needed them most!

She turns to Lindsay. "My dear, it's true I've witnessed some changes. But the act of photographing has never changed. It's always been about realism. About truth. If I've fallen short, it's not for lack of trying."

"Who could say you've fallen short?"

"You'd be surprised. Now, if you don't mind, I'd like to rest a bit. I tend to tire easily these days."

She closes her eyes, leaning her head on a cushion that she brought along for this purpose. This will be her last time visiting New York, she realizes, because even the driving is too much. Barely forty minutes in and already she feels sapped. She can hear the purr of the engine, the rhythmic swoosh of the tires making their rotations. Lulled by the repetitive sounds, she half-dozes, drifting off into memories of Manhattan, of striding around with her camera bag in one hand and tripod in the other, stalking scenes of urban beauty. She feels a wave of happiness at the memory. Oh, but how she'd been on fire back then!

Manhattan—light shining through the elevated train tracks, dappling the streets below with brilliant triangles. The shabby glory of the piers. And the skyscrapers, those soaring behemoths, rising like sea gods from waves of lower buildings. A city in flux, changing so fast you could hardly keep up; layers of history jostling each other, accreting.

New York: the place of her most searing agonies and, conversely, her greatest triumphs. When she'd finally moved—first to Boston, then Maine— it was like abandoning a lover whose intensity she could no longer take. The electricity was addictive, but it was eating her alive.

The rest of the day passes in something of a blur. At some point, just before crossing into New Hampshire, they stop to buy gas and eat lunch. Lindsay finds a diner that serves a good cup of coffee and a surprisingly tasty chicken potpie. Then they're on the road again, going through southern New Hampshire, and when she's not dozing she's having flashbacks to the road trip she and Liz took in 1935, trying to fulfill Liz's dream of doing a book on the forty-eight states. An over-ambitious project, for sure, and predictably they'd failed to win any grants. Still, it had been wonderful to tour the small towns and cotton fields, the boredom of driving mixed with the thrill of being with Elizabeth. A woman she'd already decided to love for as long as possible.

At one point, she wakes up and sees a sign for Springfield, Massachusetts, and thinks of Butchy again—this time, with a burst of admiration. All that time Liz spent slaving over articles for the *Springfield Republican*, treating each one as reverently as if it were going to be edited by Pulitzer himself. Dear, clever

Elizabeth—Liz, who never made it to the top rank, but had enough friends to fill the Museum of Modern Art. Which is not such a bad thing, after all—and in the end, might be the greater achievement. At her memorial service, there were speeches by curators and painters, editors and political friends. And by Berenice, of course—though the oblique references she made to their "great, deep friendship" barely scratched the surface of what they'd meant to each other. It tore her heart out to be treated as one of many eulogists.

At last, she wakes to find that they're on the outskirts of New York City. They're stuck in traffic, driving through suburbs with chain stores and squat, ugly apartment blocks. She looks at her watch: twenty past three. Just about on schedule, if the traffic eases up.

Then they're on the Henry Hudson Parkway, and she's watching *her* city appear, redolent with memories. The George Washington Bridge, the Empire State, the Chrysler, the Rockefeller Center. And there are new landmarks, of course: the sleek Metropolitan Tower, the angled Citicorp Center. The World Trade Center Towers, dominating the downtown skyline like skinny, uninspiring salt and pepper shakers.

At Forty-Second Street, Lindsay turns off the highway. "I'm going to drop you at your hotel," she says. "You'll have a couple of hours to rest, then I'll pick you up at six."

"Fine," Berenice says, though her head is throbbing from the city's sensory assault. How funny that for so much of her life she was enthralled by urban life! She doesn't crave it at all now, quite the opposite. The city seems sordid, with its fumes and graffiti, its aggressive pigeons pecking at plastic containers on the streets.

They cross over to the East Side and Lindsay drops her at her hotel on Fifth Avenue. She has asked for a room on a high floor, and the hotel has obliged. She can see to the east, across to Grand Central Station and the Chrysler Building, all the way to Queens and the piers where she used to walk, stalking views of the city.

So many memories, most of them good. She's had to struggle, yes, but it made her who she is—stronger than she would have been if success had fallen like a ripe apple into her lap.

By the time Lindsay comes back, Berenice has bathed and dressed in her formal wear, a gray skirt suit with a blue silk shirt. She's feeling refreshed, no longer as enervated as she was when they entered the city. *Bring it on*, she thinks, *I'm ready*. In a rare concession to glamor, she has put on lipstick.

"Take my arm," Lindsay says as they negotiate the crossing at Forty-Second Street. "The road's uneven. I wouldn't want you to fall."

And so it's in this way, clutching the arm of a younger woman, that Berenice encounters the main building of the New York Public Library. As elegant a building as exists in Manhattan, with its neoclassical facade and the two imposing lions flanking its entrance. And there, hanging the length of its pillars, are the banners announcing the show. BERENICE ABBOTT: A MODERN VISION. The type plain and unadorned, as she requested, no flourishes to distract from the words themselves.

So here it is, the exhibition that encompasses her life's work. From Paris to Maine. From horses and buggies to the space age, as Lindsay would say. A triumph, something she's achieved despite being cast into the wilderness for years after Aspen; despite sequestering herself in Maine. Of course, this exhibition is at the public library, not MoMA or the Met. But she no longer cares about such distinctions. Her only regret is that Butchy is not here to see it.

They stop for a while to admire the building, the banners flapping in the breeze. Leaning against Lindsay's arm, Berenice nods as she takes it all in. "Looks good, doesn't it?"

Lindsay laughs. "Looks terrific. And wait until you see inside."

The park behind the library is shadowy and threatening, a well-known hangout for criminals and addicts. But nothing can take away from the library's Beaux-Arts magnificence, its striking grandeur.

And then, as the wind buffets them from behind, making her clutch Lindsay's arm more tightly, Berenice blinks and frowns. Surely they weren't there a moment ago, those people massed on the library steps? Looking at them, her heart gives a mighty, rolling thump. There they are all: Lilian and Johnny, Djuna, Sylvia Beach. She can see, peeking from the back, Duchamp, and next to him Man Ray and a sultry-looking Kiki. Stieglitz is there—unsmiling, of course—and there's Hippolyte with Tylia on one arm and Bronia on the other. Standing nearby is Rod with his children, and next to him Maggie Bourke-White in an aviator's cap. Holger Cahill, Beaumont Newhall; marvelous Elsa, wearing a live boa constrictor around her neck. Her sister—dear, practical Hazel, who had been such a comfort to her after Liz died. Who made sure to visit her annually, whether in Cambridge or a frozen Maine.

And of course, in front of them all is Elizabeth—not wan and weak, as she was in her last years, but restored to her fully vibrant self. Robust, effervescent. Her eyes shining with pride.

For a moment Berenice just stands there, shaking her head at the wonder of it all. Tasting the cool air, the moment's bittersweetness. And then, when the vision has passed, when the necklaces and bow ties and sequins have faded and the steps are revealed again, she pats Lindsay's arm. "Okay, kid," she says, "I'm ready. Let's go in."

ACKNOWLEDGMENTS

Many people helped bring this novel to fruition. Jennifer Cody Epstein was there from the beginning, and has been a tireless cheerleader, mentor and colleague: thank you. Carole Rosenthal, Ellen Conley, Sue Mellins, Susan Stern, Joachim Frank, Alison Lowenstein, Maura Sheehy, Julia Lichtblau and Courtney Zoffness were the most supportive workshop groupmates a writer could hope for. Susanna Einstein offered key advice and encouragement. Nicola Coleman, Vera Coleman, Julie Brown, Amy Sanidas, Susannah Gardiner, Michael Epstein, Matthew Sharpe, Michele Page and Whitney Otto read early versions and made useful comments. I am indebted to the team at Silverwood Books, especially Catriona Dickie for her careful stewardship of this book through publication. Last but not least, my amazing husband Dan put in many hours of childcare so that I could have time to write, and my children Nathan and Zoe were sources of light and inspiration. Nate, to your question, "When is your novel going to be published?" there is finally an answer: "Now!"

FURTHER READING

Berenice Abbott: A Life in Photography, Julia Van Haaften, W.W. Norton, 2018

Berenice Abbott, Photographer: An Independent Vision, George Sullivan, Clarion Books, 2006

Berenice Abbott, Photographer: A Modern Vision, NYPL, 1989

Berenice Abbott, American Photographer, by Hank O'Neal, MacGraw Hill, 1982

Berenice Abbott, Thames & Hudson Photofile, 2010, Introduction by Hank O'Neal

New York in the Thirties (Changing New York), Dover, 1973

Republic of Dreams: Greenwich Village: The American Bohemia, 1910-1960, Ross Wetzsteon, Simon & Schuster, 2002

Being Geniuses Together 1920-1930, Robert McAlmon and Kay Boyle, North Point Press, 1984

CPSIA information can be obtained
at www.ICGtesting.com
Printed in the USA
LVOW03*0213221117
557218LV00003B/6/P